HEART OF IRON

HEART OF IRON

OF

IRON

ASHLEY POSTON

An Imprint of HarperCollinsPublishers

Balzer + Bray is an imprint of HarperCollins Publishers.

Heart of Iron

Copyright © 2018 by Ashley Poston

ISBN 978-0-06-265285-0 (trade); ISBN 978-0-06-284485-9 (special edition)

Typography by Sarah Nichole Kaufman

18 19 20 21 22   PC/LSCC   10 9 8 7 6 5 4 3 2 1

❖

First Edition

TO THE STARRY-EYED GIRL
WHO DREAMED OF BECOMING AN AUTHOR—
WE MADE IT

Far above the crown of stars,
there lay a kingdom cast in shadows
until a daughter born of light
drove the night away.
And so the Great Dark waited
a thousand turns around the sun
and promised on its heart of iron
to once again return.
—"Origin of the Moon Goddess,"
The Cantos of Light

I

IRON THIEF

ANA

Nine hundred and ninety-nine candles lit the Iron Shrine.

Ana curved a crescent moon across her chest—in honor of the Goddess she didn't believe in—to disguise tucking three coppers from the offering tray into her burgundy coat.

Di gave her a long look as he sat in the pew beside her.

"What? It's called an *investment*," she told her best friend. "Don't give me that look."

Di—short for the serial number D09 inscribed at the nape of his neck—gave a human-looking shrug. His voice sounded like garbled static from a damaged voice box. "I am not sure what you are referring to."

"The judgy one you're giving me right now."

"I am incapable of giving looks."

"Says the Metal giving me a look." She shifted uncomfortably, and then sighed. "*Fine*. I'll go put the money back when we leave."

"Do not be chivalrous on my account," he said in his monotonous, staticky voice. If he had emotions, she thought he would've said it dryly—like a joke.

As if he could tell one, she thought, amused.

He sat forward, elbows on his knees. His hood was pulled low to disguise the slats and plates that made up his face, without a nose or ears or eyebrows. He was more dented than other Metals, having fallen through mine shafts on Cerces and been shot at by mercenaries on Iliad. She felt bad for a particular ding on his forehead, but she had apologized a thousand times for accidentally running him over with a skysailer.

He still refused to let her drive.

An abbess passed down the almost-empty aisle. Ana could hear her humming a sad, lonely hymn from *The Cantos of Light* as she swung a thurible, carrying with it the heavy scent of moonlilies. At the head of the shrine stood the statue of the Moon Goddess, seven men high, her arms outstretched as she looked to some distant point in the domed ceiling, where murals of the Moon Goddess's story, the kingdom of shadows and the girl of light, were painted. The entire space station of Nevaeh felt empty in the shrine, as if the world only existed between the alabaster pillars and stained-glass trappings, so quiet she could hear the electric hum of Di's wires and functions, as soft and soothing as a song.

She figured most of the kingdom's citizens were at home or at the pub, glued to their holo-pads and newsfeeds. Today, the Grand Duchess would choose her heir—and the thirtieth Emperor of the Iron Kingdom.

So naturally, with everyone distracted, it was a good day for a heist.

As the abbesses in their shimmery silver robes roamed the

aisles, two older women scooted into the pews a few rows up. "May the stars kep us steady, and the iron keep us safe," they murmured as they drew crescent shapes across their chests and sat. One of them had a mechanical hand—a sign that she had been infected with the Plague twenty years ago.

The woman's friend glanced back to Ana, and gave a start. "Goddess save me," she said in a hushed whisper to her friend, "I think a *Metal* is behind us. Do you think it's HIVE'd? I hope it's HIVE'd."

The HIVE was the Iron Kingdom's way of dealing with misbehaving, or rogue, Metals. Instead of imprisonment, the kingdom stripped Metals of their free will and assimilated them. Then, with them obedient and unthinking, the kingdom used them as guard dogs—Messiers.

The woman with the mechanical hand looked back, too, before quickly turning around again. "No, its eyes aren't blue."

"They all give me the chills. To think our Iron Adviser created them to *help* people, and then they go and do that dreadful thing seven years ago."

"Not all of them are bad."

"Please. It probably gave that girl those scars, poor thing. They should all be HIVE'd—they're *unpredictable*."

So were humans, Solani, and Cercians, but the kingdom didn't try to control *their* minds.

They'd probably feel differently then, Ana thought, absently pulling a pendant out from under her collar and tracing her thumb around it. Her good luck charm. She'd had it for as long as she could remember, a dragon or a snake molded into an open circle. Once, it might have been a fancy brooch, but whatever had burned the left side of her face had also melted the brooch. She wished she could remember who gave it to her—she always felt safe with it on—but her head ached every time she tried.

Captain Siege had found her and Di in an escape pod in the wreckage of a cargo ship. It had been set upon by mercenaries. No survivors—except for them. She didn't even have pictures of her parents, and her own appearance didn't give her any clues. She had warm bronze skin and wide golden-brown eyes, full lips, and a heart-shaped face. Her hair was as dark as space itself, but it always curled into tangles. She wore it atop her head in a long braid and shaved the sides. She was moderately tall, solidly built for a life of evading death at every turn, and wore hand-me-down coats like the red one she wore now and darned trousers that never fit right. She looked like a girl from any part of the Iron Kingdom—and nowhere all at once.

She loved the crew of the *Dossier*, Captain Siege's ship. They were her home. But Di was her only family—her best friend—and if it wasn't for him, she wouldn't be suffering in this stuffy shrine, listening to old ladies who couldn't mind their own business.

Di glanced over to her as she rubbed her thumb and forefinger around and around the melted circle pendant.

"You are nervous," he said.

"Am *not*," she lied, but when he flicked his eyes down to her pendant, she dropped it back underneath her shirt and admitted, "Maybe a little. I wish I could be more like you. Not programmed for emotions. To have a clear head. It sounds great sometimes, you know?"

"I am unsure. I know nothing else." He flicked his white-eyed gaze to her. "If you are nervous, then we could leave—"

"We're staying."

"But the captain did not want us to pursue—"

"The *captain* didn't want us to come because Mokuba did her over on the last deal," she interrupted, lowering her voice as an abbess walked by. "And I'm not going to pass up this opportunity just because some two-bit information broker screwed Siege out of a few coppers. We're running out of time. We have to fix your memory core—your glitches are getting worse."

"I have had them since we were found by the *Dossier*. They are not so bad—"

"You glitched for *three hours* last night."

"But I rebooted," he replied simply, and she wanted to throttle him.

"And what happens when you glitch hard enough you can't reboot? The mechanic on Iliad said you're getting worse, and your memory core won't just *magically* heal itself."

"Could we not simply pay the info broker instead of stealing the coordinates?"

"If we had that sort of money, I wouldn't be stealing from offering trays, Di."

His moonlit gaze—optics blazing in his eye sockets, looking like tiny stars—bored into her and almost made her feel guilty. *Almost.*

"Besides, we're not stealing it from Mokuba. You never steal from your info broker—that's bad business. We're stealing it from the Ironblood he's *selling* to," she went on. "Some rich kid isn't going to do one over on us."

"I am more worried about the captain. She frowns on outside jobs."

Ana rolled her eyes. "Di, we live on a ship that pirates other ships, transports illegal goods, hunts lost treasures, escorts Ilidian underground kingpins—"

"—The captain promised we would never do that again—"

"—and smuggles weapons. We don't have *job* descriptions, except for being outside the laws. And hey!" She held up her hands. "We're outside them. So stop worrying so much."

"My worrying keeps us alive."

"Your worrying is giving me a headache. This is worth it, Di. Trust me." She reached for his gloved hand and squeezed it tightly—more of a comfort to her than him. As the medic on the *Dossier,* Di's hands had stitched her up more times than she could count. "If these coordinates lead to your creator's lost fleetship? We won't need another fix. The Adviser's lab was destroyed in the Rebellion seven years ago—nothing survived. Except this ship. The *Tsarina.* Which might *happen* to hold a key to fixing you. Maybe a spare memory core. Maybe an empty Metal to transfer you into—*something.* Anything."

"But I rather like this body."

"Even the dent?" She grinned, her gaze straying to the light scuff on the corner of his forehead.

"We do not talk about the dent." The slats around his mouth

rippled into a frown. "Ana, the likelihood these coordinates lead to the *Tsarina* is dubious at best."

"It's called hope, Di."

"The probability of this hope of yours is point-oh-four percent."

"But there *is* hope," she pointed out, and knocked her shoulder against his—

Movement caught her eye. A tall, burly gentleman in a stained long coat and trousers, the seams frayed and boots greasy.

She'd know his curly peppery-gray hair anywhere—Mokuba.

He was moving down the far side of the shrine, against the mosaic windows, away from her, until he was completely obscured behind the pillars.

She leaned forward to get a better view.

Between the marble pillars, the buyer in question shook hands with Mokuba. He glanced over his shoulder, and piercing sky-blue eyes peered out from beneath his dark hood as he quickly surveyed the shrine. He was definitely an Ironblood, she could tell by that *ridiculously* lavish coat. Blue, with floral embroidery along the cuffs and collar, the buttons so polished they blinded. And he carried a lightsword on his back. Well dressed *and* well armed. Not a combination she saw often.

Except the poor Ironblood probably didn't know how to use the sword.

"Okay, Di, now's our chance," she whispered, easing herself to her feet slowly, so as not to attract attention. But Di didn't go with her. "Di?"

No answer.

She glanced over.

He stared straight ahead, elbows almost touching his knees, as if he'd been beginning to rise to his feet but time froze before he could. His moonlit eyes flickered like a lightning storm.

Glitching—*again.*

"Goddess's spark," she muttered, earning a scathing look from the elderly ladies in front of them. She grabbed him by his coat sleeve. Tried to shake him—but it was like trying to budge a six-foot all-titanium boulder.

The Ironblood and Mokuba were departing now in opposite directions. If she didn't go after that Ironblood now, she'd lose him.

Panic crawled up the back of her throat, tasting sharp. "Di, I'll be right b—"

With a crack, the heavy shrine doors flung wide.

She ducked instinctively, turning back toward the entrance. A skysailer landed just outside. The gust from its wings roared into the shrine, blowing out the candles that lined the Goddess's outstretched arms and the chandeliers overhead.

A patrol of six Messiers appeared in the doorway. They were sharp, metallic. Made of planes and slats she knew well, because they looked like D09. Like Metals.

Because once, they had been.

Now HIVE'd, the Messiers' blue eyes blazed like virtue incarnate. They moved in unison, their blue-and-black uniforms pristine, shined boots making solid thumps on the masonry floor as they marched into the shrine.

Cursing, Ana took Di by the shoulder and with all her might shoved him onto the floor so the Messiers couldn't see him, and covered him with her body. She and Di were wanted in at least twelve different districts across the Iron Kingdom, never mind Cerces. She was sure the entire mining planet had them on a watch list.

Goddess-spitting rotten luck, she thought, pressing her forehead against Di's unmoving cheek. If the Ironblood bolted she'd *never* catch up to him.

"We pardon the intrusion," the head Messier said, its Metal voice pleasant and melodic—how Di's should have sounded if it hadn't been damaged years ago.

Another Messier—she could tell from the brief pause—went on, "But we are looking for one—"

"Mokuba Jyen," finished a third.

They completed one another's sentences, since they were all part of the HIVE mind, and the effect was so eerie it made her shiver.

Why were Messiers after Mokuba? How in the blasted Dark had they tracked him down? Mokuba was the best at what he did—he never left a trail.

Are they after the coordinates, too? she thought, alarmed. How did they know he had them?

"Come on, Di," she muttered, knowing he could hear her.

Hoping, at least. Hoping he could work through this glitch.

She didn't want to think about what would happen if he couldn't. She didn't have time to worry whether this glitch was his last.

The Messiers passed her aisle, moving toward the towering statue at the front, and she slowly got onto her knees to peer over the pew in front of her. One of the abbesses—the only one not petrified by the Messiers' entrance—shuffled up to greet them.

On the other side of the shrine, still inching toward the side exit, was the Ironblood with the coordinates chip she needed.

She waited another moment, hoping Di could fight through his glitch, as the abbess pointed to Mokuba, who shifted nervously in the corner of the shrine.

Think, Ana, she told herself, exhaling a calming breath, tuning out the whispers from the other worshippers—and *especially* the crones in front of her—trying to think of what to do. Maybe she could sneak after the Ironblood and—

But Mokuba will be arrested and sent to the mines on Cerces, her guilty heart reminded her. And she had heard enough about those mines from the crew on the *Dossier* to know Mokuba would die there.

Goddess *blast* her conscience.

She reached into her coat, hoping she'd brought at least *one* of Riggs's flashbangs in her mad dash off the *Dossier* this morning. Her fingers wrapped around a small oval canister, and she brought it out, thumb slipping under the pin.

At least she had a little luck.

"Di, don't move," she told her glitching Metal.

The Messiers reached for the shiny Lancasters at their hips. "Mokuba Jyen. You are under arrest for—"

She flicked out the pin and jumped to her feet.

"Hey, *spacetrash!*" she shouted, and the Messiers turned in unison.

Giving it a good-luck kiss, she lobbed the flash grenade high into the air. It arced across the domed ceiling—and exploded in a dazzling blast of solar white. With a wail, the blast from the grenade blew out the candles, the smell of burned wicks sweeping through the shrine.

ROBB

His mother always said he longed for trouble.

It was never a compliment. She said it while looking down the bridge of her nose, her mouth too refined to snarl, like the time he invited "special" entertainers to his brother's coming-of-age party, only to find the house burgled the next morning and the topiary bushes crudely defiled. She said it when the headmaster at the most prestigious Ironblood private school, the Academy of Iron and Light—the Academy for short—busted him for running a perfectly reasonable gambling den underneath the school. And the time he challenged Viera Carnelian to a duel in only their knickers on the rooftop of the dorms . . .

Robb Valerio *did* long for trouble—

But this . . . was *not* the kind of trouble he liked.

The flashbang brought tears to his eyes. Disoriented, he caught himself on a stone pillar, blinking. Spots danced in his vision as candle smoke filled the shrine.

Goddess-spitting rotten luck, he thought, rubbing his eyes.

In the middle of the aisle, the Messiers pressed back against one another, their vision resetting. That was smart, to trick Metal optics with a flashbang *and* use the blowback to wipe out the candles. Assuming it was on purpose.

It probably wasn't.

The shrine was almost completely dark now, the only light the colorful streams coming through the mosaic windows.

He blindly took another step back toward the side exit. Almost there. Then he could call for his skysailer and ride it off into the sunset like nothing had happened.

The coordinates chip in his pocket felt heavy, weighed down by all the years he'd been searching for Lord Rasovant's lost fleetship. He couldn't lose it now. He had somewhere to go— somewhere to find *answers*. After seven years of searching, he *deserved* them.

The person who must have thrown the flashbang was grabbing Mokuba by the hand. Tattered burgundy coat, a Metroid at her hip, long black hair in a renegade braid, and looking like she hadn't bathed in a week—the girl must've been an outlaw.

With Mokuba in tow, she turned to pursue the person with the coordinates—*him.*

Yeah, he needed to leave like three seconds ago.

Pressing the comm-link pinned to his lapel, he snapped, "Ride. I need a ride!" and made a mad dash for the side exit.

Ten feet, five—

A shadowy figure stepped in front of him, hood pulled low.

Robb collided with it—a brick wall would've had more give—
and stumbled back, holding his nose.

"*Goddess!*" he cried in pain.

The figure raised its head slightly, white eyes gleaming.

A chill curled down his spine. A rogue Metal, of *all* the
things. Its soulless gaze flickered toward Robb's hand inching toward the lightsword on his back, as if daring him. For a
moment, he actually hesitated. The Metal could break his arms
in two moves if it wanted to.

I'll chance it.

With a cry, he reached for his sword—

The girl tackled him from behind and slammed both him
and the Metal into the door. It gave a groan and swung outward
onto a staircase and into the grimy alleyway. He grappled for
the railing, trying to catch his footing, but his ankle bent. He
tumbled down the steps, striking his head against the cement.

The world split with pain and he gasped, gagging on his
own breath.

Beside him lay the girl—the one who'd thrown the flashbang. Mokuba rushed down the steps, the Metal bending the
door handles inward so the Messiers couldn't follow.

Robb rolled onto his knees, world spinning, and pulled himself to his feet. His head pounded. He wanted to vomit.

Worth it, it's worth it, he tried to convince himself as he heard
the sound of a skysailer drawing closer. His ride. He reached
his hand up, higher, higher—

"Stop!" the girl cried, standing quickly. "I need those coordinates!"

The skysailer broke over the buildings. It came in low, tilting sideways.

"No hard feelings," he told her as one of his family's guards leaned out and took him by the hand as the ship passed, its fan-like wings almost scraping the ground.

The girl screamed for him to wait—why, so the Messiers would catch *him* too? Great Dark strike him, he'd rather *not*.

The guard heaved him into the skysailer and banked the boat upward, so sharply Robb's head spun. He lay down on the backseats, trying to keep from vomiting.

"We're late to your brother's announcement ceremony, sir," said the guard. He was older, with a graying mustache, the most loyal to Robb's late father—and *more* loyal with a sack of coppers to keep him from tattling to Robb's mother. "Your mother will not be pleased."

"I've got my entire life to kiss my brother's ass when he's crowned Emperor. I think I can be late to one more party," he muttered, fishing in his coat pocket for the coordinates chip Mokuba had sold him. He held it toward the skylight, its insides sparkling green.

The guard eased into Nevaeh's flying traffic. Skysailers zoomed past them, the sound of the congested airwaves enough to drown out his thundering heart. "What shall the excuse to Lady Valerio be this time, sir?" asked the guard.

Once, a Solani who claimed she could read the stars had told Robb that his silver tongue would be his undoing, and he took that as a compliment. Lying was an art form. He simply had perfected it.

"I was paying my respects to the Goddess," he replied, and curled his fingers around the coordinates chip as the skysailer rose toward his family's floating guarden in Nevaeh's man-made sky.

ANA

The skysailer with that stupid Ironblood climbed into the air, leaving a cold feeling in Ana's gut. There went Di's last chance, disappearing into the Nevaeh sky right before her eyes.

Behind her, the shrine's side door buckled out with the force of the Messiers on the other side.

Di pressed his back against the door to keep it closed. He must have stopped glitching after she lobbed the flashbang.

"That door won't hold," Mokuba said nervously, taking her by the arm. "Kid, you gotta get out of here before they break through. If they catch you *or* your Metal, then Siege'll skin me alive. You were stupid to come after those coordinates. I told you *no* to begin with—"

"I have to!" She twisted out of Mokuba's grip. "Di, we need to call Jax."

"On his way," Di replied.

She gave a relieved sigh. "Goddess, I'm glad you didn't glitch long."

"My"—*Thud!* The door shook again—"apologies."

"Kid, don't go after it," Mokuba begged. "It's cursed. People have died for those coordinates. You don't understand. This whole thing is—"

A lightsword sliced through the door beside Di's head. He ducked out of the way, but not quick enough before it tore through half of his hood.

Sweat prickled on Mokuba's upper lip. "Ana, you have to run."

"But—"

"*Now,*" the info broker snapped. His black eyes were frightened and desperate. She had never seen Mokuba like this before. "Siege'll kill me if anything happens to you."

"What'll you do?"

"Distract them."

Alarmed, she shook her head. "They'll catch you. They'll—"

The Messiers kicked the door open, and it fell outward with a terrifying crash.

Hurtling over the railing, Di landed at the bottom of the stairs and curled his cold gloved hand around her wrist. He pulled her down the grimy alleyway before she had a chance to argue, leaving Mokuba to face the Messiers alone.

JAX

As a Solani, Jax prided himself in knowing two things: how to fly absolutely anything, and how to stay out of trouble. The first was a breeze. He had a knack for flying, and when he closed his eyes he could feel the stars orbit around him no matter where he was, so he could never get lost.

The second, however, was proving to be a problem. Along with his *excellent* way-finding skills, he was taught at a young age to stay out of conflict. Solani were good at that: sticking to their heritage, never leaving their homes, growing old under the stars, and coasting under kingdom radar—

But being Ana's getaway driver made staying out of trouble very, *very* difficult. Maybe he should have picked an easier job instead of being the most talented and respected pilot on the wrong side of the law.

Still, on days like this, he wondered if it was worth a lifetime in jail. Solani didn't fare so well in dark places.

Gunfire exploded through the alleyway below. He leaned

over the skysailer, squinting down into the mess of Nevaeh. Ana and D09 sprinted down the alleyway. A few yards behind, gaining speed, six of the kingdom's mindless legion pursued them.

"You were supposed to babysit her, metalhead, not send her into the middle of a firefight," Jax muttered, tugging at his leather gloves—a nervous habit—and swooped into the no-fly airspace below.

The sailer purred like a kitten, its silvery wings fanning up on either side of the hull, soaking in the solar light coming through the harbor high above them. Wind whistled through the cracks in the cockpit shield as he ducked out of the airstream, gliding toward Ana and her boyfriend—

Metal, he corrected himself. *Metal* boyfriend.

Warning signals sprang up on his console. *NO FLY. RE-TURN TO ROUTE.* He swiped them away with a flick of his finger. If he was going to get arrested for anything, it wouldn't be because he was flying in a *no-fly zone*.

In twenty yards the alleyway broke out into a crowded market square. Nervous sweat prickled the back of his neck; he only had one shot at this.

He unlatched the shield and shoved it up.

"Ana! Di—*Ak'va!*" he cursed as a bullet ricocheted off the dash. He pushed on his goggles, his long silver ponytail swirling up like a streamer in the wind.

D09 grabbed Ana by the waist, skidded to a stop, and lifted his hand—

Jax jerked the helm left. The ship tilted sideways, diving

into the alley. The left wing scraped the ground, leaving a trail of sparks.

He outstretched his free hand.

Fifteen yards, ten—

Di caught ahold of his arm, and as the ship burst into the market square, Jax used the momentum to swing them into the cockpit and right the ship. The sailer grazed over the top of the crowd, rising sharply, and burst out from between the buildings, higher and higher until the Messiers were dots with glowing blue eyes.

Ana scrambled to her feet, and grappled for the back of his chair. "We have to go after that skysailer! Did you see it? It's—"

"I saw it," Jax interrupted, looking up at the ship rising through the slipstreams of traffic. "And that means you *don't* have the coordinates."

D09 inspected his cut hood. "We ran into some problems."

"Obviously."

Even if the Messiers got a good look at their skysailer, thanks to his paranoia it looked like every other standard-grade skysailer in the kingdom. Recognizable, but easy to mix up between his and the one in front of him in traffic.

Above them, the pinprick of the skysailer in question swirled up into the underbelly of one of the floating Ironblood gardens, and his heart sank. Anywhere else. The Ironblood could've gone literally *anywhere* else.

"Love," he said, easing back on the helm, "I think your Iron-blood's late to a party."

Ana stared up at the floating patch of greenery. "That's not . . ."

"Astoria. The Valerios' garden estate," D09 confirmed. "Where the Grand Duchess is scheduled to announce her heir."

"Well, we gave it our best," Jax said lightly, turning the skysailer toward the harbor. "Who's up for a round of Wicked Luck when we get ba—"

"We're going, Jax," she said stonily.

"Come again?"

"It is not wise," Di agreed.

"See, when the Metal agrees with me, we have a problem," he noted dryly.

She glared at both of them. "Either we're going or I'm kicking you both off this ship," she threatened, the tone in her voice making his stomach twist like it did when he stared at the stars for too long.

He never liked that tone. It usually ended with them trapped in a mine on Cerces, or caught in the middle of a territory war between mercenaries. She wore trouble like royalty wore the Iron Crown, and it fit her a little too well.

"It's the *Valerios'* garden," he stressed. "They're worse than any mercenary group out there."

"We're going," she repeated.

He quickly looked away, chewing on the inside of his cheek.

She went on, "And if I don't get the coordinates this time, I'll stop—I promise. Just give me one more chance."

He didn't want to point out that if she got caught, there

wouldn't *be* a next time, but trying to argue with Ana was like trying to tell the stars to stop shining. Sighing, he pulled at his long, pale ponytail, trying to convince himself this was a good idea, and turned the ship up toward Astoria.

ANA

The closer they drew to the floating garden, the louder her heart thundered in her ears. Crashing an Ironblood's party couldn't be *that* difficult. She'd gone through worse. The mine on Cerces was worse. This would be easy. This was just a garden.

Just a few Ironbloods.

The floating gardens of Nevaeh were renowned across the kingdom for their beauty and exotic flowers. Ironblood-owned, and Ironblood-funded, the islands rose and fell over the cityscape like the cycles of the moon, and anyone who didn't have pretty noble blood couldn't visit.

And sneaking onto the *Valerios'* floating garden . . .

She wasn't sure if she was just desperate—or foolish, too.

Anxiously, she checked the bullets in her Metroid .56; an older pistol Captain Siege had given her three years ago when she turned fourteen.

"Count your bullets and remember where they land," Captain Siege had warned. She put a hand over Ana's to steady her aim. "Once you steal a life, you can never give it back, so easy on the trigger. Exhale. Feet apart."

Ana did as she was told and let the captain fix her posture, straightening her back and crooking her elbow, and she found her aim easing toward the target, her finger effortlessly squeezing the trigger. Bull's-eye.

"On your way to being a fine captain, I'd say," Siege had said with a grin.

Ana still remembered that moment, how those words filled her with pride.

She hadn't killed anyone yet, hadn't started counting her bullets, but she'd come close. How desperate was she for those coordinates?

The skysailer slipped between the lines of traffic toward the underside of the garden. From this high up, the people in the streets looked like dots of moving sand. Or bugs. If the Moon Goddess existed, did she look at humans that way? As faceless little termites scurrying around, ruining perfectly good foundations?

Ana had never believed much in the Goddess. She only knew the origin story, as sweet as a bedtime lullaby. How, in a kingdom of shadows, the queen bore a daughter of light who chased the Dark away.

But would the Moon Goddess protect an outlaw like her?

Ana prayed anyway, like the old women had in the shrine. *Goddess bright, bless my stars and keep me steady.*

"Twenty-five feet and closing," Jax told them, and added, "Try not to get yourselves killed."

"It is a priority not to," Di replied, earning a glare from Ana as she spun the barrel of her pistol shut and holstered it.

The skysailer coasted into the marina under the garden, where guests' skysailers sat parked in rows upon rows of ship ramps. The plan was to go in through the service entrance—hopefully unannounced. The Valerios' guests used the main entrance on the garden level, so the odds of being found down here were slim to none. Besides, Ana rather liked going in the back door—she didn't have to knock.

"Remember," she said through the comm-link to Jax, watching him drop away into traffic again, "keep low until I get the coordinates, and then—"

"It's not my first rodeo, love," he interrupted, laughing.

"I do not like this," Di protested as they hurried across the docking ramp toward the service entrance. "There should be more security—"

The door to the service entrance slid open.

A Messier, clad in uniform blue and black, stepped out. It shifted its blue gaze from her to D09, and lingered on him. Ana went silently for her gun. She didn't like way the Messier stared, as though nothing ticked inside its metal head. Nothing thought.

Ana glared at Di. "Happy now? *Security.*"

"You are trespassing," the Messier said, and turned its HIVE'd eyes to Di. "And you are rogue."

"I am," Di agreed, then punched his hand into the weakest part of the Messier's torso and ripped a small glowing square out of its body. Strings of optical wires came with it, stretching like sinew.

With one final tug, the wires popped away. The Messier's eyes flickered out, and it dropped onto the docks. D09 pushed the body over, and it fell and fell and fell into the city, until Ana couldn't see it anymore.

She looked back at the glowing square—the Messier's memory core. It was so small, no bigger than a sugar cube, like Di's, sitting damaged in his metal chest. It held everything a Metal was, everything they could be. But this one was dark, barely glowing at all—HIVE'd.

He crushed it in his grip, and she flinched.

"Are . . . are you sure you needed to do that?"

"I lack the capacity to be unsure. It was already HIVE'd. Shall we continue?"

"But—"

"This way." He led her through the automatic doors and into a dimly lit hallway. Irrigation pipes above their heads hummed with water, leading them toward what smelled like the kitchen. Floating garden cuisine used only produce grown in the garden. It must have been nice, having food that wasn't dry-sealed and tasting like dust.

The smell of baked goods and meats led them to the kitchen, and up a staircase to the garden. There wasn't door at the top but a curtain of honeysuckle vines. From between them came the sound of a full string quartet playing lively melodies over the chatter of high-society gossip. She relished the noise for a moment, and the scent of magnolias and chocolate twisted into a perfume that made her mouth water.

She peered out between the vines, not daring to move them, afraid of being seen. Ironbloods were only *Ironblooded* because their lineage could be traced to the Goddess's court—or so the *Cantos of Light* said. But in the midst of lavender roses and orange daffodils, green grass and ivy vines, the Ironbloods looked almost ethereal in their glittery dresses and jeweled coats.

"How do you plan on infiltrating the party?" Di asked. "We are hardly Ironblooded."

"I didn't get that far. Gimme a minute," she muttered. Grease-stained trousers and a patched frock coat were't quite *Ironblood* attire. She chewed on her bottom lip, glancing into the kitchen at the cooks.

Di began, "Perhaps we can—"

Coming out of the kitchen, a waiter with a tray of champagne flutes stopped dead in the doorway. He wore the crimson-and-gold colors of the Valerio house, and a black collar around his throat, humming gently.

A voxcollar.

She'd only seen them on prisoners in Cercian mines to keep them silent, to stop them from inciting a rebellion. Why were they on the Valerios' *waitstaff*?

The waiter gave a long, slow blink. He looked about her height.

She slid her burgundy coat back to reveal her pistol. "Sorry, but I'm going to need your clothes."

·) ● (·

Ana finished tucking the crimson dress shirt and bib into too-loose pants and swirled her hair up into a bun. She figured they had twenty minutes before someone found the waiter they'd locked in the pantry—she hoped, at least. He couldn't scream with that voxcollar on unless he wanted a thousand volts of electricity straight to the neck.

She grabbed the tray of champagne flutes as she left the kitchen and hoisted it onto her shoulder. Di waited for her at the top of the stairs, the curtain of honeysuckle vines a vivid green and yellow against his still frame.

In the garden, Ironbloods chatted to one another from behind delicately laced fans and white-gloved hands, their pleasant smiles like masks.

To hide all the rot underneath, Ana thought bitterly as she searched for that damned Ironblood in the crowd. It didn't help that she'd barely gotten a good look at him. Sharp jaw, crooked smile. Goddess, all the men looked the same in their starched evening coats the rich color of flowers, accented with brassy buttons and family insignias. Jesper. Carnelian. Malachite. Umbal. Wysteria. Valerio . . .

It was a viper den.

She pursed her lips before finally saying, "I think you should stay in here and look for the Ironblood underground. He could try to give me the slip."

"He does not even know we are here, and I will be of more assistance to you in the garden. I could pose as a Messier."

"And what's the chance of you glitching again soon?"

He did not respond for a long moment. "Seventy-four-point-six percent."

"It's getting too high," she said softly. "Don't be difficult, please."

"I am being pragmatic. It is a large party and—"

She turned around and grabbed ahold of his hands, looking up into his moonlit eyes with all the conviction she had.

"I'll be *fine*," she said. She genuinely believed it, too. "You know I won't get into trouble without my best friend."

"That is not as reassuring as you may believe."

She squeezed his hands tightly, even though he couldn't feel it. "I'll always come back for you," she whispered, reaching up on her tiptoes to press her forehead against his cool metal one. "I promise you on iron and stars."

She wanted him to promise, too—but she knew he wouldn't.

Metals didn't have emotions, so how could she love something that would never—*could* never—feel the same? She often told herself, when her heart fluttered or her cheeks burned, that she didn't love him.

That she *couldn't*.

But, every time she tried to picture herself without him, there was only a great darkness in her head. She didn't know who she would be without him, and she never wanted to know. Her heart beat, and his wires hummed, and they were Ana and Di—and there were no words for that.

So she pressed her lips, briefly, against his metal mouth, and whisked herself out through the vines and into the party.

Goddess, she needed fresh air.

D09

A kiss.

One-point-three seconds—and gone.

He touched his metal mouth even though he could not feel—neither physical touch nor emotional. Ana had never kissed him on the mouth before. On the cheek, yes, when she'd drunk too much of Wick's Cercian ale. But never on the mouth. Her words echoed through his processors like a virus.

I'll always come back for you. I promise you on iron and stars.

It was more than a promise—it was an oath. Unbreakable. Strong like iron and steady like stars.

It was said that such promises could never be broken; the Goddess would not allow it. The probability of a supernatural binding was less than one percent, but the vow stuck with him all the same.

Because Ana had never promised on iron and stars before.

The Ironbloods did not notice as she passed into the party. They laughed among themselves, leaning against statues of the Goddess, her marble gown flowing freely in a stone-petrified breeze. The Goddess always looked up. He recalled how Ana hated that. But if she looked down, she would have seen men and women sipping on rose-scented champagne, oblivious of the poor living below this floating garden.

The Ironbloods were too self-absorbed to notice Ana as she waded between them, deeper into the garden.

He watched her for 7.3 seconds longer—until a signal pinged his processors. It was faint, easily hidden under the garden's security radio chatter. Could it be the HIVE? He had never picked up the HIVE's frequency before. Only Messiers could.

The signal began to grow louder.

Easing down the stairwell again, he pressed himself against the wall and sank into a shadowy corner between the kitchen and the hallway.

An older man, graying beard braided down his chest, appeared at the far end of the hallway. Dark eyes and deep wrinkles and ghostly-pale skin. The clank of decorative medals on his breast accompanied his footsteps. He was dressed in a simple royal-purple evening coat with uneven tails, gilded buttons and filigree across the collar and sleeves. He carried with him a thin piece of glass with scrolling data—a holo-pad—that illuminated the hallway as he walked.

Di recognized the man from countless newsfeeds and history books.

Lord Rasovant. The creator of Metals.

D09 had never seen him in person before, at least never a time his damaged memory core could recall, and it could not recall anything from before the *Dossier*.

The strange signal was so close now, bouncing off the steel walls like ricocheting bullets.

"Then *find* those coordinates," the older man stressed in a sharp tone. "Surely one of the Messiers managed to get their faces."

"As luck would have it, they did not," replied the girl who trailed behind him. She walked with the grace of a dancer, floating without a sound. The pins in her flaxen hair matched her black dress. Floor-length, high collar, the insignia of the crown on her sleeve. She was a royal servant, and yet she spoke so informally to him that Di thought it strange. "Rasovant, this ship is not worth our time."

The Iron Adviser stopped in the middle of the hallway and turned back to her. "Mercer stole that ship, and I want it back. Find it. Do whatever is necessary."

"Whatever necessary?" The signal turned sharp and grating. It made D09 shudder, rattling his code. "Are you sure?"

"Yes, Mellifare," Lord Rasovant replied.

This was not part of the plan. If Rasovant was looking for his own fleetship, then Di would let him find it—without interferrence. This was not worth the trouble it entailed, and he had promised Siege to keep Ana safe. This was not, in any definition of the word, *safe*.

Finding a way to fix his memory core was not worth Ana's life.

The servant girl, Mellifare, smiled. "My pleasure—"

From the far end of the hallway came a guard, clad in the

royal purples of the crown. A Royal Guard. If the Royal Guard were here, then so was the Grand Duchess. The odds of him or Ana escaping decreased by the moment.

"My lord, a moment," said the guard. She was tall, with white-blond hair and arrowhead-shaped markings under her eyes—heritage markings for certain Cercian clans. The woman must have been from one of the few Cercian Ironblood families, as only Ironbloods could join the Royal Guard.

"Royal Captain Viera," the Adviser greeted her. "What can I do for you?"

"There may have been a breach in security," Viera replied, a hand resting on the lightsword at her hip. She was young to be the Royal Captain. Eighteen. If not for the Plague that had decimated an entire generation twenty years ago, he doubted she would be in such a position.

"A breach?" asked the Iron Adviser.

"Yes, a waiter was found tied up in the pantry without clothes. We believe we have an imposter in the garden, and the Grand Duchess is not safe. Should I notify her or—"

"That will not be necessary. I will tell the Messiers to assist you so you can deal with this quietly."

"I don't need their assistance, my lord—"

"Of course you do, Captain. Messiers are here to protect, after all."

"Yes, sir," replied the Royal Captain, trying to disguise the downturn of her mouth as she gave another low bow and left.

If the guards found Ana in the garden, she could not fend them off alone—and there was a 93.7 percent chance that she *would* fight. She did not know how not to.

The signal spiked again, tugging at his code. D09 jerked—and his metal elbow hit the wall with a resounding *ding*.

Rasovant's assistant snapped her gaze over. Her eyes narrowed.

D09 went rigid as he raised firewalls against the signal. Another glitch picked at his code, pulling like kite strings.

"Is something the matter?" asked Lord Rasovant.

The young woman shook her head. "Nothing important. Let us go—the Grand Duchess should be announcing her heir soon. . . ." She grabbed her elder by the hand and tugged him along the hallway. She did not look back.

The spiking signal faded, until only an echo remained.

He sank to his knees, twitching as his programming righted itself again. If that assistant saw him, why did she not say so? The glitch tugging at his processors ebbed, giving him access to his own functions again.

"Jax?" He sent out a comm-link to the skysailer. There was no answer for a moment, and then—

"Messier. Stupid—gotta—trying hard—marina!"

That did not bode well.

Rerouting his energy to his legs, he got to his feet. He would not glitch. Not now. Not yet.

He must find Ana.

ROBB

The cityscape of Nevaeh passed below, a grid of grimy, dilapidated buildings.

Nevaeh had been the only safe haven from the Plague twenty years ago, so everyone who was not infected had moved here—including Ironbloods, who created the gardens to separate themselves from the citizens. An extra layer of protection from the Plague. But soon the space station fell into disarray, with too many citizens and too little space and no money left to buy land on-world on Eros or Iliad after the Plague was eradicated.

At least the view from the floating garden was still beautiful, he reasoned, as he rotated the piece of iron ore his father had given him between his hands. It was an old habit, and he always felt closer to his father when he did it. The ore rusted in his grip.

His father had given it to him the night he'd left for the Iron Palace seven years ago, mere hours before the Rebellion, when the palace's North Tower went up in flames. The fire killed the royal family and—as rumors went—his father as well.

"Keep it safe until I get back, son," his father had said. Robb still remembered the way he looked in the light that leaked through the cracked doorway into his room, thick beard and blue eyes and a lightsword on his back. "Don't let anyone know you have it. I'll be back by morning."

Then he'd kissed Robb's forehead and was gone into the night.

It was the last time Robb ever saw him.

In the seven years since, Robb still couldn't puzzle out why his father had given him a *rock*, reminding him every day of what he was not. It was a piece of the same iron that made the crown, and like the crown, it rusted for everyone who touched it. Except those chosen by the Goddess to lead the kingdom. For the last thousand years that had been the Armorov bloodline, until they died in the Rebellion.

Would it rust for his brother, a Valerio?

Would it even *matter*?

Erik was the next in line, despite not being of Armorov blood. The Valerios were related to the Armorovs by marriage— their late aunt had married the late Emperor. But when they died in the Rebellion, the Grand Duchess became the interim ruler until the Moon Goddess chose another Emperor.

The Moon Goddess never did.

So now, what alternative did the kingdom have other than Erik Valerio? Besides, the other side of the Armorov bloodline, the Aragons, had gone reclusive after they'd lost their only daughter to outlaws.

Emperor Erik. The title made Robb sick.

The Valerio family was the wealthiest in the kingdom and ruled over twenty-three districts on Eros and Iliad, and a mining continent on Cerces, so they were expected to present themselves with a certain flair—especially at parties.

He straightened his vintage blue evening coat—it was his favorite, but after that altercation in the shrine there was a tear at the elbow. He hoped the flowers covered up the stench from the back alley of Nevaeh and no one would pay attention to the scratch on his cheek. He smoothed back his brown curly hair and took a calming breath.

"Please remove that unpleasant look from your face, darling, people are watching," said an arsenic-and-honey voice.

Robb jumped, almost dropping the ore. He quickly pocketed it, rubbing the rust off on his dark trousers.

His mother came to rest against the railing beside him, her tea-length crimson dress, diamonds sewn into the lace, glittering like a bloodred sky.

"Was it too much to ask for you to be on time to a party for once?" she asked.

"Forgive me, Mother," he said with a short bow. "I lost track of time."

"And where were you this time? The horse races? A gambling den?"

"A shrine."

She waved her hand dismissively. "The less I know about whatever you do these days, the less I'll dislike. But you can at *least* be present at your brother's celebration," she added after a moment, pursing her red lips. "Your brother will be named heir to the Iron Throne—"

And crowned on the thousand-year anniversary of the Iron Kingdom, on the morning the three planets of Eros, Iliad, and Cerces aligned—Holy Conjunction—as if his brother could *get* any more insufferable.

The coronation next week couldn't come fast enough.

"—and you need to start acting like the head of this family," his mother finished.

The words made him pause. Feel nauseous. "Forgive me, what?"

"It's only natural when the new Emperor takes the crown that he abdicates all family ties, and as the Goddess must have foreseen," she said with an air of bitterness, "I have a second son."

Robb bit the inside of his cheek before he could say anything he regretted. He wasn't like his brother. At nineteen, Erik Valerio was dashing, popular, and conniving in a way that granted him whatever he wanted. He looked like their mother—tall and olive skinned, a sharp face, with straight dark hair and a smile that made you want to trust him. He was made to lead.

And as the second son, Robb never thought he would amount to much. He looked the most like their father, broad shouldered and stocky, with hair that curled like the lies that fell from his tongue.

Goddess save him, the *head* of the Valerio family?

That was his father's position. His father's title. Not his.

"Right, of course. *Naturally.*" He turned to flag down a waiter for a glass of champagne. "The rose blend," he began—and paused.

The waiter wore a black collar around his neck. A voxcollar. Robb tried to keep his face placid, even though the sight of one of those horrible things made his blood boil. His grandfather had created them to control the prisoners on Cerces, but taking away one's voice was a punishment no one should endure.

"Oh yes, I've been wanting to try that one—make it two," added his mother, and the waiter bowed and left. Then she frowned. "I would much prefer Messiers at our next engagement. They do not gossip. I'm sure Lord Rasovant would let us borrow a few."

"Is that why we're using voxcollars on our employees?" he asked, keeping his voice level. *To keep them from gossiping?*

"Do you disagree with my choices?" his mother asked, narrowing her eyes. "Voxcollars keep my employees loyal."

"Humans can't be HIVE'd, Mother—"

"No but they can be quiet. As Valerios, we need to be mindful of what people say, especially once our Erik takes the throne."

Because if word got out that the crown rusted for Erik Valerio, his legitimacy would be questioned, and instead of finding someone the crown *didn't* rust for—including a citizen not of the nobility—the Ironbloods would rather choose their own. It was easier to control a kingdom that way.

But if he said as much to his mother, he wouldn't have a tongue.

"And once he *does* take the throne," she went on, "I will see to it that the Academy will forgive your prior misdeeds and welcome you back. I cannot have an uneducated son running my family."

Prior misdeeds, as if his failures were simply part of a laundry list to be expunged, like every other smear on the family.

He pushed himself off the railing. "Excuse me, Mother, I think I hear my name being—"

She took his right wrist and pressed into the thin flesh to grind the tracking chip into the bone.

He sucked in a painful breath.

"I know you are still searching for him, Robbert," she said, her eyes more steel than blue, marbles behind kohl lashes. "You will put an end to these heedless fantasies. Your father is dead, and we have a legacy to pursue. *Toriean el agh Lothorne*"—their family's motto, carved into every crest and every insignia with their name—"Glory in the Pursuit. Understand that. Be the man your father couldn't, or you will ruin us all."

She pressed for a moment longer, grinding, grinding, thumb digging into his skin, before she released him.

He drew his arm away quickly, rubbing the tender flesh. He couldn't meet her icy eyes. The tracking chip had been a precaution years ago, implanted permanently into both of her sons so she'd never lose her family again.

At least that was what she'd told them.

He could run, slip through the asteroid belt surrounding their kingdom, and disappear to the farthest reaches of the galaxy, but he could never escape her.

"Yes, Mother," he replied as the waiter came back with their drinks. He pushed the glass of champagne away apologetically, trying not to stare at the voxcollar. "Can we pick this up later? Mother, it was a pleasant chat. We must do it again soon."

He managed to control his gait as he left, careful not to let his anger dig into him until he was out of her sight. If she thought he would stop searching for his father now that he had a lead, she was sorely mistaken.

He was about to take the stairwell hidden behind a curtain of honeysuckle vines when his brother's voice drifted up from the roses. "What do we have here? A rodent in the bushes?"

Robb's feet slowed to a stop.

"Haven't seen you around before. I think I would've noticed someone like you," his brother went on—and one of his lackeys laughed. "And she doesn't have a voxcollar! You really aren't supposed to be here, are you? Trying to sneak in to get a better look at your new Emperor? Go on, take a good look."

Now he understood why his mother had wanted the wait-staff voxcollared.

"Let go of me, *asshole!*"

He froze. He knew that voice—the outlaw from the shrine. The one with the rogue Metal. She had followed him *here*? How could Rasovant's ship mean *that much* to a criminal? When caught, she'll be arrested—at the very *least* for trespassing.

How had she escaped the Messiers, anyway?

The good Valerio part of him said to get the guards and call it a day, but his feet remained rooted to the spot.

"Oh, *let* you go?" Erik went on. "Or what? Where'd you get that uniform, sweets?"

"From your mother's corpse, you *pig*."

His brother laughed. "Aren't you spunky—"

Turning toward the voices, Robb inhaled a little bit of courage and rounded a particularly dense rosebush to find Erik with a hand clamped tight around the girl's wrist, his knuckle rings glinting. He never went anywhere without them.

She tried to twist against him, but his brother was stronger, thicker. Struggling was useless—Robb had sported enough black eyes in his lifetime to find that out.

Erik glanced over at him and grinned. "Oh, look who finally arrived. How's it, brother? Do *you* know who this little ferret is?"

"She's with me," Robb lied easily, and the girl shot him a sharp glare.

"*You?*" his brother scoffed.

"Come now, is it that hard to believe?"

Erik's lips curled into a sneer. He gave the girl another once-over, lingering on her scar that stretched from eyebrow to chin, and released her. "Of course not. You always made poor friends."

It was a stab Robb tried not to flinch at. Everyone knew about the Umbal boy at the Academy—or they thought they did. But no one knew, not really, how deep that wound ran. How Robb had tried to talk him out of the window, laying their entire relationship bare to all the nosy, shitty people who watched from below. How the words didn't matter.

And how, after, Robb himself felt like he had fractured on the ground, too.

With one last sneer to the girl, Erik Valerio snapped his fingers and left with his cronies, off to flirt with some unassuming Ironblooded girl. Erik was good at wearing masks—he'd tricked the entire Ironblood society with an amiable smile and a few choice words, so that even the knuckle rings he wore looked polite. They didn't see what they didn't want to, the real person underneath.

Once Erik and his escorts were gone, the girl turned to him with a scowl. "I didn't *need* your help, Ironblood."

He pulled his fingers through his curly hair. "You shouldn't have followed me."

Her eyes widened. "You're that Iron—"

The orchestra struck up the royal march—the Grand Duchess's entrance cue. His ears prickled. *Already?* If his brother could see through this outlaw's disguise, he didn't want to chance the Royal Guard getting a look at her.

He'd opened his mouth to tell her to leave when she grabbed him by the forearm and pulled him into the shrubbery after her.

ANA

Through the gates, half a dozen royal guardsmen proceeded into the garden, white-gloved hands resting on the hilts of their ornate lightswords. In the middle of them, her gait slow like the moon rising over the sky, was the Grand Duchess.

The threads of her gray gown shimmered with the colors of Nevaeh's dusk in a beautiful array of oranges and pinks, like the surface of an opal.

Ana drank the woman in, from the delicate wrinkles across her face to her silvery-white hair pulled back into a simple bun, making her cheekbones look sharp enough to cut. Her skin was the color of soft earth and speckled with age, her hands bony knobs. She looked old, but in a terrifying and timeless way, the way mountains looked old but immovable.

The Grand Duchess wasn't a true Armorov. She was an Aragon by blood. All the royal women had married into the family, because the crown had sired only boys for the last thousand years.

Until a daughter was born seventeen years ago. The

Goddess returned, everyone said. But then she died with the rest of her family in the Rebellion.

Blood or not, the Grand Duchess was the last Armorov of an era that would die with her. And to Ana, that sounded a little sad.

And lonely.

One by one, the Ironbloods knelt. She'd never seen an Ironblood so much as nod before—it was always the galaxy bending to them.

Ana and the Ironblooded boy were trapped in the shrubbery, surrounded on all sides by men and women in billowy dresses and too-bright suits. She caught the boy's elbow when he tried to sneak away, pinning him with a dangerous look.

If they moved—or so much as snapped a twig—the silence would tell on them.

"My friends, my court," the Grand Duchess began, extending her hands. "Please rise."

And like a tide, the Ironbloods swelled to their feet again.

"There is a story we tell our children. Once, I told this story to my beloved granddaughter. So in honor of her memory, I will tell you the story today."

Even though her voice was small, Ana felt herself drawn toward it, hanging on her words in a strange, intoxicating way.

"Far above the crown of stars, there lay a kingdom cast in shadows. . . ."

Ana knew the story—everyone did. It was the beginning of *The Cantos of Light*. Of a kingdom in darkness and a girl of light. The Ironbloods mouthed the words they knew by heart, as far below citizens knelt in creaky pews of old shrines, praising the Goddess who had birthed the Iron Kingdom. It was said that after a thousand years the Goddess would return to defeat the Great Dark again. Ana quite liked the story. The thousand-year anniversary was a week away, during the alignment of the Holy Conjunction, but there was no sign of a *Great Darkness*, whatever that meant.

It was a bedtime story—some illuminating metaphor—for young kids and dusty old scholars.

As the Grand Duchess told the story, Ana's cheek began to ache, and she massaged her scars against the pain, wondering if Di was all right. She hoped he'd found a good hiding spot.

"Thank you, my friends," the Grand Duchess went on, nodding, "and thank you, Lady Valerio, for inviting us to your beautiful garden. It is a wonder, full of ancient heirlooms and new blossoms. It reminds us that from death we can bloom anew."

Lady Valerio looked wicked, from her bloodred lipstick to her bloodred dress, as she gave a gracious bow. "It was my honor, Your Grace. These are difficult times."

"Indeed they are," the Grand Duchess agreed, "but we must push forward. Twenty years ago, a Plague ravaged our peaceful kingdom, taking with it the best and brightest of its age, including my husband, Emperor Nicholii I. But just as we thought the kingdom would perish under the rot of the Plague, our Iron Adviser came to us with a salvation—Metals. They tended to the sick, for the Plague was too easily spread, and helped those infected pass in peace until the Plague was eradicated."

There was a rushing, festering whisper that swept across the crowd. Because Metals were no longer anyone's salvation. Metals were looked down upon. Kicked at. HIVE'd. For creations that had saved the Iron Kingdom, its people sure knew how to express their gratitude.

"For thirteen years, we rebuilt our kingdom. We entrusted Metals to jobs, to lifestyles, for although they could not feel emotions, they could think as we could, and converse as we could, and some of us even found friendship in them.

"But we soon found out that Metals could also be callous, and hateful. On the eve of the nine hundred and ninety-third anniversary of the Goddess, Metals laid siege to the Iron Palace and burned the North Tower where my family slept, destroying the heart of our kingdom." Her voice broke under the weight of the words. "They took my family—my son, Emperor Nicholii Armorov the Second, his wife, Selena Valerio Armorov, and their four young children. Those Metals took your Emperor, and your future. They burned the first daughter born to our kingdom in a thousand years—she was to be the coming of the Goddess, the savior predicted in our *Cantos of Light.* It is an unspeakable tragedy to lose the light in our lives."

Ana scowled. "Does everyone really believe this trash? There are other tragedies, too," she muttered to herself.

"None as great," the Ironblood argued in a hushed whisper.

"None as *great*? What about the shantytowns in Nevaeh, or the crime-ridden cities on Iliad, or the mines on Cerces. Those people don't matter, do they? All that matters is this one girl, who probably *wasn't* the Goddess."

The Ironblood opened his mouth to say something, but a cheer rose up across the garden, and whatever he was going to say sank into the noise.

"But we will not crumble into darkness," the Grand Duchess continued with conviction. "For the last seven years, I have steered our kingdom the best I could, and our faithful Iron Adviser, Lord Rasovant, created the HIVE so the kingdom could be safe again."

Safe. Ana had felt a little less than safe when the HIVE'd Messiers were shooting at her not an hour ago—and she hadn't even done anything to *warrant* being shot at. The kingdom was only safe to the snotty Ironbloods, who could pay for that sort of protection with their own private guard.

Like the Valerios.

The Grand Duchess looked toward the stars high, high above, past the harbor and the thousands of ships docked there. "But we will grieve no longer. I have finally chosen my successor. Our Ironbloods are strong, and I have selected the one who embodies our greatest qualities—resilience, courage, and strength."

The Grand Duchess reached out her hand to one of the men standing in the crowd. "Erik Valerio, ever since your father passed in the Rebellion, you have led your family through the hardship like very few young men I know. You have embodied all that it is to be Ironblood. Will you follow as Armorovs have for a thousand years? Will you be resilient, courageous, and strong? Will you be loyal to the Iron Crown?"

The dark-haired man in question stepped forward, swooping

a low, low bow. Just looking at him made her skin crawl. It was the young man who had grabbed her wrist earlier, called her a *rodent*.

"It would be an honor, Your Grace," Erik Valerio replied.

He was to be their new Emperor? He didn't embody any of those traits, unless the Grand Duchess wanted a resiliently strong *asshole*. But the way he bowed to the other Ironbloods, a fixed smile of absolute sincerity on his face, she could see how they'd be fooled. How anyone could be.

And what about the Iron Crown? It rusted for everyone the Moon Goddess didn't choose. Wouldn't they test it on Erik Valerio? To see if he was worthy? It would rust for him—it *had* to.

A cheer erupted through the garden, his name on the lips of every Ironblood.

"Long live Emperor Erik!"

"Long live the Iron Kingdom!"

The cheer was so loud, she didn't hear the Ironblooded boy until he grabbed her by the arm. "You really have to leave."

"Not without what I came here for," she snapped, and shoved him as hard as she could. He tripped back over his feet and landed flat on his back. She dove on top of him, slipping a hand into his pockets for the coordinates chip.

Around them, Ironbloods applauded over the sound of their scuffle. Trumpets sounded as the Grand Duchess departed, so no one heard Ana slam her fist into his face.

Then she took the chip.

"No hard feelings, though," she added snarkily, echoing the

very words he had said to her in the alleyway, before he grabbed her by the uniform sleeve.

"Please!" the Ironblood gasped, his lip bleeding against his pearly-white teeth. "I need—"

"There she is!" someone cried. From the honeysuckle-vined exit, a woman in royal purple emerged, arrowhead-shaped Cercian markings etched under her sharp eyes.

Great Dark take me, Ana thought, recognizing the Royal Captain of the Guard. Viera Carnelian.

Messiers spilled out from behind her, swarming around her like a legion of ants, their placid blue eyes on no one but Ana.

"Goddess's *spark*," she groaned.

ROBB

Viera Carnelian. Top of her class. Graduated a year ahead of him, perfect test scores and an infuriating knack for fencing. She always said she would be part of the Royal Guard. He hadn't expected her to be the *Royal Captain*.

Then again, Viera Carnelian never did anything halfway.

And if she or the Messiers caught that girl, there went any chance of him finding his father. Goddess, he hated his luck. He hated it *so much*.

Struggling to his feet, he knew there was a servants' entrance on the other side of the garden. Less used, the shrubbery thick with gardenias and moonlilies. The Messiers drew closer, burrowing into the Ironblood crowd like the roots of a tree.

If he could drag that girl across the garden to that exit, it would be a straight shot to the docks—

"You reported me!" The girl spun back to him, face blazing with anger.

"When would I have had a chance to do that?" he asked incredulously.

"I'm going to run you through with—"

"Sounds nice." He grabbed her by the arm, wiping his bloody mouth on his coat sleeve. He hauled her through the nearest hedge, twigs and thorns catching on his favorite evening coat, as they plowed over rare flowers in a mad dash for the unused exit.

A hand shot out through the bushes and grabbed her, knuckle rings glinting. Erik hauled the girl against him with a snarl. "You aren't leaving."

She struggled, but he twisted her arm behind her back to keep her close.

Robb reared his fist back for a punch—

The girl slammed the back of her head into his brother's face. Erik gave a cry and she twisted her wrist out of his grip. Blood poured from his nose and onto his dapper crimson evening coat. He would *definitely* be angry about that in a minute. Robb didn't want to stick around for it.

"Get them!" the Royal Captain shouted to the Messiers. "Don't let them escape!"

That sounded like a challenge.

Taking her by the hand again, Robb pulled the outlaw between a row of hydrangeas and escaped down the stairs. As they passed utility and storage closets, he grabbed his light-sword from where a servant had propped it up by the coat check and slung it over his shoulder. It was a safe weight on his back, and he instantly felt better with it on. More in control.

Because Goddess knew this was spinning out of control— *fast.*

"I have to find Di," the girl was saying frantically. "I have to find him before the Messiers do!"

"Then give me the chip," he replied.

"What?"

"The coordinates! And you can go find—"

At the end of the hallway, the marina doors yawned open. On three Messiers.

Robb shot up his arms in surrender. *This is okay. This is fine*—who was he *kidding?* He didn't have enough luck to get away with all this.

"Surrender the coordinates," one Messier said.

"Or *what?*" the girl challenged, making Robb sorry for everything he'd ever done in his life to deserve this moment.

The Messiers did not even pause as they raised their Metroids, ammunition humming brightly. "Or you will die."

The girl paled. "Now wait a minute—"

Goddess, this was a bad day.

Reaching back, he pulled out his lightsword and slammed the superheated blade into the middle guard, carving a line down its front like it was soft butter. The Messier's eyes flickered as he sliced through the android's torso and it dropped in two pieces, wires sparking.

The other two Messiers swung their Metroids toward him. He flinched—

A blur rushed past him, grabbing one Messier by the head.

Robb stared dumbfounded. It was a Metal—the *girl's* white-eyed rogue Metal.

It spun the Messier around under its arm and anchored its

fingers under the Messier's chin. And pulled—one time, then again, wires snapping out of the Messier's neck like rubber bands. Then the rogue Metal tore the Messier's head clean off.

Oh, Robb thought, *I'm going to die.*

The last Messier standing adjusted its aim to the rogue Metal.

"Di!" the girl cried, stealing the lightsword from Robb's grip. With an appalling lack of skill, she hacked at the Metal, carving a gouge deep into its chest. The Messier's eyes flickered once—twice—before she toppled it to the ground with a kick. Robb snatched his sword back.

The girl's Metal said, "We need to leave, Ana."

"You *think?*" the girl—Ana, apparently—snapped, and turned to Robb with a glare. "I don't need your help, Ironblood."

He returned the glare. "You're welcome—"

The distinct stomp of Messier boots echoed down the hallway—the heartbeat of an unrelenting monster.

The three of them fled into the marina.

The metallic smell of city exhaust flooded Robb's nose, washing away the stuffy aroma of flowers and Ironblood perfumes, as if the garden had been a dream.

Astoria hovered at its zenith—over five hundred feet in the air, closer to the skyline than the city streets below. A terrifying height, people so small that they blended into the streets, neon signs like twinkling stars.

Her Metal overrode the marina keypad, locking the doors to buy them time. His skysailer was two docks over—but it was trackable. *Everything* he owned was trackable. *He* was track-able.

But the girl seemed to have her own plan as she fled down the longest dock into the middle of the marina, the cityscape hundreds of feet below.

"What are you doing?" he asked, following. "It's a dead end—"

She grabbed him by his coat collar and whipped him around, forcing him to the dock ledge. His heels teetered off precariously.

Oh.

Oh, so *this* was her plan.

He felt light-headed remembering the window at the Academy. Remembering the moment the Umbal boy let go.

If he fell—if she dropped him—he would die before he hit the ground, wouldn't he?

Had Aran Umbal?

"Why do you want the coordinates?" she snapped, and when he didn't answer, she shook him.

"M-my father w-went missing," he said, holding on to her wrists, so if he fell he'd be damned sure to bring her with him. "I think—I think he was on Rasovant's ship."

"You *think*?"

"Why do *you* want the ship?" he asked.

Messiers were at the door now, trying to override the lock. Any moment they'd break through, and whatever hole he dug himself into would quickly bury him.

"Ana," her Metal said when he caught up to them, "we can ask later."

She narrowed her eyes.

The door buckled and collapsed, and the Messiers stepped through in perfect unison. Their eyes blazed with the glory of victory. Royal Captain Viera elbowed through the line, the ammunition in her Metroid glowing like starlight.

Goddess, this day was spacetrash.

"Release the young lord safely," the Royal Captain said, "and we will not harm you."

Well, *that* was a lie.

But the girl took the bait. She swung Robb off the edge and let go of him, turning to face the Royal Captain with her hands up in surrender. Her Metal followed suit.

Robb fixed his coat collar. *Seriously?* They *believed* that?

Viera crept closer, her face as stoic as those of the Messiers who followed her. "Now lower yourself onto the ground. . . ."

Ana glanced over at Robb. "You might want to hang on to something."

"Why?" he asked, confused, as a hum began to vibrate up into the marina. "What's that?"

A gust of wind rushed up from the city below, sending his coattails fluttering. The docks gave a heave, skysailers bumping together with sharp thwacks. He pinwheeled his arms to keep his balance, jerking his head around to find the source of the wind.

A skysailer rose up above the docks, windshield flipped open. The pilot, his long starlight-silver ponytail whipping like a ribbon in the wind, pulled up his goggles and gave him a wink.

Robb stared.

Goddess's spark, was he already dead?

"Down!" cried the girl, grabbing him by the arm, and jerked him to the ground as the pilot tilted the skysailer forward.

The wind howled. Roared. Scraped over them. It tossed the skysailers out of their parking spaces like toy boats and sent the Messiers and the Royal Captain flying backward.

The next Robb knew, the Metal had him up by his coat and was tossing him into the sky. To his death. One moment there was the dock—then the cityscape far below. This was how he was going to die.

He knew it.

Metals could never be trusted.

Until the skysailer came into view.

He covered his face with his arms a split second before he slammed into the backseat of the sailer with the wind knocked out of him. He scrambled to his knees, trying to catch his breath. His body shook.

The pilot glanced back at him with eyes the color of lilac flowers. Silver hair, violet eyes—a Solani. "Buckle up, little lord. Don't want your pretty ass falling out."

Robb pulled himself to sit up as the girl and her Metal jumped next. They quickly sat, fishing for their seat belts as if his request wasn't an exaggeration at all. Seriously? Robb had never buckled himself into a skysailer in his entire l—

A bullet pinged off the dash.

He glanced back to the source and found Viera struggling to her feet, smoking Metroid in her grip. A thin line of blood ran down her forehead. There was a gleam in her eyes—dark, feral, resolute—that made him shiver.

She shot again.

This time the bullet struck through the grates to the engine. Red warnings flared up across the dashboard as the engine gave a whine, sputtered—

And died two thousand feet above the city of Nevaeh.

The skysailer fell straight through the marina, between the lines and lines of traffic, spiraling. Wings fluttering, wobbling, useless. A scream tore out of the girl's throat as her Metal planted a hand over her lap to keep her secure.

The ground came at them fast.

Too fast.

And above them Astoria shrank and shrank, until it was a disk above them, shining like a silver sun.

Robb had the distinct feeling that he should've stayed in the garden. He shouldn't have saved the girl. He should've stopped looking for his father years ago. He should've listened to his mother.

You will put an end to these heedless fantasies, she had said. He should have listened. And now he was going to die.

The pilot grabbed tightly onto the steering wheel and pulled up, trying to jump-start the engine again. If a bullet hit a spark plug, they were dead. Or an exhaust pipe. Or—literally *anything else*—they were dead.

Goddess bright, please don't let us die—

The engine gave a start and hummed to life again. Wings fanned up, tried to catch the wind, to slow them down. They were falling too fast—no matter how hard the Solani pulled on the controls, it wouldn't make a difference. He couldn't force the helm back far enough for the wings to right themselves.

Numbers flashed across the dashboard.

Three hundred feet. Two fifty. Two hundred.

They were dropping like deadweight. They'd land smack in the middle of Nevaeh, a lump of splattered guts and rogue Metal.

And Robb was vain enough to want a better eulogy than *My son killed himself the way his late father did—with a Metal and a misguided sense of duty.*

Like *hell* he'd let his mother write *that* eulogy.

As the wind screamed up around them, he dove over to help the pilot—buckling up be *damned* if he was dead. He reached his arms around the Solani, who was a lot taller than he realized, to grab ahold of the steering wheel. Pressed his back against him, feeling the bumps of his spine. He smelled vaguely of lavender.

"Pull!" Robb shouted over the roar of the wind.

He and the Solani pulled back together. More. More. Until—

A loud crack burst across the skysailer. The wings rippled, bulging with air, as the aircraft finally caught itself. Slowed. Robb gripped the driver's midsection as he reached forward and overrode the propulsion controls.

The ship shuddered, slowing to skim over punctured and rusted rooftops, leaving the floating garden far, far behind. After a moment, Robb let go. He stumbled back. Dizzy. He couldn't get a deep enough breath, for some reason.

"Next time, we should at least trade names first," joked the Solani. He had a charming face, long silver eyelashes, and sharp cheekbones. *A nice face*, he thought a moment before the smirk dropped from the Solani's pretty lips. "Goddess, you're *bleeding*!"

He became distinctly aware of the pain in his side. Why did it hurt to breathe? He looked down. Blood stained the right side of his favorite evening coat. Was—was that *his* blood?

"Oh . . . ," he laughed, but it sounded more like a wheeze. "I'm shot."

The pilot looked alarmed. "Someone catch him before he—"

Darkness ate his vision, and the last thing he knew, he was tipping over the side of the skysailer.

II

IRON SHIPS

ANA

The *Dossier* was a ship of beauty.

The Cercian-7 transportation vessel was from an era before Metals and Rebellions. Close to a century old, the black-and-chrome girl was retrofitted, so it looked like a patchwork of old parts and new spares. Too many firefights had run its three black solar sails ragged, and still it kept sailing like a dead man in the night. The ship wasn't as fast as newer models, but it was quiet and durable and its solar engine purred sweet as nectar. It was finicky to fly, so most pilots couldn't handle it properly, but Jax flew it like a dream.

The cargo bay could fit a skysailer and crates for goods and their latest haul, connecting to an infirmary and an engine room. Up a rickety set of rusted stairs was the crew's quarters, the galley, the captain's room, and the cockpit where Jax spent most of his time. The ship constantly hummed from the golden solar energy core at its heart, a sweet and low song that Ana couldn't sleep without, and the ship always smelled like recycled air, rust, and gunpowder.

There was never enough privacy, the showers were always colder than the darkest recesses of space, and you could hear someone whisper from *anywhere* on the ship. But her bunk was warm, and her mattress lumpy to fit her curves, and the crew was like her—forgotten, exiled, orphaned, refugeed. Her family.

Home.

Her jittery nerves leveled off the moment the *Dossier* came into view in Nevaeh's harbor. After Jax caught the Ironblood from falling out of the sailer, Di had tried to stop the bleeding on the way back to the ship—and avoid ruining Jax's newly upholstered backseat. Ana sincerely hoped the rich boy wasn't dead. Or dying.

She didn't want anyone dying on her watch.

The cargo doors of the *Dossier* closed them inside, sucking space out with a sharp whistle, before Jax pushed up the windshield of the skysailer. Di scooped the Ironblood into his arms like a rag doll and hurried him into the infirmary.

A small cube-shaped robot met them, hovering at eye level. The bot was the newest addition to the ship. It kept the guns calibrated, the programs updated, the solar engine humming— and its nose in everyone else's business.

The robot beeped, hovering over Ana's shoulder, but she pushed it away absently. "Not now, EoS."

It buzzed around them anyway.

"We should've dropped him at a medic ward instead," Jax said, tugging at his gloves.

"Then the Messiers *would've* caught up to us," Ana replied, closing the skysailer windshield after them, and followed Di into the infirmary, "and you know Di's the best medic."

"We have a bloody *Ironblood* on this ship, Ana. What if he's a Carnelian? Or—or a *Valerio*?"

EoS blipped.

"See, the bot agrees."

"The bot cannot think for itself," Di replied, rolling the Ironblood onto a gurney.

The boy groaned. He was alive, at least.

Di went on, "The bot is merely an instrument—"

"At least it obeys," came a cool, stern voice from the front of the cargo bay, where a set of stairs led up to the first level of the ship.

Ana grimaced at the voice and slowly turned to her captain. "I can explain. . . ."

The middle-aged woman did not look amused. Dressed in a loose blouse and dark trousers, she looked like she might've been relaxing—and Ana hated that she had interrupted that. The captain's black hair framed her brown face in wild, electrifying curls, glowing with interwoven fiber optics, simmering orange like a stoaked fire—

Oh, Ana could tell by the color that she was *mad*.

The kingdom feared Captain Siege. She was ruthless and she was smart. She never surrendered a ship, never shied away from conflict. No, she didn't eat her enemies' hearts for breakfast—but seeing her rage, Ana realized the captain might start with hers.

"Were you followed?" asked the captain, her voice surprisingly calm despite her wildfire hair.

"There is a ten-point-seven percent chance that we were," said Di before Ana could respond.

Jax scowled. "Thanks for the vote of confidence, metalhea—"

"Jax," the captain interrupted, making him wince, "get us off this Goddess-*blasted* space station before the entire Messier military arrive. The rest of the crew has already returned from shore leave."

The Solani ducked his head. "Yes, Captain." He gave Ana his practiced *I told you so* look before hurrying up the stairs, past Siege, and toward the cockpit.

When he was gone, Captain Siege turned her green eyes to Ana. "My cabin—now."

"But—Di needs help with the Ironblood—"

"Now!" she snapped, then disappeared into the corridor, too.

Ana hesitated for a moment, not wanting to face it—any of it. The events were finally settling into her bones, and they were heavy. Mokuba, the info broker, had been arrested—might be dead. The garden, Erik Valerio's knuckle rings . . .

The boy groaned on the gurney again, his face creased in pain. He tried to grab at his wound, but Di gently pried his hand away. She could almost pity the Ironblood. Almost. Until she remembered that he was an *Ironblood.*

"You should go," Di said as she hovered in the doorway to the infirmary. He took a medical kit from one of the cabinets. "EoS can help me with the Ironblood."

EoS agreed with another blip, using one of its spindly arms to fetch a suture pen from a rack on the counter, and handed it to Di.

"But—" she began.

"Lord Rasovant knows about the coordinates to find the ship," Di interrupted, peeling open the plastic around the suture pen, as the bot disinfected the boy's wound. "I overheard him talking with a royal assistant. He is now looking for it as well."

"We'll beat him to it, then."

"Ana, I am not worth—"

"I need to go see the captain," she excused herself, and hurried up the flight of stairs to the main level.

Ana, I am not worth the trouble, he was going to say.

What did she have to do to prove to him that he was worth any price?

The sound of the parking clamps knocked back, and the *Dossier* left the docks. Ana steadied herself against the wall, the vibration of the backward thrusters humming through the ship. It would take a while to leave the clearance of the harbor, when Jax could deploy the solar sails and send them on their way.

Hopefully before the Messiers or the Royal Guard regrouped.

At the end of the hallway, the door to the captain's quarters slid open with a *blip*. The cabin smelled old and musty, decorated with knockoff tapestries of the rolling landscapes of Eros and star charts of the kingdom dating back five hundred years. There was a small nook where a tiny bed sat hidden beneath mounds of dusty books, a coatrack where Siege's famous bloodred frock coat hung from a peg, and an old mahogany desk too big for the room. On the corner of the desk floated a hologram of the solar system. Three planets—Eros, Iliad, and

Cerces, and all their moons—spun around the sun, trapped inside an asteroid belt. The Iron Kingdom.

The coordinates to Rasovant's lost ship could lead to any-where. Any shadow. Any place the kingdom had forgotten.

Di's fix had never felt so close before, and yet so far at the same time.

Captain Siege, already sitting behind her desk, pointed to the seat opposite her. Ana found her butt in the chair quickly.

"There is an Ironblood in my infirmary," said the captain.

"I can explain!"

"I'm sure you can, darling." The captain took a cigar out from her desk drawer and lit it, the smoldering orange end matching the fiber optics in her hair.

"I know how to fix Di's memory core, Captain. Here—the coordinates." She fished out the small square chip from her borrowed Valerio uniform pocket. "To Lord Rasovant's lost fleetship, the *Tsarina*."

"Mokuba's coordinates," the captain said flatly. "Ana, I told you not to go after them. We have no business—"

"No *business*? Rasovant's ship could save Di and that's *not our business*?"

"That ship is dangerous."

"But we do danger every day!" Ana argued. "Why is this any different? If there's a chance we can save D09? I'll risk—I'll risk *everything*."

"I know," Siege replied, massaging the bridge of her nose. "But what would you have done if you were arrested? If D09 were arrested? *Jax?*"

"They wanted to come—"

"I'm sure they'd follow you to the ends of the stars," the woman replied wryly, "but that doesn't mean you take them there."

She bit the inside of her cheek. "I know, Captain, but I had to try. If anything can tell us how to fix Di's memory core, or point us in the right direction, it's that ship. I *know* it."

The captain sat forward in her chair, cigar wedged into the corner of her lips. "There's lots of rumors about that ship, darling—unsanctioned Metal projects, missing tech, long-lost kingdom secrets—but in my experience, rumors aren't true and that ship's nothing more than a death trap."

"But what if you're wrong? Wouldn't you do anything to save me?"

She puffed on her cigar, chewing on the end. "How did you even get the money Mokuba was asking for it? No—don't tell me. The Ironblood bought it and you improvised."

Ana gave a half shrug, not quite disagreeing, and held out the small green chip to the captain. "Can we at *least* see where these coordinates point? Please. I've never asked for anything before."

She'd never needed to—and she'd been so thankful for that.

But now she was asking.

The captain's hair shimmered a deep orange—the color Ana knew well as "no." But then Siege leaned forward and took the chip out of Ana's outstretched hand. "On one condition," the captain said. "You do what I say whenever I say it—no matter what. Do we have a deal?"

"That's a terrible deal—is this because I didn't tell you I was going to meet Mokuba?"

"Do we have a deal?" repeated the captain.

Ana chewed on the inside of her cheek. If she said yes, she wouldn't have any power if the captain decided to go—but at least they'd be *going*, right?

If it was to save Di, she'd do anything.

"Fine," she agreed.

"Good." The captain inserted the chip into the holo-pad sitting on her desk. The glass screen flickered to life, swirling into a map of the solar system. It zeroed in on a small pinpoint at the edge of the kingdom. Near Cerces.

Ana's chest tightened. *Oh no.*

Palavar.

Desperately, she said, "*Please.* Reprimand me, ground me, take my wages—I don't care. We have to go. I can't lose Di. I—"

The small intercom box lit up, and Jax's voice punched through the receiver. "Captain," he said, and there was something strange in his voice. It put Ana on edge. "We're being followed."

JAX

Careless. He'd gotten too careless.

Eros took up most of the starshield, a blue-and-green planet wrapped in layers and layers of bone-white clouds. In the corner of the starshield was a small video feed he kept his eye on, relaying the space behind them. Nevaeh floated against the backdrop of infinite space like a bulb about to bloom, and from it pursued an Artem-1S schooner. Bright silver, solar rocket propulsion. One of the first ships not to rely on solar sails. It was fast, and it was trouble.

He was good at losing Messiers. They had a one-track mind, and all he had to do was be unpredictable—but he'd never had the privilege of losing the Royal Guard before.

The captain burst into the cockpit like a firestorm.

"Report," she said, resting a hand on the back of his chair. "Flying any colors?"

"Purple and silver, the Royal Guard," he replied tightly as Ana eased through the doorway to the cockpit, staring wide-eyed at the pursuing ship on the screen.

"What did you *do* on Nevaeh, darling?" the captain asked Ana.

"We . . ." Ana, for the first time, was at a loss for words. "I . . ."

Jax tapped his thumbs on the controls, watching the rear screen. Something was wrong. The Artem-1S schooner was still a good distance away, and he knew it could be a lot closer by now. Why was it waiting?

"We might've caught the attention of the Royal Captain," Jax filled in when Ana didn't answer. "The Carnelian one."

"*Viera* Carnelian. Good," the captain said, clearly believing the opposite. "This is good. Perhaps she just wants to be invited aboard for cup of tea."

"We have *tea*?"

"Not for troublemakers." She glared at him. "Any sign of hostility?"

"Not yet—"

A spark ignited from the pinprick of a ship. The whorl of white light drew closer. Warnings flashed across the starshield. *INCOMING PROJECTILE.*

"*Ak'va,*" he cursed, and flicked off the autopilot, pulling up the helm from below the console. He swiped away the warnings, opening up the intercom to the ship. "All hands, *brace!*"

The white-hot missile spiraled closer. He spilled the sails and drew them back into the sides of the ship, banking the ship left as hard as he could. The missile screamed past them like a streak of white and exploded. The blowback knocked the ship toward Eros, rattling the old girl like a tin can full of nails. He quickly steered it out of the gravitational pull of the planet.

Captain Siege leaned over his chair and pressed the inter-com button again. "Stations!" she snapped. "Riggs, give me a damage report when you get down to the hull."

"Aye," came the staticky voice of Riggs a few seconds later.

"Jax, get us out of here."

"Where?" His fingers skimmed along the controls as he tried to check for internal damage, but the blast had just knocked the dust off the rafters. "We can't outrun that thing. We're a *row-boat* compared to an Artem-1S—"

"Aren't you the best pilot in the kingdom?"

His mouth went dry. "I . . . of course I am."

But there was no way to outrun a solar schooner. Those ships were faster, with better maneuverability than any other ship in kingdom space. But they were also heavy.

And the *Dossier*, one of the oldest ships still using solar sails, was very lightweight. Well, he had an idea, at least.

INCOMING PROJECTILE, the starshield read again.

Ana anchored herself in the doorway. "Jax," she warbled, "Jax, it's about to—"

At the last possible moment, he slammed down on the controls. The ship dove toward the blue-green expanse of Eros. A few thousand yards behind, the missile exploded, knocking the *Dossier* lower into the atmosphere. Its wings glowed a brilliant orange, friction against the sky.

If he rode too close to the mesosphere, gravity would drag them in, burning their sails, and all they could ask for then was a soft landing in the Biteryi Sea.

But I know this ship.

He could use Eros's gravitational pull to slingshot around the planet and launch them out into space. The Royal Guard couldn't keep up once gravity took them, and they'd lose the *Dossier*'s signal in the magnetic field of the planet. He just had to stay in the thermosphere and not hit any satellites. Easy.

So easy he could do it *blindfolded*.

. . . Not that he would want to try at the moment.

The taste of excitement—like the moment before you plummet off a cliff—was sharp on his tongue.

A series of small holo-screens lining the console, reading off altitude and speed, deepened to a frantic red. He kept an eye on them as the lights flickered. Space and atmosphere swirled around them, so loud it roared.

Just keep her steady, he coaxed himself, as the ship began to shake violently.

The cockpit was silent as the ship crested against the dark side of the planet, taken by the pull of gravity. Behind them, viewed from a small video feed in the corner of the starshield, was the glint of the Artem-1S following in close proximity. He could almost see the pilot in the cockpit, the solar thrusters on its wingtips flaring as bright as stars.

Come on, he thought frantically, *give up already.*

The *Dossier*'s altitude dropped lower, and lower, and lower until—

The Artem-1S veered up, deflecting into space again so it wouldn't be dragged into Eros. Good, just as he thought it would.

The *Dossier* went lower.

The power flickered and sent them into darkness. The starshield melted into oranges and golds, flames tingeing the corners of the ship's shield like a sunrise. No readings, no data, no warnings.

Nothing.

He tightened his sweaty grip around the controls, reminded of how this was like the skysailer. How he almost hadn't gotten that under control, either.

But he *had*.

He concentrated on the feeling of the ship moving through space—the stars spiraling around them, turning, turning. He was never lost in the stars—he always knew where he was. And it made him a damn good pilot.

Concentrate. He waited for the sun to rise across the horizon. Waited for that spark of light. Only his breath kept him company. Inhale, exhale.

The Captain gripped the back of his chair harder.

Inhale.

Exhale.

All this trouble because of some coordinates and a stupid *Ironblood*? Great Dark take him, he would've spaced the idiot by now.

Inhale—

Light broke across the horizon.

The ship moaned, roared, cried. The planets aligned in the distance—the Holy Conjunction—looking barely more than bright stars to the naked eye. And ahead in the distance glinted Nevaeh, a silver bud about to bloom.

Now.

With a thunderous *pop*, the *Dossier*'s sails snapped to full mast, catching the solar winds.

The ship groaned, cables straining against the sails, lighting the solar core belowdecks. Powering it. The starshield came back to life with a burst of blue light.

The *Dossier* shot out of the gravitational pull of Eros and into the stars. The crew cheered from their stations across the ship, but he didn't celebrate yet.

He checked the radar to see if that solar schooner was still pinging them, but the communications were silent.

It worked.

Finally, he pried his shaking hands from the controls. Waited for a moment, making sure he was still breathing and functional, and then thrust his fists into the air. "And who is the best pilot in the kingdom?" He turned his thumbs toward himself. "This sexy pilot *right here!*"

The captain patted the back of his chair, as close to a congratulations as he'd get. "Nice flying, Jax."

"Go on, tell me more." He grinned. "So, where to? Iliad? Patoor Mav Station?"

For a moment, the captain didn't respond, and the fiber-optic wires in her hair flickered, dimming to a burnt orange. "Set a course for Palavar," she said at last, and in the doorway he heard Ana's breath catch.

He turned to look the captain in the face to make sure she wasn't joking. But then he remembered the captain never joked. "That's . . . Captain—*Palavar?*"

Cerces's dark moon. It orbited around the third planet from the sun in such a way that it always fell into the planet's shadow. No light reached it—and that meant no energy. Ships couldn't function for long, tech would power down.

Not to mention Cerces had at least three separate bounties out for the *Dossier*. If a patrol caught them in Cercian space . . .

"Captain," Jax said, "Palavar's suicide—" And then it dawned on him. "It's where those coordinates point, isn't it? The ship's on the dark moon."

"Aye," she said, and leaned over Jax to the intercom. "Congratulations, crew. I hope we're all in one piece. As most of you have probably already guessed, Ana took it upon herself to steal a few things—an Ironblood included."

Jax wanted to point out that none of them would steal an Ironblood willingly—not even the gorgeous one currently in the infirmary.

"She also stole coordinates to Rasovant's missing fleetship, the *Tsarina*. She thinks there might be something on it that can fix Di's memory core, but there's a good chance someone'll follow us. I don't like the odds"—she paused, pursing her lips—"so speak your grievances now, or you're coming with us. To Palavar."

The captain leaned back and waited. The speed from the maneuver propelled the *Dossier* along so quickly, the ship vibrated, and if Jax's anxiety wasn't already peaking, it might have felt nice—like a massage.

Finally, the intercom crackled and Talle's sweet voice came in from the galley. "Sounds like trouble—I'm in, Sunshine."

"Aye," came the voice of Riggs. Then Lenda, Barger, and Wick. Finally, Jax nodded, too. Even though it was a *given* he'd come along.

Who else would fly the ship?

"Then we're on our way to Palavar," said Siege, and ended the transmission. Jax heard her sigh. "Remember our deal, Ana."

"Thank you!" Ana cried, and tore away from the doorway, her footsteps pounding against the floor as she fled down to the infirmary to talk to Di.

Jax cued up the autopilot. "Looks like we'll be there in seven hours and some change. Are you sure about this? It's Palavar."

"That it is."

"So you think Ana might be onto something, then."

The captain clicked her tongue to the roof of her mouth. "I think love is a powerful thing, Jaxander, and it sometimes makes us blind. We'll need someone monitoring the frequencies all night, at least until we reach those coordinates. You should take a break. I'll look over the cockpit for a while."

He pushed the controls down under the console. "Goddess, *thank you*. I think I'm going to take a nice cold shower because Goddess forbid the heater's working—"

But the captain caught him by the jacket as he went to leave. "—I have a favor, first."

He tried not to wilt. He'd expected as much.

D09

As D09 finished the last suture, the Ironblood awoke with a gasp. D09 anchored a hand on the boy's shoulder and shoved him back down onto the gurney.

"Let me go!" the Ironblood wheezed. "Let me—"

Reaching into the medical kit, D09 drew out a sedative and pressed it into the boy's neck.

"Let me . . ." The Ironblood's eyes rolled into the back of his head and he went limp.

E0S, tending to diagnostics on the medical computer, gave a beep of disapproval.

"He struggled," D09 told it as he disinfected the boy's wound again before wrapping it over with gauze. People were easier to treat when unconscious, he reasoned. He had not sedated the boy because he was more than a little annoyed at their current predicament. He did not become annoyed.

He was Metal.

The sedative would wear off in approximately twenty minutes

and thirty-two seconds. Di would be gone from the infirmary by then.

As he pulled off his bloodstained gloves, the door to the infirmary opened, and he turned just as Ana flung herself at him, arms wrapping around his neck in a hug.

"We're going!" she cried with a laugh. "We're going to the ship!"

"So I have heard."

"We survived *and* we're going to the ship. We're going to fix you! We're going." Smiling, she pressed her forehead against his and closed her eyes. "We're going."

She was so close he could count every dark eyelash.

"Yes, we are," he replied.

He knew how to sew a wound. How to mend bone. He knew the deepest intricacies of flesh and blood, and yet he did not know how to repair himself. That made him insufficient. If his memory core had not been damaged, Ana would not have to endanger herself for him. If he was not there, she would not have to cheat death.

It was logical.

But the way she pressed her forehead against his, and opened her golden-brown eyes, and looked into his as though he was the sun her life orbited around, stopped him from ever saying as much. So he simply stood, his forehead pressed against hers, looking into the face he knew better than his own circuitry—and *that* he had blueprints for.

She took a deep breath, and finally drew away from him.

"It's nice to just listen to you for a moment," she said.

"I did not think I sounded like anything."

"You sound like a symphony of electrical currents," she explained, and began to hum, as if in tune with it, and grabbed his hand to dance. She had not stopped smiling yet, and if he told her that there was a 17.3 percent possibility that they were still being followed, he was sure the smile would drop from her lips.

And he did not want that. Not yet.

"Am I interrupting something?" asked Jax. He leaned against the doorway, a single silver eyebrow raised.

"Why're you here?" Ana asked. "Who's piloting the ship?"

Jerking straight, he gave a gasp. "I'm the *pilot?*"

Ana rolled her eyes. "Very funny."

Jax grinned. "Siege's got the helm for a while. I'm apparently stuck babysitting this troublemaker." He jerked his chin toward the Ironblood.

"Lucky you."

"Mmm. Talle wants you in the galley, by the way, to help set the table. Beef stew tonight, your *favorite.*" Jax poked her in the stomach, and she made a face.

"Come on, Di," she said. "You can help me chop onions."

"You mean do it for you," D09 retorted, letting her pull him out of the infirmary—until Jax put a hand to his shoulder, stopping him. Ana glanced back, confused, but Jax waved his hand for her to go ahead.

"He'll be up in a sec," he told her. She shrugged and went on ahead without him. When she had climbed the stairs, Jax bent in to D09. "I know you love Ana—"

"I cannot love—"

"Well I can, and I do, and I don't want to see her hurt. We both know that ship probably won't have anything—*if* it's even out there. You need to prepare her for that. Trust me, you'll want to say good-bye."

Di could not quite compose a response.

"Metalhead, hurry up!" Ana called from the top of the stairs.

"Think about it." Then Jax let go of his shoulder, and Di left the infirmary.

Ana smiled down from the top of the staircase, her braid pulled over her shoulder, a thorn scratch on her cheek.

He did not need to compose a good-bye yet. He had time.

ROBB

Robb's head was pounding.

What did he *drink* at his brother's celebration? Nothing that he could remember. There was the champagne, but then there was that waiter with the voxcollar, and the outlaw masquerading as a waiter and—*Goddess's spark.*

He snapped his eyes open and looked around. He was in an . . . infirmary? It smelled like disinfectant and gunpowder. The sharp halogen lights made everything bright and blurry. His head swam.

"Get up, Ironblood," singsonged a voice, and poked him in the side.

He sat up with a hiss, holding his ribs. How had he—

Nevaeh. Blood staining his favorite evening coat. Falling out of the skysailer.

The *outlaws.*

Robb scrambled off the gurney, away from a young man with violet eyes. A Solani. The one from the skysailer. He must've been close to Robb's age, but his silver hair made him look old—ancient—and his skin shimmered as if starlight hid just beneath. He wore a ruffly purple evening coat, golden filigree decorating the collar to match the lining, and buttons so polished they gleamed. Underneath that insufferably garish jacket was a silk shirt, stained with what Robb figured was his blood. A pair of goggles sat around his neck.

The Solani was impossibly tall—they all were—with a square face and sharp jawline. His eyes were narrow, eyebrows slivers of silver to match his thick and messy ponytail, his lips pressed into a thin, impatient line.

Robb grabbed the first thing he could find—a suture pen—and held it to attack. The pain in his side was a dull roar, but it was quickly sharpening. "Where am I?" he wheezed.

"The *Dossier*," the Solani replied, "and put that down before you embarrass yourself."

"Last time I woke up, a Metal sedated me."

"D09 rarely likes people who try to get Ana killed. In fact, I don't like those kinds of people, either."

Robb steeled his shoulders, because *Ana* hadn't been the one dangling a thousand feet over Nevaeh's slums. "Fine. I assume I am your prisoner. Where're you taking me?"

"*Taking you?*" The Solani bit back a laugh. "Ironblood, you're just along for the ride."

Embarrassment tinged Robb's ears. "Then where are we going, *star-kisser?*"

The Solani's face pinched. "I have a name, little lord. You could ask me for it."

Robb bit his lip. "Where are we going?" he repeated, trying

to look anywhere but at the Solani—at the cabinets, the rusted walls, the flickering halogen lights of the infirmary.

"The *Tsarina.*"

He gave a start. *"What?"*

"It's Rasovant's lost—"

"Fleetship. The coordinates. Yes, I know. We're going?"

The Solani crossed his arms and leaned against the dormant medical console. "Yes, we are."

I'm prisoner on a ship going to where I need to go, Robb realized. How lucky was *that*? If he played his cards right, he could use these *pirates* to get what he wanted. He just had to survive until then.

There had to be a catch. "Where do the coordinates point?" he asked.

"Palavar."

Ah.

Cerces's dark moon. Of course. It made sense. Where better to hide a solar ship than a place no solar light could reach?

"And no one's following us?" he asked. "Not the Royal Guard or . . ." *My mother*, he thought, rubbing his thumb over the chip in his wrist. It hadn't been activated yet, so his mother either didn't know he was missing or didn't care.

The Solani rolled his eyes. "Please, we lost the Royal Guard. Well, *I* lost them. Modesty is overrated."

"And Vier— Captain Carnelian?"

"Lost her halfway around Eros. She's eating my space dust."

I wouldn't count on that, he wanted to say, because if he knew Viera Carnelian at all—and he knew her better than most—she was viciously stubborn. And righteous.

The Solani inclined his head. "Now come on, we're not stay-ing in the infirmary."

"*We?*"

"Yes, we. Someone has to keep an eye on our esteemed *guest*, and I drew the short straw. What's your name?"

Did no one know he was a *Valerio?*

Am I really this lucky? he thought, putting down the suture pen. These criminals *had* bandaged him up. . . . Why would they do that if they wanted to kill him?

He said the first name that came to mind.

"Aragon."

The Grand Duchess's maiden name. Most of their descen-dants had died of the Plague, so these outlaws would be hard-pressed to catch him in the lie. And when lying, it was best to stick as close to the truth as possible.

"Robb Aragon."

"All right, *Robb Aragon.* I'd say it was a pleasure meeting you, but I can't lie."

"What's your name?"

The silver-haired boy cocked his head, as if debating for a moment. "Jax."

"No last name?"

"Not one that matters. Now follow me." Then Jax pushed himself off the old console and left the infirmary.

Robb—feeling like he didn't have much of a choice—followed. The dried blood on his shirt crackled when he moved. The pain was horrible, but the smell was worse—rotten eggs and iron. He tried not to gag.

Of all the people to get hit by a stray bullet, it had to be him. *Goddess*, he was cursed.

The stairs hurt. Walking hurt. Even breathing hurt. On the first level of the ship, the Solani showed him to an empty bed in the crew's quarters. Two bunk beds sat on either side of the room, with a communal meeting area in the middle. His bunk was apparently across from Jax's. The quarters were small—smaller than any room he'd ever slept in before—and smelled like fresh linens. A row of bookcases lined the far wall, filled with medical texts and ratty adventure books, the covers so worn they were falling off. This . . . wasn't the type of living space he imagined when he thought of outlaws.

The rest of the crew were somewhere else on the ship—Robb could hear them shouting. He'd rather not meet them, but he knew he would eventually.

They'll gut me and eat my insides, he thought, remembering the stories from the Academy.

"Here," said Jax, handing him some clothes from a trunk.

Robb stared at them.

"Unless you want to go around smelling like a corpse, little lord."

Little. A muscle in his jaw throbbing, he took the shirt and breeches. They smelled like lavender, reminding him of the skysailer, pressing his chest against the Solani's back—

He swallowed thickly and turned his back to the silver-haired boy.

Unbuttoning his shirt, he winced as pain spiked across his

ribs again, racing up his side. He managed to get one sleeve off, but it hurt to move his right side. After his third try, he noticed the Solani watching, sitting on the edge of his bunk with one leg draped over the other.

"Do you need assistance?" asked Jax, amused.

"I can do it," he snapped, and to prove it, he unlaced the other sleeve and tore off the shirt, dried blood crinkling, and pulled the new shirt on. It was too baggy. He hesitated before he took off his breeches. "Do you mind?" he asked, giving Jax a pointed look.

"Mind what?"

"A bit of privacy?"

The silver-haired young man grinned then, toothy like a cat. "Afraid I'll judge too harshly?"

Robb narrowed his eyes.

"*Fine.*" Jax sighed, turning to look toward the wall instead. "You know I've always heard Ironbloods were never any fun. Glad it wasn't a lie."

I do have fun, he thought angrily, quickly changing into the new breenches, and sat down to lace up his boots again. The trouser legs were so long, he had to roll them up to his ankles.

"And I'm glad to know that all Solani—" Robb went to stand again when black spots ate at his vision. He swayed, trying to catch himself on the side of the cot, but the Solani caught him first and set him down on the edge of the bed again.

Robb was afraid to move until his head stopped spinning.

"You'll pull your stitches if you don't slow down," the silver-haired boy cautioned, and rerolled Robb's left pants leg.

"I'm fine."

"I'm sure you are," replied the Solani, and leaned forward, "but just a word of warning: if I catch you lying to me or the rest of the crew about *anything* you've said, I promise you'll wish I'd let you fall out of that skysailer on Nevaeh. Do you understand?"

Robb sat back, distancing himself from that fierce violet-eyed glare. His chest wound tight—from panic. It was definitely panic—

A shrill bell rang across the intercom.

Robb jumped.

Jax quirked an eyebrow. "It's the dinner bell, little lord. Stop being so jumpy. You act like you're expecting company." He stood, dusted his knees off with his leather-gloved hands, and left the quarters.

Once he was gone, Robb finally got a chance to catch his breath. The lingering smell of lavender was suffocating.

The sooner this band of space pirates found the fleetship, the better. He hoped this antique ship had enough of a head start to the *Tsarina* before his mother tracked him down. What happened after—to these outlaws, to that Solani and that girl Ana—didn't matter.

His father mattered. Finding him mattered. And the answers were on the *Tsarina*, Robb was sure of it. He was sure he'd find his father. Or find out where he'd gone—find *something*. He had to.

He'd spent seven years searching, and he wouldn't let anything stop him now.

ANA

Ana rubbed her half-melted pendant, contemplating the playing cards in her hand.

The crew sat around the cramped galley table, playing a round of Wicked Luck after dinner. A scoreboard hung on the far wall of the galley with little tick marks under each of their names to signify who had won previous nights. Jax was leading by forty-seven wins.

But no matter how much Ana tried to concentrate on the queen, jack, and three aces in her hands, she couldn't, too afraid that the Royal Guard were still in pursuit and that all of this would be for nothing. She barely ate any beef stew. Her stomach was tied in knots, and hers wasn't the only one. Beside her, Lenda—who normally ate three helpings—hadn't even touched her food.

Please, don't let this be for nothing, Ana thought. *Please let the* Tsarina *be there.*

"Five hours until we reach our destination," Di's voice rang out over the intercom.

"Seriously?" Lenda groaned, brushing back her floppy dishwater-blond hair. She was solid, with narrow brown eyes and tawny skin with rosy undertones. She displayed the scars on her arms like trophies—battles won in the fighting arenas of Iliad. Lenda was twenty and unafraid of everything—

Except, maybe for Palavar. "We've only been traveling for two? It feels like *years.*"

"Eh, don't bother me. Three jacks," said Barger, a stout man in his mid-twenties with a ginger mustache. His fingers were always grease stained, nails ripped short, the signs of a tireless weapons mechanic.

Lenda frowned over her cards. "You can't have three jacks," she told the ginger-mustached man across from her.

Barger snorted. "You ain't gonna call Wicked on me, Len. Hey, *Solani*, your turn."

At the far end of the table, Jax tossed two cards into the middle. "Patience, you heathen."

The object of Wicked Luck was to lay facedown however many cards you had of that pair, and lie your way to zero cards first. If someone caught you in a lie—by saying "Wicked"— then you got the entire pile of discarded cards.

And there was nothing like calling someone a liar to ruin friendships and solidify lifelong grudges.

Jax tossed two cards facedown onto the pile. "Two aces."

"Wicked!" Lenda called, pointing to Jax. "Wicked, Wicked, *Wicked!*"

Jax rolled his eyes and flipped the two cards over. "I can't lie, Len," he said, and the crew roared with laughter.

Lenda raked the entire pile of cards toward her end of the table and sorted through them in her hand.

Ana patted her on the shoulder sympathetically.

At the head of the table, beside the captain, Talle—short and thin, with black hair in a pixie cut and hands so steady she could slit a throat clean while navigating the skyways of Nevaeh—sliced a piece of bread in half with one of the dozen knives from her belt, and buttered it. Siege leaned forward and ate it out of her hand. "Sunshine! That was mine."

"*Ours*," Siege replied, kissing her, and played her hand—three twos. No one called Wicked against the captain. No one ever did. Except Talle.

Talle and Siege had been married longer than Ana had been part of the *Dossier*. She always wondered how they'd met, but it was a secret—like Siege's last name.

Di once said that it seemed surprising that two people who were so opposite could fall in love, but he didn't see that while Siege was the flame, Talle was the shadow. One could not exist without the other.

Ana wished she could explain it. She wondered, often, if he would feel the same about her if he was programmed to have emotions.

Talle leaned over to the old engineer beside her. "Riggs, I think you're up, sweets."

"And get your damn leg off the table and play," Barger grouched.

Riggs, fiddling with a ball bearing in his mechanical leg,

grumbled a reply and heaved it off the table, setting it on the bench beside him. He'd lost his right leg to the Plague twenty years ago—cut it off himself right above the knee. He lost his family to the disease on Eros, and kept a photo of his daughter in a silver locket around his neck. Sometimes at night, Ana heard him talking to her in his dreams. He picked up his cards, fanning them out, and set three down. "Three fives—"

"Wicked!" Lenda roared.

Barger threw up his hands. "You gonna call it all night?"

"Sorry," she muttered sheepishly. "I'm just real jumpy. I don't like Palavar."

"No one does," rumbled Wick, who had a habit of being quiet. He listened, and that made him a talented communications specialist. He absorbed languages like a sponge, so many that Ana could only hope to wrap her tongue around a quarter of them. He was Cercian by birth, the markings under his eyes so faded Ana couldn't tell which clan he hailed from, and he never told, having left that life years ago. His skn was a shade darker than Siege's, with a warm hue to it—like the dawn. "This is dangerous."

"My leg's hurting, too," Riggs added. "It always hurts before a fight."

"Your leg always hurts," Talle replied dryly.

"Yes, but it hurts *more*," the engineer said defensively, and Wick nodded in agreement—but he always agreed with Riggs. They'd spent years in a Cercian mine together. "Palavar is *dangerous*."

"Palavar will be easy," Siege assured them. "We're on the quietest ship in space, and we've got the best crew in the kingdom."

"Yeah, but what about that Ironblood?" Barger jutted his chin toward Robb, who went still in his chair. The Ironblood hadn't touched his food, potatoes sitting congealed on his plate. "What if he sends out our coordinates? Tattles?"

"Well, then we can space him," Jax replied, reorganizing his hand.

The Ironblood choked on a sip of ale.

"We're not *spacing* him," Ana said, tossing two cards down. "Two tens."

Barger took two cards out of his hand. "Two queens—"

"Wicked," Robb called.

Barger shot him a look that Ana could only have described as death incarnate. The table was quiet until Wick leaned forward and flipped Barger's two cards over for him. A nine of spades and a three of hearts. Wick shoved the stash of cards in Barger's direction.

Smoothly, the Ironblood leaned forward and dropped his last four cards onto the table. "Four queens."

Jax gave him a side-eye. "I think I'm going to call you."

"Then do it," Robb replied.

"You can't have four queens. You can't be *that* lucky."

"Technically, I can— *OW!*" Robb gave a cry and clutched his right wrist.

The captain leaned forward worriedly. "Something else hurt?" she asked, Jax and the rest of the crew echoing the concern.

Ana didn't like the way the Ironblood turned pale. Or the way he straightened up again, a rigid set to his eyebrows. "No—no, I'm fine."

"You don't look fine," said Jax.

Robb's blue eyes turned cold. "I said I'm—"

"Captain," interrupted D09 through the intercom. His voice cut through the noise of the galley like a knife scraping against metal.

The captain finished her tankard of ale in one gulp and called up to the ceiling, "What's it, metalhead?"

"The Grand Duchess is transmitting live from the palace. She is speaking about the events on Nevaeh."

Ana's heart plummeted into her toes.

Cursing under her breath, the captain left for the cockpit in a whirlwind of bright fiber-optic-tipped hair, the rest of the crew scrambling after her. In the cockpit, Wick quickly slid into his chair at the communications console, pulling up the vid.

Ana elbowed her way through the crew to stand beside Di, lacing her fingers through his.

He slid his expressionless gaze to her, and she met it, swallowing the lump lodged in her throat. No one could have possibly identified them on Nevaeh. There was nothing to be worried about. *Nothing.*

But her heart pounded anyway, calling her a liar.

The Grand Duchess's delicate face stretched across the starshield. *"At sixteen hundred hours, a terrible act ravaged our beloved Nevaeh. A Metal and its accomplice attempted the assassination of my heir, Erik Valerio."*

Ana felt all the blood drain from her face.

"Thankfully, he was unharmed, but his kin was not as fortunate. As of four hours ago, we have it on good authority that the younger son of the Valerio family, Robbert Mercer Valerio, was taken captive by the assassins."

A photo of a young man with curly hair and sky-blue eyes appeared in the upper left-hand corner of the screen. A cold chill curled up Ana's spine. She knew that face—sat across from it at dinner.

Oh—oh no.

She quickly looked around the cramped cockpit for Robb, but he had disappeared. Had he even followed the crew here? She couldn't remember.

"Ak'va," Jax cursed under his breath. "He said his last name was Aragon."

Siege's eyes darkened. "Aragon my ass."

The Grand Duchess went on. *"This is an act of terror, and it is war against our kingdom. I will award five hundred thousand coppers to whoever returns Robbert Mercer Valerio unharmed."*

Ana could see the thoughtful looks on everyone's faces at the idea of half a million coppers. That was three new sails for the *Dossier*. An updated solar core. A quiet house on Eros. A new life.

"And to whoever brings in the rogue Metal assassin and its accomplice, I will reward you whatever you desire."

"Whatever we desire?" Barger murmured. "We could get our records wiped clean."

"I'd space you first," Talle warned, her words as sharp as the knives on her belt.

"There is no price too great for the safety of this kingdom and the security of its people. We will not bargain with terror. May the stars keep you steady and the iron keep you safe."

The connection flickered and faded to stars. Ana counted the silence—one heartbeat, two, before the fiber optics flared in her captain's hair like an inferno. But as Siege opened her mouth, green eyes full of murder, Jax dashed out of the cockpit and slammed the door closed, locking them inside.

JAX

Jax was, by all accounts, the most merciful crew member on the *Dossier*.

He also had a promise to uphold to that charming, lying sack of spacetrash who happened to be from the most hated family in the entire kingdom. He tried to forget the solidness of Robb's chest as they free-fell through Nevaeh, the warmth of the Ironblood's hands over his as they pulled the skysailer into flight, and the color of his eyes, a blue that reminded Jax of summer rain on Iliad.

Or that the Ironblood, for no particular reason, smelled like mint and honey.

He would *not* be swayed by a pretty boy.

The Ironblood had lied. Jax wasn't sure what he would do once he caught the boy, because everything sounded appealing at the moment. Strangling. Shaking. Dismantling him limb from limb—slowly, to enjoy the moment.

After all, he was the most merciful of the crew members.

But when he found Robb trying to hot-wire the skysailer in

the cargo bay—and failing—he quickly realized the most he could do was kick the poor boy's charming ass.

"The battery's shorted out, little lord," he said, surprising the Ironblood in the cockpit. "And we're far past Iliad's way-station already. You wouldn't make it even on the Goddess's good graces."

Robb gave a start—and grabbed for something under the dash—his lightsword—and drew it, stumbling out of the cockpit. The weapon glowed between them like a slice of sunlight, emitting a soft hum. They always looked a good deal prettier than they felt. Superheated, they could slice through anything like a knife through butter.

Jax raised an eyebrow. "My, what a shiny hello you have there. Found where we hid it, did you?"

"Let me leave—or I'll skewer you."

"Haven't you already tried once? Although with a smaller utensil," he added jokingly, but when the Ironblood didn't falter, Jax pocketed his hands with a sigh. "Go on then, *Valerio*. Solani bleed like the rest of you. Skewer me. I'd make a pretty shish kebab."

"Don't think I won't do it."

"I know you will."

Sweat prickled on the Ironblood's brow. With the wound in his side, the poor boy could barely stand for long, let alone *fight*. But he knew how to handle a sword, at least—lightly on the handle, loose like an extension of his arm. He knew to look at his opponent and not the tip of his own sword; he knew the fighting stance, turning sideways to be as small a target as possible. He must've been quite a lovely outcast at the Academy. All frills and sweet cologne and a bleeding heart on his sleeve.

"Why are you running?" Jax asked. "Scared that we'll kill you for being a Valerio?"

Robb tightened his grip on his sword.

"Or," Jay drawled, "are you afraid we *will* turn you in? Half a mil coppers is a very pretty picture."

"Goddess be *damned* you will," the boy snapped. "I'm not going back."

"We could just kill you—"

"Says the one at sword point."

"—but I have a feeling you'd be messy."

"Then let me go."

"Or—now hear me out." Jax tested his courage and took another step, eyeing the lightsword. "Or you stay here, and we work this out like civilized gentlemen."

"*Civilized?*" the Ironblood scoffed. "You must be kidding me."

"We're perfectly civil, thank you. I'm not the one holding an innocent man at sword point, now am I? But oh, woe, we're so *uncivilized.*"

Robb set his jaw. "You mock me."

"Only because you're being insufferable."

"*Goddess*, why can't you just let me—"

Jax heard the dedicated whir of E0S coming down into the cargo bay—probably to check on the solar engine. It did its rounds every hour, but the time must have slipped his mind.

He had to act quickly, or else that bot would go straight to the captain like the dutiful little tech it was and unlock that cockpit faster than a jewel thief out of a Cercian mine.

The sound of EOS distracted Robb for the split second Jax needed.

He lunged for the lightsword—

And underestimated the Ironblood.

Robb jumped away, spinning it behind his back to his other hand, and sliced at him. The sword flashed through the air like a bolt of lightning. Jax cursed—nothing around to block the blade—and raised his arm. Jax saw Robb's lips parting in surprise a moment before the blade slammed into Jax's forearm.

The lightsword bounced off like steel on stone. Sparks lit the air between them.

Robb stumbled back, perplexed. "What the—"

"Congratulations—now I'm mad," Jax said, pushing up his shirt sleeves. He always liked this reveal, vain as it was. Around his wrists were thick, dark bands of what looked like obsidian, reaching all the way to his elbows. He might have inherited his good looks from his mother, but his father had given him the war cuffs. An heirloom.

Robb stared at the cuffs.

Jax thumped his finger against one. "Tempered black glass, terribly sturdy, and oh so *very* uncivilized—"

"*Shut up!*" Robb swung again.

Jax raised his wrist. Deflected the attack. He couldn't keep this up forever—and judging by the thin sheen of sweat on Robb's pale face, the Ironblood couldn't either. Jax was actually amazed he hadn't passed out already, or pulled a stitch.

The Ironblood was either very determined or very, very stupid.

"How *are* you a Valerio, anyway?" Jax asked, hoping to distract the Ironblood—or at least get him angry enough to make a mistake. All Jax needed was one. "I bet your mother is *ashamed.*"

"She'll never be happy!" Robb swirled his sword around in his grip and put his weight into it this time.

The lightsword clashed with the black glass, sparks hissing between them. Robb leaned in, much stronger than he looked, but Jax did, too. One slip and the lightsword would graze past his cuffs and slice off his arm. He wouldn't look too dashing without an arm, he didn't think. His elbow ached.

"If you leave in that skysailer, Siege *will* hunt you down," Jax said, struggling in their stalemate. The lightsword was so close, he could feel the heat against his skin. "And when she catches you? No one will save you."

"I don't need saving." Robb's hot breath fell against his lips. Their faces were so close Jax could see the fire burning in the Ironblood's sky-colored eyes, and his skin prickled.

"We all need to be saved, *Lord Valerio.*" Jax bent closer, an electric, warping energy between them. "You just have to choose who you want saving you."

In a single motion, he looped his leg around Robb's and jerked his feet out from under him. The Ironblood fell onto his back with a yelp. The lightsword skittered away underneath a crate and flickered out.

"Am I interrupting?" asked a voice.

Both boys glanced toward the entrance.

D09 stood in the doorway, holding E0S hostage under his arm, downturned so the little bot couldn't see anything and tattle back to the captain. So D09 had managed to override the lock on the cockpit. Of course he had. D09 was a computer, after all.

Behind Jax, he could hear the Ironblood struggling to his feet again. *You should've stayed down, little lord.*

Jax told D09, "Give me a moment?"

Then he turned to the Ironblood and coldcocked him right in that smug, perfect jaw of his, sending him back to the ground. The Ironblood didn't get back up.

"All right," Jax said, and tugged at his worn leather gloves. "Take him to the captain. I'm done."

As the Metal came over and grabbed Robb by the arm, Jax turned away to fix the mess of wires in the skysailer.

ROBB

Robb awoke with a sudden pain in his side. Sharp. Throbbing. He sucked in a hiss, jerking to sit up, only to realize that he was already sitting upright in a chair. He really needed to stop waking up like this. Could it be, just once, from a really nice dream?

He shifted to alleviate some of the pain, becoming distinctly aware of the burning sensation in his wrist too.

The tracking chip.

He quickly pressed his wrist against his thigh so no one would notice the telltale glow of the activated chip. A signal on its own wavelength, manufactured so that no other radar could pick it up. Jax thought Lady Valerio didn't care about her second son—but he was mistaken. She cared too much about her legacy to lose him.

Goddess's *spark*, not yet. Not *yet*.

He blinked the blurriness out of his eyes.

The room was dark, rust colored, with a holographic map of the kingdom rotating on the corner of the desk, throwing stars onto the walls. Siege's hair lit up the room like an inferno. He squinted at the brightness, the ringing in his ears loud enough to make his head feel thick.

"He had this in his pocket, Captain," the Metal said, extending the iron ore. It didn't rust in Metal hands. Well, *obviously* it didn't—but it was still peculiar. By the Goddess's scriptures, whoever the crown didn't rust for was destined for the Iron Throne.

Oh, the kingdom would combust into rage if a *Metal* claimed that right.

The captain's eyebrows shot up as she took the ore. "An iron ore? Where'd you get this, son?"

His jaw hurt to move, and he tasted blood in his mouth from where Jax had knocked him good. "How long was I out?"

"Ten minutes and twenty-seven seconds," replied D09.

"Now where'd you get this?" pressed the captain.

Robb gave her a flat look.

"Ah, so we answer your questions but you don't answer ours? Typical Valerio," she added under her breath, and waved her hand to dismiss D09. "Give us a minute."

The Metal did, but Robb noticed another face in the doorway.

"You too," the captain said to Ana, who was hovering just outside. "Don't think I don't see you there."

"But Captain—"

"*Out.*"

He couldn't meet Ana's withering glare. She had trusted him, stuck up for him against her own crewmates. A Valerio shouldn't care, he reminded himself. Valerios *didn't* care.

Sulking, Ana closed the door behind her.

And left him alone with the homicidal captain. Siege was terrifying even without her bandolier and golden-trimmed murder coat. In a plain nightshirt and breeches, she still looked like the walking emblem of death.

"So, why Aragon?" she asked, rolling the iron ore between her fingers. Rust came off, painting her fingertips a reddish brown.

He shrugged.

"Start talking or I'll cut off your ears first. Then your lips. Then your nose—"

"What am I supposed to say? *Sir*," he added.

"You're a Valerio," she replied, setting down the iron ore. "Let's start with that. The younger, right? You can't be more than, what, fourteen?"

"Seventeen."

"You should be graduating from the Academy, so why aren't you there?"

I was kicked out, he thought, remembering the weight of his shame as his peers stood against the banisters and watched him leave the great hall. The look of pity from the professors, the sneers from the other students. It seemed that even with perfect test scores, the Academy frowned upon low attendance. He spent too much time sneaking away to find some clue—any clue—to his father's whereabouts. He told himself he didn't care that the Academy kicked him out.

And when he found his father, it wouldn't matter what anyone else thought, either.

"With all due respect, why do you care?" He tried to keep his voice level, to stop the shaking, but it was impossible. He was so close to answers, and now he was going to be spaced because these pirates weren't as dumb as he'd hoped. "I'm a Valerio, so I doubt you'll believe whatever I say. You already have your ideas about me."

"Same can be said about us. Your brother's about to be Emperor, and we're the thorn in his side. I have communications with at least half a dozen other vessels in the same line of work, and they all report to me. You've got your ruler, and your kingdom, and your crown, and we've got ours. Me. And life'd be a lot sweeter if the kingdom got rid of me. So how do I know you aren't trying to bring me in? Or kill me? I'm right here, so what's stopped you?"

Well, that was a simple answer. "I don't care about the kingdom."

"But it's your legacy—"

"My *brother's* legacy," he corrected. "Not mine."

"And what would your father say about that?" asked the captain, as if she knew what he would and wouldn't approve of. Who was she, a *criminal*, to judge?

A muscle in his jaw twitched.

She went on. "He was killed in the Rebellion, wasn't he? You would've been, what, ten?"

"They never found a body."

"Never found the bodies of the Armorov boys either, but that doesn't mean they aren't mixed in with the ashes," replied the captain. "Your father could've burned in the palace, too."

The carelessness in her voice made Robb fist his hands to

control his anger, the pain in his side becoming a numb throb. "He didn't—I know he didn't. The *Tsarina* was the only ship docked in the moonbay that wasn't accounted for after the Rebellion. If there's a chance he took that ship . . . if he's *still* on it . . . if he escaped . . ." His words caught in his throat, because this was his hope. This was what helped him sleep at night, the thought that his father hadn't *burned*, that he had survived. "My father didn't die in the palace, *sir.* I will bet my life on it."

"You're stubborn like your father," she replied offhandedly, putting her elbows on the desk. She steepled her fingers. "But now Ana's the most wanted criminal in the kingdom and we've got half a million coppers on our head."

"To be frank, sir, *she's* the one who stole from *me.* I bought those coordinates fairly. None of this would've happened if she hadn't followed me to my family's garden. So pardon me, but I think she deserves it."

"Then why did you help her? On Astoria?"

He didn't know why he had saved Ana. It was something a good Ironblood *wouldn't* do. "I needed those coordinates," he heard himself saying. It sounded truthful enough.

"I would've let you bleed out in some back alley of Nevaeh if I were her—"

"Then *space* me already," Robb snapped. "You think you're better because you cheat and steal from Ironbloods, but you're no different than us. You just do it under different colors. So if you're going to kill me, *do it.*"

Now he *definitely* was going to be spaced, jettisoned out and bounced against the wing tip of this shithole of a ship. Fear stung in his throat, feeling a lot like the telltale sign of tears.

The captain stared at him for a long moment and then sat back in her creaky leather chair. "We'll be arriving in three hours to the *Tsarina*. Best you get some shut-eye before we get there."

His fear became a cold knot in his stomach. "You're . . . letting me live?"

"We aren't all like you Ironbloods, Robbert Valerio. Sometimes, people make mistakes," she replied, and his cheeks burned in embarrassment. She held out the iron ore. "But a word of warning: if you ever decide to take someone else's last name again, make sure you don't already have one first."

Nodding, Robb took the ore, wrist burning from the chip. He should tell her about it—

But if he did, he would be off this ship faster than he could blink, and then he wouldn't be any closer than he was before to finding his father. And besides, he was sure this terrifying captain and her crew could take on a few Valerio soldiers.

Of course they could.

Whoever his mother sent couldn't be *that* close behind.

I have time, he told himself, and for the moment he believed it, his side aching a little more with each passing moment. It was a different kind of pain this time. Sore. Shuddering. It hurt to breathe. He put his hand against his side instinctively.

He escaped the captain's quarters as quickly as he could, not seeing Ana eavesdropping by the doorway until it was too late.

They collided, and the rock went skittering across the floor.

"Sorry—ow, ow, *ow*—" he hissed, clutching his wounded side, before he remembered the iron ore. "*Shit*, where did it—"

"This?" She picked it up.

"Oh, careful, it . . ." His words trailed off. The iron ore didn't rust against her fingers.

A chill raced down his spine.

Was her hand artificial? It looked real enough, and a cut on her finger looked recent, freshly scabbed over.

He studied her, trying to jog some long-repressed memory from his childhood, waiting to recognize her—or for her to recognize him.

If the *Tsarina* had escaped—if his father had escaped . . .

He racked his brain to remember the princess. He'd always played with her older brothers, so their paths had never crossed much. Dark hair. Golden-brown eyes. Always running around barefoot.

He would have recognized her, wouldn't he?

Ana eased away from him. "You okay?"

"I—I'm fine," he quickly replied, looking away. It was just a trick. What were the odds? He shook his head, holding out his hand for the ore. "Just . . . wishing I wasn't a Valerio right about now."

Her mouth twitched. "At least you've got a last name."

"You don't?"

"The captain found me and Di in an escape pod. I don't remember much." She handed the ore back. Still, her fingers had no rust on them, while the ore left a trail of burnt red across his skin. "My parents were ship traders. The captain said they died in a mercenary attack."

"Oh." So she was not the lost princess. The princess had died—the entire royal family had. "I'm—I'm terribly sorry." He put the ore back into his pocket, other hand still holding tight to his side, and leaned against the wall as she left for the crew's quarters.

His head was buzzing too much to think, a jumbled, tumbling mess. There was a girl on this ship who didn't rust. A ship merchant's daughter who didn't *rust.*

He sucked in another painful breath. Had he pulled a stitch?

Jax emerged from the stairwell, tugging his ponytail, until he noticed Robb leaning against the wall. He quirked a silvery eyebrow. "The captain let you off easy, did she?"

"Do you want a thank-you or something?"

"An apology will do."

"Ha—is that all?"

His fingers were wet, but he didn't want to draw his hand away. His side hurt so badly it brought tears to his eyes, but he would be damned if he cried in front of Jax. "You knew that if I stayed, the captain would give me another chance."

"I wasn't lying. I can't lie."

Robb pushed off the wall. "Is that the spiel you give every . . ." His head swam, words floating away. The ship tilted—or was it him? Weakly, he grappled for the side of the wall to steady himself, but his hand slipped against it, slick with blood.

Jax lurched forward and caught him by the arm before his face met the floor, and steadied him.

Everything was spinning. And smelled like lavender and blood.

He hated lavender. He wanted to hate it.

"You *did* pull a stitch—or twelve," said the Solani, and it was strange because all cocky pretense was gone, leaving his voice soft and lilting—like a song. "Can you make it to the infirmary?"

Robb nodded, and the Solani helped him—slowly, with more patience than he would have thought—to the infirmary downstairs. The lights flickered on, so bright he had to squint. He hated infirmaries. Especially this one. He would be happy never to see it again. Jax helped him up onto the gurney and retrieved a medical kit, pulling Robb's shirt up on one side.

Everything made him dizzy, so he trained his eyes on Jax's gloved fingers as they pressed a piece of gauze against the wound, soaking up the blood seeping through the stitches. The Solani's face was blank, his hair falling across his shoulder, reminding Robb of starlight.

He used to love looking at the stars, but he couldn't remember the last time he had. Not since Aran Umbal.

"Do you know what you're doing?" he asked dimly.

"Scared that a star-kisser'll screw you up?"

He felt the tips of his ears reddening. "I'm sorry I called you that. And I meant because you're a pilot, not a medic."

"Don't put me in a box, little lord—I might just surprise you. Hold still—"

"Aah!" He cried out in pain, trying to pull away as Jax took out the broken stitch. He blinked and tears stuck to his lashes.

Perfect, he was crying in front of a Solani. Valerios didn't *cry*. Not from pain. Not at funerals. Not even for Aran Umbal. *Goddess strike me.*

He gritted his teeth, willing himself to stop. "Numbing it first would be—be *grand*."

"Oh, must've slipped my mind," the Solani replied off-handedly, taking a numbing agent from the medical kit and administering it around the wound. "Do you know where the word comes from? 'Star-kisser'?"

The pain ebbed with the medicine. Robb took his first full breath. "The stars?"

"My, you're a genius." Jax began to restitch the wound with the suture pen. "Long before we came to the Iron Kingdom, my people learned how to see the future in the stars. What may be, what will be, and what will never be. With this knowledge, we created a great empire and prospered for thousands of years."

"Really?"

"That's what the stories say. Until one day, the stars began to blink out, and the *D'thverek*—what your lovely people call the Great Dark—came for our sun. We had relied on the stars for so long that we didn't know how to defend ourselves, so we took what remained of our people and fled to where the stars pointed—here."

"So . . . you *can* read the stars? Like the rumors say?"

Jax snorted. "Please. We can barely read our own mother

tongue anymore. Over the generations, we fell in love with humans and Cercians, and we forgot."

"But, theoretically, if there were any Solani who never married Erosians or Cercians . . . they still could?"

Jax raised his eyes to Robb's. They were more red than violet—like a dying star—and Robb felt as if the Solani was telling him a secret in that stare, one that his mouth could not form words to. The smell of lavender was making him light-headed for a completely different reason.

"Theoretically, anything could be possible," the Solani finally said, cutting his eyes away. He took another strip of gauze from the medical kit and wrapped Robb's wound again. Jax's long, gloved fingers felt whisper-soft, making goose bumps shiver across Robb's skin. "And . . . we're all done. Better than the Metal, if I do say so myself."

Robb tugged down his shirt and sat straight again. If a Solani couldn't lie, he found himself asking, "If you—if you *could* read my fate in the stars, do you think I'll find my father?"

The silver-haired boy blinked. *"Truthfully?"*

"Truthfully."

Jax reached up. Robb winced, thinking he'd slug him again, but Jax brushed his thumb across Robb's busted bottom lip, so gently it sent a shiver down his spine. "Please don't ask," he whispered, and left Robb alone in the infirmary with a plea that sounded more like an answer.

D09

Two hours and four minutes and seven seconds.

Recalculating.

Fifty-eight seconds.

Recalculating.

Two days and four hours and thirty-two seconds—

D09 sat drumming his fingers on the pilot chair's armrest, space passing by in a blur of stars and nebulae. He kept a counter running in the back of his computing, constantly recalculating the time until he would no longer function. He had first begun the calculations when they had visited the mechanic on Iliad, who told him about his damaged memory core, but the countdown was not logical. It sped up. It slowed.

But it never gave him enough time to figure out how to say good-bye.

Perhaps it would be best if he were *smashed* instead—the slang for destroying a Metal's memory core. Not murdered, or killed, but smashed like a child's plaything. Metals had been useful during the Plague in keeping those infected quarantined from the rest of the kingdom, but now that the threat was no longer an issue, they were not needed.

Perhaps that was all Metals were supposed to be— impermanent tools. Means to an end.

On a star map pulled up on the cockpit monitor, a white dot moved toward the third and farthest planet in the kingdom, Cerces. It was his duty to watch the cockpit while Jax slept.

Nights were quiet. They gave him time to mend temperamental fuses in the ship or find ways to lock EoS in service closets.

Where was the troublesome robot, anyway?

He keyed up the video feeds to look when footsteps echoed down the corridor, activating his motion sensors. He shifted in his chair. No one should be awake.

The captain stepped into the cockpit. "Any news since the video feed from the Grand Duchess?"

"No, sir. There has been no sign of the Royal Captain or the Messiers on the radars or comm-links," he relayed. "There are only two freighters and a passenger ship in our immediate vicinity, but they are not a threat."

"ETA to Palavar?"

"An hour and forty-seven minutes."

She spun the communications chair around and sat, draping one leg over the other, propping her chin up in her hand. "I don't like it, metalhead. It's too quiet."

"Yes," he agreed. "It is."

Sighing, the captain shook her head. "You're usually so much better at keeping her out of trouble."

"Forgive me," he replied, bowing his head. "Accompanying Ana to Nevaeh was a mistake. But I . . ."

The weight of the memory in the garden, the kiss, the promise . . . made him hesitate. He looked at his hands, at the wires glowing between the plates.

"I could not let her go alone," he finally said. It was the best answer he could find.

"Ah."

"I do not understand why. I am endangering the crew even now. I am a liability. After the *Tsarina*, I will leave. I do not want to put Ana at risk—"

"That won't be necessary," replied the captain, her curls turning red. "You aren't going anywhere."

"But what if these glitches are impairing my judgment?"

"I don't think it's the glitches doing that." She stood and kissed him on his metallic forehead, leaving a bloodred lipstick print, and retired back to her quarters.

He turned back around to face the starshield, and caught his reflection, a red lipstick print on his forehead. He rubbed it off. He wanted to tell her that she was mistaken. That it must be the glitches. A virus—malware corrupting his judgment. Something deep inside murmured to him. It was an echo he could not place—even though he had run numerous virus scans over the years—a piece of code from before the *Dossier*.

From before the captain found him and Ana in an escape pod.

But those memories had been damaged; the data was gone. Gone as though it—and whatever he was before—had never existed, and only this echo remained. Calling. Beckoning. Like a voice through a long and narrow tunnel. He knew he had been something before, but he was not programmed to be curious, to care.

Or to be afraid of what he used to be.

Yet the echo remained, beating like the cadence of a heart.

On the starshield, a blip pinged the *Dossier*. A second long. He turned back to the starshield, but the radar did not receive the signal again. An anomaly? He slid out the control panel to investigate—

Someone knocked on the doorway to the cockpit.

He glanced over his shoulder as Jax ducked in. "Evening, metalhead," the young man greeted. "How's the night been?"

D09 turned his moonlit eyes back to the starshield. "Something just pinged us."

"That's not good."

"It only happened once."

Jax frowned and leaned on the back of the pilot chair, squinting up at the starshield's readings. "Are you sure?"

D09 gave him a blank look.

"Right, of course you're sure. Well, let's not worry about it. It was probably a glitch. I'll take it from here," he added, motioning for Di to get up.

He did, and the Solani fell over the armrest into the seat with a sigh.

"Ah, *home*. You know what would be better? If you could keep the seat warm for me, too. Literally warm."

"I am sorry I do not have heaters installed in my rear," he

replied, and left the cockpit as Jax cackled gleefully.

The rest of the crew were still asleep in the quarters. Riggs muttered in his sleep, but it was almost inaudible under Lenda's snoring. He made his way down to the engine room to run diagnostics on the solar core before they arrived. It kept him busy, so he did not concentrate on the recalculations in the back of his head.

Seven minutes and fifty-three seconds—

Recalculating.

Two minutes—

Three hours and—

As he made his way down the stairs, a shadow moved in the open skysailer. It looked like legs sticking up out of the backseat. He recognized them, went over to the sailer instead, and peered inside.

Ana lounged across the backseat, legs sticking up over the headrest, as she read through the newsfeed on a holo-pad. The blue glow paled her face and hardened the lines on her puckered cheek. She glanced up when she saw him.

"Oh, hi, Di."

"Why are you awake?"

She shrugged and righted herself in the backseat. "Couldn't sleep. I guess we're almost there."

"Almost." He climbed into the backseat with her—and felt something akin to a jolt. A jerk in the back of his code.

A glitch.

Two hours and thirty-seven minutes . . . , the counter read.

Another jolt. Numbers skewing.

Twenty seconds . . .

Ana turned off her holo-pad. "I have a question."

"I may have an answer."

She pulled her braid over her shoulder, beginning to unravel it with her fingers. "Do you think if—*when*—we repair your memory core, you'll remember who we were? Before the *Dossier*?"

He shook his head. "I do not know."

"Do you think . . ." She hestiated. Her fingers snagged on a knot, and she gave up. "Do you think you'll remember who *I* was? Who I am?"

In reply, he took her hair out of her hands and began to braid it for her, meticulous and patient. "I know who you are," he said. "You are Ana of the *Dossier*. You are everything you need to be."

She smiled at that and closed her eyes. "Stop brownnosing."

"I do not have a nose, so that would be impossible," he replied, knowing it would make her laugh—and it did. She laughed, light and melodic, her entire body shaking with it.

He knew her better than he knew his own circuits and wires. They had been a team for as long as he could recall. He had never been without her, and she never without him—and even when they were apart he thought of her, as though a piece of her had been written into his code.

But did a piece of him run through her as well? Organic things were different. They operated on thoughts and feelings. They made rash decisions. They evolved—they *changed*. He never would. When he expired, would Ana change too, slowly, until he no longer lived in her thoughts?

At the edge of his consciousness, he could feel the glitch spiking, like when the starshield lost reception. He tried to sequester the code. Trap it.

Two minutes and—

Thirty-one seconds—

His fingers slowed. "Ana?"

She turned her golden eyes to his, curious. "What is it?"

Another spike of code seared through his programming. White noise.

He thought of what Jax had said about good-byes. Perhaps he could say it now. Find the right words. He opened his mouth to try when Jax's voice rang out over the intercom. "We have committed a heinous deed and are now in one of the kingdom's no-fly zones. Add it to your résumés, children. Destination ahead, fifteen minutes and steady. Everyone, report to the cockpit. Let's board this lost ship."

Ana sat up and turned off her holo-pad. "Let's go, Di—you ready?"

Two minutes and thirty-eight—

Nine hours and three—

He nodded. He still had time. "Yes."

JAX

So it was there after all, the *Tsarina*.

Jax tugged at his gloves. The entire ride had been too quiet. Too easy.

Through the starshield, the kingdom's largest planet, Cerces, loomed like a dying sun. It was a planet of deserts, and underground cities built of topaz and emeralds, and the infamous prison mines that supplied rare jewels to the rest of the kingdom.

On the other side of the planet, in its shadow, rotated Palavar, Cerces's largest moon. What a *dreary* place to park a starship. Aside from the ruins, nothing had existed on the dismal dark moon for the last thousand years.

As the crew filed into the cockpit, a small silver ship materialized ahead in the darkness. The uneasiness that had settled into the crew turned electric. He could taste the anticipation like a sharp drop of lemon on his tongue.

This was *Rasovant's* fleetship, and even if the Iron Adviser didn't know where his own ship was, Jax hardly thought the old man would sit around twiddling his thumbs. For all he knew, a Messier fleet was right behind them, and Jax wasn't sure he could get get away this time.

You're just worrying too much, he told himself, sliding out the controls from under the console to take the ship off autopilot, slowing the *Dossier* out of its sailing speed with a sigh.

"How's it looking?" asked Lenda, fitting on her shoulder armor. The crew wore a hodgepodge of raiding gear, mismatched and worn. It wasn't the look that mattered, but whether it saved your hide. LED lights hummed against their chests— their comm-links, live and ready.

The captain came into the cockpit last, helmet under her arm. "All right, crew. Hope you had a little catnap after last night's . . . *ordeal.*"

Robb winced, embarrassment tingeing his cheeks, although Jax had to admit the color looked rather good on him. It matched his lips.

Jax turned back to the console and brought up a diagram of the *Tsarina.* "I've scanned the ship already, and it seems to be abandoned. Can't say how long it's been without solar power, but on the dark side of Cerces, it'd take a miracle to get that thing running again."

"Nothing living?" asked Wick.

"There is only a two-point-seven percent chance of anyone surviving for seven years on residual power," said Di.

Jax glanced over at him, hoping Di had heeded his warning to say good-bye to Ana.

"But there *is* a chance someone could be alive," Robb pressed.

"There has to be a chance."

"It is unlikely."

The look Robb gave Di could have melted steel.

The captain massaged the bridge of her nose. "All right, noted. We won't have much time either way. Without solar light, we'll only get about thirty minutes before the *Dossier* powers down, so we'll have to tackle this like we did the one near Eros a few years back. Jax'll swing around, and we'll board from the stern and make our way up to the bridge. Di, what are we looking for?"

"A memory core," the Metal replied.

"Oh, is that all?" Talle scoffed, crossing her arms over her chest. "They're so small—how on earth is anyone going to find one?"

"They will probably be in the ship's mechanical bay," said D09, "or a lab."

"Are the ones in active Metals still off-limits?" Riggs asked. "I hate to be the one to say it, but if worse comes to worst, you could just upload yourself into one of those."

"That'll overwrite and kill the Metal already in that memory core," Ana argued. "I mean, as a last resort—"

"No," D09 interrupted.

Ana pursed her lips. Jax could see the disagreement in the creases of her brow. It had always been an option—kill an innocent Metal to use its memory core. He wished they could use a Messier, but the HIVE took control of the memory core—and no one knew how to un-HIVE a metal yet.

Goddess, Di really was a beacon of morality. If uploading Di into some other Metal's memory core could save him, then Jax didn't see why it couldn't be an option—especially since Metals couldn't *feel*. It wasn't like Di could feel guilty over rewriting some stranger's code.

"All right, and if we can't find an empty memory core, loot everything you can. Let's make this trip worth it. The more dangerous it looks, the better."

Talle chewed on the inside of her cheek. "I'll stay back on the ship with Jax, then, in case we need to break and run."

"That might be for the best," replied the captain, glancing up at the schematics of the *Tsarina* on the starshield one last time. Her hair blazed like sunshine. "Everyone should keep your wits about you. May the stars keep you steady."

"And the iron keep you safe," they echoed, and dispersed, leaving Jax alone in the cockpit again.

He turned back to the starshield, tapping his fingers impatiently on the armrest as he studied the drifting ship.

Something wasn't right, and it made him feel things he would rather keep locked up, his father's voice telling him in that slow and confident cadence, *Stalo ban ach van'en*. Stars are not afraid.

Screw the stars—he was *terrified*.

He heard the captain stop Ana in the hallway. He paused, about to summon the grapplers to hook onto the *Tsarina*, and listened. "You're staying with Jax to monitor the radio frequencies."

"I'm *what?* Captain, you can't do that!"

"We had an agreement. I'm leading this mission, and I tell you what we do."

"I'm not *staying!*" She stomped her foot. Jax winced. "I'm your best shot! You can't honestly want me to stay? Get Riggs to stay! I need to go—Di, tell her I need to go."

"He's staying, too," the captain informed them. "There might be something on the *Tsarina* that could compromise you, Di."

"I understand," D09 replied.

"*Understand?*" Ana raged. Angry Ana was a meteor who left craters in her wake. "Bullshit! Nothing can compromise *Di*! And I suck at radio chatter—I *need* to go, Captain. You can't stop me—"

"*Can't?*" Siege's voice cut like a knife.

Oh, she can, Jax thought, slowly turning back around in his chair so he could say that he hadn't been there to witness Siege plunging her hand into Ana's rib cage and ripping out her still-beating heart. Even with his back turned, the changing color of the captain's hair, from yellow to fiery orange, snuck in from the hallway and cast a shine over the starshield.

That was her super-angry color.

"Ana. You are *staying.*" Then, with thinly controlled rage, Siege left to go meet the rest of the crew in the cargo bay.

Out of the corner of his eye, Jax watched Ana take a seat in the communications chair, staring out at the starshield with a defeated look, as he prepared the grapplers.

Obviously Siege was right to keep Ana on the ship, but it wasn't to monitor radio frequencies. Ana was being reckless. She wasn't thinking straight. When you cared for something too much, you tended to do impulsive things.

. . . Such as sneak into an Ironblood garden to steal coordinates to a ship that might be a seven-year-old death trap just waiting to be sprung.

Ana turned to him. "Jax, is there another way onto the ship?"

"Ana," D09 warned.

"No, *we* should be going," she snapped. "We're the only ones who know what to look for. Jax, you know this ship better than anyone. Is there another way onto the *Tsarina*?"

He hesitated, because he couldn't lie, and Ana knew that with a vicious certainty.

"There is, isn't there?" she went on. "I can see it on your face."

On *his* face? That was funny, when desperation was written in the crease of her eyebrows and the downward slant of her bow lips. If there wasn't a fix for Di on that ship, he wondered who she would be without him.

For a moment, he wished he could read Ana's stars just so he would know.

I'm going to regret this, he thought, tugging nervously at his gloves.

"I . . . would probably check where the emergency air locks are on the *Tsarina*—left side, by the way—and jump from one of ours onto the other ship. It's tricky, and I'd never attempt it, but if I wanted to get on the *Tsarina*, that's how I'd do it." He whipped around in his chair to her. "At least *try* to hit an air lock on the other ship and not splatter your brains all over it, okay? I don't want your death on my conscience."

She smiled, and he hated how much he loved it. "Thank

you!" Springing out of the communications chair, she rushed toward him.

"No, no, no, no!" he cried, flinging out his arms to stop her.

She stopped herself mere inches from him and eased back sheepishly. "Sorry, I forgot you don't like being touched."

"Not that I don't love you," he replied tightly.

"I owe you. This is going to be a breeze!"

"A breeze?" D09 asked. "How hard a breeze—"

She pulled him out of the cockpit with her but not before he caught Di's moonlit eyes and knew that the stubborn Metal hadn't done what he'd advised.

Di quickly looked away and let Ana pull him out of the cockpit. He breathed out a sigh of relief. Too close.

She'd come much, *much* too close.

A holo-screen blipped up in the corner of the console, and he turned to inspect it. Which *would* have been D09's job. Of course he was stuck doing all the grunt work. He frowned at the console. It was a signal—from a *long* way off. A ship? No, it couldn't be. It didn't have the right permissions. And the frequency wasn't like anything he'd ever seen before. It made every program on the ship blitz.

And if it pinged the *Dossier*, then it also pinged—

"*Ak'va*," he cursed, turning back to the scans of the *Tsarina*.

And like fireworks bursting across the schematics, from one room to the next, blinking on like a long-slumbering monster, the ship awoke.

D09

The *Tsarina* was a Class-4 Armada retired thirty-four years ago for private use, but it did not show its age. On its side, in royal purple, was the Rasovant family crest, a nine-tentacled octopus.

There had been only a 10.4 percent chance the ship would be here. But he should have known, as with everything else Ana touched, probability did not matter.

Still, the advice Jax had given him resounded in his head. Humans were emotional creatures, so he must say something in case the *Tsarina* did not hold what they would come to find.

"Jax, we're at the emergency chute," Ana said into the comm-link as she rubbed her melted pendant. For good luck. It was the only thing she had kept from the escape pod where Siege found them. He could not recall a moment when she was without it. "Jax?"

The link was quiet.

"Is he responding to you?" she asked Di.

He shook his head. "I believe the comm-links have gone dark due to magnetic interference from the moon."

"Perfect." She put on her helmet and was reaching for the latch to open the air lock when he stopped her.

"Ana," he said, "I wish to talk to you for a moment."

"*Now?* Di, whatever it is, you can wait until we get back."

"No, it must be now."

"All right Di, what is it?" She turned back to him as the *Dossier* rotated into position. There was a soft *whoosh* as Jax deployed the ship's grapplers, puncturing the side of the *Tsarina*, and proceeded to reel the ship in.

In the red emergency light, he could see the impatient set of Ana's mouth. She was always one to leap first, ask questions later. She never looked back. He hoped she never would.

He said, "I need you to promise me that if this ship has nothing, you will let me go."

Her mouth fell open. "Di—"

"I am a tool built of metal parts," he interrupted. "I can be cloned, reprogrammed, and dismantled, and it will not change my core functions. I am not unique. When you lose me, you will find another. Promise me. Please," he added, because it was always the word Ana used when she wanted to get her way.

Her thick black eyebrows furrowed as she shrank away from him. "No."

"Ana—"

"You don't think you're worth saving?" Her voice grew louder with every word. "Because you aren't flesh and blood? Is that it?"

"No, I am merely saying that if you lose me, you will find another—"

"I'll *never* find another you, Di."

"Please, Ana."

She did not *understand*, and she needed to. But the look on her face through the clear helmet shield, the mix of hurt and pain and something he could not identify—a look that sent a spike through his programming, fraying the glitch, feeding it—made him *want*—no. He did not *want*. Could not *want*.

But he did.

He wanted so badly to exist a little longer beside her. But if he could not be fixed, perhaps on the *Tsarina* he could learn how to say good-bye.

"You are *more* than the sum of your parts, D09, and I'm going to save you," she said, and reached for the latch to open the emergency air lock.

ANA

The universe roared in, sucking the oxygen out of the air lock in a puff of frozen white. The door popped open and tore away so fast, it looked as though it disappeared completely.

Space itself ripped Ana and Di out of the air lock, grabbing them by their very molecules. They shot toward the fleetship across the fifty-yard expanse. The access port grew larger by the moment.

They were coming in too fast. She'd miscalculated the gravitational fields between the two ships.

Improvise.

Drawing her pistol out of its holster under her arm, she shot the latch off the *Tsarina*'s emergency air lock. Di grabbed her by the waist and spun around just in time for his back to slam against the round door.

It crumpled inward and gave way into the starship.

The buffer of artificial gravity slowed them, so when Di hit the floor, Ana on top of him, it was like falling from ten feet instead of a thousand. Pain still spiked through her backbone and shoulders and knocked the breath right out of her.

An emergency cover slid over the open access port.

She coughed, rolling onto her knees, and clawed off her helmet to suck in a lungful of breath. The ship's air tasted stale, as though it hadn't been recycled for a while. That was a good sign. Abandoned, like Jax said.

Di got to his feet first.

"Thanks for that," she gasped, taking his hand to help her up. She pressed the keypad to open the door to the small maintenance air lock they'd landed in and stepped into a corridor. "See? This is why we make such a good—"

The halogen lights overhead flickered on, humming.

"I thought Jax said the ship was running on emergency power," she muttered.

"Perhaps there is an internal generator belowdecks."

"Fancy."

The halogen lights popped on one at a time, illuminating the long corridor. It was white, lined with silver doors glowing with red keypads. Locked. At first glance, the ship looked immaculate, but there was a thin layer of dust on the tiled floor, showing their boot prints as they traveled down the corridor.

"Where do you think we should start looking?" she asked, testing the nearest keypad. She punched in a random number, and it beeped red.

ACCESS DENIED.

"Hey, do you think you can override these locks?" When he didn't answer, she glanced over her shoulder. "Di?"

He cocked his head, as if hearing something.

"What's wrong?"

Slowly, his eyes slid toward the door in front of her, and he reached for his gun. Instinctively, she did too—

The door slid up, revealing a silvery figure, too tall and too thin to be human. It looked like Di, from the slats around its mouth to its polished chrome body—new. But Metals hadn't been in production for twenty years. After the Plague, the Adviser stopped manufacturing them.

"Halt," it said, voice deep and melodic—like a bell. "Put your weapon away, brother."

Ana took an involuntary step back. Its eyes were red. "Brother? Di, does it know you?"

"It should not," Di replied.

"And why are its eyes red?"

The red-eyed Metal answered instead. "You are not welcome here." Then it aimed its Metroid at Ana's head.

In alarm, Ana grabbed the Metal by its wrist and shoved its aim toward the ceiling. It fired, and a light burst above them.

The Metal turned its blazing red eyes to her.

A chill curved down her spine.

She twisted the android's wrist to dislodge the weapon. But it wouldn't let go. Instead, she slammed her foot up, connecting with the Metal's jaw. It released its gun, falling back into the room it came from. Fuses hissed from its neck.

Ana quickly disarmed the weapon and threw it down the hallway. Her hands were shaking. "Jax said there weren't any active Metals—*why* are there active Metals? And why are they attacking us?"

"I am unsure."

The red-eyed Metal righted itself. "You are an intruder."

"We're only here for some answers!" She drew her Metroid and flicked off the safety. She aimed it at the Metal. "I mean it—I don't want to hurt you. You're not HIVE'd, so what *are* you?"

"Ana, I do not think it will help us," said Di.

The red-eyed Metal lurched forward to attack.

She squeezed the trigger. One shot bit into the Metal's right shoulder, then one into the left, but bullets didn't stop it. She gritted her teeth and turned her aim toward its chest. To its memory core.

Her aim shook.

The red-eyed Metal reached for her throat.

Count your bullets, Siege had said. *Remember where they land.*

In a blink, Di grabbed the Metal by the arm. He twisted the Metal around, its back pressed against his chest, and jammed his hand into the center of its body—like he had done in Nevaeh.

But when Di pulled his hand out, it was empty, knotted with stray wires.

No memory core.

Without warning, the Metal hammered its elbow into Di's face, sending him stumbling back against the wall. Ana aimed her pistol. But if she shot now, she could hit Di, too.

Damn it!

Di dodged as the Metal's fist sailed past his cheek and sank into the wall. He planted his hand on the side of the Metal's head and spun it under his arm into a headlock. The Metal didn't even have a chance to parley before Di gripped it by its jaw and ripped its head clean off. Wires and fuses sparked, spilling out of its neck.

The Metal twitched once. Twice. Di let go, and it fell prone at his feet.

The cold dread in her stomach numbed her. "Why'd it call you 'brother'? *How* did it call you brother? If it doesn't have a memory core, then . . ."

"Without memory cores, Metals cannot function, so it is safe to assume it was a puppet," he replied, testing the joints in his jaw where the Metal had punched him. "The signal that was controlling it is coming from the bridge."

"The bridge? But the ship was dormant when Jax scanned it," Ana said as Di began to go down the corridor toward the bridge. She followed, shaking her head. "I don't *understand.*"

"Perhaps the signal is not from the ship but outside interference."

"Outside? Like someone took control of the ship the *moment* we boarded?"

"Yes," Di replied, and tried to access the next door down.

The keypad blinked red.

"Like a program. A sentient program like the HIVE?"

"I am unsure, Ana," he said shortly, and tried another combination of numbers to hack it. The keypad blinked red again.

"Or did Rasovant create something to protect this ship? Or what if this is why the ship was never fou—"

Di whirled around to her. "I am unsure, Ana," he repeated. His eyes burned brightly, wedging her words in her throat.

She'd never seen him look so frightening before.

Gunshots echoed down the hallway.

She gasped. "Di—Di, the crew!" She turned around to hurry back down the corridor, but he caught her by the arm.

"We must find the bridge and disable the program."

"But what if it's more Metals? What if they're attacking the crew—"

"Then they will keep attacking unless we find the bridge and disable the program that is controlling them."

Another round of gunfire pierced the quiet, a staccato, sharp tune. Her heart tore, but Di was right. "Okay. Lead the way."

As if on cue, the door Di had been trying to enter slid open.

They glanced at each other, and with a silent agreement they went through. It led down another hallway, and up a lift to the next level, and down another long and white corridor. Each one seemed longer than the last, but that was only because of the anxiety that began to creep into her shoulders, bunching the muscles around her neck.

The *Tsarina* could easily fit five *Dossier*s. At full capacity, the ship could house two, maybe three hundred people. She'd never been on a ship this big.

"I don't like this—we have to go back to the crew," Ana said. "We have to—"

"Keep moving," he interrupted, shooting the keypad to the door at the end of the way. The door popped open.

She stopped him by the arm before they moved on. "Why're you being so short, Di? What's wrong?"

Before he could answer, a door behind them slid open and a Metal stepped out, eyes blazing red. It cocked its Metroid. Aimed. She reached reached for her holster, but Di lurched forward, hand outstretched, and slammed it clean through the Metal's skull.

She winced.

He unraveled the wires from his fingers as the Metal sank, slowly, to the floor. Then Di shifted his gaze back to her, and the way he looked—moonlit eyes bright, unyielding, curled a sliver of fear up her spine. Because his gaze was cold. And calculated.

"I do not mean to offend," he finally said. "I simply want to survive this."

She swallowed the knot in her throat, along with her fear. "Me too." They made their way to the lift to the top deck, where the bridge was located, and closed themselves inside. "Are you getting the feeling we're being herded?"

"Yes."

The lift clanged to a stop, and the doors opened wide to another red-eyed Metal.

"Hello, brother," it greeted them.

Ana brought her boot up and connected with the android's center, knocking it off balance. Then she took her Metroid and shot three rounds into its head.

Di gave her a slow look.

"We're in a hurry, right?" she asked, holstering her gun again, and they continued down another corridor lined with tarnished silver doors. And at the end of the hall was the entrance to the bridge, painted with the peeling crest of a nine-tentacled octopus.

The red keypads to the doors clicked green as they passed.

Di put a hand on Ana's back. "Do not look back," he said.

"Lemme guess, there are Metals coming out of those doors?"

He looked back. "I suggest we run."

They did. The hum of Metroids filled the hallway. A bullet pinged off Rasovant's crest, leaving a smoldering black hole. Another bit at her heel. Ten feet—five—

The door to the bridge slid open and they hurried inside. She spun around and slammed her hand on the keypad again.

The door clamped shut with a vicious snap.

She let out a breath. "Goddess's *spark*, that was close. Let's find the off switch to this killer ship and—"

Di spun her around.

There were no charts or navigational systems. There wasn't a pilot chair or consoles, as there were in older models like the *Dossier*. This ship ran on holographic maps and input coordinates. The outer wall was a glass shield that looked out onto the darkened surface of Palavar. There was a tone—a long beep—and the bridge awoke. A sharp whiteness rose across the shield like a sunrise. Ana winced, shielding her eyes with a hand, as the light illuminated the bridge, casting their shadows long against the floor.

Then a voice came from everywhere and nowhere—from the air itself.

"Hello, Ana."

ROBB

This was how the captain would kill him. Not by her own hand, but by dragging an injured Ironblood onto a murder ship to be *shot full of bullets*. It was an ingenious plan. So much so he doubted she'd thought that far ahead, or maybe to the captain he was a replaceable fill-in for Ana, who'd luckily stayed back on the ship.

When they had traveled across the starbridge—a thick cord with a zip line machine—tethered from the *Dossier* to the cargo bay air lock on the *Tsarina*, Riggs had deactivated all the alarms. They hadn't tripped *anything*. Everything was going according to plan, the crew boarded, and then—

Well, then half a dozen red-eyed Metals showed up and started handing them their collective asses.

Now he and the crew of the *Dossier* were sitting ducks behind stacks of cargo crates.

Beside him, Riggs murmured a prayer to the Goddess and kissed the silver locket around his neck. His mechanical leg hummed loudly. "Didn't come to the stars to die for this," Riggs said. "Didn't come to die this way."

"What, not up for a little firefight in the morning?" Robb asked, and the old man gave him a long, wide-eyed look.

"Goddess save us, I'm gonna die beside a smart-ass."

On the other side of Robb sat the Cercian, Wick, muttering to himself in his native tongue as he checked his bullets. The words were sharp like knives. When he caught Robb staring, he kissed the tip of his gun.

"I live for this," he said, spun, and shot over the top of the crate.

Nailed a Metal square in the chest—bull's-eye.

He whooped, but the Metal simply shook off the gunshot and fired back. Wick dropped back again. *"Cecous!"* he cursed.

The Metal should've dropped like a rock. But it kept going.

"It doesn't have a memory core," Robb realized. Metals without cores? So they weren't sentient at all. Something must be controlling them. He shouted to the crew, "Aim for the head!"

"The head?" asked Wick.

"Just do it!" He turned to Siege, shielded by a crate on the other side of the cargo hold. "Captain, aim for its head!"

Captain Siege nodded, rose from cover, and finished off the wounded android. Its face crumpled in with a bullet, and it slumped to the ground, red eyes dying. But another one came through the door to replace it.

Cursing, she reloaded her gun. "Goddess's blasted *spark*, where're they all coming from? It's getting back up!"

Robb glanced over the side of the crate to see for himself.

The headless android twitched and began to rise. If he believed in the Moon Goddess, he'd be praying right now. He'd be praying really, really hard.

And he'd be praying something like, *Merciful Goddess, if you exist, please hand my ass to me some other day. I don't want to die. I haven't kissed Jax yet.*

That last revelation sent a cold chill down his spine.

He wanted to *kiss Jax.* He wanted to taste the starlight on his skin and press his lips against the cool curve of his collarbone—

"Screw this!" Barger shouted, and abandoned cover. He turned tail and ran back into the air lock where they'd boarded. He reached to press the button to open the hatch—and the override to open the outer air lock.

The captain roared at him to stop—he'd kill them all, suck them out into space.

Barger didn't care. He reached for the button.

Robb pulled his gun—Goddess damn him later—when a bullet pierced Barger's chest. A flower of blood bloomed on the grease-stained back of his space suit. He began to reach for the wound, confused, before melting to the floor.

It was the first time Robb had ever seen anyone die. Even at the Academy, when Aran Umbal let go from the window, Robb hadn't been able to watch—but now he couldn't look away. Barger was staring at him, mouth half open, as the light dimmed from his eyes until they were nothing but marbles.

Finally, Robb pulled his eyes away, wanting to vomit. The captain lowered her smoking gun and gave him a dangerous look. She had . . . she had *killed* one of her own crew. If he hadn't seen it firsthand, he would have thought it was a stray bullet—but it was *her.*

Captain Siege had saved them by killing one of her own.

Robb didn't want to die, too, so he *definitely* wouldn't tell.

He cocked his Metroid and glanced over the steel crates. A bullet bit into the steel inches from his face. He ducked for cover again.

"We need to retreat, sir!" Riggs shouted. "This ain't worth—"

"*You can't.*" Jax's voice came through the comm-link. *"Ana's onboard."*

"What?" the captain snapped.

"I told her and Di to use the emergency air lock, and then I lost connection with them. I can't get a signal through. The ship's going haywire and I can't do anything because the Dossier's *losing solar power on the dark side—I'm sorry."*

The captain sent out another string of expletives, checking the ammunition in her gun again. "What d'you propose we do?"

"We need to shut down this ship's solar core. We cut that, we likely cut the power to the ship and whatever's controlling these androids—but you're gonna run into those Metals. They're everywhere. It'd be suicide."

Robb watched Siege debate, as another bullet slammed against the top of the cargo she huddled behind. They were all going to die. Including him.

But not before he found his father.

Robb swallowed his fear. "Captain, I'll go. Take the rest of the crew back."

"Not a chance," Siege snapped. "We stick together."

"We're dead if someone doesn't shut down the power," he argued, and the captain pressed her red lips together because she knew he was right. He pressed the comm-link. "Jax, can you lead me?"

"It's suicide—"

"Can you lead me?" he asked again, this time sternly.

The Solani didn't reply for a moment, and then, *"Yes. I have the layout in front of me."*

"Okay, I'm going." Robb hated to gamble his life on the hope that cutting the power source would *likely* disconnect these murderous Metals. Not that he had much of a choice. If he wanted to find out what had happened to his father, he had to play the game.

He turned and began to move around to the other end of the crates, closer to the wall where there was more cargo to hide behind.

"Robb," the captain called, and he looked back to her. She gave a serious nod. "Be careful. We'll cover you."

In agreement, the crew gave an "Aye!"

That actually makes me feel better, he thought in surprise. He'd never imagined outlaws would have his back.

His hands shaking, he checked to see how many bullets he had left in his gun. Four. Great, *four.* After that, he'd have to improvise.

If he ran into any more resistance.

Knowing his luck? It was a given.

"Now!" the captain roared. The crew opened heavy fire.

Robb launched himself over the first crate as the door to the interior of the ship slid open and a Metal stepped out, flashing a hefty Messier-grade blaster. It turned its gleaming red eyes to him. He cursed and dropped like a rock behind the nearest crate. A bullet snagged the corner, pinging away with a sharp *crack.*

Pretend you're at the Academy. This is just a drill, he thought. He always made better marks than the other Ironbloods. It was part of being a Valerio—you had to excel in everything. Like not dying.

He peeked over the top of the crate to see if the Metal had moved into the cargo bay. Nope. It stood, like a sentry, right in the Goddess-spitting doorway.

"Didn't you always complain the exams were too easy?" he muttered to himself. "Might as well earn your marks now—when else will you? You'll either die here or on that damn pirate ship."

"Do you always talk to yourself?"

Robb jumped at the sound of Jax's voice. "*Goddess!* Don't. Do. That."

"Sorry." Although Jax didn't sound sorry at all. *"I created a separate comm-link for us so we won't distract the crew. Okay, there's a door in front of you—"*

"With a Metal standing guard."

"Let me finish," the navigator hissed. *"Now, to your left is a ventilation duct. Or there should be. Do you see it?"*

Robb glanced to his left. There was a wall of steel crates—but between them there was a horizontally slatted grate, like the ones he used to crawl through on his mother's ship when he was little. "You think I can fit through *that?*"

"Don't make me crack a short joke."

"Fine," he grumbled, steeling his courage. His side was throbbing, but if he didn't pull himself together he'd be worse—dead. No. He could *do* this. He was a Valerio, for Goddess's sake! Valerios never died in firefights.

Holstering his gun, he unsheathed his lightsword, the hilt loose in his grip, and spun out from cover, watching where the android aimed. He deflected the bullet and leaped for the vent, tucking into a roll. A bullet pinged off the armor on his borrowed space suit, leaving a stinging hiss against his shoulder blade.

"Surrender," the android ordered, moving out of the doorway, toward him. Its footsteps clomped on the steel floor, closer and closer.

Stabbing the grate through with his blade, Robb cut a square hole and kicked it in, then sheathed his sword. He scrambled into the vent, but the android grabbed him by the foot to drag him back out. Yelping, he slammed his other foot into its face and kept kicking. It didn't let go.

Twisting around, he reached for his pistol in its holster, took it out, and blasted three bullets into the android. It let go and he clawed farther into the vent shaft. The robot couldn't follow; it was too large and too heavy. It peered inside, its red eyes glowing.

It couldn't reach in, but—in a wave of pure terror—he realized it could still shoot at him.

"Blasted festering useless Great Dark–sodding hunk of—" He rattled off a string of curses as he rolled onto his knees and shimmied around the first sharp turn in the shaft. He waited a breath. Then two.

But the android never shot.

After a moment, it turned away from the grate and clomped away.

He let out a sigh, trying to not think about his aching body. *Push through it*, he told himself, absently massaging the burning chip in his wrist. It had not stopped burning since dinner, and had begun to make holding a gun painful. Just moving his fingers hurt.

"Okay, Jax, I'm in the damn thing. Now where?"

"It took you long enough."

"Shut it. Where do I go?"

"You should be able to head straight for the engineering room."

Robb began to do as directed, then paused. "Should?"

Jax hesitated. *"Well, these are supposed to be the* Tsarina*'s scans, but some things don't . . . add up."*

"So what you're saying is they're not accurate," he deadpanned.

"Well, that's why it's called an adventure."

"Remind me to kick your ass the next time I see you."

"A kiss'll do."

For a brief moment, he was glad he was in a dusty, stale ventilation shaft being followed by a bloodthirsty Metal if only so Jax couldn't see him blush.

Stop it, you can't kiss him if you die thinking about kissing him, he chided himself, crawling through the ventilation shaft.

"Do you think anyone could survive out here for seven years?" asked Jax, but Robb was thinking it, too. *"With these murder-bots?"*

"I don't know. I don't think these androids have been activated for long. Maybe they were triggered when we came onto the ship. Some sort of defense mechanism?"

"I . . . don't know. The Dossier *got a weird ping before the ship lit up like a firework. It had a weird code, weird permissions."*

Robb paused to rest for a moment, holding his side painfully. It wasn't bleeding yet, but if he didn't pull another stitch crawling through these vent shafts, it would be a miracle. "So you think someone woke these androids up and is now *controlling* them? Seriously?"

"Seriously."

"We don't have that kind of tech— I'm here."

Through the slats in the grate, he could see a warmly lit room. There was a small glowing orange ball in the center of the room, clamped into place by four prongs on the ceiling and floor.

A solar engine. Fusion-based. Rare, and high-tech. He'd read schematics on them at the Academy, but he'd never thought he would see one in person. At its full power, if the ship was not hidden behind Palavar, the core would've shone as bright as the sun.

He squinted as he looked through the slats at the rest of the room, but it seemed to be empty.

I want it to stay that way, he thought, and quietly kicked the vent cover out. It clattered to the ground and he slid out, landing on his feet.

Pain shot up his side again, making him grit his teeth.

"We have to turn off the power," said Jax through the comm-link. *"There should be a few wires coming out of the engine."*

"Here we go with the *should* again," he muttered, rounding the solar core—when he noticed a person sitting at the engineering console.

Quickly, he drew his sword.

"Don't move," he called, "or I'll kill you."

"What? Who are you talking to?"

The shadow in the chair did not make a move to reply. In fact, the person did not move at all.

Robb flicked his eyes over to the screens above the console. An emergency notification blinked with the status of the escape pods. For a ship this size there were two, but only one was accessible on the screen. The other was outlined in red: *EJECTED.*

"Valerio? You still there? Robb?"

Ignoring Jax, Robb crept up to the engine console and jabbed the corner of the chair to turn it around. It rotated, slowly, but the body didn't move. He fell back a step. A dead man slumped in the chair, his face so mummified Robb couldn't recognize it, skin dried to the bones, with what was left of a beard and short-cropped dark hair.

The dead man still held a hand to his stomach, where the suit was black with dried blood. Robb checked the breast pocket for some sort of identification. A holo-pad with an ID, or an Ironblood insignia—

The corpse's clothes were stiff like cardboard from where

the man had bled out. It was a slow death, it seemed. Robb checked the man's cuffs, his other pockets, and finally his lapel.

It was discolored, as if a pin should have been there. A broken circle to anyone who didn't know what the missing pin looked like.

But he knew.

The Valerio family crest, a snake eating its own tail. An ouroboros. There were only four in existence, passed down through the family line. One belonging to his late aunt, his mother, his brother, and . . . his father.

Robb took an involuntary step back.

This wasn't how it was supposed to go. The ship was supposed to be abandoned. He'd have to follow clues to the next place and find his father alive and well, living happily in a small town on Iliad—

"Robb? You really *need to turn off that power!"*

He pried his fingers under the communicator on his space suit and ripped it off. He didn't want to hear any more. He didn't want to answer.

Grief coiled inside him like a snake, squeezing his insides. All these years, he'd known his father was dead. He'd *known*, deep down, but he'd never wanted to believe it. His mother had told him. His brother had insisted. But Robb held on to the sliver of hope that maybe—*maybe* . . .

Yet here his father sat, abandoned on the *Tsarina*, his casket empty in the Valerio cemetery.

All because—because *what*? He'd decided to die *here* instead of fifty years from now, at home on the Valerio estate?

Abandoning his family, his wife, his sons—*him*?

All those years, his mother had been right. Mercer Valerio was dead. He was dead because he went to the Iron Palace on the wrong night and got swept away in the Rebellion.

Deep down there was the little boy who thought his father was invincible. The boy who remembered sword training in the floating garden on Nevaeh, long weekends learning how to pilot a skysailer. The faces his father made behind his mother's back when she scolded Robb. His father's wide shoulders, and the way he hugged with all of his body, and the laugh that rolled and rolled like mountains—

Robb couldn't stay here anymore. In this stupid room. It was suffocating. And the corpse was staring at him. He tore out into the hallway, his eyes burning—

There was movement behind him a moment before he heard the voice.

"Halt," it said.

He gripped his lightsword tightly and turned toward two red-eyed Metals. They stood guard at the end of the corridor. His anger pulsed through him like white-hot magma. These Metals had killed his father. These heartless *things*.

One of them raised a Metroid.

With a furious cry, he lunged for the monsters as they opened fire.

D09

"Who's there?" Ana called out, spinning around on the bridge that was not a bridge. She swung her pistol around the room to find somewhere to aim, but there was no one else here. "How do you know my name?"

"I must know."

D09 inclined his head. The signal surrounded him, waves of commands attempting to sink into his mainframe, but he put up walls to block them. If he had not had a memory core, the program could have easily overriden him. He was 94 percent positive that was why the other Metals had attacked. They lacked the sentience to command themselves.

But why had the Adviser created Metals that were not AI?

The walls were seamless; the door they had entered by had disappeared. The corners of the room blended into one another, an endless expanse of white melting into the bright glow of the starshield. It tricked his optics, made colors that he knew were Ana dance and blur together. There were no readings on the starshield, no commands. But he could feel where the signal was strongest and turned to the center of the room.

It grew louder the closer he stepped. The signal throbbed—scratching at his firewalls like white-hot talons. He had felt this sort of invasion before, just once, but much subtler.

On Astoria.

The signal cracked the walls he'd put up and wormed its way into his code. The counter he kept in the back of his head, the time until his next glitch, fluctuated under the stress of it.

Two hours and thirty-seven seconds.

Four hours and—

Three minutes and thirty tw—

Forty-seven seconds—

He could not glitch now. It would put Ana in too much danger.

Her golden-brown eyes darkened as she looked around the bridge. "Di, where is this thing?"

"You wound me, Ana. I am not a thing."

She visibly tensed, spinning on her heels with her weapon ready—but there was nothing. There was nowhere to shoot. "We're not here to hurt you," she said, but her voice trembled all the same. She holstered her weapon and raised her hands. "See? We're not. Are you a program like the HIVE? Did Rasovant create you?"

"Did the Goddess create light?"

The program breached his last wall. The foreign code threaded through his own, not disturbing or intrusive. Gentle. Prodding. Searching. "Ana, I believe it is not a program, but malware. And it is trying to hack me."

"*Please* tell me you're joking."

He reassured her. "It is having difficulty."

"*One-zero-one-one-one-zero-one*—" It read off his data. "*You are broken, brother. Your code is ruined.*"

Ana's face pinched in pain. "That's why we're here to fix him."

"*You have ruined him.*"

"I *know!*" she cried. But she had not ruined him. He wanted—tried—to say as much, but the program clamped down, suffocating him. "My crew—please, they don't mean harm. Stop attacking them. We just want answers—"

"*You should have burned.*"

Her eyes widened. ". . . What?" she whispered.

"Ana—" Di forced out, and the foreign codes in his processors seized. He made a noise, and the program dropped him to his knees. The counter in the back of his mind clicked to zero. He froze.

Glitched.

"*He should have let you burn. And now he is ruined.*"

"Di!" Ana fell to her knees beside him, grabbing him by the shoulders. "Di, snap out of it—"

He twitched, trying to override it, but the spikes of code disrupted him again and again. He could not stop it. The intruding numbers pulsed, breaking his data byte by byte. He was losing himself. What he knew. Information. Facts.

Deteriorating.

The program was breaking him.

Trying to take control.

No—

It.

Would.

Not.

"Stop it!" Ana cried. "Stop whatever you're doing to him right now or I'll shoot this whole place up until I find you!"

"There will be others like him. They will be better. Do not fret."

"Like bloody *hell* they will!"

The voice laughed. It would never let them escape, Di knew. The signal—it came from the center of the room.

If the malware could sink into him, he could travel the same path. He could reach it, but he could not come back.

"I'm getting you out of here," she said, curling her arm into his. She tried to pull him up, to get him on his feet, but he was too heavy.

She did not understand. They would not escape.

In the signals, the wires, the pulses of white-hot talons that clawed into his code, he followed the malware's trail. It was large—foreign. It had not had time to infest the entire ship, only the androids. He spread across its programs in zeroes and ones like the roots of a tree. He forced the console to reveal itself.

A thin cylinder rose in the center of the room, a mass of mainframe and wires, and a hard drive at its center. Festering with the virus.

"Di?" Ana asked as he drew himself away from her. Her voice was thick with worry. "Di—what's happening? Did you do that?"

"Stop struggling, brother. You are ruined. We will remake you."

"You are mistaken," D09 said, willing himself to move, over-riding protocols, breaking his own systems beyond repair. He staggered toward the console, not looking back at Ana, because if he did, he would recalculate his decision. "I am more than the sum of my parts."

"Di." He registered her voice but could not look back. "What are you doing? Don't—stop—come back!"

He hesitated for a moment—long enough to realize there were no good good-byes.

Then he shoved his hand into the console, wrapped his fingers around the hard drive, and pulled. The program retaliated, digging into his mainframe, clawing him apart. There was no pain.

But the moment before he crushed the starship's hard drive, not long enough by any quantifiable standards, he knew he would miss Ana.

He would miss her more than iron and stars.

ANA

As Di's moonlit eyes darkened, the shattered hard drive of the ship fell out of his ruined hand and plinked onto the floor like drops of hail.

"You . . . will burrrr . . ." The voice grew distorted until it faded with a hiss of white noise as it died. And then nothing.

For a moment, Ana didn't realize what had happened, until the silence sank in.

"Di . . . ," she croaked, getting to her feet, and shuffled over to him. "I think it's dead. I—I don't hear gunshots anymore. Di?" She shook him, but he didn't move.

His eyes were dark. Dead like the bridge, hollow like the ship as it lost power, the lights above her flickering, flickering, then out, until only the light came from the emergency halogens, painting their shadows across the floor.

"Di?" she asked again, shaking him harder. He moved then—or so she thought he did—but it was just gravity as his body fell over onto its side with a terrible *thunk*. "Wake up, you stupid metalhead!" Her eyes stung, searing with tears. "No—I didn't mean to call you stupid. You're not stupid. You're my best friend. Please answer me, please . . . Di? *Di?*"

She repeated his name, louder and louder, shaking him, but he was stiff, and dark, and cold. She screamed his name for so long, the word tore at her throat like daggers. He was just glitching.

He would wake up. He had to. She would wait until he did.

She hadn't said good-bye.

A figure appeared in the doorway. The captain. Hair as bright as sunshine.

Ana turned her watery eyes up to her captain, rocking back and forth. It hurt to stay still. She was afraid that if she did, her sobs would shake her apart.

"I'm sorry—I'm sorry, I'm sorry," Ana repeated, her words choking on each breath. "I'm sorry, please, let's—please let's do it again. I won't—I won't—won't leave this time. I won't—I won't c-c-come here. . . ."

The captain's bloodred lips curved down as she knelt next to Ana. "C'mon, darling."

"We should wait—he's just glitching. He'll wake up. He'll—he'll come back—he *always* comes back. He . . . he . . ." Her voice wavered as the reality finally sank in. Her sobs grew louder until she could barely breathe. She pressed her face into her captain's hair, which smelled like gunpowder and smoky cigars, and wailed.

"Shhh," the captain murmured, kissing her forehead. "We need to leave. The Metals are dead."

As Siege helped her to her feet, a great steel groan rumbled through the ship. The shards of the broken hard drive slid across the floor as the *Tsarina* tilted.

"Captain—Captain! Can you read me?" Jax's voice crackled through the comm-link.

Siege responded. "Aye. I have Ana. What's happening?"

"Thank the Goddess. You need to get out of there. Now that the ship's without power, it's being pulled into Palavar's orbit. We'll be dragged down with it if we don't disconnect. Is Robb with you?"

"No, I haven't seen him. We're leaving." The captain began to pull Ana with her, but she refused to move. "Darling, we have to go. Ana!"

Ana snapped her eyes up to meet Siege's green gaze.

"I can't carry you if I'm going to carry him, okay?"

Him.

Di.

The captain wasn't going to leave Di. Because he was going to wake up. They wouldn't leave him to wake up alone.

The captain grunted as she heaved D09's frame over her shoulder. Di's pistol lay abandoned in the corner of the room. The ship tilted farther, red emergency lights flaring on in the corners of the room, as she followed her captain out of the room—and paused.

Turned back.

She grabbed Di's pistol, the barrel still warm, and took it with her, the sound of her heart beating in her ears when it should have broken on that bridge with the rest of her.

JAX

Grabbing an extra helmet from the rack in the cargo bay, he swirled his ponytail up into a bun and shoved it on. The air lock sighed and opened, bringing with it Riggs and Wick, carrying—

"Goddess, *Barger*," Jax gasped, staring at the lifeless body between his crewmates.

A gaping hole was carved into the center of Barger's back. Panic seized Jax's insides and twisted, because he'd lost contact with that blasted Ironblood a few minutes ago. What if the Metals had shot him, too? What if he'd accidentally led the Ironblood straight into harm's way? Goddess, he hated the Ironblood, but he hated the thought of him bleeding out somewhere alone even more.

"Have you seen Robb?" he asked, trying to disguise his panic.

Riggs shook his head. "Not since he ran off to go cut the power. You can't possibly be going on the ship—it's about to toss itself into Palavar."

"How can a ship toss itself?" Wick muttered, but Riggs waved him off.

"You know what I meant—Jax!"

But the Solani was already latching his helmet on to his suit. "Look, whatever awoke the ship is ninety-nine-point-for-sure coming after us, and the Ironblood's not answering his *fucking* comm-link."

"Leave him," Wick grunted, earning a sharp look from Riggs.

"What about the ship? You're the pilot," said Riggs.

"Wick, you can take the helm, yeah? " Jax asked, and the Cercian nodded. "Good—if you don't hear from me in five minutes, leave," he added, stepping into the air lock.

Great—he was even *sounding* desperate now. But he wasn't. He simply wanted to look after his investment. Yes, that was it. He'd saved the Ironblood's life once. He didn't want that rich brat to die *now*.

The door closed behind him and the air lock decompressed. He opened the outer door and grabbed onto the starbridge, hooking the safety strap onto his suit, and flicked the switch. Humming, the machine hauled him across the expanse toward the other ship.

The *Tsarina* made him feel much smaller than he already did as he traveled across the line between the ships. His heart thumped louder against his rib cage the closer he got to the air lock, the only sound save for the voice in his head telling him that he shouldn't get attached.

You'll regret it, the voice warned.

It sounded suspiciously like his father's.

The zip line came to a stop with a whine, and Jax heaved himself into the *Tsarina*'s outer cargo air lock and closed the door behind him.

The ship's cargo bay looked like a war zone. Half a dozen Metals lay sparking on the ground; a trail of blood was smeared across the floor in front of the cargo-bay doors. Barger's blood. He wondered, faintly, if Ironbloods bled the same, and the panic made him frenzied.

"Lenda!" he called, taking off his helmet. The air in the *Tsarina* tasted like metal and dust. "Lenda! Where are you?"

The blond woman peeked up from behind one of the cargo crates. Her eyes were bloodshot. "What're you doing over here?"

"Have you seen the Ironblood?" he asked, pretending he hadn't noticed she had been crying.

"Not since before the ship lost power," said Lenda, wiping her nose with the back of her arm. "The captain's gone looking for Ana."

"I know—*she* at least answered *her* comm-link," he grumbled, and whirled around toward the opposite hallway, trying to remember what the ship's map looked like. He'd told Robb to go into the ventilation shaft over there—the one with the destroyed grate—then that meant . . .

He went that way.

"Don't wait for me. Once you see Siege and Ana, get off the ship!" he shouted back to Lenda, and took off running toward a door at the other end of the hull, grabbing a helmet off the floor—assuming it was Robb's.

If the ship had powered down, that meant its emergency functions were depowering, too. He did *not* want to be swimming around on this ship in zero gravity. He hated zero gravity.

I'm going to kill Robb if he's just not answering his comm-link, he thought, tripping on his own feet, as he followed down the hallway Robb would have shimmied alongside in the air shaft. It was dark, and he could barely see.

I'm going to kill him when I find him.

But in his head, *kill* sounded suspiciously like another word.

Foolish, self-centered Ironblood! And, just as vehemently, *Foolish me.*

The engine room must be somewhere in this area. He would search through every corridor until he found it. The ventilation shaft hadn't taken Robb far. Just a few rooms, but the longer Jax ran, the farther it seemed to be.

Finally, he slid into the next hallway—and stopped.

It was a dead end. His heart plummeted like a rock into his toes. He was lost—was he lost? No, he couldn't be. Solani were never lost. Solani knew exactly where they were exactly when they needed to—

Someone stepped out of the room at the end.

Dark, curly hair, sun-kissed skin, a lightsword in his hand illuminating the corridor like a flickering star. The boy lifted his sky-colored eyes to Jax.

"*Ma'alor,*" he breathed in relief, then a little louder, "Robb!"

His legs went faster than his mind, darting down the corridor before he could gather what little decorum and dignity he had left. The Ironblood looked flustered to see him.

"What are you—why are—"

"Here, put this on," Jax interrupted, handing him the helmet. "Why weren't you answering your comm-link?"

A sigh whooshed through the ship as the gravitational systems shut off. Jax felt his stomach float first, then the rest of him. He tried to claw his way toward a wall.

Robb seemed perfectly at ease to float—he didn't seem in a hurry to leave at all, actually. "Why're you here?"

"Is that how you say thank you?" he asked, incredulous. Even with his long limbs, the walls were too far away. He couldn't grab ahold of anything. Unless he wanted to grab ahold of the Ironblood. "I'm trying to save your pretty ass."

"I didn't ask you to—and stop with the backhanded compliments," Robb snapped. "Leave me alone."

"You honestly want to die here, then? On the forgotten side of Palavar?"

Robb finally looked up to Jax, eyes rimmed red—as if he'd been crying. "My mother would say I deserved it. Like my father."

Jax recognized the note of bitterness in his voice, and despite his carefully built walls, his heart gave a lurch. *You found him, then.* "Robb . . ."

"Mother would say this was the *legacy* I earned." His eyebrows knit together. "So yes, I want to die here. I *deserve* to die h—"

Jax took Robb by the face, fingers in his hair, so this

insufferable Ironblood could look nowhere else but at him. Every speck of stardust in his being told him to let go. Being so close was a hazard, the thin gloves of his space suit the only thing separating skin from skin.

What Robb didn't realize was that Jax knew something about *legacy*, too. How stories were never all true or all lies. How the Solani gift to read the stars had slowly faded over a thousand years into one of those many stories, and how he was the last bit of truth left.

"Screw *legacy*," he said, the space between them barely a breath, but just enough to not touch, just enough to orbit without ever colliding. He pushed a curl behind Robb's ear, but it sprang back. "I was worried about *you*."

For a moment, it felt like the words didn't register.

Robb blinked. Once. Twice.

Then the Ironblood bridged the gap between them and pressed their lips together.

Robb's mouth was hungry and desperate, tasting like honey and salt and surprise. Jax's skin buzzed at their nearness, and he wanted to sink into the kiss and rebel, to be closer and a thousand light-years away. He braced himself, waiting for the inevitable—

For a second, a second more before—

Solani could read the stars, but it wasn't through the sky. It never was.

There was a jolt—like touching a live wire. A burn. A hiss. Then the star-stuff inside Robb swirled, brighter and brighter, sending his fate through Jax with the sharpness of a knife.

A black collar. A marble palace. Ana touching iron. Moonlilies. The glint of knuckle rings. A bloodied crown—

With a gasp, Jax tore himself away, the taste of Robb still on his tongue, the visions filling his head like sand. His lips stung. The pull of the stars was so strong it made him dizzy and weak.

"Goddess," he said, breathless, shaking. "You—you have—you're going to . . ."

"You said a kiss would do, remember?" Robb replied. He must've seen something odd on Jax's face, because he looked away a moment after and fastened her helmet on. "Before we go, I want you to see something."

Jax felt numb, trying to box away the images, but they were so fresh and raw. He hadn't seen someone's stars—*touched* someone—in ten years . . . and *this* was how he broke his streak?

"Did you hear me?" Robb said, and nudged his head back toward the door at the end of the hallway, where two Metals lay. "I said I've found something."

"W-what?"

"Just trust me—you have to see it." He took Jax by the arm and pulled him into the room at the end.

The room was pitch-black until Robb drew his lightsword, and it illuminated the small room. Dim holo-screens lined the walls, flickering as the ship used up the last of its energy, monitoring levels of oxygen and hydrogen and other vitals—like a hospital room.

The thought of Robb's stars quickly fell to the back of Jax's mind.

He fastened on his helmet, suddenly wanting to be anywhere

else. He hated dark spaces. "*Ak'va*, what is this?"

"It's in here," said the Ironblood, motioning to a long white box in the middle of the room. It reminded Jax of the caskets used to jettison deceased crew members into space. Robb planted his feet at the base of the casket, worming his fingers under the lid, and with a heave lifted it open. The steam from dry ice spilled out and quickly swirled in zero gravity, like snaking clouds.

"It's creepy, just so you know," Robb warned.

"What is it? Some sort of new tech? Frozen animal? A *weapon?*"

"Worse." Robb hovered his lightsword over the opening.

Jax peered into the box, not wanting to see what was inside. Wanting to leave. To get the taste of Robb's stars out of his mouth.

But when he looked closer, his heart began to race.

Inside the box was a young man.

He looked slightly older than Jax—maybe eighteen—with a brush of freckles across his shoulders, and deep-red shoulder-length hair. Jax quickly pressed his fingers against the boy's throat, but his skin was cold even through Jax's gloves. And there was no heartbeat—

He quickly took his hand away.

"It's a Metal," said Robb before he could freak out, and turned the android's head to the side to show him a small circle of grooves at the base of its neck.

A port.

"I think it can help Di. Will you tow it over to the *Dossier* with me?" Robb's sky-blue eyes met his, and in the shine of the sword light Jax saw something in them that looked like hope.

And Jax didn't have the heart to tell him that hope was not in his stars.

Instead, he pressed the comm-link on his chest and radioed Wick. "I found Robb. Keep the *Dossier* idling. We're bringing something over."

"Yep. Captain's returned, too. Standing by," Wick replied.

Then Jax reached in and grabbed the android under the left shoulder, and Robb grabbed its right, and they pushed their way out of the hidden room and down the hallway, hoping this Metal—whatever it was made of—didn't mind floating naked in the harshness of space.

ANA

The *Tsarina* fell into Palavar.

It sparked—small, like a flare—before the darkness of the moon swallowed it whole. The *Dossier* was heading to a way-station on the far side of Iliad. There they'd lie low for a while. Figure out what to do next. Ana held her breath, watching from a porthole in the galley, clinging to a reality when Di wasn't . . . when Di was . . .

But he was never coming back.

The crew sat around the table, their heads bent and their faces somber. The loss of Barger and Di left holes in the crew like bullet wounds. The only sound was a soft sniffle from Lenda as she dabbed her eyes.

Barger's gun, a polished Lancaster .47, lay in the middle of the table. Ana set down the other, a scrappy one dark with age. Di's.

It had cooled in the last hour. Now it was nothing more than cold and twisted metal. Like the corpse of her best friend, stowed in the infirmary with Barger's corpse.

Ana took a seat on the other side of Jax and Robb. She couldn't look at the crew or the pistols on the table, or the empty chairs. The sound of Barger and Di playing Wicked Luck filled her ears, Barger accusing him of counting cards. She could still hear the laughter, the moments of reverie, now swallowed by this suffocating, blackening cloud.

The captain retrieved an old bottle of bourbon, opened only for rare occasions, and set out five shot glasses, filled them, and slid them to the crew. The liquid looked brackish, like rainwater left out too long, and smelled like the richest spices on Iliad.

"To Barger, the finest mechanic I knew."

"Aye," agreed the crew.

"And to Di"—the captain's voice broke—"who was the best damn medic—no, the best *person* this kingdom had to offer. He was more human than the rest of us combined." She raised her shot glass. "To those who set sail into the night, may the stars keep them steady . . ."

"And the iron keep them safe," the crew replied, drained their shot glasses, and slammed them onto the table.

Ana did not drink.

After a moment, Lenda said, "That ship was cursed. That ship was cursed and we should'a never gone."

"We didn't know," Riggs replied, and Wick nodded quietly.

Lenda turned a tear-filled glare toward him. "Didn't *know?* Everyone knew about the *Tsarina!* It was *lost* for a reason! And now Barger's *dead* because of those bastards!"

"And Di," Jax reminded her softly, and the words felt like

a punch to Ana's stomach, stealing all her breath away. "Di's dead, too."

At the other end of the table, Robb shifted uncomfortably. He looked as though he wanted to leave the galley, too.

"And what do we got to show for it? " asked Lenda, fisting her hands on the table. "That weird . . . *thing* Jax and that Iron-blood brought onboard?"

"It's a Metal," Robb corrected her.

"A *Metal*?" Riggs balked. "It looks human."

Robb nodded. "I think Rasovant was trying to keep it hidden. There were red-eyed Metals guarding the room it was in before Di"—he faltered—"before the ship went down."

"But why would Rasovant hide something like this on that ship?" Jax muttered, a finger tapping his bottom lip thoughtfully. "It's not illegal or anything. There are human-looking robots in all the best dens on Iliad."

"And why would he have guards protecting it?" Robb added. "Unless it was different somehow."

"So basically it's just an upgraded version of Rasovant's killing machines," Lenda concluded, her voice dripping with bitterness. "Half of us were already shot at by Metals—it'd be a real treat for that thing to wake up and kill the rest of us!"

Siege gave the young woman a warning. "Calm down, Lenda."

"*Calm down?* Barger is dead!"

"So is D09—"

"He was never alive!"

"Yes, he was!" Ana pushed back her chair with a loud *crack* and stood. "And I loved him!" Her voice echoed off the metal walls at every place Di would never be again. She heard her own breath hitch, a sob escape her lips—and tore herself away from the table.

"Ana, wait," the captain called, but she was already out of the galley, her eyes blurring with unshed tears.

But there was nowhere for her to go. Nowhere to escape to. Every corner of the *Dossier* reminded her of him. Every cranny, every nook. She couldn't get away from his ghost.

The ache in her chest was so heavy she couldn't breathe. Why didn't the pain stop? When would it *stop*?

The door to the infirmary slid open with a quiet blip. On the floor in the corner lay Barger in a black body bag, the smell of blood soaking the air in a dark perfume, and beside him was the strange red-haired *thing* Robb had brought aboard. She couldn't even look at it. If Di had survived, maybe it could have been an answer.

But now there wasn't even a question.

On a gurney, not even human enough for a body bag, lay the shell of her best friend.

She could still hear the clank of his feet as he shuffled around the room, the deft way his hands worked, like a surgeon— precise. Exact. The sound of his core humming, the soft swish of electricity through his wires, the buzz of parts, the crackle of life, sweet and lovely—

She couldn't set foot inside the room; she wasn't strong enough.

The *whoosh* of the solar sails sighed through the ship as they caught the solar winds, bringing the ship into motion. She could feel it as sharply as she felt cuts and bruises.

She didn't hear the captain until Siege was already behind her. "We'll have the funerals tomorrow, darling. We have to keep moving now. The malware that took control of the *Tsarina* could have reported us to whoever created it. We'll take our time to say good-bye on Iliad. I promise."

Ana closed the infirmary door, locking Di inside. "Okay." She pressed her back against the cold, solid metal, slowly sinking to the floor.

"Maybe, during the funeral, if you want you could say a few words—"

"Okay."

"I could help if you—"

"I said *okay!*" Ana snapped as tears burned at the edges of her eyes.

Siege knelt beside her. "Darling, I know it hurts—"

"No you don't!" She angrily wiped her tears away with the palm of her hand. "I just wanted to save him. I just wanted to save him and I ended up killing him. I kill everyone! I probably killed my parents too, didn't I? Everything I touch I ruin—"

The captain took her by the shoulders. "Don't you *ever* say that."

"Even if it's true?"

"Ana—"

She slapped Siege's hands away. "Leave me alone!"

"But Ana—"

"*Please,*" she sobbed, curling her legs up to her chest. "Please leave me alone."

For a long moment, Ana thought she wouldn't leave. She pulled herself tighter into a ball, looking anywhere but at the captain, thinking that maybe if she pretended Siege wasn't there, she'd go away.

And eventually, the captain did, and left her alone on a too-quiet ship in a too-quiet universe.

She sat against the infirmary door, waiting, waiting to hear her heart break.

Like heartbreak was supposed to sound. Like a mirror cracked in half, like a world tearing in two, like a galaxy crumbling, stars falling, crashing around her in the realization that tomorrow would not have Di. Or the next day. Or the day after that. That she could never see him again, never hear his voice, never press her cheek against his cool shoulder and savor the humming cadence of *him*.

He was gone. Not lost. Not broken. Because he didn't have a soul. He wasn't alive. D09 was simply gone. Gone in a breath, in a blink of an eye.

Gone.

And her heart beat on in a universe without him, a sad and useless organ in her chest.

ROBB

It was an hour after the rest of the crew went to bed before Ana came back into the quarters and crawled into her bunk. Robb wanted to tell her that he knew what it was like to lose the one person who meant the world to you. Because he knew it better than most people. He still felt it, the hole in his heart now taped over with the image of his father's corpse on the *Tsarina*.

But he was a Valerio, and he doubted she'd want condolences from him.

He waited one minute, two, until her muffled sobs sank into silence and he was sure she was asleep, before he shimmied out of his bunk. Jax was huddled underneath his covers, a pale hand peeking out from beneath the pillow. Robb had never seen him with his gloves off before. Long, thin fingers. No scars, no horrible burns. But all the same, the Solani looked fragile without them. He could still taste their kiss, soft and bitter, and the horrified look on Jax's face moments after.

He hadn't thought a kiss would hurt Jax. He hadn't thought the wounded look would hurt *him*. He . . . didn't know *what* he thought, actually. That Jax's words were sweet? That, for a moment, he wanted to taste them. He wanted to trap them, claim them as his.

No one had said they cared about him before, not with the kind of protective look in those violet-red eyes.

Another throb of pain pulsed from his side, reminding him why he was up to begin with, and he slipped out of the room and down into the infirmary to find some more painkillers, ignoring the body bag in the corner, the red-haired robot, and the Metal on the gurney.

Finding some pain medicine in the first aid kit, he tore the cap off with his teeth and slammed the needle into his side and bit in a scream as he pressed the medicine into his skin.

The ache dulled to a sore throb.

He wished it would numb the burning in his wrist, too, that was making it hard to move his fingers. But it wasn't that pain that bothered him. It was the other kind—the betrayal that tightened his chest, made it hard to breathe. Even if he wanted to, he couldn't take the chip out without doing permanent nerve damage to his entire sword arm.

And it was just a matter of time now before someone found him.

The sound of metal hitting the floor made him yelp, and he spun around, toward the gurney—

But it was not D09.

EOS hovered over the Metal, using small, thin arms to mend the broken wires in the android's hand. It made the same clattery noise when another piece of Metal hand fell to the floor.

Guilt ate at Robb's conscience—if he had just cut the ship's power when he was supposed to, if he hadn't been so selfish . . . Ana's Metal D09 would be alive. And if D09 hadn't destroyed the program controlling the androids and deactivated them when he had, then those Metals in the hall would have killed *him.*

So he owed his life to D09. He was not the same as those other coreless Metals on the ship.

D09 was good, and the world could have used a little more good a while longer.

Annoyed, he shoved at EoS. "Hey—hey, it's useless. He's *dead.*"

EoS didn't acknowledge him, connecting another severed wire.

Gritting his teeth, Robb shoved it away. It bleeped angrily. "He's *dead,* you stupid can opener! He's not coming back. Don't you *get* that?"

Like his father. Never coming back—no matter how much Robb wanted him alive.

EoS whirled back to D09's ruined hand. Couldn't it just take a *hint?*

He grabbed it out of the air—and froze, noticing a dull light pulsing from the smashed Metal's chest. D09's memory core.

It wasn't smashed.

The ship must have only fried D09's body.

A plan formed in his head, one that sounded more and more impossible the longer he thought about it. He couldn't save his father—unless he could reverse time—but maybe he could try to make *one* thing right.

The bot wiggled out of his grip and whirled up noisily, beeping every expletive in its one-tone vocabulary.

If he transferred the code in D09's memory core into the other Metal—the human-looking one—would it work? Memory cores were nothing but data, so he should be able to scan a copy into somewhere else. Namely, the humanoid Metal.

What was there to lose in trying?

As a Valerio, he should just let his mother find him and be a good son. He was more than likely in enough trouble already.

He didn't need to poke around in lives that weren't his.

But . . . D09 had saved him—all of them. Could he not at least try to do the same?

Damn the part of him that was his father. *Damn it all.*

Rushing out of the infirmary, he found a toolbox in the back of the skysailer and hurried back to D09, then rifled through it for an omnitool.

The Academy taught basic programming and science. Boring stuff. He never showed up to class, partly because he couldn't stand the spit-spewing teacher, and he still received the highest marks.

As a Valerio should, his mother always said.

But he didn't realize until much later how rare that sort of brilliance was. And that his mother would always see him second to his brother.

He found the tool and forced open the paneling in D09's

chest, revealing a cube. It pulsed, like a fading heartbeat, when usually functioning memory cores lit up white.

He extracted the core, carefully setting it on the infirmary computer's scanner.

The old computer was used more for research and bone scans than anything else, but as long as it didn't overheat, he was sure he could transfer the Metal's memories.

Now was the hard part. He exchanged D09 on the gurney with the humanoid Metal on the floor, feeling a little more awkward than he should that the android was naked. He'd seen naked boys before.

He's not a boy, he reminded himself.

EOS swirled over, inserting a computer cord into the small port at the base of its skull, almost hidden in the hairline. Smart bot.

In theory, the only way to successfully transfer a Metal's data was to write over another memory core. It was probably why D09 never wanted to try it—because it would essentially kill another Metal.

But this one was empty.

After a few quick keystrokes, the scanner flickered blue, trying to pull data. He waited, folding his arms over his chest, for the computer to read the cube—if it could. The algorithms could be too complicated for this piece of junk console.

After a moment, he gave a sigh. It was worth a try—

Data ignited across the wall-size monitor in zeroes and ones, so suddenly Robb jumped back. Memories, made with numbers. Ana's entire life with D09 in these jumbled sets of digits.

He glanced at the small cube. A light inside it pulsed gently, like a distant star.

With shaking fingers he keyed in the command to copy the data to the humanoid Metal.

"Uploading data," the computer relayed. *"In three, two, o—"*

A thunderous boom ricocheted through the ship, pulling the *Dossier* out of traveling speed. Robb pitched forward with the sudden stop as the screen crashed to black, red emergency lights blinking on in the corners of the room.

And he knew without a doubt it was his mother come to find her lost son.

ANA

Ana bolted upright in bed.

An explosion thundered through the ship, the lights flickering, dimming to a terrifying emergency red. The rattle was so fierce, it shook the empty glasses off the community table. Riggs's leg, propped up next to his bed, fell over. From the highest shelf, D09's favorite book clattered to the floor. It lay there, open to a bookmarked page about medicine and scar tissue. She quickly jumped out of bed to close it and put it back. The other crew members crawled out of their bunks, rubbing the sleep from their eyes.

"What's it?" Riggs muttered, as Wick pulled him out of bed and handed over his mechanical leg.

"An attack," replied the Cercian.

The sails quivered with the extra weight, rattling the ship.

Still in her crumpled clothes from yesterday, Ana ran for the cockpit, her hand skimming along the wall for balance.

Lenda stumbled out after her, hopping into her boots. "We're in protected space!" she cried, short blond hair sticking straight up in a cowlick. "Who's shooting at us? Is it the Messiers? The *Royal Guard*? Should we suit up?"

For a brief, terrifying moment, Ana thought it was the *Tsarina* come back to finish her off, even though it had crashed into Palavar hours ago. It couldn't be the malware—Di had destroyed it. The memory was burned into her retinas every time she closed her eyes.

The ship jolted again, and threw her against the wall. A shuddering rumble followed, and the sound of an air-vac, sharp like an inhale somewhere belowdecks, sucking a breach in the ship secure again.

She made it to the cockpit, where Jax sat with a map of the cosmos lit up around him. Wick, tucking in the tail of his shirt, slid into his comms station, trying to decode the message blasting across their feed.

"Jax, report," ordered the captain as she stormed into the cockpit, sliding into her bloodred frock coat. She put a steady hand on the back of the pilot chair.

"Two klicks and closing, sir. It's an Armada, class seven." An Ironblood ship. "Faster than it looks and heading straight for us."

"Can't we outrun them?"

"Right sail's punctured, putting strain on the left, so I can't steer worth shit—*damn it*," he cursed as another missile tore through the same sail. Warning lights glowed red against his determined face. "I didn't even *see* the ship before they attacked. No warning, no nothing—"

Another explosion rattled the *Dossier*, so close to the cockpit it threw Ana off her feet. Her shoulder slammed into the floor. A shower of sparks spewed from one of the control panels. Wick yelped, shielding his face.

The cockpit plunged into darkness before flickering back to life with emergency power.

"Captain!" Jax righted himself in his chair again. *"Captain!"*

Dizzy, Ana scrambled over to the captain lying on the floor a few feet away, grabbing a fistful of Siege's coat to roll her onto her back. A nasty gash bled down her forehead, soaking into her black hair. Talle, bracing herself in the doorway, rushed over to her wife and pressed the back of her hand against Siege's mouth.

"Breathing," Talle said in relief.

"Good. Ana, get in a seat," Jax instructed. "We're in for a bumpy—"

Another blast hit somewhere starboard. More warning lights. Emergency lights.

Wick gave a shout. "Message incoming! It's—" His eyebrows furrowed, and he turned around in his chair to face Ana. *"Toriean el agh Lothorne."*

Even as the ship blared its warning sirens, a silence sank over the cockpit. They had all heard the phrase before. Seen it carved on the hulls of derelict ships and on the foreheads of unfortunately spaced men.

The Valerio motto.

"They're asking permission to board," Wick added.

"Let me guess," Jax growled. "On the condition of our *surrender.*"

"Yeah," replied Wick.

Riggs slammed his metal foot into the side of the ship with a sharp *ping*. Another line in the solar sails snapped off, leaving them barely able to coast.

"Right sail down," reported Jax. "Left's at forty percent—we're sinking. Fast."

"What do we do?" Talle asked, kneeling to put Siege's head on her lap. Her fingers were curled around the captain's coat collar protectively. "I can't get her to wake up."

Riggs was shaking his head. "We have to escape! We don't surrender to Valerio ships. In fifty years, I never have!"

"How?" Wick shifted nervously. "We're sitting ducks, Riggs."

"I *knew* that Valerio kid was bad luck. Barger did too!" Lenda raged, slamming her fist against the doorway she had braced herself against.

Ana couldn't take all the noise. Her chest was tightening, making it hard to breathe—the cockpit narrowing, walls squeezing together—

"We gotta outrun them."

Jax scowled at Riggs. "You wanna drive? I'll let you—"

Lenda argued, "We should fire back!"

"Against *that* ship? Good luck hitting it—"

"Stop arguing!" Ana shouted, and the cockpit plunged into silence.

Di would've known what to do. He would've calculated the odds and figured out how to—to what? *Escape?* Keep them alive? But Di was dead, and it was her fault. All this was her fault.

And now the rest of the crew was going to die.

"We have to accept the terms," she heard herself say, voice wavering. "We don't have a choice."

Because there was no way to escape. Because if they tried, they would die. The crew of the *Dossier* had been through enough chases and firefights to know the endgame. They knew the story of a ship with a punctured sail in the middle of open space. They'd seen it happen to others before.

Ana had never thought the *Dossier* would become one of those ships. And it was all her fault.

"We don't have a choice," she repeated, her voice tight. "I don't want anyone else to die."

Wick leaned forward in his chair and radioed in their surrender. Jax eased the *Dossier* to a stop and sat back, releasing the controls, as the screens in front of him dimmed, showing their coordinates. There were no more explosions, no more noise, except for the Valerio creed that echoed in Ana's ears like a siren.

Even though she didn't know the Old Language, she knew the words.

Toriean el agh Lothorne.

Glory in the Pursuit.

JAX

Valerio guards swarmed the *Dossier* in a sea of crimson.

It would've been nice to have seen this in Robb's stars, Jax thought bitterly, raising his hands to show that he was unarmed.

A burly woman yanked him out of his seat and stuck a gun against his back anyway. Another took Ana by her braid, pulled Siege up by her coat. Their captors bound the crews' hands behind their backs with strong wire and led them back to the cargo bay.

Goddess, when he got his hands on that slimy little shit-stain of Valerio spacetrash, he'd—

The guard forced him to his knees in the cargo bay beside Wick, then Lenda, the sting of his kneecaps hitting the floor sending a hiss through his teeth.

On the other side, a guard shoved Ana down beside him. Her face was blank, as if she'd already given up. She'd given up the moment Siege brought her back to the *Dossier.* He had told Di to prepare her—*hadn't* he? But now there was a sinking suspicion in his gut, like a bird falling from the sky, that things were about to get a whole world worse.

The decompression chamber sighed, and the air lock slid open to reveal a woman whose boots struck the floor like swords, making the guards stand straighter at attention.

Tall and thin, with olive skin and graying brown hair swept into a bun, cheekbones so sharp they could cut ice. She wore a finely detailed coat and trousers, a Valerio crest pinned above her heart. She appraised the small crew with shrewd blue eyes—he knew that color. He knew it achingly well. The color of Erosian skies.

This nightmare of a woman must be Robb's mother.

Jax had never felt such vitriol for anyone before.

"And where is the captain?" asked Lady Valerio.

"Here, milady," replied the commander as two men dragged the captain into view. Siege's head lolled against her chest, unconscious. The gash on her forehead smeared blood down half her face, lipstick smudged. Jax couldn't remember a time her unruly hair hadn't glowed.

"*This* is the frightful Captain Siege?" the Valerio woman asked with a sneer. "I would have expected someone a little more . . . *frightening*. And what a dreary little crew. Smaller than I would have suspected. And young." Her icy eyes rested on him. "And what do we have here, a *star-kisser*? What is his charming little name?"

Jax pressed his lips together. Swallowed. He couldn't lie— he couldn't *lie*.

"Well?"

Wick and Lenda leaned forward protectively. Wick snarled,

"You don't deserve to know it, *knrachne*."

Jax wasn't sure what *knrachne* meant, but he had a feeling it was one of those names you didn't want to call anyone—or be called.

The woman's stone facade flickered—like a candle—with anger. Jax could see it resting behind her marble eyes, dangerous and explosive. Her deep-red lips had begun to form into words when a thin voice interrupted her from the infirmary.

"Mother." Robb pushed through a line of guards, tripping on one of their shoes. Despite himself, Jax tried to rise to his feet to catch the Ironblood—but stopped himself. *Foolish. He doesn't care about you.*

The flicker of anger beneath Lady Valerio's gaze dissolved as she turned to her son. "Robbert, my dear. It's wonderful to see you alive."

He stood straight, lips pressed into a thin line. "Of course I'm alive."

"You were kidnapped, my sweet. I was worried."

"I wasn't *kidnapped*—"

"And you can *gladly* have him back. You have no cause to keep us," Jax snapped before he could bite his tongue. "We're in protected space. You have no right to be on this ship."

The woman's eyes flicked to him. "I have *every* right. Who will tell me no?"

"I just did" was Jax's shrewd reply.

So the woman took Siege's pistol out of its holster and fired a bullet into one of her own guards' knees. The guard gave a shriek, collapsing to the floor, before two others dragged him back to the other ship, leaving a smeared trail of blood.

"It seems, dear Solani," Lady Valerio said coolly, "that you attacked first. Therefore, I boarded your ship."

She cocked Siege's pistol again and aimed for his head.

He barely had time to blink before she pulled the trigger, and Wick shoved him to the floor.

ANA

Gunshot was louder on the *Dossier*—or maybe it was the silence after that made it so loud.

Wick looked at the hole in his chest and gave a gurgle—wet and gasping. Ana could only watch in horror, her hands bound behind her, as the man who'd taught her how to clean a pistol and speak Cercian, and darn her own socks, slumped onto the floor and went still.

The air stank of gunpowder and iron. It suffocated her.

"Seems you pirates do have honor after all," Lady Valerio said, amused, and handed Siege's gun to one of her henchmen to reload. As if she couldn't care to load her own bullets, while the captain had taught Ana to count each one.

Remember where they land.

"You killed him," Ana heard herself saying, her voice calmer than she expected. "You killed him!"

The shock that quivered and quaked inside her began to turn, coiling into bitterness, tightening, until it was hot and angry. She glared up through wet lashes and found herself gazing down the barrel of the woman's pistol.

"You'll be next if you don't hush up. Do you even know who you're speaking to?" asked Lady Valerio.

"A dead woman," Ana growled in reply.

The lady's expression shifted—just slightly—but it was there. The twitch of an eyebrow. Ana knew she'd struck a nerve. "Robbert, who is she? She looks familiar—wait. Isn't she the assassin? I seem to recall a Metal as well. Where is it?"

"Smashed, Mother," Robb replied, his voice tight. "The body is in the infirmary."

His mother looked to a guard for confirmation. Lady Valerio didn't even trust her own son?

"He's correct, milady. There's a Metal on the ground and two body bags—one on the gurney."

"What a pity," said the woman. "Dead crewmates, a smashed Metal . . . did you outlaws run into *trouble*?"

When no one answered, her lips twisted with impatience.

"Robbert, pray tell, what did they come all the way out here to find?"

He pursed his lips. Ana didn't think he had it in him to be quiet—the spineless piece of spacetrash he was.

But he didn't answer—and neither did anyone else. The woman snapped her fingers. In two steps the Valerio commander had taken Lenda by her hair and forced her head back, pressing a blade to her neck.

"It was the *Tsarina*!" Ana said, her voice quivering with

thinly veiled rage. Lady Valerio raised a single sharp eyebrow and motioned for her commander to lower her weapon. "We— we were looking for the fleetship. We wanted to loot it. You know us *outlaws*."

"Yes, I'm well aware. And I don't believe you."

"I'm not lying."

Lady Valerio waved a hand dismissively at Ana, her diamond rings glinting in the halogen lights. "Robbert, take your newfound *friend* here to one of the holding cells on the ship. We have a reward to collect, and she will do."

Talle rose to her feet. "Don't you dare take her—" The Valerio commander slammed the hilt of her blade into Talle's gut, and she slumped to the floor again.

Robbert Valerio came and tok Ana by the arm.

He was perfectly careful to keep his face impassive—as though he wore a mask. Or maybe his expressions before had been the mask, and this was the real monster underneath.

All Ironbloods were monsters—she didn't know why she ever thought one could be different.

"Don't make this difficult," he warned her, pulling her away from her crew.

Ana looked back at Jax, Talle, Lenda—but all she could see was Di the moment before he died. She had heard the stories of what happened to outlaws, to the forgotten and the unwanted and the broken. They didn't matter in this kingdom.

They didn't exist.

"Take the star-kisser too. Question him about the *Tsarina*.

The Solani will break if he's left in the dark long enough. Do what you want with the rest of them," Lady Valerio ordered her commander.

"You can't do that!" Ana cried. "We surrendered!"

"My girl"—the Ironblood woman shook her head—"we are not *pirates*. We don't follow rules."

Then she waved Robb away with a flick of her wrist.

Ana bucked against him as he dragged her into the air lock, where an elaborate starwalk, like a long tube, stretched the ten feet from the *Dossier* to the Valerio ship. The starwalk groaned as they entered. She jerked against him, fighting, and with every movement his fingers dug deeper into her skin. In the air lock on the other side, two Valerio guards waited with drawn Metroids.

If Robb dragged her onto that ship, she would never escape.

Gritting her teeth, she grabbed her left thumb, and pulled— she pulled so hard it popped out of joint. She bit her tongue so she wouldn't cry as she tore her hand out of the wire binding, skin scraping away.

Robb's mouth fell open. *Never* underestimate an outlaw.

She reared her fist back and took a swing at him. He ducked, caught her bloody wrist, and twisted it painfully behind her.

"You punch like my brother," he said against her ear, squeezing her arm so tight she couldn't move. "Please don't make this harder than it is. I don't want to hurt you—"

She thrashed against him, getting her hand free of his grip, and grabbed at his side where his stitches were. He let out a painful gasp—and that only made her curl her fingers into the wound, squeezing harder, until blood soaked the shirt Jax had lent him.

"Great Dark take you, you son of a b—"

Something cool and sharp pricked against her neck, and a lazy honey feeling washed over her, numbing her into darkness.

III

IRON BLOOD

ROBB

His mother's ship, the *Caterina*, sailed as silent as it was swift, thrusters spitting white-hot sparks that left trails of light behind them. The ship sped through the expanse between Cerces and Eros, toward the Iron Palace on Eros's third moon, Luna. It was a straight shot, thanks to the Holy Conjunction— the alignment of the planets. A journey that, the last time he'd traveled it, had taken the better part of a week; they'd now arrive in less than a day.

As he left the *Caterina's* medical ward, he popped two pain-killers into his mouth. They tasted like chalk but gave him a nice, dull buzz so he didn't have to think much. Not about the *Dossier* now controlled by Valerio men, or that humanoid Metal he hid in a body bag after he failed to upload Di, or Jax captured by his mother, Ana down in the holding cells, or how it was his fault that—

Stop. Thinking.

He rubbed his thumb against his chip, which was no longer hurting, though he wished it still did.

Jax should have left him on the *Tsarina* after all.

The starboard observation deck was empty, thankfully, not that he knew of anyone else on the *Caterina* who liked this room. Only he, and his father, stretched out on the two benches overlooking the passing stars.

He'd avoided windows ever since the Academy, but he couldn't think of anywhere else to go.

He sat on the left bench with a hiss, the ache in his side as sharp as ever, and watched space slowly move by. He didn't notice the Messier in the corner of the room until it asked him, "Do you need a refreshment, Lord Valerio?"

Robb jumped.

The Messier looked so much like D09, he thought for a moment it was the android. But this Metal's eyes were blue, and its uniform pristine and pressed. D09 never looked anything short of just-hit-by-a-skysailer.

"Would you like a refreshment?" the Messier repeated.

"No—no, thank you. I would like some privacy, though," he said.

The Messier's blue eyes flickered. It bowed and left the observation deck.

Robb was sure he'd see more of them in the future, now that he was the soon-to-be Emperor's brother. Wherever the Emperor went, Messiers followed. Their mindless blue-eyed gaze should've been a comfort after the red-eyed androids from the *Tsarina*, but it made him squirm nonetheless.

He ran a hand through his curly hair. This was the first time he had truly been alone since Astoria, and it was too quiet. It made the doubt and disgust in his head too loud.

You killed them—the entire crew.

What did they do to deserve that? Why do you care?

The reflection in the window tiredly stared back at him.

He didn't recognize himself at first.

His cheeks looked thinner, and he needed a shave—but he'd seen that face before. It hung above the hearth at the Valerio estate of a man who'd died on the far side of Palavar.

His father was dead, and now the only people who had treated Robb remotely like a person were going to die, too.

And it's all your fault, his shame whispered in the silence.

Resting his face in his hands, he squeezed his eyes closed, trying to push down the shame that clawed up his throat— Siege's grin during a game of Wicked Luck, the crew mourning over their dead, the look Ana always gave her Metal, the taste of Jax just after their kiss. . . .

But the guilt bubbled up and up, because he had used them for his own selfish gain. He'd screwed up over and over and still they'd given him another chance.

Those outlaws don't matter, he tried to convince himself, but the words morphed, twisted to *You betrayed them—they mattered.*

And there in the solitude of the observation deck, he cried. He wanted so badly to be his father's son, but he had so unwillingly been everything his mother always wanted.

ANA

Great plumes of fire reached toward the marble ceiling. She coughed, unable to catch a deep-enough breath, as tapestries dropped from the walls and flowers in rich Erosian vases shriveled in the heat.

It was a nightmare.

She knew it was because she had never seen this place before in her entire life, but she recognized the corridors from the newsfeeds—the veiny marble walls and the melting golden trim.

The Iron Palace.

The ash tasted familiar on her tongue—and she wasn't sure how.

Archways of fire stretched across the ceiling, crackling and smoldering against the white marble. Screams echoed down from the distant corridors. She wanted to save them, but someone had grabbed ahold of her wrist and led her away.

He was tall and broad shouldered, with thick dark hair and a beard. But she quickly realized that he wasn't very tall at all— she was short. A child. She couldn't see his face; it was blurred like rushing lights. Her heart pounded in her chest with fear—

But it's a dream—this is a dream.

"It'll be okay," he said, his voice echoing like he was shouting to her from the other end of the hallway, even though he was right there. He bent to her and pinned something to her nightgown—a brooch in the shape of an ouroboros. "As long as you wear it, it'll protect you."

But the fire was too hot—suffocating. She could barely breathe.

There was a great shudder above them, and she looked up. The ceiling, heavy with fire, gave a groan.

The man grabbed her arm and darted through the flames, but she twisted out of his grip. He dove through the flames alone.

And then the ceiling collapsed.

She winced, closing her eyes, when someone scooped her up into its arms—except it wasn't a person at all, but a Metal. And it was so hot—burning, bubbling hot—she tried to scream but nothing came out. The side of her face lit with unimaginable pain.

It hurt, it hurt so fiercely she could feel the fire against her cheek as she tried to claw it away. She felt her nails dig into her skin, scratching, drawing blood, but she couldn't wake up.

She wanted to wake up.

And then the Metal monster who had burned her let go, and there was a broken look to the Metal's face, something familiar, like a memory she couldn't quite place. She thrashed away from it, but the android grabbed her wrists, moonlit eyes shining.

"It is a dream, Ana. Wake up," he said in Di's damaged voice. "*Wake up, Ana.* Wake up!"

· ☽ ● ☾ ·

She lurched awake.

The memory of the fire prickled her skin. She couldn't catch her breath, dizzy from the smoke in her nightmare. It had been so real—there were faces now in the burning hallway. There were words and voices. Where had they come from? Her hair stuck to the back of her neck, slick with sweat, the taste of ash still in her mouth. And—and there was Di.

Frantically, she looked around. She'd heard him—she knew she had. He was right there in the fire, telling her to wake up. But the further her nightmare slipped into the past, the fainter the memory grew. Because it couldn't be Di.

Di was dead.

Her eyes focused—

She was in a small room. Steel walls. Worried Erosian-sky eyes watched her. He had a hand wrapped around her wrist, as if he'd shaken her awake instead. Robb Valerio. Her last memory on the *Dossier* came flooding back. Her crewmates were dead—or dying—and she was about to die, too.

She quickly jerked her hands out of his grip, and his worried expression fell away to an indifferent mask again.

The cell door opened behind him, and two Valerio guardsmen entered.

"We're here," Robb said, his voice steel and stone.

"W-where?" The guards pulled her to her feet, binding her hands behind her back again. Her thumb was sore, but it had been reset, and Wick's blood had dried on her pants. How long had she been asleep?

"The Iron Palace," the Ironblood said as he adjusted his disheveled coat, "to turn you in."

ROBB

The Iron Palace looked like a shard of black glass against the otherwise pale landscape of the moon, a gloomy fortress. The North Tower looked like the other three, but it stood as a hollow shell with burned insides. It had never been rebuilt, and instead the doors were locked—the halls never to be trod in again. The rest of the palace, however, was immaculate in its marble walls and golden trim—the pinnacle of opulence. Surrounding the palace lay terraformed gardens blooming with moonlilies, and in the largest garden stood the kingdom's first Iron Shrine.

Robb hadn't been back to the palace in seven years, but he quickly realized as he stepped out onto the docks that nothing had changed. It was frozen in time—a broken relic from a terrible rebellion.

He wished he were anywhere other than here.

Two of his mother's finest guardsmen led Ana down the length of the docks to the waiting Royal Guard, passing large starships with sails that shone like spun gold. They were all warships built in a time of peace, as if Ironbloods ever had to worry about *battle*.

At least not the physical kind.

At the end of the docks, Royal Captain Viera waited, a bandage on her cheek from their run-in a few days ago. She looked just about as pleased as a wet cat.

Robb caught up with the Valerio guards escorting Ana and dismissed them. "I can take it from here," he told them.

"But Lady Valerio said—"

"Did I stutter?"

The two guardsmen gave each other hesitant looks before relinquishing Ana to him, her hands bound with wire behind her back, greasy hair stuck to her face and neck, clumped together with sweat and dried blood. She looked like a dead girl walking.

He turned back to the Royal Captain, inwardly cursing his luck that Viera Bastard-Born Carnelian was the Grand Duchess's *Royal Captain*.

He gave a slight bow. "Vee, it's a pleasure."

"I am glad you managed to apprehend her," replied the Royal Captain, knowing very well that he had escaped with Ana instead of *after* her.

"One of us would've caught her eventually."

"Of course."

Royal Captain Viera led them into the palace gates and through the empty square, the palace towering over them like a shard of black glass. The palace doors opened into the great hall, lined with pillars as thick as three men. The hall seemed endless, or maybe it was just his wishful thinking.

He had spent several hours on the observation deck, trying to puzzle out how to fix this, how to save Ana—but it had been staring him in the face this whole time.

You can do this, he told himself, remembering the moment Ana had picked up the ore, when he realized that it didn't rust in her hands. *It's just another way to get in trouble. You're good at trouble.*

That still didn't calm the twisting, clawing panic rising in his stomach. Because what if he failed?

At the end of the hall was another set of double doors as big as the ones at the entrance. These were carved with moons and stars, the motto of the Iron Kingdom in gold across its length.

Dvarek et su Lait.

In Darkness We Shine.

The Royal Captain planted a hand on each door and pushed them wide.

Robb winced as light flooded the hall, a blinding spectacle of beautifully gilded floors and antique tapestries. A plush purple runner trailed its way up a small set of stairs to the Iron Throne, and behind it stood an imposing ancient statue of the Goddess. She almost looked alive, the way Her hair and robes floated in an imagined breeze, as She stretched Her arms out, Her eyes looking up, and up, and up, toward a pinpoint in a sky no one could see.

The statue made him feel infinitely small.

The royal-purple tapestries on the walls fluttered in a breeze that made the lanterns overhead bob and sway, warm swaths of yellow-orange light moving over the people in the room like light under the sea. In the corner of the room stood Messiers, as still as statues, their blue eyes glowing, watching.

Viera took her place on the left side of the throne, while the Iron Adviser stood to the right, his long beard braided halfway down his chest, dressed in the kingdom's finest—a black suit with draping tails, swirls of silver and purple sewn into the broad sleeves and fluttery hems, and a shimmery gorget around his neck. Lord Rasovant, the shadow who haunted the corners of the room and whispered in the Grand Duchess's ear.

Robb bowed to the woman perched on the metal throne. "Your Grace."

The Grand Duchess inclined her head.

The throne swallowed the old woman. Large steel beams spiked out from the chair's back like sun rays, and she the center. Her glittering navy-colored dress accented the warm brown of her skin, ancient and soft. Her dress was all sharp lines and pointed shoulders, as though it was her choice of weapon against the universe.

Do you want to take this gamble? a voice whispered deep inside him. *Is Ana really who you think she is?*

Ana didn't look like the Goddess returned, as the late princess was supposed to be. The girl of light. She simply looked like a tired and lost outlaw.

"I was promised a Metal," the Grand Duchess said with mild disdain. "Where is it?"

"Smashed, Your Grace," Robb replied. "In an accident—"

"So I suppose for bringing the girl here your family wants a reward?" the Grand Duchess went on, leaning her head on her hand, elbow propped on the armrest. "Tell me, Robb Valerio—your brother is about to be crowned Emperor of the entire Kingdom, and he will have all my worldly possessions, so what could you possibly want?"

He glanced back to Ana.

If his father had survived the Rebellion, if he had escaped, then couldn't she have, too?

The room was quiet; the only sound was his thundering heart. There used to be people at these hearings. Hundreds of Ironbloods and citizens alike lined the throne room, waiting on the Emperor's words with bated breath. His father used to stand with him by the door and whisper things only he knew about the Emperor—they had been best friends, along with Lord Rasovant's son, Dmitri, and Marigold Aragon. They'd grown up together. They'd gone on adventures together.

He used to envy his father; he used to wonder what that sort of friendship was like.

And for a moment, in a rusted old transport ship with shoddy black sails, he'd known.

"*Well?*" prodded the Iron Adviser impatiently.

"I want to tell Your Grace a story," Robb said, looking back at Ana, a dirty outlaw with blood staining her shirt, and burn scars on her face, and the eyes of an Imperial bloodline, "of how Princess Ananke Armorov of the Iron Kingdom survived."

ANA

Princess Ananke Armorov.

She—Ana—couldn't be. She had no recollection, no memory, no *proof.* She was Ana—she was the daughter of ship traders. They had died in mercenary raid, and she and Di had escaped. Siege found them drifting on the far side of Iliad, and healed her wounds, and raised her.

She was *not* an Ironblood.

Princess Ananke Armorov had died in the Rebellion. She had burned to death, and Ana pitied the girl, because she knew what it felt like to burn.

Her stomach clenched in fear.

Burns. Like the burns on the side of her face. The scars. But hers were from the raid. Siege said they were from a *ship explosion.*

Siege said.

"There was once a fire," Robb said, his voice so loud it crackled, "that set the North Tower ablaze—"

"*Silence!*" the Grand Duchess hissed, and turned her

scrutinizing gaze to Ana. "What game is this?"

"No game, Your Grace—"

"My granddaughter is dead, young Valerio."

Robb lifted his hand to Ana. "She survived, Your Grace."

The old woman looked as if she wanted to break Robb in two on her knee, the rage on her face was so potent. "Then how did the girl escape?" She turned her vicious gaze to Ana. "How did *you* survive when no one else did?"

Ana's mouth went dry. Because there was a gap in her memory, an expanse of blurry images she couldn't make out. "I—I don't—I don't know, Your Grace. I can't remember—"

"A convenient excuse," said the Iron Adviser dryly, "for a girl pretending to be—"

"I don't *pretend* to be anyone I'm not," Ana snapped, her voice rising, echoing off the walls, remembering the words Di had told her the evening before when he'd braided her hair. It felt like a lifetime ago. "I am Ana of the *Dossier*—"

"Send the young Valerio on his way," the Grand Duchess interrupted. She was shaking, so old and brittle she could fracture apart from her anger alone. "And you, girl—you are a terror to this kingdom. I have seen enough. On my word of iron and stars, you, Ana of the *Dossier*, are found guilty of treason—"

"No, Your Grace!" Robb cried.

"—and hereby sentenced to death."

Before she could take a breath, Messiers swarmed toward her like a tidal wave to seize her. She struggled against them, but there were too many, and each time she tried to push away, they held on tighter. This was not how she thought she'd die.

She wanted to die fighting. On a ship. Surrounded by nothing but light and space and sky.

She wasn't *royalty*—she wasn't the *Goddess*. The girl of light. If she were, then she could have protected Mokuba. She could have shut down Lord Rasovant's ship, rescued Barger.

She could have saved Di.

But she hadn't. And there would be no tombstone, no grave—and no one would remember him.

Where was the justice in *that*?

The thought broke something inside her, something so deep it reverberated through her soul. Where was justice at all? Where had it ever been?

If there was justice, Lady Valerio would be here, answering for Wick's death. Lord Rasovant would be standing here in judgment instead, answering for the monsters he'd created on the *Tsarina*.

She was *innocent*.

Count your bullets, Siege had said, but the count was still at zero and yet here she was. Sentenced to death. For trying to save her best friend?

There was no justice in that.

With a scream, she tore against the Messiers that pulled her away, their grips bruising her. They clamped on harder, but she knew their weakness—like she knew Di's when they trained in the cargo bay. She slammed a foot into one of their knees, and the Messier buckled, and crashed into the one beside it, knocking them both off balance, and she twisted out of their grips.

She spun back toward the doors, toward the exit, toward

freedom, but a hand snaked into her hair and grabbed ahold of it near her scalp.

And pulled.

The Royal Captain dragged her back and pressed a lightword against the side of her neck. "Be *silent*," she hissed.

Tears pooled at the edges of Ana's eyes. She would *not* be silent. It was not a virtue she'd learned from Siege.

"She's a *murderer!*" Ana shouted up to the old woman on her throne, the Royal Captain pulling harder at her hair, the blade sizzling against her skin. "You HIVE innocent Metals, and you kill everyone who disagrees with you. That's not justice— that's being a coward!"

"*Silence!*" the Royal Captain barked, slamming the hilt of her sword into Ana's jaw, sending her to the ground.

"Ana!" Robb cried as Messiers caught him, twisting back his arms, and held him back. He squirmed against them, but from the look of pain on his face, his side must've started hurting again. "Your Grace, please—"

The Royal Captain raised her blade, readying to strike.

The Grand Duchess raised a hand. "Wait, Viera."

The Royal Captain paused.

Ana glowered up at the Duchess and spit a mouthful of blood onto the plush runner, her hands bound behind her tight and uncomfortable.

The Grand Duchess studied her.

Just kill me, Ana thought. *Just get this done with.*

"Fine—if Robbert Valerio truly believes a dirty little girl like yourself could be my granddaughter, then who am I to call him a liar?" asked the Grand Duchess. "The Goddess will show me the truth. Fetch the crown."

The Adviser gave a start. "But Your Grace—"

"I did not ask for counsel, Gregori."

Yielding, the Adviser gave a short bow and left through the back hallway, as the Royal Captain forced Ana to her feet, unlocking her handcuffs. She rubbed her wrists so no one would see her hands shaking.

A few moments later, Lord Rasovant returned with the circlet of metal, the rust like bloodstains across its pointed edges.

The Iron Crown.

She had never seen it before. It was said that a thousand years ago, the Armorov bloodline had carved the crown from the Goddess's heart, and only those worthy could wear it without its rusting. But Ana had never seen the Goddess in all the seven years she'd flown across the kingdom. Not in the sky, or in the worlds, or in the stars—she'd never seen the Goddess anywhere.

If she was the girl of light, then there was no Goddess.

But what if you were looking in the wrong places? a voice in the back of her head asked.

The Grand Duchess took the crown, and rust bloomed across her fingers where she held it. "Come, see if this crown fits; and if the Goddess decides you are *unworthy*, then both you and the Valerio boy will be sentenced to death."

"But Robb's innocent," Ana argued, even though he probably deserved death just for dragging her into this. "He shouldn't be—"

The old woman extended the crown. "Take it."

She glanced back at Robb, and he nodded as if to say, *Go on.* She wanted to punch him. She wanted to drive his face into the Goddess-damned *floor*. How could he bet his life on the crown *somehow* not rusting for her? Because it would.

Wouldn't it?

She was afraid as she took the cold metal crown. It was heavier than expected, and colder, too, the tines sharp enough to cut. A small crowd had gathered in the doorway, mostly servants and royal guardsmen, and they leaned in, holding their breaths, waiting for her death sentence.

Her hands shook.

This was the end, and she wished it weren't here. She wished it were somewhere in the stars, beside her best friend. She just wanted to see him one more time. Being near Di had filled her with so much light and goodness that every moment without him felt like suffocating in space. He was gone, and there was no rescuing him. There was no way back. If she'd never boarded the ship, if she'd stayed on the *Dossier* like Siege had asked, maybe Di would be alive.

And maybe they would have had more time to say good-bye.

Goddess bright, let me see Di again, she prayed for the first time in her life, and pulled one hand away.

Her breath caught in her throat.

"It didn't rust," murmured the Royal Captain—and the young Cercian fell to her knees, touching her forehead against the cold marble floor. "Your Grace."

She stared in awe at her fingers, dirty with blood but clean of rust. There was some mistake. She was still dreaming. She was not . . . she could not be . . .

But then one of the servants in the entryway fell to his knees, then the Royal Guard, then Robb, like dominoes tipping over. The Iron Adviser lowered himself to the floor and pressed his face to it, and the Messiers bowed with him.

And finally, the Grand Duchess stood from her twisted throne, and bent as low as her old age would let her, until Ana was the only one left standing.

DI

"Stand by. . . ."

There was a light.

"Rebooting . . . Importing memories zero through zero-zero-zero-seven-five-eight."

He blinked—blinked? Darkness, light, darkness, light—

Warmth spread through his wires, igniting fuses, as data rushed into dormant programs, bringing them to life with a single spark. Another line of data joined it, and another, piecing together like swirls of DNA. The warmth connected synapses, united links, corrected damage, reassembling something that had broken on the far side of Palavar.

"Forty-five percent complete . . . fifty-five percent . . . sixty percent," the computer relayed.

Memories—a word. A word meaning events. Meaning moments. History. But whose history? His eyes wandered the room. The immaculate cabinets. The rusted metal walls. Thoughts filled the darkened crevices, lighting them, expanding energy to his fingers and toes. He raised a hand over his face to block the bright light. His fingers moved when he told them to.

"Eighty-nine percent."

His hands began to shake.

Memories—oh, oh, *memories.*

History. His history. Moments. Seconds. Days. Years. They took shape, every missed opportunity and fractured moment and borrowed minute. The anythings, the somethings, the everythings, so vast and so full and it—it was overwhelming.

"Ninety-five percent complete," the computer chimed. *"Stand by."*

He cringed—pressed his hands against his face, trying to stop it.

It hurt.

Everything hurt like despair hurt, an ache so deep in his chest, it felt like a hole at the center of the cosmos. Like hope hurt, too, rising, suffocating, a tingling in the back of his throat. Everything hurt like laughter hurt, all over his sides and abdomen. Like anger hurt, nails buried into his palms. Like happiness, rushing across his fiber optics like fizzy soda. Like heartache.

Like love.

Longing.

Remorse.

Hate—

His body went rigid, tensing, reactions he couldn't control, couldn't stop.

"Ninety-nine percent complete. Installing rationalities."

The hurt doubled, tripled, the *whys* and the *hows* colliding. His head felt like it would explode. Empty and full at the same time, the pain dissolving all his thoughts while filling him full of—of something else entirely.

Of so many *memories.*

He—he wasn't sure he wanted to know them anymore.

Those seven long years. The fit of a pistol, the weight of induced gravity as the starship sped through the finite expanse, the night watches he spent alone in the cockpit, and the moments sailing across the stars, the way his fingers folded between someone else's—but *whose?* He remembered another code invading him, scrambling him, making him less and less and less until he was nothing at all.

He remembered that he hadn't thought about himself in those moments, that there was something else spread in the space between those seven years ago and now.

Something curious, and something rare.

"One hundred percent."

Then—the memories stopped.

"Transfer complete. Subject is now free to disconnect."

He squeezed his eyes tightly closed and groaned. His head throbbed.

"Subject is now free to disconnect," the computer repeated.

Something cold and metallic bumped up against his cheek, bleeping.

"Subject is now—"

"I heard you," he rasped, and rolled over onto his side, pressing the heels of his hands against his forehead, afraid to open his eyes because the light was too bright. It made his head ache.

It . . . *It what?*

Hesitantly, he tried to open his eyes again. His vision, blurry at first, focused. He looked at his hands. Flesh. He told himself to move his fingers, and the fingers in front of him moved. Those fingers—his fingers? His hands?

He sat up, slamming his head against something hard. He hissed in pain as EOS whirred up, beeping angrily at him. It yanked something out of the back of his neck—a cord.

The infirmary—why was he . . . why was he *here?*

He rubbed his head where they'd collided, and hissed against his throbbing headache. It *hurt*—no, that must have been the wrong word. His programming must be corrupt. He tried to think, but his processors felt heavy and sluggish, as though his head was full of molasses.

Molasses. There it was again. A metaphor. *A metaphor?*

Something was wrong.

He tried to slide off the gurney, but his legs tangled in a black tarp. A body bag. He was in a body bag. With a cry, he scrambled out of it, but his legs didn't want to cooperate. They slipped out from under him. He caught himself on the medic console and pulled himself back up.

Something was *very* wrong.

EOS nudged his cheek.

"I do not understand," he told it—and with a jolt, his hand went to his throat. His voice?

Not metal. Not broken.

"Reflection," he said to the infirmary's computer console,

and a screen swirled into color, showing an image. A serious face, strong cheekbones, shoulder-length red hair. And incredibly naked. When he bent closer, the reflection did too, dark eyes staring at him. He blinked.

So did the reflection.

He recoiled, his foot bumping up against something on the ground. Something dull and silver. A silver arm. A bent shoulder. A Metal face. *His* Metal face.

Staring down at himself, he trembled.

This was not right—he was malfunctioning. Glitching. Everything in his system was chaotic. He scratched at the side of his head with his fingernails—why did he scrub at his head? Why did he have *fingernails?*

Why was he *here?*

He. D09. But . . . not. Not D09. That was quite evident by the skin, the length of his fingers, the sudden dire need to find clothes, and the collision of thoughts and emotions in his head. Not D09—not anymore. But who, then? Who was he if not—

Just thinking about it made his head hurt worse.

At least he was on the *Dossier*, but how had he gotten back here? The last thing he remembered was being on Rasovant's fleetship. He remembered the malware, he remembered it screaming as he pulled out the ship's hard drive. . . .

And then the program invaded. Told him things. Whispered. He remembered it whispering, but he couldn't remember what it said. Its cold code creeping into his functions like a virus, curling around his processors, and—

And like a sunrise, he remembered Ana.

Pain blossomed in his chest. A pulling, constricting kind that tasted like panic. She had to be alive. She *must* be.

EoS bumped into his shoulder, beeping.

"Where is everyone?" he asked it. "What happened? Did you do this?"

The bot began to beep again when they heard a voice from the cargo bay.

"C'mon, Captain, just tell us about the rest of your fleet. I know you got some outlaw friends, don't you? No?"

—And then the sound of something being struck.

"Sixteen," replied a familiar voice. Siege. Captain Siege.

He pressed the lock on the infirmary door, and it slid up. He followed their voices, EoS hovering over his shoulder, and hid behind the skysailer.

On the other side of the cargo bay, the captain knelt in front of two guardsmen. Crimson uniforms. The crest of a snake eating its own tail—Ouroboros insignias.

They were Valerio guards.

One of the guards struck her in the face again, but the captain did not even let out a sound. She licked her busted lip, glaring up at the man. "Seventeen," she kept counting.

"I can start breaking her fingers," the other Valerio guard said—a female. "Or I can start killing her crew. It's all she got left, isn't it? I heard she used to be an Ironblood, but she deserted them."

"You're shittin' me."

"That's the rumor. I could start with her wife—"

"Our orders are to turn them in, not kill them."

"But she isn't *talking*. She's just counting." But then the female guard sighed. "*Fine*, I'll start with her pinkie finger." She moved around behind Siege to untie her hands. "You know, Captain, I can break your fingers so you can never fire a gun again. Or you can just tell us about that fleet of yours."

The captain stared straight ahead. The wires in her fiber-optic hair flared a bold orange.

Di hesitated behind the skysailer. What could he do? He did not have full control over his body. He did not even *understand* his body. Despite that, he searched for a weapon.

There was nothing around he could use as a—

The female guard began to bend Siege's pinkie finger. "One . . ."

He grabbed EOS out of the air and threw the bot at the female guard. With a pitiful *bloop*, it struck her in the side of the head.

It must have been with more force than he realized, because the female guard slumped to the floor, unconscious.

"What the—" The man spun toward him, drawing his gun, when Siege swung out her leg, knocking him in the back of the knees, sending him onto his back. She grabbed his hands, and pressed her knee against his throat.

"One, two," Siege began counting as the man beneath her struggled. "Screw this, I'm impatient." She slammed her fist into the man's face and knocked him unconscious.

Then Siege unholstered the guard's gun and stood, turning it toward Di. He froze, quickly raising his hands into the air.

"Not another step," said the woman, her green eyes flat like sea glass.

"Not a single one," he agreed.

She narrowed her eyes.

Captain Siege had always been imposing—the way she stood, feet apart, shoulders back, giving off the impression that she was taller than anyone else in the room—but he had not *understood* it. Now, in this body, while he stood a good inch taller than her, he felt short and infinitely inferior.

"How did you wake up?" she growled. Dried blood painted the side of her face from a nasty gash hidden under her flickering fire-colored hair. "Who rebooted you? What are you?"

"I . . . do not know."

She clicked back the hammer. "I'll ask one more time—"

"I just woke up," he interrupted, his voice wavering. "I do not know. Captain, I am not your enemy—"

"Piss you aren't!" she said. "Barger's dead, Wick's dead, my crew's hostage, and my ship's been taken over by Valerios. It's awfully suspicious that a Metal the Ironblood found on that *cursed* ship isn't against me, too."

"I am not."

"And I'm supposed to believe you?—"

Voices came from the top of the stairs.

Cursing, the captain grabbed him by the arm and pulled him back into the infirmary. She slammed the butt of the pistol against the door lock, which slid shut, and pressed the barrel against his ribs.

"I am on your side," he stressed, "and there is a ninety-three point four-seven percent chance that the others will find those two guards soon if we do not act now."

"Then what do you *suggest?*"

"I can hack into the ship's computer from the console in here and reverse the video feeds so we can see what we are up against."

"How do I know you aren't lying?"

Because I am D09, he wanted to say, but how could he prove it? He was *not* D09, and the fear of a bullet wound was much too strange. He swallowed. "Trust goes both ways, Captain."

Siege studied him before lowering her pistol. "You double-cross me, and you'll get a bullet straight to the heart, got it?"

If you can find it, he wanted to reply, but simply nodded.

The computer in the infirmary was simple at best, but it seemed someone had used it recently anyway. A memory core—it must have been his—sat on a small scanner, pulsing ever so slightly. Was that how he had been transferred? Through *this* computer? He was lucky that whoever did the procedure had not scrambled his code. The cube—his memory core—looked so small and weak—the source of his glitches.

It was how all this trouble began.

Bitterly, he pushed it off the scanner, and it clattered to the floor. The computer hummed to life.

Fingers skimming over the keyboard, he broke into the internal server. He knew the ship's antiquated computer system better than the back of his hand. There were at least three fire-walls and a viral system, all of which he himself had installed with the utmost security. And now he bypassed them without even a second glance. He ventured a guess that it was from an upgrade to this body.

It frightened him a little, to think how easily he could undo his own work.

He reversed the video feeds into the *Dossier*'s rooms, instead of out of them.

A holo-screen blipped up with a map of the ship.

"All but two Valerio men are in the galley, and they are . . ."

Another holo-screen flicked up.

"In the showers? Oh, *two* in the showers." He squinted at the screen. "Captain, I could be mistaken, but are they . . . ?"

"My poor, defiled ship," she scowled, drumming her sharp fingernails on the console. "How many bullets do you think you can handle before getting dead?"

"I do not wish to find out," he replied dryly.

"Do you think you can fit through a ventilation shaft?"

An informational file blipped up in the back of his head, a file of knowledge. He bit his bottom lip, wondering what good it would do, but did as it commanded. He raised his hand to the screen.

"What are you doing?" the captain asked. "You didn't hear a word I said, did you?"

A tingling spread across his fingertips, and instinctively he lowered his hand to the ports on the computer's dash. An electric sensation coursed over his skin, and he found himself— his code, his programming—pulled toward the console like a magnet. Then he was rushing across the electrical currents of the ship, spreading across the motherboard, sinking into the programs. He was the ship, but he was also in his body. He was soaring through space and staring at the holo-screens. A hundred places at once, seeing everything.

The couple in the bathroom, heavy breathing, moaning.

Close the door.

The door slid shut. The keypad gleamed red. Locked.

Sixteen men in the galley. Refrigerator door opened. Letting cool frost onto the floor. The pop of beer tops. The crack of bottles onto the floor. Laughter. Pork roast and potatoes. Chewing like pigs. He closed the refrigerator door, and one of the humans complained. Pushed the guy beside him.

Lights.

The orange glow of the neon turned dark. Bloodred. Men panicked. One of them tried to exit the galley.

Close.

It slammed shut. Almost took off a hand—

"Hey!"

Someone pulled him away from the computer. The connection weakened, but it didn't sever. He could still see. Still feel.

Lock the door. Turn out the lights. Cut off the ventilati—

There was the distinct click of a pistol.

He blinked and refocused on the room. The heady power eased out of his programming and sank back into the computer. The naked couple in the bathroom, trousers around their ankles, banged their fists against the closed door, shouting for someone to let them out, but no one could hear them.

He did not realize what he had done until he pulled away. He had closed the doors. He had controlled the lights. It reminded him of the moment he had infiltrated the *Tsarina's* corrupted intelligence. Being everywhere at once. Doing everything. Had his memory core absorbed that function? Or was it new?

He looked at his fingers, then back at the ports. What *was* he?

"Sorry . . . I—" He turned around, and Siege pressed the barrel of her pistol against his forehead.

Slowly, he raised his hands.

"*Who*. Are. You." She enunciated each word, through clenched teeth.

"I—I do not know—"

"*Bullshit.*" She drew the hammer back. "I'll give you to the count of three. One . . ."

He opened his mouth, but nothing came out. This was not like him. He never had problems with words. He knew every word in the known language. He knew the Old Language. He knew Cercian. Solani. He knew synonyms and antonyms and a waterfall of adverbs and adjectives and—and—

"Two."

EoS beeped frantically, banging on the door outside the infirmary.

"Thr—"

"I could not let her die."

The words slipped out, the only ones that came to mind. And they would not suffice. He squeezed his eyes tightly closed, waiting for the sound.

But Siege never pulled the trigger.

He cracked open an eye.

Her face went slack, eyebrows rising, hair shimmering with

bright yellow strands. "What did you say?"

"I—I could not let her die. On the ship. The malware that infected the *Tsarina* wanted her. It wanted to kill her. So I . . . I destroyed it first." I—I did not say good-bye. I did not know how to say good-bye.

She dropped her gun. ". . . D09?"

"I—I think?" he replied, searching for the right words. "I do not know. D09 was my serial number, but I am not in that body anymore, and I . . . I do not feel like D09. Because I . . . I *can* feel. I can feel and I believe I am ninety-three point seven-eight percent sure that I am scared and—"

Siege lurched forward and wrapped her arms around him, squeezing him tightly. He stiffened at the feeling, being embraced, her scratchy coat against his skin, until she let go and took his face in her hands, looking into his eyes. "How did you get in this body? Goddess, that *face*. When Robb brought this Metal over, I didn't get a good look, but . . ."

"Is it offensive? I do not think I can change it—"

"No, no. It's fine. Just reminds me of someone. Here, put this on." She shrugged out of her red coat and handed it to him. It smelled like musty cigar smoke and gunpowder. Exactly how he thought Siege might smell. "Let's go see where they put the crew, yeah?"

"The quarters, I think."

"Then let's look there, and go save Ana."

Wrapping the coat around him, he followed the captain out of the infirmary and up the stairs, EOS trailing behind them, flying in happy circles.

JAX

He hated the darkness.

He tried to blink the dizziness out of his eyes and pressed his forehead against the side of the cell, the cool metal wall soothing against his hot skin. He didn't remember much after they had dragged Ana away. Someone had cuffed him upside the head. He was lucky he stayed conscious—but he couldn't even begin to guess what awful level of the Valerios' ship he was on. Whichever it was, his cell could use a little more light. Solani never did live well in darkness. The sickness felt like a dry well that went into some deep part of him he couldn't quench with water or food or air.

How the darkness crept closer and filled his lungs with shadows. How it made him frightened, calling upon old memories he hadn't thought about in years.

It is never far away, the Dark and the decay, the children in his memory sang, sipping on hot cider, staring at the stars and not knowing what it meant until they were older. *First it tastes, then it waits, and then it will consume.*

He curled his fingers into his palms, feeling his gloves tighten. Not that his gloves had helped him when Robb had kissed him.

Goddess, he wanted to kick himself. If he hadn't been so afraid of his gifts, maybe Ana wouldn't be captured. Maybe he could've saved Wick. Barger. Maybe things didn't have to end this way. But he knew, deep down, they did.

All fates in the universe connected in a river, and that river flowed only one way.

The door opened and a shaft of light streaked into the bare room. A silhouette stepped inside.

"Oh—oh, *dear,*" said the man. His deep voice held the same Erosian accent as Robb's, but slithery. Like oil in molasses. "Mother must have forgotten to mention to the guard you star-kissers don't like the dark. You're like plants that way."

Jax looked up through his greasy silver hair and recognized the Valerio jawline and sky-colored eyes. "You must be the other brother. Erik." He shifted so he could be in a little more of the light. The weakness in his body ebbed, making him keenly aware of how close the broad Ironblood was. "I can't say it's a pleasure."

In response, the elder Valerio grinned. "Oh, I doubt anything will be a pleasure for you ever again, star-kisser. Our little Robbert is leading your friend to her death as we speak. She might already be convicted by now. Maybe bleeding out, riddled with bullets."

A muscle in Jax's jaw fluttered. This Ironblood was more insufferable than Robb, and he didn't think that was possible.

"I'll tell you what," Erik Valerio went on. "I'll leave the door open if you tell me what was on the *Tsarina*. And when I'm Emperor, I might even let you go."

"You won't be Emperor."

"Oh, won't I?"

Jax drew himself up to sit tall, even though he did not feel tall or imposing, his favorite trousers stained with his crew-mate's blood. "You won't be *anything*—"

"Lord Valerio!" a guard called from down the hallway, coming to a stop in front of the cell. He was sweating—quite profusely. "Lord Valerio—there's been—that girl has—"

Erik hissed, "Spit it *out*!"

"The lost princess has been found!" the guardsman gasped. "I—I ran here as fast as I could!"

"The *what*?"

"The prisoner, sir! She's the lost princess!"

Jax thought he had heard incorrectly. The darkness was getting to him. Ana? *Ana* was the lost princess?

"You won't be Emperor," he heard himself say, remembering the bloodied crown in Robb's stars.

With a rage-filled cry, Erik went for Jax's throat. "I'm going to *kill* you—"

"Erik," chided a calm voice from the doorway, and Erik stopped in his tracks. Jax squinted toward the door to the thin figure blocking the light. Graying brown hair, olive skin, Ero-sian blue-sky eyes—Goddess *damn* him, couldn't he catch a *break*?

He slumped against the wall, again. He just wanted a little

light. Just enough to breathe easy.

"It's not true, is it?" Erik asked his mother. "The princess is *dead*, and we know it."

"She is not," Lady Valerio replied, "and as luck would have it, your brother found her."

"Then what about *me*, Mother?" Erik asked. "What'll *I* do? He did it on purpose, Mother. You know he did. He never liked me—"

"Quiet. Nothing is set in stone. As for you, C'zar Taizu"— she turned to address Jax, who felt about as far from a C'zar as the stars felt from the sun—"I expected to find you in better company than in the riffraff on the *Dossier*."

"*C'zar?*" her son asked, baffled. "The Solani named *him* C'zar?"

"Surprise," Jax muttered. She'd probably known who he was the moment she'd laid eyes on him on the *Dossier*.

"What's he the prince *of?*"

"Nothing," Lady Valerio replied. The word struck him in the stomach and twisted.

The prince of *nothing*. No, he was a prince of less than nothing. Of things forgotten. Of a people who couldn't feel the stars anymore. Of a people who treated the one who could as a weapon.

She turned to leave. "Come, Erik. We're needed at the palace."

Dutifully, her son followed, and the sliver of light began to close.

Panic rose in Jax's throat, tasting like the sharp bitterness of

Robb's kiss. And with it came the glint of knuckle rings, an image from Robb's stars that felt like a knife slicing deep into his gut. If Ana was the lost princess, then the bloody crown meant *her* death. It had to. Robb's brother was going to kill Ana.

Jax had to do something. He didn't want her to die.

But what can I do?

The glimpses of Robb's stars were supposed to be beacons to be followed, not stories to be changed.

What would happen if I tried? He swallowed the knot of panic in his throat. *Could I?*

As the Valerio woman left, he realized he would be damned if he didn't. Ana was family. Ana was *his* family—more than his mother or father had ever been. She was one of the only people he'd ever cared about in his life. One of the only ones who truly mattered.

Princess or not.

"I can read your stars," he called out after Lady Valerio, even though when he did read someone's stars, it drained away a little more of his life. "I—I'm the only one who still can, and I'll read yours."

Lady Valerio stopped in the doorway. She inclined her head, listening.

"Don't you want to know?" he asked, trying to balance all his deceit with nothing but truths. "A powerful woman like yourself could use a little hint. You might find me useful."

"Mother, it's an old wives' tale," Erik scoffed. "You don't actually believe that star-kissers can tell the future, do you?"

But the longer the woman stayed silent, the more his panic

ebbed. Ironbloods didn't believe in Solani superstitions, but Robb had said his mother valued legacy. At least that was what he was counting on.

With a sharp flick of her hand, she dismissed Erik. He tried to argue, but she sent him away again, and turned back toward the darkened cell, her blue marble eyes gleaming in the shadowy light.

Jax spread a grin across his teeth to mask his fear. "I'm glad I've got your attention. Let's make a deal."

ANA

Everything she knew was a lie. Her parents. Her history. Her scars—had Siege lied to her, too? Had Siege known who she was all this time? She must have—she found Ana, after all. It must have been why Siege didn't want her on the *Tsarina*. The realization hurt deeply, somewhere in the center of herself, carving out a hole like a bullet wound.

She was a lie.

People flooded into the throne room, more than there had been a few moments before, kissing the back of her hand, pressing their foreheads against her palms, telling her how happy they were that she was alive. But she wasn't so sure she was anymore. She didn't remember the faces of these Advisers who knew her name, or the servants who bowed to the floor, or even the Grand Duchess, who disappeared so quickly after everyone had risen to their feet in the throne room that Ana almost believed that she had been a ghost.

"Don't overwhelm Her Grace," a short man with a gray mustache said, shooing the Advisers away. Her thoughts were a blur, spinning. "I'm sure she is very tired. Would you like to retire to your room, Your Grace?"

"My . . . room? Who're you?"

"I am the Grand Duchess's, and now your, steward. And yes, Your Grace, your room. You are home."

She was very far away from *that*. Glancing around the throne room for Robb, at a loss for what else to do, she realized he was gone. Of course he was. He'd probably left the second he could.

"Yeah," she replied, defeated. "Yes—please."

The steward excused her from the throne room, and in the hallways she could finally breathe. Large potted plants grew against the walls, flowering with moonlilies and roses and purple dragon-tongues.

A small patrol of Messiers accompanied her and her steward to her room. She doubted they were guarding *her*. The crown might not have rusted, but she had just been convicted of treason not an hour ago.

But at the moment, she was too tired to care.

The steward showed her to a room somewhere in one of the towers. Hallway after hallway, each lit with bobbing lanterns that floated in an invisible river above them. When the steward finally stopped at a room at the end of a long corridor, and the Messiers took up position on either side of the door, she was lost. There was a crest above the door—the Armorov insignia.

A crescent moon with a sword down its middle.

Inside was a queen-size four-poster bed with a silken white canopy draped over the mahogany bedposts. The breeze from the open balcony window fluttered the silks so they danced in the evening light and drew shadows across the marble floor. There was a dressing table against the far wall, filled with opulent perfumes and pearl-studded accessories, and a wardrobe so big she could live in that, instead.

The bedroom was so large she felt like a mouse inside a lion's cage.

Through a connecting door there looked to be a parlor of sorts, and beyond that a study—there were certainly a lot of expensive-looking books. None of them must have been very good—the best stories were the ones with cracked spines and dog-eared edges.

"If it is not to your liking, please don't hesitate to say so, Your Grace," said the steward, his gray mustache twitching. "There is so much to be done before your coronation—"

"My coronation?" She wanted to laugh—or cry, she wasn't sure which. "You barely know me! And you're going to give me a *kingdom*?"

"You're the lost princess, Your Grace. You are the Goddess returned—the girl of light who will lead us out of the darkness of the last seven years. You arrived exactly when you needed to," he added smugly. "And on the morning of the Holy Conjunction, you'll be crowned Empress to the kingdom."

One week, she thought.

She had one week to escape this madness.

"Don't fret," the steward said as he backed out of the room. He must have sensed the desperation seeping through her sweat glands. "Ruling is in your blood. The Goddess will never lead us wrong—and neither will you."

He closed her in this foreign room, promising to retrieve her for dinner.

As if she could *eat* at a time like this!

Her stomach twisted, nauseous at the thought of food.

Was this real? Or was she still in that terrible nightmare? Why had the Grand Duchess let her touch that crown? She was a citizen—Ironbloods would *never* let a normal citizen touch it. They were unworthy.

But you aren't a citizen, she realized. *You are Princess Ananke.*

She needed to get out of here—now. Hurrying out onto the open-air balcony, she looked down at the drop into the gardens. Ten feet—she could handle that. Hiking one leg over the rail, she began to climb over when a voice made her pause.

"What are you doing, Your Grace?"

She glanced up. It was a servant girl.

"How did you get in here?" Ana asked, perplexed.

The servant girl waved toward a panel in the door that was still cracked open—a servants' entrance. She'd heard Di read about them in his books about the palace. There was an entire network of secret corridors within the very walls of the palace. Maybe . . . maybe she could escape that way?

The girl was fourteen, maybe fifteen, with spun-gold hair pinned up behind her head, her dress the deep, deep purple of the royal family.

Ana had begun to loop her other leg over when the bushes rustled in the garden below her, and as if called by some remote dog whistle, a Messier came to stand underneath her. Its blue eyes watched patiently.

Frustrated, she climbed back over the rail and cleared her throat. "What do you want?"

The girl curtsied. "Your Grace, I was assigned to be your handmaiden. My name is Mellifare. I will see to your personal needs for the immediate future."

"I don't—I don't need anyone to help me dress or anything."

"Then I can assist you with other daily matters. Altering your clothes, deciding what to wear, bathing—"

"I don't need that kind of help, either."

"It is my job," the servant girl replied, her dark eyes flickering down the length of Ana, making her keenly aware of just how filthy she looked. Dried blood stained the knees of her trousers, her braid half fallen out of its tight coil. "The Grand Duchess has asked me to see to your needs. Is there anything you would like?"

To leave—to get as far away from here as she could. To change clothes and—

"A bath," she heard herself saying, feeling the dried blood beneath her nails. "A warm bath."

"Of course, Your Grace."

With a bow, Mellifare left through the far door.

The moment she was gone, Ana peeked over to the balcony again, but the Messier was still below, watching her with its vacant gaze.

So she'd have to find some other way to escape.

There was another way, wasn't there?

The strangeness of the day was wearing thin, unveiling an itchy panic in her chest. From her balcony, she could see the stars and the other moons and Eros—but it didn't quell the uneasiness broiling inside. If she couldn't escape, she'd be trapped here—*forever*. In rich silks and beautiful petticoats and marble hallways—

She'd rather be in a Cercian mine. At least that *looked* like a prison. This wasn't the *Dossier*, and she missed the ship so much.

But all these years, Siege had lied to her. What if the rest of the crew had, too? And Di?

He wouldn't lie to me, she reminded herself, but she hadn't thought Siege would lie to her, either. Jax couldn't, but she didn't remember ever talking about family with Jax. It wasn't something that mattered.

Family was the *Dossier*.

And family had lied.

"Your Grace?" her handmaiden called, and she followed Mellifare's voice into the far room, to a bath made of marble and ornate golden carvings, a tub that was more like a pool, bubbling and hissing, pouring the aroma of moonlilies into the air.

When Mellifare left, Ana undressed herself, peeling off her clothes, hearing the crackle of Wick's dried blood, her eyes burning with tears. He was dead. The fact sank in, like an anchor into the sea. He was dead, and Barger was dead, and Di was dead—

Stop thinking, she told herself, dipping her foot into the bath. It was so hot it tore the thoughts right out of her.

Slowly, she sank beneath the water and stayed under for a

long time letting the hot water sting her cuts and wet her curly hair. She stayed under for so long, her pulse leaped into her throat, but the sound calmed her. It was the same one she'd heard since the *Tsarina*.

A broken heart beating on.

She didn't know who she was anymore. She wasn't that orphan girl from the stars. She wasn't the girl who Siege raised, who shot beer bottles out of the air and knew every word to Wick's drunken lullabies. That girl was part of a lie that no longer existed, a ship that sailed across her memories like a phantom, leaving a cold room in its wake.

But she was not an Armorov either.

Her lungs shuddered, so she pushed out of the water, sucking in a breath. The air tasted sweet—like moonlilies. She washed the blood from under her nails, and the stains from her skin, scrubbing until she was raw, and finally stepped out of the bath, pulling her hair over her shoulder. Her scalp still ached from when that Royal Captain had grabbed her.

She still remembered the patient way Di took hold of her hair, cool fingers twining each lock, as if he was built of all the things she lacked.

Di would never braid her hair again.

Her fingers fell away from her damp hair. It hadn't hit her until that very moment. All the things they would never do again. All the moments she would miss. All the ones he would never again be part of.

She stared into the steamed bathroom mirror, at the blurry image of a girl with warm bronze skin and golden-brown eyes and black hair that fell in tangled curls across her bare, muscular shoulders. She didn't have the body of someone dainty—fit for royal balls and beautiful dresses. She was hard, and strong, her hands covered in calluses and her fingernails bitten to the quick. She had always wondered where she came from, but now she picked herself apart, trying to find which parts were Valerio, and which were Armorov.

But all she could see was herself—and she didn't feel like Ana anymore.

She searched through the drawers in the bathroom until she found a small razor, and sharpened it on a flint, the way she had back on the *Dossier* when she needed to shave up the sides of her head. Then she turned back toward the mirror, wiped the steam away, and pressed the razor to her scalp.

Di was gone, and so was the girl Ana used to be.

ROBB

Two Valerio guardsman led him through one of the many identical hallways of the palace, following the gentle ebb of the lanterns overhead.

Erik's going to kill me, he thought morosely, realizing that he'd annihilated his brother's chance at the throne. *He's going to hire an assassin and literally kill me. And wear my skin as shoes.*

Although he hadn't been to the palace in seven years, he still remembered his way around well enough. The guards were leading him to the South Tower and not, say, somewhere to be inconspicuously offed. The corridors were tall and narrow, filled with ornate filigree and golden molding. A blue-eyed Messier stood like a statue at each corner, and as he passed them he couldn't help but shiver, remembering the Metals from the *Tsarina*. The guards showed him to a nondescript room in the middle of the hallway and left without so much as a nod.

"Good-bye to you, too," he muttered, wrapping his fingers around the doorknob, and pushed it open.

And instantly regretted it.

His mother perched on one of the floral fainting couches, and standing just behind, like a shadow, was a Valerio guard. He wanted to cry in relief—it wasn't his brother. He'd live a little longer.

"Robbert. Come, sit down," she welcomed him, motioning to the other couch.

He took another hesitant step into the room when he recognized the guard. Silver hair, lanky build, red-purple eyes that glared with enough intensity to stab him right through.

Jax.

He was dressed in a formal crimson uniform, epaulettes gleaming gold in the low lighting, the Valerio insignia pinned to his sleeve. But even the collar of the uniform couldn't hide the glint of a black voxcollar, its nodes sparkling with electricity, the faintest glow against his sparkly skin.

Robb's breath caught in his throat. He couldn't tear his eyes away from the contraption, how it hissed and hummed against Jax's skin.

Robb had done plenty of things in his life he regretted—after all, his mother had said he longed for trouble.

But this was far worse than trouble.

And it was all his fault.

Robb tried to rein in his emotions, but it was far more difficult than ever before. "Why . . . why is the Solani here?"

"Every outlaw needs a second chance. Now come, sit down," she repeated.

Cautiously, he came to stand by the vacant couch, unable to bring himself to sit, every nerve ending inside him like a live wire the closer he came to Jax. He'd thought he would never see Jax again. He'd thought his family's guards had turned the Solani in to the Messiers, that the Solani had been left to rot in some mine on Cerces for the rest of his life.

Robb had never expected to see him *here*. He could still taste Jax's lips, and it was starting to curl, rotten. First Ana, now Jax.

His mistakes felt haunting.

"I must say I am impressed, Robbert," she said. "Your father would be, too. He always liked doing the *right thing*. Tell me, did you think about the consequences of returning the princess?"

"Consequences?"

"Of returning her to the kingdom? She wasn't raised in the palace—she knows nothing about politics or economy or how to govern a kingdom. I doubt these outlaws taught her literacy, never mind understand the complexities of the government."

"But she's the lost princess, Mother, *and* my cousin—"

"And now, when the kingdom has its Goddess returned, the royal line will be reborn and where will we be, Robbert?"

Too close to marry, too far from the throne, he realized, and numbly sank down on the couch. His mouth opened and closed in shock. "You *knew* she had survived the Rebellion."

"I did not," his mother said. "I thought she had died with her brothers."

"But you recognized her on that ship, didn't you?"

"I had a feeling. I had just hoped you would not do the imbecile thing you just did. You need to curry favor with the Grand Duchess and the other Ironbloods if you ever wish to return to the Academy."

"You'd have *killed* her."

"We all make sacrifices for our kingdom, dear," she replied coolly.

He'd believe that his mother had sacrificed *anything* when the sun caved in on itself. She was calculating and coarse. That was why she herself came to retrieve him. To make sure he did exactly as she wanted. She'd even thought he would turn Ana in at the palace—but he hadn't.

He had surprised her.

"Ana isn't a *sacrifice*—"

His mother's lips pursed. "Do we damn one to save a thousand, or damn a thousand to save one? As Valerios, we do what is necessary."

"Ana is half Valerio! She can learn to be a good ruler. She's resourceful, and she's smart—"

"She is soft," his mother snapped, rising to stand. She towered over him, her icy eyes looking down the bridge of her nose, making him feel like the ten-year-old who was expected not to cry after losing his father. "You have disobeyed me once, and made me look like a fool—you will not again. We will fix this problem, and you will not get in the way. Do you understand?"

"Mother, you can't honestly want to kill her—"

She grabbed his wrist and dug her thumb into the chip, as she had done in Astoria, as she always did to remind him of who he was. His mother never needed to brandish threats, because they were quiet and subtle, laced into her bodice, sewn into her seams.

"You will not interfere. Do you understand, my son?" she repeated.

He could feel Jax's violet eyes on him, but he couldn't meet them; he was too ashamed. All Robb wanted to do was go back to those moments on the *Dossier*. He wanted to do it all differently. Maybe then they wouldn't have ended up here.

"Yes, Mother," he replied softly, and she let go of his wrist.

"Good. Come, Solani, we should leave Robbert. He's had a long day and I am sure he needs his rest," she said, and Jax silently followed, leaving Robb alone in the room with the realization that he hadn't changed Ana's fate after all.

Because of who he was, he had damned her all the same.

DI

He hovered his hand over the lock to the crew's quarters and tried to remember how to reach inside again. He concentrated, letting his programming slither into the keypad, and threaded himself through the code. He twisted his hand and the lock responded, beeping green—

And as the door opened, he dodged Riggs's mechanical leg.

"LET US GO, YOU PIECE OF— *Captain!*" Riggs cried, eyes growing wide as he looked past Di to Siege. "You're *alive!*"

Lenda dropped her makeshift weapon—a stool—as Talle leaped at Siege, swinging her arms around her, kissing her on the mouth, her nose, her cheeks.

"Goddess, I thought you were dead!" Talle, with dark circles under her eyes and clothes rumpled, sobbed into Siege's shoulder. "I thought you'd gone to the stars!"

Siege pulled her wife into a hug. "I'm here, starlight. I'm fine. How is everyone?" Her green eyes wandered over the three of them. "Where's Jax?"

"They took him," Riggs said as Di handed his leg back to him. "And . . . Ana is . . ." He shook his head. "Why didn't you tell us, Captain?"

"Tell you what?"

Talle said, "That Ana is the lost princess, sunshine."

Di was not so sure his sound receivers were working properly. "The what?"

Talle fussed with Siege's coat buttons. "It's not true, right? She can't be. You'd have told us."

Behind her, Lenda agreed, folding her thick arms over her chest. "It's all over the newsfeeds. She's *Ananke*—"

"Didn't you use to work in the palace?" asked Riggs. "Why didn't you recognize her?"

"I never saw her. They always kept the princess locked up so we *plebeians* couldn't see her—"

As the crew bickered, Di backed out into the hallway. One step. Then another. There was a mistake. His thoughts raced so fast he could barely compute them all. Ana was not—she could not—there had to be some—

The other crew members voiced the same thoughts. That she was not, that she could not be, because the princess was dead, because the princess had burned.

But those scars. Those *burn scars.*

How did it suddenly seem so probable when it had not been a possibility ever before?

No, no, no—

He grabbed Siege by the back of the coat and yanked her

through the doorway and into the hallway with him. He needed to think—just two seconds alone—and suddenly there was a swift click in his head—

And the door shut to the quarters with a loud *snap*.

Locking the crew inside.

"D09!" Siege barked, catching herself on the wall. Her hair blazed a bright, angry red. "What in the *bloody*—"

"You found us stranded in an escape pod," he interrupted. "The palace does not have escape pods."

The captain pursed her lips. "It was a ship's."

"Like from a—a transport vessel? A merchant ship? From the aftermath of the Rebellion?" he asked desperately, searching Siege's face for the truth.

After a moment, Siege shook her head. "No."

He went numb.

In the seven long years he had been Ana's, he had never known. He had never even thought to question it. He was *Metal*. Metals did not care. The probability of her being the princess was .0034 percent. It was not enough for a rational computer to consider. And he was a computer. He did not *care*.

But then why were his hands trembling?

His functions were going strange. His code jittered.

"You saved her," the captain said, as if that was supposed to bolster him. "The crew found your pod floating in the dead space between Iliad and Cerces, and when we opened it up, there you both were. The little girl in your arms was badly burned, and you asked to use our infirmary. You told only me who she was, and you asked me to protect her."

"I asked you? I *remembered?* Why can I not now? What were you supposed to protect her *from?*"

"You didn't say. You struck a deal with me to protect her and wipe your memories. We didn't realize she'd lost hers, too, until after I'd already wiped yours."

"My glitches," he realized. "That was why my memory core was glitching. Because you tampered with it."

She nodded. "And I was to dump you at one of those way-stations for a Messier to find and HIVE."

"But you did not."

"I don't kill innocent people."

"But I am not a person."

She massaged the bridge of her nose. "Di, how many times do I have to tell you— Are you okay? Metalhead?"

"I cannot feel my legs—" he said a moment before his knees went numb. Siege caught him and slowly eased him to the floor. "I—I am malfunctioning. I cannot think straight. You . . . agreed to take her in? But for what? What did I make a deal with you for?"

She squatted beside him. "It doesn't matter—I never collected. I shouldn't have kept this from either of you, I know, but . . . I was selfish. She was happy, I thought . . ." Her brow furrowed. "She was mine. For a moment she was mine."

He pressed his palms against his temples. He did not know how to process the information. The whirls and whorls inside his head ground louder and louder, beating in repetition like a drum.

I am, I am, I am, never quite completing the statement. "I—I stole her away. I never returned her," he said, dread coiling in his middle. "What if I am the villain? What if I had set that fire—"

"Metalhead," Siege said gently, "you saved her. She's alive now because of you."

But who—or what else—could have caused the fire? Reports said it was a Metal—

He pulled his hands through his hair. "The malware on the ship said it wanted her to burn."

"It . . . did?"

Realizing it at the same time, Di and Siege exchanged the same look—a growing horror.

"Oh, *Goddess*," he said. "It knew her—the *Tsarina* knew her and it told her to burn. There is a ninety-seven-point-three-eight percent likelihood that it was a part of or knew about the Rebellion. I would have returned her if she had been safe. Oh, *Goddess*," he repeated, and crawled up the wall to his feet again, legs wobbly. "We must rescue her. We must—"

She caught him by the arm as he tried to leave for the cockpit. He whipped back, the taste of a fight on his tongue—

"The door, metalhead" was all she said.

Oh.

There was a click in his head, a shift, a command, and the keypad turned green. The door slid open. The crew, having heard the entire conversation from the other side, leaned out hesitantly, afraid it'd shut again.

Talle cleared her throat. "So, let me get this straight . . . you are . . ."

"D09?" Lenda ventured.

"But he's *smashed*," Riggs argued. They headed toward the cockpit after the captain. "And this is the Metal from Rasovant's ship. How do we know he isn't a trick?"

Di began to explain how he could not possibly be anyone else, ready to divulge all their darkest secrets, when a whirring came up and knocked him gently on the back of the head. He glared at EoS.

Lenda blinked. "Yeah, that's him all right."

"EoS'd know."

"Can't fake that kinda thing."

Di gave them an incredulous look. "You believe *that* thing?"

Talle clapped him on the shoulder as they ducked into the cockpit. "Don't take it personally, D09—"

"Di—please," he said, somewhat awkwardly. "D09 feels . . . it does not . . . I am not . . ."

Talle grinned, and kissed Di on the forehead. "Di, then."

"No one's gonna talk about the door-slamming-shut thing back there?" Lenda asked. "Anyone?"

"It is a glitch," Di replied absently.

Siege sat in the navigation chair—Jax's chair—and whirled around to face the crew, crammed elbow to elbow into the tight space. "All right. We're going after Ana. I'm not asking any of the other ships, so we're going to be on our own. Anyone who doesn't want to risk their lives can get off at the waystation and transfer to the *Illumine* or *Scorpius* with my highest regards."

The crew looked at one another, but no one objected.

Talle took Siege's hand and squeezed it tightly. Di had never noticed before how they looked at each other, as though the stars orbited around no one else.

"Sunshine, my Sunshine," Talle told Siege, "Ana's our family. We don't leave family."

"At least not without a fight," Riggs added with a grin. "Wick would've wanted that."

"Barger, too." Lenda agreed.

The captain looked relieved. "All right. Di? Your new upgrade kept you fluent in communications?"

"I believe so."

She jutted her chin toward Wick's empty console. "Then would you mind?"

Di opened and closed his mouth, not knowing what to say. "It . . . would be an honor," he finally managed, and took his position at the console.

Siege ordered the crew to go to their places, spinning back around in her chair. They needed to drop off the Valerio guards, restock their supplies, mend the sails, and somehow infiltrate the Iron Palace. But Siege said it with a grin, all teeth and daring courage, and it made Di want to ignore the 87.34 percent chance of failure.

And that was a strange feeling, not to care about facts.

Do not think about it, he thought, absently touching the port at the nape of his neck, feeling the indentations, wondering what parts of him were less Metal, less wires, less data, and more . . .

More.

Because Ana meant something. He felt it. Deep, burning,

dawning like a sunrise. Ana meant something and he was not sure what to call it. But it was something, and it was expanding.

It was a light.

The sails billowed out with a thunderous roar, catching the winds. The starshield lit up with their destination, a waystation nearby where they would drop off the Valerio guards and mend the sails. In the meantime, Di pulled up the feeds to search for some way—any way—to infiltrate the Iron Palace.

And survive.

ROBB

He made his way through the palace toward Ana's room, rubbing his aching wrist where his mother had pressed the tracking chip. She'd find a way to get Erik on the throne, even if it killed her.

And Jax . . .

His mother couldn't have known what Jax meant to him—

Could have meant, he corrected himself.

He had screwed up more times than he cared to admit, and whatever he had felt on the *Tsarina* for Jax—whatever he had tasted in Jax's words, felt against his lips—meant nothing if he could not fix this.

His mother was not going to win. Not this time.

As he hurried down the Messier-lined hallway, he began to form a plan. But it would take Ana's help—*if* she ever forgave him.

Ana's royal bedchamber was at the farthest end of the South Tower, well away from the skeleton of the North one where her bedchamber—and those of the rest of the royal family—used to be. Yellow lanterns bobbed above him, floating through the air like rafts on a river.

In the summers when he was a child, he'd run through the halls with the Armorov boys while their kid sister sat in her room, forbidden to run through the palace or dig in the garden. She was always separated from the rest of them. She was the Goddess—she wasn't allowed to have a childhood.

But on the *Dossier*, everyone embraced her with open arms. They loved her—unconditionally. Not because she was the Goddess . . .

But because she was Ana.

Two Messiers stood by a door at the end of the hallway, ignoring the poor Royal Captain banging on the door.

"Your Grace!" Royal Captian Viera yelled. "I implore you to unlock the door!"

Robb pocketed his hands. "Is there a problem, Vee?"

Startled, the Royal Captain spun around to him—and scowled. "No, Lord Valerio. Everything is fine."

"Yeah it is, so shove off!" came Ana's reply on the other side. "*Both* of you!"

Robb couldn't help but grin. "I see you have your hands full. I'll come back some other time."

"Please do," Viera ground out, her cold eyes following as he turned to retrace his steps down the hall.

So, Ana had locked herself in her room, which meant either she wasn't coming out—

Or she was planning an escape.

He needed to get to her before she tried *that*.

The hallways were vacant as he made his way toward the kitchen, where he dismissed the lone chef busily prepping food for the Grand Duchess's dinner. He took a large napkin from a drawer, piled it full of foods in his immediate reach, tossed in two napkins with silverware, and tied it tightly into a makeshift basket.

Then he set off toward a small door hidden at the back of the kitchen. If he remembered correctly, the servants' corridors led to all the suites in the palace.

He pushed on it with his shoulder, and the door swung inward to a narrow and dark corridor. Dust hung in the air like slow-moving snowflakes as he felt his way through the darkness until he came to what he *hoped* was the right door. He pressed his back against it. The wall gave way, and the door swiveled around into the room—

A pillow bounced off the wall beside him, clearly aimed for his head.

"It's me!" he called, holding up the basket in surrender. "I brought food!"

Ana paused in the middle of reaching for another throw pillow from her bed—and threw it anyway.

It nailed him in the face. He stumbled back. "*Goddess*, stop that!"

"I'll murder you!" she threatened. "You *and* your mother! You were her *pawn* this whole time—"

"Her pawn," he deadpanned, catching the third pillow out of the air. "Why does everyone think I *like* my mother?"

"Because you're *like* your mother."

"I don't like anyone," he snapped in reply, and paused, finally getting a good look at her. Her hair—the braid—was gone, her head shaved clean. It made her face look sharper, her golden-brown eyes brighter. Where she'd been soft edges before, she was broken glass now. Of course she didn't wear any of the beautiful nightgowns in her wardrobe, but a simple pearl-colored tunic belted at the waist, and dark trousers.

He held up the bag of food. "I deliver nutrients. So you don't starve."

One look and she turned her nose up at it. "I'm not hungry."

Of course you are—you haven't eaten since yesterday, he thought, annoyed. "Look, I'm not here to pick a fight, okay? We need to talk—"

"I have nothing to say to you."

Pursing his lips, he moved around her to the balcony that looked out into the moon garden. It was a short drop, so he climbed over the railing.

"What are you doing?" Ana asked, coming over. "Where are you going?"

"For a walk. Isn't it stuffy here?"

"No. We're on a balcony."

He gave her a pointed look. "Wouldn't you like to stretch your legs?"

"No."

He smiled tightly and mouthed, "Let's talk *privately.*" Ana hesitated. He held up the cloth basket of food again. "And you have to be hungry."

"Well I'm not—"

Her stomach grumbled. He raised an eyebrow.

Embarrassed, she folded her arms over her middle. "I mean—I'm fine. I don't need your charity."

"Believe me, it's not charity," he replied, and let go of the banister, dropping into the bushes below.

"Wait!" she cried, rushing up to the railing. "There's a Messi—"

When he landed, he whirled around and came face-to-face with a Messier in the bushes. He gave a start, leaping back, but it didn't make a move to apprehend him. He slunk around it, out of the shrubbery, and its blue gaze followed him the whole way.

He pulled a leaf from his curly hair and gave Ana a wave.

"I can't go down there!" She eyed the Messier.

He rolled his eyes, stepping out onto a cobblestone path. "It's not going to hurt you—it *works* for you. Now come on."

The palace's moon garden wasn't like his family's garden in Astoria. There weren't exotic flowers or mazes of thorn-bushes. The palace's garden was simple, with topiary bushes in the shape of the Goddess and crescent moons and stars, and willow trees lining the edges. A stark black moondial stood in the middle of the garden, counting the rotation of Luna around Eros, and rising up from the edge of the garden was an Iron Shrine, its windows warm with candlelight.

Most of the garden could be seen from the palace—except for a small grove near the East Tower. The eldest Armorov, Rhys, had shown him the spot years ago, although back then it had been used to get away from their tutors.

Behind him, he heard Ana land in the bushes and creep around the Messier. "Why isn't it *doing* anything?"

"What's it supposed to do? You're the heir, so the palace is yours. It's not like it's going to *arrest* you."

She caught up to him, picking a twig off her shirt. "I still don't like it. Why couldn't we talk in my room? What, it isn't good enough for a spoiled-rotten Ironblood like you?"

"It could be bugged. Someone could be listening. Can't you trust me a *little?*"

"*Trust* you? You *lied* to me. You led your mother straight to the *Dossier*! And now that I'm apparently royalty, you probably want to marry me so you can get the throne—"

"We're cousins, and you're not my type."

The anger on her face dropped. "Cousins?"

"Your mother was my aunt—my mother's sister," he confirmed, and ducked under a low-hanging willow branch and into the hidden grove. Small white buds sprouted from the ground, and he made sure not to step on them as he found a spot to sit.

She stood stiffly at the edge of the grove. "I'm *not* a Valerio. I'm not like you. You killed my friends, my *family*—"

"My *mother* did that," he corrected under his breath, and then added louder, "Jax is alive."

The anger on her face fractured into hope. "He is?"

"Yes, and he's here. My mother won't let him out of her sight. I don't know *why*—" She spun to leave the grove. "Wait! What are you doing?"

She threw a glare back at him. "I'm going to *order* her to release him."

"You can't do that—"

"Can't? Or you don't want me to?"

He bit the inside of his cheek. *A little of both.* "If you bring attention to him, it'll put a marker on his back for the rest of his life. A Solani protected by the Empress? He'll be a walking target, I promise you."

"Then what do you expect me to do? Just sit here while your mother does *who knows what* with him?"

No, but if Ana ordered his release, then his mother would know that he was talking with Ana; and if Ana did nothing, there was a very real chance that things *would* get worse for Jax—and that was the last thing he wanted.

"Let me save him," he heard himself saying before he realized what exactly he meant. Ana blinked, just as surprised.

She scoffed. "Like how you saved *me?*"

"My mother won't suspect it coming from me. She doesn't expect much from me at all, really."

She debated for a moment, shifting from one foot to the other.

It was a look Robb had seen a hundred times before. In ballrooms. Parties. Framed in a window, leaning back, just before letting go.

But you're a Valerio, they all said.

He unbuttoned the cuff of his right sleeve and bent back his hand to show her the dormant tracking chip. "This was how my mother found the *Dossier*. I didn't tell her. It was activated just before the Grand Duchess made her announcement—my mother came looking for me."

"Then why didn't you tell anyone about the tracker?"

"I messed up." It was the only answer he could give. "I—I didn't know she'd come herself. I thought she'd send one of her commanders. And I knew you would throw me off the ship if I said anything. I had to find out what happened to my father. Believe me, if I could pry this from my wrist, I would, but if I did, it would cut the nerve endings in my sword arm."

And then I wouldn't be able to fight off Erik, and the thought of being helpless against Erik made his chest tighten with panic.

"Oh, forgive me if I don't feel bad for your precious *sword arm*," she snapped icily.

"Please, Ana. I *will* get Jax out of here, you have my word. My mother has won her game a hundred times before, but she won't win this one—I promise."

Ana hesitated, but he knew she was smarter than anyone gave her credit for. She knew he was right and came to sit down beside him. "I still don't believe you, but I don't have a choice."

He untied the basket of food, unwrapping the silverware, and studied her. "It's more than just Jax, isn't it?"

She nodded. "Whatever took control of the *Tsarina* and killed Di is still out there. It knew my name—it might've known I was the heir to the kingdom, too." She riffled through the food until she found a jar of olives, twisted it open, and popped one into her mouth. Empress Celene loved olives, too. "It told Di he should have let me burn. I think it was there the night of the Rebellion."

Robb sliced up the bread and took a wedge of cheese from a small wheel. "But Rasovant said all the Metals who stormed the North Tower were destroyed—"

"How can Rasovant be sure of that?"

He shoved the piece of bread and cheese into his mouth. "He was the only survivor—until you."

She blinked.

"On the night of the Rebellion, he was called to the North Tower when the Metals stationed there attacked—he said they wanted to kill the Goddess. Um, *you.* Then a fire broke out and everything went to shit. Rasovant barely made it out himself."

"Don't you think it's odd that he's the only survivor? And all we have to go on is his word?"

"Ana, he *saved us from the Plague.*" He's a hero, one of the kingdom's best. Why would he lie?"

"Because he wasn't a *hero* when he created the HIVE. If he just wanted to control Metals, why did he give them free will in the first place?"

"Maybe he wished for the best?"

"But not *every* Metal tried to kill me—"

"Who's to say the malware after you isn't a Metal he created? If they were all HIVE'd, this wouldn't be a problem."

She slammed down the jar of olives. "If they were all HIVE'd, then Di would have never existed."

He looked away, uncomfortable. "I'm sorry. You're right."

She mumbled something under her breath and grabbed the bread knife, spearing a slice with a little too much force. He tried to imagine that it wasn't his head, but it was hard to think of anything else. "Even though I can't remember it, I need to find out what really happened the night of the Rebellion. So if you were going to investigate, where would you start?"

"Probably the visitation logs from that day? You seem dead set on disbelieving the Iron Adviser, so we can check there first. Who came to the palace, who left—maybe we can pin down what happened that night and who met with the Emperor, and which Metals were in the Tower when they attacked. The palace's libraries should have some sort of record-keeping archive." He cocked his head. "I can start there."

She raised a single black eyebrow. *"You?"*

"Yeah, me." He met her gaze. "I want to know just as much as you. For some reason my father thought he had to run as far away from the palace as possible. I want to know why."

"So do I. I'll start nosing around to find some info on Rasovant and your father, and you figure out a way to free Jax." She outstretched her hand. He looked at it blankly. "Well? Are you with me or not, Valerio?"

"To the end." He took her hand, and they shook.

She grinned, snagging another piece of cheese. "Don't say things you don't mean. . . ." Her words trailed off as Eros's second moon drifted into view above them, casting a silvery light across the garden. And one by one, the small white buds around them bloomed to soak up the moonlight.

Her lips parted in awe. "Moonlilies?"

"They *are* the Goddess's flower."

She plucked one and stuck it behind her ear. "What do you think? Do I look Goddess-like?"

"You look—" The moonlight glinted against a pendant around her neck. It was slightly melted, a shadow of itself, but it was still there. A snake eating its own tail.

His heart began to race. "Where . . . where did you get that? Around your neck?"

"This?" She touched the pendant. "It's my good-luck charm. I've had it as long as I can remember—"

"Ananke?" an old, crackly voice called from across the garden. The Grand Duchess ducked beneath a low tree limb, eyes flickering across the grove. "Ah, it seems you have company."

Robb quickly scrambled to his feet and gave a low bow. "Your Grace. I was just—"

"Enjoying the moonlilies, as we all are," the Grand Duchess replied, and turned to Ana. "I am sorry for interrupting, but I was on my way to the shrine when I heard voices, and you sounded so much like your mother. . . ." She faltered. "Forgive me. I'll leave—"

"Wait." Ana began to rise to her feet, but Robb snagged the edge of her tunic.

"What are you *doing*?" he whispered.

"If we're going to find out about that fire, where do you think's the best place to start?"

Point.

The Grand Duchess turned back, strangely curious. "Yes?"

"Can I come with you?" Ana asked, swiping his hand away, and rose to her feet. "To the shrine?"

"Of course!" The Grand Duchess looked pleased. Robb had never seen the old woman look anything besides dour. "It would be an honor, Ananke."

"Great," replied Ana, and without even a good-bye, she followed the woman out of the moonlily grove.

She's definitely adapting quickly for a girl found in an escape pod, he thought—before he realized exactly how his father's pendant had ended up around her neck.

The screens on the *Tsarina's* engineering console.

The ejected pod.

Goddess's spark—his father's missing brooch. It had been staring him in the face this whole time.

His father had sacrificed his life to save Ana.

But if the Metals who had ignited the North Tower had been destroyed, as Rasovant claimed, then why hadn't his father and Ana escaped to the rest of the palace, like Rasovant? What were they running from? And if Metals had burned the tower, why had his father trusted D09? And if that malware was a Metal from the Rebellion, then how had it survived?

Ana was right.

Rasovant had lied.

ANA

The last time Ana visited a shrine, Messiers tried to kill her, and this time she willingly accompanied the woman who'd almost handed her a death sentence.

If the Goddess had a sense of humor, Ana didn't see it.

Inside, long stone pews stretched up to the pulpit, and behind it towered a statue of the Goddess, twenty feet tall. Ana searched the face of the Goddess, trying to find herself in the nose, the cheeks, the lips—but the face was as foreign as the rest of the palace. The statue loomed over them, lit with the glow of nine hundred and ninety-nine candles, one for each year that had passed since the girl of light drove away the Great Dark.

The Grand Duchess made a crescent shape across her chest and kissed her palm. Ana did the same, and took a seat beside her on the first stone pew. She hoped she hadn't made a mistake by inviting herself here.

"This place brings me peace," the Grand Duchess said, her lips perpetually curving downward into a scowl, accenting the lines in her tired face.

"I . . . guess," Ana replied.

"You do not remember me, do you?"

Startled, Ana turned to look at the Grand Duchess. "What?"

"Do you remember anything?"

She shook her head.

"Perhaps it's for the best," the old woman said. "I was not the best grandmother, and when our family died, I was the only one left. I am an Aragon by birth, married into the Armorov family, so I could not wear the crown. I was never supposed to rule." Taking a locket out from underneath her collar, she pried it open with her long nails and offered it to Ana. "This is the last picture of our family and you."

At first, Ana didn't want to take it. She didn't want to look at a family that wasn't hers. But curiosity got the better of her.

The portrait was so small she had to squint. The Emperor, clad in royal purple, had a hand on his wife's shoulder. He looked like all the pictures she'd seen in the newsfeeds. Golden-brown eyes and rich brown skin, like the Grand Duchess, a full beard over a strong face. Beside him, his wife, the Empress, smiled out of the portrait, brown curly hair and Valerio-blue eyes. There were three boys in front of them, all with heads full of dark curls. The youngest had his mother's eyes.

Tobias, a voice in her head whispered. *Rhys, Wylan, and Tobias.*

Names she'd heard on newsfeeds before, in articles, passed around on people's lips with "Goddess bless them" and "tragic loss." They were names that still meant little to her, and that made a hollow part inside her ache.

She was supposed to remember them, and she didn't.

Beside the youngest boy stood a girl. Dark hair and warm bronze skin, as though an expert painter had taken the best colors from her paints to make her, with eyes that Ana had seen every day of her life. She stared hard at the locket, trying to find herself in the picture, to remember that scratchy dress, the way it always pinched her under her arms—

She handed the locket back quickly. "I'm sorry that you lost them."

"They were a good family," the old woman said, staring up at the overpowering statue. "I should have looked for you—but I left you in this kingdom alone to fend for yourself against those *heathens*—"

"They were kind and they loved me. Captain Siege—"

The Grand Duchess tore her eyes away from the statue to gaze at Ana in horror. "That *criminal?*"

"I love her," Ana said, wishing she could go back in time and apologize for yelling at Siege outside the infirmary. Instead, Ana would have let the captain hug her, and cried into her shoulder. She would have apologized, over and over, until her voice went hoarse. "She raised me and she loved me—"

"She did *not* love you," the old woman replied, her voice lower, quieter. "She probably knew who you were. That was why she kept you hidden. As ransom, or bait, or—"

"She wouldn't do that. She's my family—"

"*I* am your family, Ananke."

A flash of anger lit inside Ana. She jerked to her feet. "I'm *not* Ananke."

"You are the first daughter born to the Armorov bloodline in a thousand years," said the old woman, and the gleam of the candle lights showed the desperation in her eyes. "You are most important—and *you* are the one who survived. You will fight the Great Dark."

"The Great Dark doesn't exist," Ana argued. "It's just a *story.*"

"All stories are built from the bones of something true. You are the daughter of iron and stars. You are the symbol of hope in a time when light only shines from things that burn."

Ana gritted her teeth. "The Armorovs burned. So are you saying that was hope? That they *burned?*"

"It was a tragedy I will forever mourn, but we finally saw those Metals as the heartless beasts they are—"

"Metals are not *heartless,*" Ana snapped.

"Do you truly believe that when you look at your face, my darling?" asked the Grand Duchess, raising a hand to Ana's scarred cheek.

Ana slapped her hand away. "I'm going to bed. Good night." Then she turned out of the shrine, but she couldn't escape the Grand Duchess's words quickly enough. Metals were not heartless.

She knew it firsthand.

Di was not evil.

Somehow, she found her way to the great hall, and the gilded doors she had come through earlier that day. Beyond them was the courtyard, and then the gates, then freedom—it seemed so far away.

Two Messiers stood on either side of the door. They turned their heads toward her, watching, as she approached. Guarding.

But this was *her* palace. If she was the the heir, she could go wherever she wished—anywhere in the kingdom.

She reached to open the doors when one of the Messiers grabbed her wrist. Not harshly, but just to stop her.

"It is not safe outside," it said, and let go of her wrist.

The other one added, "It is best you stay inside."

"But I want to leave," she argued.

"It is best you stay inside," the same Messier repeated. "It is pleasant inside the palace."

She took a step back. Then another, a knot forming in her throat.

Robb was mistaken. The Messiers were not here to guard her. They were here to keep her inside. To keep her prisoner. They didn't report to her at all, but she was certain who they *did* report to—Rasovant.

While she was inside this palace, she was a sitting target for the malware from the *Tsarina*—and whoever was truly behind the Rebellion seven years ago.

JAX

Jax stood in a hallway in the East Tower, positively lost. He hadn't moved since Lady Valerio told him to stay put, but still he was lost. There were too many hallways, and too many rooms. He leaned against a window that looked out onto the moon garden, tapping his gloved finger impatiently on his forearm. A few moments ago, Ana had fled the shrine, and he watched as the Grand Duchess followed, as slow and steady as a funeral procession.

A Messier stood like a statue outside the room Lady Valerio went into—she was meeting with Lord Rasovant. She tried to keep it a secret, but honestly, he was a prisoner, not *stupid*.

The Messier's blue eyes didn't flicker as it stared straight ahead. Even Di's eyes flickered.

He tugged at his voxcollar.

Of all the ideas his pretty little brain could come up with, *this* was the best he could do? Offer to read Lady Valerio's stars in exchange for . . . Oh, it didn't matter now.

"However, I do not trust you'll keep your word," Lady

Valerio had said. "I knew your father, after all, so to ensure your end of the bargain, I will agree on one condition."

He had not thought that condition would be to wear a vox-collar and be at the lady's personal beck and call.

With a silent sigh, he leaned farther out of the window, to soak in as much starlight as he could. It made him feel better. The palace was cold and drafty—downright spooky, really. Eros loomed outside the window like a monstrous shadow, a ring of light surrounding it, shifting shadows across the hallway.

If he closed his eyes, he could feel the stars rotating, spiraling, across the great black expanse. And if he concentrated further, he could feel the blackness itself. Encroaching.

Ah ba'tha nazu mah, the Darkness whispered, like a sigh. *Ah ba'tha nazu morah.*

I am coming from the edges, it translated from the Old Language. I am coming from the end.

The call was stronger tonight. It was stronger than it had ever been. Was it that close already—how could he not have heard it?

Because you never wanted to, he thought bitterly, clenching and unclenching his gloved hands into fists.

When he opened his eyes again, something in the moon garden caught his eye. A distinct, bright flicker of red. A pair of eyes.

The hair on the back of his neck stood on end—

"Well, look who I've found. The star-kisser."

He glanced over his shoulder at the familiar voice. Erik Valerio smiled.

ROBB

He made his way down a darkened hallway in the East Tower, back toward his room, when a voice caught his ears, low and quick, coming from around the corner. Erik.

Of *course* Erik had to be at the palace, too.

"So how do you do it, then?" asked his brother. "Do you suck blood? Sacrificial ritual?"

Who was he talking to? Cautiously, he peeked around the corner. Erik had Jax up against the sill of the window that looked out onto the moon garden, his fingers wrapped beneath the voxcollar. The Solani's red-violet eyes snapped to Robb's, first frantic—and then stone.

Erik went on coolly, "Admit it—you can't do it. You'll tell my mother the truth—"

"Leave him alone." Robb stepped into the hallway.

Erik unraveled his fingers from around the collar. "Oh, look," his brother drawled. "It's the spare, on time to ruin my fun as usual."

"Leave him alone, Erik."

His mother wouldn't let the Solani out of her sight unless she was indisposed.

Erik shrugged. "Why're you so *defensive?* I simply found a friend in the hallway and decided to say hello—we are friends, aren't we, *star-kisser?*"

The Solani glowered at him.

"*Leave,*" Robb said levelly.

Erik's eyes sparked. "Ooh, I hit a nerve."

"LEAVE!"

"I'm going, I'm going." Erik raised his hands in defeat. As he passed Robb, he paused and bent close to whisper, "But you know I'll always end up breaking your toys."

Then his brother was gone, down the hallway and out of sight.

JAX

Robb was a *terrible* sight for sore eyes.

Jax tugged at his voxcollar, wiggling it back into a comfortable position from where that egomaniacal lord had messed it up. The collar was already rubbing a rash on his neck. He didn't need permanent scarring, too.

Then—remembering—he glanced back into the garden, but the red eyes were gone. It couldn't have been a trick of the light, could it?

"Are you okay?" Robb asked. "Did Erik hurt you?"

Jax turned a glare back to the insufferable Ironblood.

"Oh—right. You—the voxcollar. Listen, I . . ."

Jax waved his hand dismissively. He would rather not have pity. Groveling wasn't all that attractive, anyway. Besides, Robb was the last person he wanted to see. If it were up to him, he'd toss the Ironblood out of the window, but then he was sure Lady Valerio wouldn't keep him around. He wasn't here for his own revenge fantasy, and remembering that made

Robb a little more bearable.

Until, of course, Robb fell to his knees and pressed his head against the floor. "I'm sorry," the boy said. "I'm so sorry. I'm going to get you out of here. As soon as I can. I'm going to—"

He was *what?*

Jax grabbed the Ironblood by the shoulders and dragged him to his feet again, glaring at him with all the hatred he could muster. *"No,"* he mouthed, "you won't—"

The voxcollar zapped, and he flinched away from Robb. The sting went all the way down to his toes. He bit his tongue so he wouldn't make a sound.

"Please," Robb said desperately, *"let me help."*

And *ruin* his plans? Oh, Darkness damn *everything.*

He shoved the Ironblood backward.

Robb stumbled but found his footing. His face fractured with hurt before he could reel his emotions in and hide them behind that charming stoic Valerio mask. Good—emotions didn't look nice on Robbert Valerio, anyway.

"I *will* get you out of here," he said with conviction. "I promise you. On iron and stars."

About to shove the Ironblood away again, Jax froze. His hands began to tremble.

The door opened again and Lady Valerio stepped out, pausing when she noticed Robb in the hallway. Her eyebrows rose just a fraction. "Dear, did I not tell you to go to bed?"

A muscle in Robb's jaw twitched. "Yes, Mother." He bowed

to her and left without another glance.

Jax watched him go, the sound of the unbreakable vow ringing in his head, sweet and strong, like a gold chain woven through strings of glass.

ANA

The next few days were filled with classes and lectures and learning. The gray-mustached steward from the other day rattled off her schedule while Mellifare poured a cup of morning tea. Ana hadn't even gotten out of bed yet, her eyelashes still crusted with sleep. The steward seemed to think that she was as dumb as rocks. No, she'd never been to school before, but she was not illiterate.

The *Dossier* was where she'd learned. Her maths were made up of the perfect calibration for Riggs's mechanical leg. Her words from pages and pages of Di's favorite books and Wick's word-scramble games. Her history lessons were learned in every world they visited, every city they slept in. Her decorum from every shore leave on Nevaeh, every waystation hustle.

The steward told Ana that she had to learn the proper history of the kingdom. No less was expected of a future Empress, as if everything she'd learned as an outlaw was inferior and dangerous. She needed to be taught. She needed to be groomed and polished, like silverware to set a table.

"You only have a handful of days before the coronation," the steward went on, "so if Your Grace has any questions, I would be more than happy to answer them."

"Have you heard anything about the *Dossier*?" she asked, surprising him. It wasn't the question he was expecting, but it was the only one on her mind. Robb had said he had over-heard his mother talking about how her guards lost the ship and ended up in a mine on Cerces.

He looked happy. "Absolutely nothing. If we're lucky, that old ship is finally done. You see, it's been a pain in the king-dom's rear for quite some years, Your Grace."

"Oh," she said.

It felt like a story now, those years on the *Dossier* when she had been happy.

·❭ ● ❬·

The Grand Duchess had ordered Viera to be her personal shadow. So Ana did the only thing she could think of—she made the Royal Captain swear her loyalty under penalty of death. Since Viera didn't seem like the kind to break her oaths, Ana only mostly believed her.

The Royal Captain was merciless in her job as she followed Ana around the palace. Between classes, between meals—everywhere. Ana couldn't even shake her to go exploring.

"You have tutoring beginning in a few minutes, Your Grace," said the Royal Captain, following Ana down another long and winding corridor toward the North Tower. "We should return before your tutor informs Her Grace of your tardi—"

"Lord Whatever-His-Name can wait," replied Ana, coming to an intersection. She watched the lanterns bob above her. They seemed to turn left, so she did, too.

"Understanding Iron Law is a crucial part of ruling, Your Grace."

Ana rolled her eyes. "I'm a criminal. I think I know something about Iron Law."

"Learning to evade the law isn't the same as learning to pass judgment inside it," the Royal Captain replied. "At the Academy, we spend years going over the doctrines. There are intricacies and amendments that take years for scholars to understand—"

"You've never broken the law, have you?" Ana stopped, turning back to face her bodyguard.

"I'm not like Robbert *Valerio*."

"I bet he knows the law better than you. Captain Siege always taught me that you learn the law so you know how to break it." She paused, looking down an adjacent hallway. It was a lot wider than the others, and at the end stood an intricately carved set of doors that were padlocked and sealed tight.

Two Messiers guarded the doors, one on either side. She started to turn down the hall when the captain stopped her.

"It's the North Tower, Your Grace," said Viera.

"Why's it still closed off? It's been seven years."

"Lord Rasovant thought it best that the North Tower be kept as is, a monument to what we lost."

"Even the Metals?"

"Hmm?"

"Are the Metals who burned my family still in there, too? Since none survived?"

The Royal Captain faltered. "I . . . am not sure, Your Grace."

The Messiers that guarded the empty tower kept staring, staring, and for the first time Ana actually thought they were looking at her instead of past her. As if daring her to come investigate.

"And why are there Messiers standing guard over it if it's just a monument?"

"They stand guard everywhere," the Royal Captain's replied. "Now please, Your Grace, we must get back before anyone notices you're missing."

Because Ana was *just so scared* of that. But she didn't want anyone gossiping about where she was snooping, and if she came back later than usual, someone would be nosy enough to find out. So she gave in and followed her guard back to her room in the South Tower, unable to shake the attentive gazes of the Messiers as she left.

·❭●❬·

Every evening, Robb would come to her room and they would have dinner out in the garden. They never went to the moonlily grove again, but ate on the benches beside the moondial, the stoic shadow of Royal Captain Viera keeping watch over them.

Robb couldn't seem to find the visitation logs for the day of the Rebellion.

"It's like they've disappeared," he said between mouthfuls of roasted chicken.

"Or someone destroyed them," Ana replied, turning back to the captain. "Do you know who has access to the palace's records?"

"Only the highest personnel," replied the young captain. "Myself, the Grand Duchess—"

"And a good majority of the Iron Council," Robb finished for her before explaining, "The Iron Council's only called in a crisis. It's composed of the heads of all the Ironblood families, so anyone could have taken or destroyed those records."

Ana felt like they hit a barrier at every turn.

She couldn't get any answers from her tutors either. They— and everything they taught—ran together like watercolors: history, intrigue, economics, Iron Law, policy. . . . She relentlessly asked questions about the palace, the Rebellion, her parents, but most of the stuffy-looking Advisers diverted her questions, or ignored her completely.

All except for one.

·) ● (·

Lord Machivalle, her royal demeanor and conversation tutor, never seemed to shy away from *any* question. Ana often overheard her other tutors gossiping about him. He wasn't even from a proper Ironblood name, they said. He had skin baked dry from the sun and wore so many jewels he glittered like the mines on Cerces. He looked Siege's age, with hair the color of starlight—like Jax's, but his skin didn't shimmer like Jax's did.

"Flattery is not something given lightly," Machivalle lectured, discussing the proper decorum for interacting with other Ironbloods. "Keep it simple and straightforward—you never like a person *that* much. Your mother was the queen of flattery. Then again, she was also a Valerio . . . but she was the best of them."

She glanced up from picking at a loose thread on her trousers. She didn't feel like herself in dresses. And she couldn't run in them if she needed to. "Did you know them? My parents?"

"Of course," replied her tutor. "They were rare. They treated everyone with as much dignity and grace as they treated each other, you see. Some say it was why they never saw the Rebellion coming. They trusted too much."

"They trusted Metals too much? Or someone else?"

Her tutor hesitated for a moment. "They had a dear friend who was a Metal, but he disappeared after the Rebellion."

"Do you think he set the fire?"

Machivalle's eyebrows furrowed, his jaw working, not sure what to say. But when he finally opened his mouth, another voice interrupted.

"May I come in, Lord Machivalle?"

Ana whipped around in her chair.

The Iron Adviser, Lord Rasovant, stood at her door, a glowing holo-pad in his grip. She hadn't seen him since the throne room, the day the iron crown didn't rust. It felt almost like a lifetime ago, although it had only been three days.

"Lord Adviser," Lord Machivalle greeted Rasovant. "I didn't

realize I had run over time. I thought Lord Charone was her next tutor?" Her economics tutor.

"I'm afraid he is indisposed today," the Adviser replied coolly.

"Indisposed or relieved?"

The Iron Adviser smiled politely. "He is sick."

"He drank too much Ilidian brandy, eh? Ah, well, we all have our vices. Some of us are just better at hiding them."

"Yes, well." Rasovant blinked and then pressed a thin smile across his lips. "Pleasant day, is it not, Machivalle?"

Lord Machivalle leaned forward and whispered, "Take note of the forms of redirection," with a wink, and closed his old leather tome and stood. "Don't forget to practice your articulations, and I'll see you tomorrow, Your Grace," he said, and nodded to the Iron Adviser. "I hope you have Charone's lessons for today. The burgeoning disadvantages of the Erosian economy thanks to the influx of Messiers will be quite a treat to talk about today, I feel."

Then he left without so much as a glance at the Iron Adviser.

Such sass. Ana approved.

Until she realized she was alone with Rasovant, and her courage spiraled into a cold knot in the center of her stomach.

"Good afternoon, Your Grace," Rasovant began, gliding toward her, and her skin crawled the closer he came. "We will *not* be going over your economic lessons today. Instead, I thought we could get to know each other a little better before your coronation on the Holy Conjunction. You need to know your duties."

She stood as the Adviser approached, a wrongness settling

in her stomach. His eyes reminded her of cut obsidian—shallow, stagnant. "What kind of duties?"

"I'm sure your other tutors have already said what's expected of you. I am here as more of a spiritual Adviser, simply to remind you of your duties to the Cantos and the Iron Shrines. We are a kingdom of many, after all. We are of different planets and different beliefs, but we will all be stronger with an army under the Goddess."

Ana's brow furrowed. "What?"

"Once you are crowned, and with your blessing, we shall begin the acquisition of all remaining Metals by force—"

"What?" Her voice was louder, brittle. The Adviser gave her an impatient look. "You can't just order innocent Metals—who have not *broken* the *law*—to be HIVE'd! What kind of army do we need?"

"In these dark times, we need to be united—"

"Dark times? Haven't they always been dark? Look around you! We're surrounded by *space!*"

"Metals cannot see the Goddess's light. They will go astray. They have already. They have the Great Dark inside them. You of all people should know that. The Rebellion cost you everything you knew."

"It's a good thing those Metals *died* in the North Tower, then," she replied, trying to keep her voice level.

"And if there are more?" asked Rasovant. "We are not safe until they are all HIVE'd."

"Why did you create Metals to think, then? If you just wanted to control them?"

The edges of the old man's lips twisted. "I was arrogant and young. I assure you, the HIVE does not hurt—"

"I said *no*," she snapped, balling her hands into fists, trying hard not to punch the old man in his crackly old mug. "I will *never* be a part of that. Find a different Empress."

She turned on her bare feet, because she refused to wear shoes in her own room, and left. Like a shadow, Royal Captain Viera pushed off from the wall and followed her out.

Why did Lord Rasovant insist that all Metals be HIVE'd when the ones who'd burned the North Tower had died? And why was the North Tower *locked*?

Because Rasovant lied about the Rebellion, and for once she hated that she'd been right.

DI

On the afternoon before Ana's coronation, citizens crowded the square in front of the palace. Siege said that at the last coronation, people celebrated for weeks after. Tents lined the broad square, food stalls and festival games, the heavy scent of ale making everyone punch-drunk by the smell alone. Di hiked his knapsack higher on his shoulder and moved his way through the crowd, slowly, cautious not to attract attention.

It had taken longer than expected to get to the palace, between repairing the *Dossier* at the waystation near Iliad, unloading the Valerio men, acquiring fake IDs, booking *legal* passage to the Iron Palace, going through security screenings, never mind the dizzying ride *to* the moon. . . .

Too much time had been wasted. They could not afford any more.

He stepped lightly through the crowded square, this body much more agile than the one before, though he missed being taller. Evening light filtered through the willow trees lining the square, creating swirls of shadows across the cobblestones.

Citizens from every corner of the worlds were stuffed into the expansive square, along with vendors selling hot pots and kebabs and sweet ales.

In his knapsack, E0S hummed against his back, the little can opener calming his nerves, and somewhere far, far above him, the *Dossier* drifted around Eros in silent orbit, waiting. The ship was too far to reach him if trouble broke out, but just remembering that it was there helped.

A little.

Nervously, he pulled at the collar of a coat he had borrowed from Jax's wardrobe. It was the only one that seemed to fit reasonably well.

"I should be down there with you," the captain said, her voice resounding in his head like an echo. She had patched herself into his receptor. It was—what was the word?

Intrusive.

"I should be helping you get her—"

I am fine, Captain, he stressed. *Besides, I have the can opener—*

E0S bleeped angrily, earning Di an alarmed look from a passing family, and he quickly moved on.

And you have seven bounties on your head, he finished, bumping his knapsack again to keep the bot quiet. *We will be safe. No one can recognize me.*

"That's what I'm afraid of," the captain murmured, because he did not look like D09, and they were all afraid that Ana would not believe him.

He squatted beside the willows, assessing the entrance of the palace. Six Messiers stood guard. Seeing a face like the one he used to have, with a placid blue gaze, made his skin crawl.

Now he realized why Ana had always been so terrified of the possibility of his being HIVEd.

Goddess, he hoped to die before ever being submitted to the HIVE.

Captain, I am in position, he said, taking off his knapsack.

"*Are you sure you want to do this?*"

Do we have a better plan?

"*Of course we do! I was gonna—*"

That does not involve coming in, guns blazing, and getting everyone killed?

"*I was going to do it at night,*" she said defensively, and sighed. "*Fine. Once you're inside, Riggs'll go park the skysailer at the docks for you—and Di?*"

Hmm?

"*Be careful.*"

Of course.

Di untied the top of the knapsack, and EoS came whirring out, bleeping happily.

"Shh!" he hushed the bot. "Remember, all you have to do is unlock that side gate, okay?"

It bobbed in a nod.

"Okay, now if you get into trouble—" But it was already whizzing away over the palace wall. "I cannot help you," he finished dejectedly.

I am upgrading EoS when we get back, he told Siege.

"*What's wrong with it?*"

It is not the brightest bulb in the light socket.

The captain howled with laughter, and he found his lips twitching up into a smile. There was a strange feeling in his throat, but he bit his cheek to keep from laughing.

As a Metal, he had been absent of feelings. But over the last few days he had come to understand a few. Anger, hatred, sadness, annoyance, *longing*. Siege had to explain that one, the pit he felt in his chest, traveling down and down and down into a metaphorical dark hole. It made him antsy and restless. He still did not need to sleep in this body, so all he did was pace, and try to work out the movement of his new limbs, and . . .

Think.

He had a lot of time to think.

Sitting against the trunk of a willow, he took a tie from around his wrist—another borrowed thing from Jax—and pulled his red hair back into a ponytail, waiting for EoS to unlock the side gate. He watched the crowd, soaking in the sound of the music and the sweet smell of the hot pots and kebabs, until an uproar on the other side of the square drew his attention.

At first it sounded like a cheer, some sort of rabble-rousing for the new Empress, but as he got to his feet again, he caught a few words in the chaos—*traitor, rogue, Metal*.

Alarmed, he abandoned his empty knapsack by the willow and shoved through the crowd toward the noise.

Siege, there is a Metal here, I believe, he sent through the comm-link, squeezing past onlookers standing on their tiptoes to see over the people gathered around whatever was happening.

"Now, Di, don't do anything rash—"

He broke out into the center of the chaos.

A Metal lay sprawled on the ground, a knife embedded in its leg. Its white eyes flickered, searching the crowd. It was not HIVE'd. "I apologize for my inconvenience," it tried to say over the crowd. "I am not here to harm—"

"Traitor!" someone cried, throwing a handful of trash.

It smacked the Metal in the face, stickiness oozing down its chin. Other people threw pieces of rotten fruit, dirt from beneath the willow trees, sticks from the kebabs sold at the stands. They pinged off the Metal's dented body, and the Metal did not even care.

Di could only watch.

"Got some nerve coming here!" someone at Di's elbow shouted.

A woman spit at it. "Go back where you came from!"

Di glanced around to see if anyone was coming to stop this, but the Messiers stood calmly at their posts, and the people outside the mob simply looked away. As though if they did not see the violence, they would not be a part of it. But he saw them. He saw all the people who averted their eyes and walked past, and all the ones crowded into the circle, spitting and hissing at a Metal who could not defend itself.

And oh, *oh*, was there an anger growing inside him. It bubbled, frothed, like a firestorm, burning so hot underneath his skin he thought he would explode.

"Murderer!" one called, before a hundred voices echoed, "Murderer! *Murderer!*" like it was the Metal's name.

"You are mistaken. I am only here to honor the Empress,"

the android tried to reason, but it was useless. It was reaching down to pull the knife out of its leg when another man with dark hair elbowed his way out of the crowd, flicking open a lighter.

"Maybe we should honor her by burning *you!*"

The temper inside Di turned his thoughts white-hot. The next he knew, he had the man by the hand and was twisting his arm behind his back. There was a *crack*.

The man gave a cry, dropping the lighter.

Di caught it, flicking the flame on, holding so tight to the man's broken arm, twisting so terribly that bone protruded from the skin. And he thought how easy it was to break them. Humans. How simple.

"Mercy," the man babbled, the whites of his eyes matching the bone Di had easily broken.

Di held the lighter closer to the man, until it singed his hair. "This will be a mercy—"

"Sir," a metallic voice cut through his ire, and he blinked, coming back to his senses. He faltered, as the human in his grip whimpered, the smell in the air matching the stain seeping onto his trousers.

"Mercy," the black-haired man sobbed.

Di let go.

Around him the crowd retreated as far as they could, many of them with looks of wide-eyed terror. Someone pulled out a holo-pad, then another person, and another, until he could feel the streams of newsfeeds lacing across him, around him, sending communications upward and outward across the galaxy.

Until he caught sight of a girl. Flaxen hair. Purple dress. He recognized her instantly—the servant from Astoria, the one who'd been with Rasovant. She held his gaze and grinned.

"Monster," she called.

Someone else echoed. "Monster!"

"Monster!" The word rippled like a rock in the ocean.

"Di?" Siege asked. *"Di, what's happ—"*

The man whimpered on the ground, the bone protruding, and Di could not recall how he had hurt him. He could only remember a white-hot rage.

The feeling in his chest squeezed, twisted, turning sour and bitter and horrible. Everything was too much—the smells of sweet ales and kebabs, the shadows through the willows, all the voices grating, ill-harmonized sounds that formed around flaps of fleshy lips—words.

I cannot do this.

Not here. Not in this body.

Monster, the humans screamed. *Monster,* said the newsfeeds.

There were so many glitches, too many sensations—he could not adapt. He hated his train of thought. The tangents. The opinions. The bias. And the *pain.* He did not like the pain. Like daggers raking through the wires of his mind. It all needed to stop—this second. Now. Now. Now.

Monster—

NOW.

A rushing, electrical charge spread out from his center, to his outer extremities, pulsing like a wave. He felt every holo-pad, every newsfeed, every comm-link like kite strings reaching into the sky—every word, every syllable, every letter—

MONSTER

—and destroyed each one.

A holo-pad burst in a woman's hand; then another exploded, another, and another, rippling out like a wave, with Di at the epicenter.

The crowd shrieked, dropping their electronics as the charges pulsed through them, singeing their skin, blackening their fingertips. They quickly forgot him, the word they repeated sinking beneath the swelling chaos.

Di turned back to the Metal and plucked the knife out of its leg. "Can you stand?"

The Metal nodded. "You are not human."

"No," Di agreed, but he was no longer a Metal anymore, either. He did not know what he was. "With them distracted, you can escape. Quickly."

The Metal nodded and limped off into the frantic crowd.

Di took one last look at the broken-armed man crying on the ground, wanting to help him, to splint the bone and—

He tore himself away, as far from anyone who had seen his monstrousness as he could. Another holo-pad exploded near him, and a woman shrieked. He couldn't stop it. The trail of electricity followed, rippling out around him in a wave.

Against the wall, the Messiers stood, dull-eyed and dormant, as if they'd been knocked offline.

A short, high beep sparked across his comm-link. EoS.

Trying to ignore the destruction he had caused, he pushed through the crowd until he reached the service door EoS had unlocked, leading into a side garden.

EoS let him inside—and suddenly jolted with a staticky, buzzing *bleep* as it got near.

"Give me a moment," he told the bot, and closed his eyes, pressing his back against the door to keep himself upright. His knees had gone numb again, his head thick. There had to be a manual for this body *somewhere*.

He was tense, his thoughts jagged as he tried to smooth them out, calm them. The sizzling, electric feeling inside him slowly ebbed, crashing back into some unknown system he did not know how to access.

EoS bleeped again, shaking off the jolt.

"Sorry," he told it. "There is a learning curve—"

"Sir, you're not supposed to have a bot here," came a voice from the garden, causing him to scramble to his feet. An Iron-blooded man stood from a stone bench, frowning underneath his brown mustache. "Say, did you just come from the square?"

Di gave the man a once-over before deciding, "I need your clothes."

"Excuse me? You aren't supposed to be here. Guards! G—"

Di slammed his fist into the man's face. He crumpled backward into the azalea bushes.

Captain, we are inside the palace, he thought loudly, shaking his sore hand. *And I found a better suit.*

"*Good. I got disconnected from you for a moment—and the live feeds from the square went down. What happened?*" she asked, sounding somewhat annoyed.

I must have hit the wrong button.

"Funny."

EoS agreed.

As he changed into the aristocrat's clothes, he added sarcasm to his list of glitches, beginning to wonder if they were glitches at all.

ANA

"I *want* answers," she snapped at her steward as she paced her room—at least she tried to pace. The voluminous ball gown kept tangling between her legs. It didn't matter how pretty the jewels beneath the frosted lace looked—this dress was a *pain* and she *hated* it.

Nothing had gone the way she had hoped it would these last few days. She thought she'd at least have more real details about the royal family's—*my family's*, she corrected herself—death by now.

"What happened out in the square? Why did all the Messiers go offline?" she asked, wrenching the ball gown from between her legs again. "What happened to the holo-pads? The comm-links?"

"I am unsure, Your Grace," the steward replied apologetically. "There was a disturbance in the square when the Messiers were knocked offline."

She turned back to him in alarm. "A disturbance? Is everyone all right?"

"Between a Metal and a few citizens, Your Grace. There were a few injuries—"

"A man had his arm broken," the Royal Captain said irately. "It was vile."

Ana frowned. "And the Metal did that?"

The old man pressed his lips together in a grimace. "We are . . . unsure, Your Grace."

"There is little evidence to indicate otherwise," Viera added.

Ana said to the captain, "For someone not there, you're awfully quick to point a finger. I know . . . *knew* . . . a rogue Metal. He didn't do anything unprovoked. It wouldn't be *logical*."

The Royal Captain looked as if she wanted to argue but then bowed her head. "Forgive me. Of course you are correct."

The steward shifted on his feet uncomfortably. Did Iron-bloods ever bother to get to know Metals? How they functioned, why? Of course not, but she could hear her decorum instructor, Lord Machivalle, *tsk*ing at her for her lack of tact.

Ana fisted her hands. "Lord steward, when you find out what really happened, please let me know—and keep me updated on the injured man's condition," she added.

The steward, clearly relieved, nodded vigorously. "Yes, Your Grace! And Lord Rasovant is investigating the disturbance as we speak. I assure you, there's nothing to be afraid of."

She bit her tongue to stop herself from saying what she really wanted to. She was not *afraid*. She was aggravated.

"I'll have Rasovant post more Messiers around the perimeter

before tonight's gala," the Royal Captain said, and the steward nodded.

"Splendid idea! The gala tonight will be *wonderful*. Your father always loved parties," he added, and left Ana's room to go track down her handmaiden, Mellifare. She seemed to run off as often as Ana herself.

Ana massaged the bridge of her nose, stepping out onto the balcony. Ships sailed over the palace toward the moonbay, carrying with them Ironbloods bound for the gala tonight and tomorrow's coronation. The air was electric with anticipation, the palace aglow with colored lights. Machivalle hadn't showed for her lesson today, so she was just more irritated than usual. She had more questions about her parents. She had questions about everything, and only Machivalle seemed to want to take her seriously.

"Do I look naive to you?" she asked the Royal Captain after a while, rubbing her pendant.

"No, Your Grace," Viera responded, "but perhaps to assert your authority you should not wear the Valerio crest tonight."

"The what?"

The Royal Captain tapped the base of her throat.

My pendant. She frowned. "I've had this for as long as I can remember. It's not a Valerio thing."

"Ah. But it is, Your Grace. There are only four in existence, and you wearing one speaks volumes without you saying a word."

She kept rubbing the pendant, trying to smooth out the jagged bits that weren't melted, but the longer she did, the more like a snake it seemed. She tried to remember where she'd gotten it, but all she could remember was that nightmare on the *Caterina*—a fire, a man pinning it onto her chest, saying it would protect her.

"It's *not* a Valerio thing," she repeated.

"What isn't?" asked a voice in the doorway.

Cursing silently, Ana shoved her pendant into her cleavage and turned to face the Ironblood.

"If it isn't you," she greeted Robb Valerio.

"Sadly, it is," he agreed dryly, cutting a thin shape in the doorway in a neatly pressed black tux. His golden cuff links, shaped into the Valerio crest, shone in the room's low light. Her pendant looked nothing like them.

Nothing at all.

"I hope you two weren't gossiping about *me*," he went on.

"Never," the Royal Captain replied.

Robb gave the captain a coy grin. "Ah, well, one can dream. Are you ready, Your Grace?"

"Wait!" Mellifare stumbled out of the servants' entrance with a box in her hands.

The Royal Captain did not look amused. "About time, girl."

"Forgive me," Mellifare said with a bow, and held out the box. "For tonight. It was your mother's crown. The Grand Duchess thought it not fitting for you to go without one tonight."

Ana hesitated, but unlatched the box anyway. Inside, sitting like a wreath of sunshine, was a golden circlet. It was the crown Celene Valerio had worn, and the Empress before that, and before that.

She drew her hand away. "This crown belongs to whomever I marry, right? My—my *consort*. This isn't mine."

"The Armorov women have worn this crown for a thousand years—"

"But I'm not the consort. I'm not the Emperor's *partner*," she replied, and closed the box. "I am the heir."

Besides, she didn't want to wear a crown. It frightened her more than the fancy dresses or tutors. It was childish and silly not to wear it, because it was only a piece of jewelry—like rings or earrings or necklaces with Valerio crests—but it was a piece of jewelry that made people look at her differently.

And she wanted people to look at her for who she was, first.

Mellifare bowed. "Very well. May the stars keep you steady, Your Grace."

"She'll have my arm for that," Robb said dismissively, and offered it. Ana took it and let him lead her out of the East Tower, through the maze of hallways she'd come to memorize by what tapestries hung on which walls and what vases stood on which pedestals, toward the ballroom where the gala was being held. The lanterns ebbed and flowed above them. Messiers stood at every door they passed like blue-eyed sentinels, and it felt as though ever since she'd first visited the North Tower, they watched her as she passed.

"So, will there be any sword fights at this gala? Duels? Drunken orgies?" she asked jokingly. "You know how we *outlaws* prefer our entertainment."

"Of course, there will be all of the above—there will even be *dancing*."

She shivered.

"Oh, what's wrong?"

"I *hate* dancing."

"Hopefully you won't dance much," he replied, glancing over his shoulder to judge how far back the Royal Captain was, before he said in a much lower voice, "I found those records in the library today—pretend like I told you a joke."

She forced a laugh, gripping his arm tighter. "Anything?"

"My father arrived at the palace just after midnight to meet with the Emperor in the North Tower," he fake-chuckled, "but I can't find a record of their meeting."

"Is that information kept?"

"Always—especially visitations from the Emperor's family."

"So what happened between his arrival and the *Tsarina?*"

"I don't know," Robb replied. His fake smile was disconcerting, it looked so real. He was terrifyingly good at pretending. "The logs are all messed up after that. It says my father called the guards to the North Tower twenty minutes after his arrival at the palace, but before they could arrive, fire consumed the Tower. I think we know what happened from there."

She found she couldn't fake-smile or fake-laugh anymore. "So all we managed to find out was that there wasn't a record of your father meeting with the Emperor?"

She wanted to *punch* something—but then Robb said, "No, we found out why my father didn't meet with the Emperor."

"Because . . . he was calling the guards?"

His eyes glimmered. "Because he found something and *then* called the guards."

They waited outside the ballroom for the steward to announce their arrival. Sweet, light music eased in through the cracks in the door, dancing with the steady cadence of gossip.

"The fire was a cover-up," she murmured.

Robb gave her a side-eye glance. "You think?"

"Something happened before the fire that we're missing. And the fire destroyed the evidence. Metals wouldn't just burn down the Tower for nothing—"

"That's the thing," he interrupted. "The logs didn't report any new Metals in or out of the palace. There was only one stationed in the North Tower during the fire, the Armorovs' personal Metal, and it wasn't accounted for after the Rebellion."

"What was its number?"

He shook his head, "Someone had stricken it out—"

The doors yawned open into the ballroom.

"We'll finish this later," he said between his teeth, as he and Ana gave the awaiting crowd a smile.

From the entrance, a grand staircase curved down into the ballroom. A canopy of ribbons fluttered above them, shimmering silver and gold. Bright lanterns bobbed underneath them, swaying to the tune of the thirty-piece orchestra in the far corner. Ironbloods clad in rich satins and laces and silks danced together in hypnotic swirls, but they stopped as soon as the steward signaled the orchestra into silence, and every guest turned to look at her.

Ana's heart jumped into her throat as Ironblood gazes pinned her like a moth to a corkboard. They stared at her face. Her scars. She raised her head a little higher so they could get a better look, unashamed of them.

They meant she had survived something no one else had.

Robb leaned over to whisper, "At least you don't have to sneak into this party."

She nudged her elbow into his, because he was about to make her lose her composure.

The steward trumpeted as loudly as his nasal voice could carry: "Our Princess Ananke Nicholii Armorov, heir to the Iron Kingdom, and Robbert Mercer Valerio, nephew to the late Selena Demitrios Valerio Armorov."

Robb laced his fingers into hers, olive skin blending with her bronze, and squeezed tightly—and at first it felt like he was reassuring her. But his hands were shaking against hers, his grip too tight. She squeezed back reassuringly, and they descended the stairs together.

The walk across the ballroom was the longest she'd ever had to endure. It wasn't because of the heels that pinched her feet, or the way her dress *still* wrapped around her legs, but because of the eyes that watched them. Waiting for her to trip, to mess up, so that they could validate their suspicions that she was not one of them.

Well, she wasn't.

So she raised her chin and stared them in the face.

At the other end of the ballroom, the Grand Duchess sat in an ornate silver chair. Lord Rasovant stood like an ever-present vulture beside her, his beard neatly braided, the multitude of medals pinned to his chest polished. Her skin crawled when his dark eyes fell upon her.

"My Ananke!" The Grand Duchess greeted her with a smile. She was dressed in yellow and orange like the sun, with diamonds sewn into swirls. "You look radiant tonight. Welcome home."

Home.

The word was like salt on her tongue.

To the girl with space in her blood and a gun on her hip, *home* was Captain Siege, smoking the last bit of a cigar while looking over a battered star chart. Home was Di patiently braiding her hair when she didn't want to. Home was Jax in his pilot chair. Home was late-night Wicked Luck games with the crew between jobs. Poker nights in the frigid cities of Cerces, half drunk on cheap ale, listening to Wick's rousing ballads and Riggs's soft lullabies.

Home wasn't always warm, and wasn't always safe, but home was hers. And it was not this prison.

Wordlessly, Ana unraveled her fingers from Robb's. She felt the Adviser's cruel gaze follow her as she stepped forward, fanned out her dress, and bowed deeply as Lord Machivalle had taught her.

"Thank you, Your Grace," she said, and tried to forget that once upon a time she'd sat in a rusty, cramped cockpit, watching as the stars danced around the *Dossier*'s black solar sails, and she had been happy there.

Happy and at *home.*

But home no longer existed.

IV

IRON WILL

ROBB

Once Ana took her place at the Grand Duchess's side, the steward trumpeted, "Introducing Lady Cynthia Malachite Valerio, married to the late Lord Mercer Valerio, escorted by her eldest, Erik Malachite Valerio."

Their names were like cold fingers racing up Robb's spine. *Please don't let Jax be with them,* he prayed as he slowly turned toward the staircase. *Please.*

Erik, charming and poised as ever, escorted their mother down the stairs and across the ballroom to the Grand Duchess, looking like a pair in matching black with silver accents. His mother's dress trailed behind like a long shadow, as though she was taller than she appeared. He must have missed the silver-and-black memo.

At least, to Robb's relief, the Solani was nowhere to be seen.

Erik and his mother bowed to Ana and the Grand Duchess. "Your Graces."

The look Ana gave them was so sharp, it could cut steel.

"Lady Valerio, Lord Valerio," the Grand Duchess greeted. "What an honor that you could join us."

"Of course, Your Grace. We only wish to serve the kingdom as best we can in *whatever* capacity we can."

"But in what capacity can I now serve you? We have given up *much*, Your Grace," Erik said, earning a sharp look from his mother.

Robb's eyebrow twitched. It wasn't like Erik to speak out and break protocol.

The Grand Duchess smiled. "Of course, I should address that lest I forget. Lord Valerio has done a great service to my family."

Lady Valerio returned her smile. "Erik will forever be a stalwart fixture in—"

"I meant the younger Valerio."

The smile dropped from his mother's face.

Robb cursed, mentally kicking himself. *Rotten, no-good, Goddess-sodding luck—*

The Grand Duchess turned her stone-cut green eyes to him, and he felt heat rising in his cheeks. "As promised, I would like to reward you for reuniting my family. Anything I can grant shall be yours, I promise on iron and stars."

Anything? What a far cry that was from just a few days ago, when the Grand Duchess had asked what he could possibly want for turning in a traitor.

Then, he had wanted to save Ana's life. But now . . .

He could ask for anything. Absolutely *anything*. Something to advance the Valerio name—a royal title for Erik, a legacy for his mother. He could ask for anything his heart wanted. Admission back into the Academy. A proper funeral for his father.

Pardons for his friends on the *Dossier*.

Friends.

A few days ago he would've scoffed at the idea, because Robb Valerio didn't have *friends*. Or if he did, he had a use for them. But Ana was unlike anyone he'd ever met. She was kind, but kind in a way most people called *brash*. She was reckless, and she followed her heart like it was a guiding star. She was insufferable, and yet she had suffered so much and it had never defined her.

Ana was different from anyone else in the entire cosmos, and a part of him wanted to be different, too.

Maybe he was already a little different, a little better than before. Whether she'd inspired it, or someone else, he couldn't explain. But he *was* different. Ever since Astoria—no, ever since the shrine.

Love was a double-edged sword. It could protect you from the worst of the kingdom, but then it could cut so deep the loss ached years later.

His mother's love had slowly been whittled down against his bone like a dull knife, and he'd thought that was the only kind of love there was. But then came Ana and the *Dossier*, using their blades to deflect instead of damage, and he wanted to do the same.

His mother looked at him expectantly. He was a Valerio, after all. He was loyal to his family, and only his family.

But what *was* a family? Did it have to be blood relatives? Or could it be people you barely knew?

And, suddenly, he knew exactly what to ask for.

"There is a prisoner," he said, "who was captured outside the Iron Shrine on Nevaeh. He's innocent, and I would like him released."

The Grand Duchess's eyebrows quirked up. "A prisoner?"

"Mokuba Jyen." The moment he said the info broker's name, Ana clutched at the folds of her dress.

"That's the Ilidian we caught, Your Grace," Lord Rasovant said to the Grand Duchess. "He was trying to sell valuable information that would put the kingdom at risk. I'm sorry, but it is not possible—"

"I think it is," Ana interrupted, and the Adviser's face pinched.

A murmur swept through the ballroom.

Ana leaned forward in her chair, one leg crossing the other, the sides of her lips tugging up. And for a moment—a second— she looked like Siege. "Iron Law states that any citizen who cannot be proven guilty of a crime is innocent. Can you prove that the info broker held valuable information, Lord Rasovant?"

The old man prickled. "Of course I can!"

"Do you have the information? Can you show us?"

His mouth worked open and closed for a moment, struggling with what to say.

Robb tried to keep the smirk off his face. *Never underestimate a criminal.*

Ana knew that Rasovant would never divulge that Mokuba's information was coordinates to his lost fleetship, because it would only lead people to ask why it was there, who stole it—*why.*

Too bad it was a shipwreck on Palavar now.

The Iron Adviser set his mouth, realizing that he couldn't win, and gave in. "Forgive me, I misspoke." Then he turned to Robb, his eyes darker and sharper than they'd been a moment before. "Lord Valerio. I will see to it that he is released."

Ana flashed Robb a smile, and he nodded. At least one of them had to wear a poker face, and it would never be her.

The Grand Duchess looked amused. "Will that be all, Lord Valerio?"

"Yes, thank you, Your Grace." With a bow, he excused himself from the ballroom. The sooner he was away from his mother, the less likely it was he would have to answer for what he'd just done.

He needed time to think up a pretty lie before that happened.

Anything—he could have asked for *anything*.

He wished he could have asked for Jax.

If his mother was here, then Jax had to be holed up somewhere in her rooms, and if he was, this was probably the only chance Robb would have of getting him out of here.

A swell of violins hummed over the crowd, and the dance resumed.

A hand grabbed his coat sleeve.

He froze, for a second thinking it was his brother, until Ana said, "Wait—I want to thank you."

"Don't. It's what I had to do."

"You didn't *have* to do anything," she replied, and undid the pendant from around her neck. She held it out to him. His father's crest. "Here. I . . . I think it's yours."

"Ana . . ."

"In fact, I'm sure it is, so *take it*. I don't remember how I got it, but I think your father saved me—from the fire. Or whatever really happened in the tower. And I think he'd want you to have it."

His throat constricted as he looked at his father's brooch. How many years had he wanted to hold it, dreamed of finding it? And here it was, so close he could take it. But . . .

"No," he said, and closed her fingers over the pendant again, "my father gave it to you. There are only four in the kingdom. As traditions go, Valerios pass them down to whoever is important to us, and you're half Valerio, after all. He gave it to you, so I want you to keep it."

Her brow furrowed. "But Robb—"

"Please."

She kissed his cheek. "Thank you," she said, before someone called her name and she turned toward the voice.

He took the moment to slip away, out of a side door guarded by a statue-still Messier, and away from the heady perfumes and romantic waltzes. The hallways were almost deserted, employees of the crown rushing from one room to the next so that the gala went perfectly. No one noticed him leave, and no one stopped him to ask where he was going—the East Tower, where he hoped Jax was being kept.

And suddenly he was so very tired of all these games. Of murder and deceit and extravagant parties. What would life have been like, he wondered, if he had been a normal boy on Eros? With a normal boyfriend and a loving family?

He had never wondered that before—who he would be if he was not a Valerio.

It might've been nice—

A shadow down the hallway caught his eye. Red eyes. A Metal body.

He blinked, and it was gone.

Breathe. He needed to breathe. He was seeing things.

First, he needed to get that voxcollar off Jax's neck before his mother or Erik did something truly horrible—and after what Robb had done at the gala, he needed to do it soon.

ANA

"Your Grace!" a young man in a navy ascot called as she latched the pendant back around her neck. It felt like a familiar weight, and secretly, she was glad that Robb had told her to keep it. It felt like safety.

The young man in question bowed. His hair was long and braided with threads of gold, making her deeply aware of her own shaved head. He had familiar arrowhead-shaped markings under his eyes. "Would you care to dance, Your Grace?"

She narrowed her eyes. "And you are . . . ?"

"Vermion Carnelian—"

"Ah." She glanced back to Robb, but he was gone.

"First in line to the Carnelian succession—"

"Viera's brother, yeah?"

He looked stricken by the question. "I—we don't—she's a *guard*, Your Grace. I'm first in line—"

"Good for you," she replied, patting him on the shoulder, and made her way over to a banquet table on the other end of the ballroom. A few Ironbloods mingled around the food, tasting the fruits and soft pastries. She ate a beignet. The rich pastry melted in her mouth and she sighed. She missed Talle. The way she hummed love ballads as she cooked. Ana stuffed another into her mouth to keep the sadness at bay.

There were so many people, it reminded her of the packed markets on Nevaeh, brushing elbow to elbow. Except everyone *here* looked like dainty pastries and wore dresses with crinoline that went on for *days*.

A group of girls twittered with laughter, cutting their eyes over to her. She looked down the length of herself—and realized the pastry had sprinkled powdered sugar down her front. Mortified, she quickly turned away, brushing off the sugar, and hurried to the other end of the table to get away from the girls. She could gut them from stomach to spleen right there, didn't they know?

But that is not proper comportment for an Empress, she thought, mocking Machivalle's tutoring.

The gala was marvelous, framed by statues of the Goddess, purple tapestries fluttering against the marble walls. They told of all the stories in the *Cantos*. The kingdom of shadows and the girl of light. The vanquishing of the Darkness. The marriage to the sun.

There were even more gossiping Ironbloods at the other end of the table, sadly. All whispering behind their hands, their eyes raking across her scars.

This party was definitely going down as one of the *worst* ever.

A young woman stepped up beside her and speared a piece

of pineapple with an expert flourish. She twirled it around in her fingers. "Good evening, Your Grace."

"Good evening," Ana replied nervously, eyeing the freckled girl.

"Lord Machivalle told me you'd probably need some company here," said the Ironblood, pushing a curl of strawberry hair behind her ear. Ana didn't need to see her insignia to know she was a Wysteria. The *Dossier* had raided one of their vineyards once.

"You know Machivalle?"

"He tutors me as well. He sends his regrets for not coming to your lessons today."

"Is he sick?"

"Oh, no," she replied, watching the pineapple piece she twirled on its toothpick.

"Then Rasovant dismissed him," Ana guessed, and when the young woman pursed her lips, she knew she'd guessed right. "Because of *course* he did."

"Machivalle told me to give you this." She took a small folded piece of paper out of her dress pocket and slipped it into Ana's hand. "He said it was 'an answer to your question'—he's vague like that sometimes."

But Ana knew exactly what question it was an answer to, and her heart quickened. She quickly pocketed it. "Thank you."

"My pleasure." Lady Wysteria smiled and turned a thoughtful gaze to the ballroom center. "It's seems quite wrong that your guests are having more fun than you, Your Grace."

Ana waved her hand dismissively at the waltzing Ironbloods.

"I don't dance—and you can call me Ana."

"Wynn, then, and come on." She took Ana by the hand—definitely not how you handled royalty—and pulled her closer to the dancing crowd. "You're an Armorov! Armorovs were *born* to dance."

Ana stumbled after her. "Well, maybe *I* was born to fight."

"You'll be surprised how much they're alike."

They stopped near the edge of the ballroom, where beautiful couples whirled around in steps Ana had no interest in learning, but she was enraptured all the same.

As though she knew the rhythm, the motion, like some far-off melody.

"I'll be the lead and you follow," said Wynn, bringing Ana's arms up into position. "It's as easy as a breeze. Now . . . left-foot-two. Right-foot-two . . ." Wynn slowly led her out onto the dance floor.

Left foot, right foot, swirling in and swirling out. Their dresses brushed together, the sound of soft sighs.

It was a lie that she didn't dance.

She danced often on the *Dossier,* to songs for cramped galleys and bold ales, bright and happy—and home. Songs Wick loved to play on the fiddle while Riggs sang along. She always dreamed of grabbing Di by the arm and pulling him to dance beside the captain and Talle. Spinning in his Metal arms, loving how he was not graceful, and not talented, but dancing with her all the same.

The dream struck her. Laughter, Di, his moonlit eyes, how it felt to smile—things she didn't want to think about. Things that made her heart ache. It was something she would never get to do now.

She'd lost her chance somewhere on the far side of Palavar.

In a blink, her feet caught onto some distant memory, tugging like guiding string in the dark, and she was spinning with Wynn across the ballroom, hands set at ten and two, elbows pointed, backs straight, sweeping across the marble floor like an old routine she'd never quite forgotten the steps to.

"Your fighting techniques are quite superb," Wynn laughed, spinning Ana again, and the orchestra changed key.

The song grew sharp, and everyone turned from their partners, including Wynn, and twirled to someone new. Ana watched her go before someone else caught her, too, folding his fingers between hers with the certainty of matching puzzle pieces.

She glanced back at Wynn, who had fallen into the arms of that golden-haired man from earlier—Vermion Carnelian. Couples spun, shifting, and Wynn was gone.

"Good evening, Your Grace," her new partner purred in a soft, sweet baritone.

She glanced up at him. Redheaded and dark-eyed, a strong jaw, and broad shoulders that filled a slightly-too-small lavender evening coat. He smiled at her—lopsided, imperfect. He looked familiar, but she couldn't place from where.

"Good evening," she replied hesitantly.

The music grew faster, sweeter, their feet sliding to the song of the violin, the sweep of the cello. Above them, the lanterns swirled, following them across the ballroom, as if they were tethered to invisible strings.

Her nearness to this stranger made her skin buzz—like electricity. So close, the individual strands of his hair looked woven with sunlight, his skin pale—but not like Jax's, more like a boy who had never seen the sun. His hands were cold, but when he looked at her, it was like finally seeing sunshine after a long night, like dawn breaking over the edge of a planet, the sharp rays of gold slicing high into the ever-night of the universe.

It made her miss sailing—miss the *Dossier*, and her captain, and her crew. It made her miss the recycled, musty smell of the ship, and Jax's witty retorts, and Di.

Oh, she missed Di with more love than her heart could hold.

And she wanted her heart to stop aching for at least a moment.

A second.

A breath.

He leaned in, closing the small gap, as the orchestra changed its tune again, ordering couples to pair with someone new, but neither of them did.

"Do I know you?" she asked. "Have we met? I—I know you."

"And I know you," he replied, and then winced, as if hearing something she couldn't, and his face hardened. He went on in a quieter voice, "Ana, you are in danger. I will explain everything, but we need to leave—"

The electric tingle across her skin turned into a cold, icy crawl. "How do you know I'm in danger? Who are you?"

"Please trust me, Ana—"

She realized why he looked familiar. The Metal Jax took

from the *Tsarina*. Red hair. Dark eyes. Pale skin. This was *that* Metal.

He must have seen the horror on her face, because he said, "Ana, I can explain—"

She twisted her hand out of his. Above them, the lanterns burst apart, drifting out of their cyclone.

"You're *Rasovant's* Metal," she hissed.

"No, wait—"

She spun away from the redheaded boy to her next partner. Anyone—it didn't matter who. *How did he get off the* Dossier? she thought. *How is he here?*

She clasped her new partner's hand.

Black suit, silver cummerbund, cold knuckle rings—

"Seems I'm in luck tonight, cousin," said Erik Valerio, and she looked up into eyes as cold and sharp as an Erosian sky. "Was that other boy frightening you? You seemed quite smitten by him for a while. Did he step on your toes?"

She tried to pull away, but he gripped her hand tighter. "I'm done dancing—"

"Just one more, Your Grace. I want to get to know my long-lost cousin."

She glanced back to the redheaded boy, but he was no longer in the waltz.

"I'm sorry, am I not entertaining enough?" Erik Valerio added bitterly.

She snapped her attention back to him. "I'm sorry, are you *talking*?"

His smile turned sharp. "You should listen." He squeezed

her hands, the rings pinching into her skin.

She gritted her teeth against the pain. "Let me go."

"You can wear all the pretty dresses you want, and shave your head, and wear a crown, but it doesn't change what you are. An orphan girl no one wants. Even your *pirate* friends didn't want you. They're probably glad to be rid of you."

"You don't know anything," she ground out.

"Or are you scared that I'm right? You destroy everything you touch, Your Grace." His breath was against her ear now as they danced intimately closer, his rings grinding her knuckles together. "You should have died with the rest of them."

"Shut up." She tried to pull away. He held on tightly. They spun faster to the music, the rest of the ballroom a blur.

"Then maybe your *Metal*, what was his name? *Di?* Maybe he would still be alive."

"I said *shut up!*" she snapped, and dug her nails into the backs of his hands.

He gave a cry and let go. "What's wrong, Your Grace?" he asked, as if *she* was the problem—until she noticed the silence.

The orchestra had stopped its waltz, and the Ironbloods all turned to her.

"Ananke?" The Grand Duchess stood from her throne, looking worried. "Are you all right?"

She could feel the way they looked at her, and her scars burned from it. She tried to speak, but no words came out.

You should have died, Erik Valerio's voice whispered in her head. She couldn't get rid of it. It resounded like a phantom pain. *Maybe he would still be alive.*

"Ananke?" the Grand Duchess asked again.

That isn't my name, she wanted to scream, but her chest was tightening, and she couldn't get a deep enough breath. Why was everyone *looking* at her? Hadn't they seen scars before? An outlaw? An orphan?

She curled her hands into fists, letting her fingernails dig into her palms, grounding herself in the pain—

Until she caught sight of the redheaded young man again— that *Metal*—hidden in the crowd. He watched her, his face the only one not judging, not appalled. But worried, as if *he* had failed in some monumental way. Not she, not she.

And over his shoulder, lens tightening, hovered—

EoS?

No, it was a bot that looked like EoS. There were thousands. It wasn't EoS. EoS was with the *Dossier*, and she would never see it again.

But what if—what if—

The crowd shifted, and the redheaded young man was gone.

You should have died, Erik Valerio's voice repeated in her head.

"Your Grace?" Erik asked, making his voice sound worried. He put a hand on her shoulder "Do you need to sit?"

She slapped him away. "Next time you touch me, I *will* break your fingers."

And Erik grinned.

Drawing her dress up, she excused herself from the ball-room as a rush of disbelieving murmurs followed in her wake.

Uncouth, wild, they said.

The Royal Captain fell into her shadow so quietly, she almost didn't realize. Ana followed the lanterns back to her room in the South Tower.

"Your Grace," Viera said, for the first time her even tone spiked with worry, "are you all right? Did something happen with Lord Valerio?"

Ana fled into her room and slammed the door before her guard could come inside and finally there was silence. She breathed in the stillness, rubbing her knuckles where Erik Valerio had ground them together, blinking to keep the tears in her eyes.

Erik Valerio was wrong. She knew in her heart he was wrong, but still his words hounded her. *He's wrong*, she repeated as she sank to the ground. Her gown crinkled—

Machivalle's note!

The answer he couldn't tell her.

She took it out of her dress pocket, and with her fingers still shaking, she unfolded the piece of paper.

His name, the note read, *was D09.*

DI

"Di, calm down." Siege's voice pierced through the fury burning in his wires. He stalked through the hallway, hands bunched into fists. Calm down? How *could* he?

The way that Ironblood—Erik Valerio—looked at her like he wanted to *break* her—he could not stand the thoughts in his head. All the ways he wanted to kill that reeking sack of human flesh—all the ways he *could*—

"Di," the captain repeated.

I am trying, he replied, but he could not seem to zero out his anger.

Nothing in this illogical body would *listen.* He was angry, but he was also confused. When they had danced, all he wanted to do was keep dancing. And kiss her. He wanted to kiss her so badly—it must have been a glitch.

She was so much *more* than he remembered, and he was exponentially less.

He needed to find another way to explain who he was. She thought he was here to kill her. She had called him *Rasovant's*

Metal—he wanted to take a shower to scrub the filth of those words away.

But anger would make him careless. That, at least, helped the rational part of him calm the rest.

"Could you go find the exit code for the moonbay?" he asked EoS once he'd calmed down enough to think clearly. "You should be able to access it from the security station in the East Tower, at the end," he added, recalling the map of the palace.

EoS bleeped and whirled away.

If he kept down this hallway, it should lead straight to the South Tower, where Ana's rooms were located.

As he passed another corridor, he heard a sharp shriek—like nails on a chalkboard.

He winced, slowing to a stop.

It was the same noise as on the *Tsarina*.

Tilting his head to listen, he turned toward the signal. Across the hall. He followed it. Yes, he was sure it was the same signal—the same frequency. It came from an inconspicuous door tucked into the corner of the hallway.

He touched the keypad, feeling for the microchip inside.

With a twist of his wrist, he visualized the data inside it and put it into the correct order. The keypad clicked green.

The door slid open and stepped inside, locking it again with a flick of his hand.

The sound was stronger now, crackling like a mistuned radio frequency.

The room looked like a study of some sort.

It was small and cluttered, with inlaid bookshelves holding

massive tomes. Books written in Erosian, the Ilidian tongue, Cercian—even Solani, he realized as he ran his fingers over the strange letters on the spines.

Separating the books sat old globes.

He spun Eros, and somehow he already knew it creaked.

This was the Iron Adviser's study—Lord Rasovant's. He was not sure how he knew, but he was certain of it. Perhaps, when he was a Metal at the palace, he had been one of the Iron Adviser's assistants. Perhaps he had helped the old man in the lab—*the lab*. Down the North Tower, at the end—

He quickly stopped the globe.

A Royal Guard's uniform hung from a peg on the wall, not worn in years. Royal badges and medals adorned the breast pockets of someone quite accomplished. The Adviser had never been in the Royal Guard.

A node of information ignited in the back of his head, culling data records from the newsfeeds. While Rasovant had not been in the Royal Guard, his son *had*. It was around the same time Emperor Nicholii II served. Why had Rasovant kept his son's uniform after twenty years?

A cold, strange feeling grew in his chest, but he rubbed it away.

Captain? he ventured through the comm-link. No response— except that grating, popping sound. Curious, Di moved around the desk to the sleeping holo-screen.

The signal became stronger, pulsing, jarring.

"Metalhead, your signal's dropping. Hello? —lo?"

The screen flickered, and words typed out across the blank

screen. They chilled him to his metal bones.

YOU SHOULD HAVE LET HER BURN.

He stumbled away from the desk, knocking over the Eros globe. It smashed on the floor.

"Metalhead? Hello? Sunshine, turn me up louder," Siege's voice pierced through the signal's shriek. *"Di?"*

The sound in his head turned scraping, red, glaring—pain spiked through his programs. There was no doubt now—he knew this terrible sound like a dead man knew his murderer.

It is here, he told the captain, hurrying to the door. *The program that infected the ship.*

"Are you sure?"

Impossibly—

Through the noise in his head, his audio sensors alerted him to the sound of distant footsteps. Thirty, no, thirty-five feet away. Walking quickly. There were no other rooms on this end of the hallway. Whoever it was, was heading here.

"I'm trapped," he said aloud.

The realization stabbed him like sharp needles in the back of his neck. If they caught him, they would arrest him, and there was an 83.47 percent chance that they would find out he was not quite human.

The HIVE might be a mercy after what they would do to him.

He tried to think of a plan, but the signal scraped across his thoughts like claws. *Focus,* he thought, but he could not—this was not like him.

He should not be distracted by a *signal.*

"I cannot think," he told the captain. "I cannot—"

"*Di, calm down,*" Siege said. "*Use that metal head of yours. I know you can. You're the smartest boy I know.*"

"I do not have many options—"

"*THINK.*"

He swallowed fearfully. *Think.* Hiding in the study was a poor choice—there was nowhere to hide. The bookshelves were impenetrable. But if he left now, he would be caught. He did not know—how was he supposed to—

He searched the room for something—*anything*—that could help.

Think.

What if . . .

His eyes strayed back to the Royal Guard uniform hanging from the peg.

The footsteps were fifteen feet away and closing. This had a 32 percent chance of success, but what other option did he have? This was Ana-level reckless.

Fitting, really.

He shrugged out of his jacket and trousers and laced up the boots, shoving his stolen clothes under the desk.

His processors recalculated his chances of success again.

Twenty-three percent.

Fifteen.

That *definitely* was not helping.

He switched off the calculations. He did not have time to listen to them.

The uniform smelled strange—musty. And, so subtly—sage.

The memory of standing in front of a long mirror, pinning badges onto his chest, straightening his collar. The fit of it snug around his shoulders, the itchiness of the sleeves. Lord Rasovant clapping him on the shoulder. Murmured words. Proud.

A wave of dizziness swarmed over him, and he steadied himself against a shelf. That was not a Metal memory—not his. *Was it?*

Pushing the memory down, he retied his hair and pushed it up into his hat, the screeching so loud he had to concentrate on walking.

He pressed his hand against the door and reached his consciousness into the keypad's microchip again, forcing it to malfunction. The microchip gave a small *pop*, and his fingers twitched with the static. The door opened, and he hurried out.

It snapped closed again as—

Lord Rasovant turned the corner, coattails fluttering, his attention on the holo-pad in his hand.

Di quickly angled his face away as he passed Rasovant, trying to be as unobtrusive as possible. The Adviser did not even look up.

"There has been a breach in security," the Adviser told someone through a comm-link on his holo-pad. "*Yes,* lock the perimeter. Lord Tvani was found in the east garden, unconscious. I don't care *how* you find the intruder, just find . . ." His voice faded as he closed himself into his study.

Captain, I escaped, but I think I have been found out.

"Goddess's spark," she cursed. *"We'll figure something else out. I have contacts I can—"*

No. If the malware is here, then I am not leaving without Ana, Di replied sternly.

He broke out into a jog toward the South Tower. The uniform boots made almost soundless clips on the marble tile. He couldn't escape the study quickly enough, but the scent of sage followed him like a haunting melody.

ROBB

Robb hurried toward his mother's chambers, feigning an upset stomach to not alarm the Messiers standing guard. Then again, he could probably punch one and they wouldn't move. He hadn't seen a single one so much as twitch.

Where is *the HIVE?* he wondered absently. *Does it have a central stationary base? What does it look l—*

A Royal Guard rounded the corner, and they slammed into each other. Robb stumbled back.

"Watch where you're—"

The guard looked at him for a moment, dumbfounded.

Robb's eyebrows furrowed. "Wait, don't I know—"

Suddenly, the guard shoved him against the wall, pressing a forearm against his neck. Robb squeaked in protest. This was not how he'd imagined tonight going at all.

"You brought her here, you put her in danger—after all she did for you on the *Dossier*," the guard hissed, dark eyes flickering white.

Realization hit Robb like a punch in the stomach. Goddess's

spark. "D09," he wheezed, tugging at the humanoid Metal's arm to try and get in a breath. "You're mad—"

"Mad? Robb, I am *furious.*"

"Let me"—gasp—"explain!"

"With that silver tongue of yours?"

The Metal was literally squeezing the breath out of him. Robb tapped on his arm to try and get him to let go. His ears rang with the dizzying pressure building in his skull. "I brought you . . . back!"

D09's face pinched, and he let go.

Robb dropped to his knees, coughing. "*Goddess* you're strong."

"You? *You* put me in this body?" the not-Metal asked. Viewing it on a gurney was one thing, but to actually see the body moving was another. He looked—weirdly, strangely—human. And stood taller than Robb, too.

He rubbed his neck. "I didn't think it *worked.* . . . Kind of wished it didn't now—"

"Why did you do this to me?"

Robb squinted up at the human Metal . . . *person.* "I thought you'd be thankful? Say, 'Hey, Robb, thanks for saving my life! I appreciate it.'"

"*Thankful?*" the Metal scoffed. "I am a great many things at the moment—"

"I realized."

"—but *thankful* is not one of them."

Robb turned his eyes to the ceiling and took a deep, deep breath. "So you'd rather be dead?"

"Metals do not die."

"Well, the way everyone mourned you, you'd think differently."

The Metal opened his mouth to respond but then closed it again, frustrated. He took off his uniform cap and ran a hand through his hair, as if he was nervous.

Robb frowned, sort of hating that D09 had better hair than him. And where had he gotten a Royal Guard uniform, anyway?

"Robb," D09 finally said, choosing his words carefully, "humor me for a minute, will you? You uploaded me into a new body without my knowledge. I had no instructions, no tutorials, *nothing*. I have had to learn it all. Can you *imagine* that?"

Robb blinked. "Every day."

D09 gave him a withering look. "You mock me."

"As much as I can," he agreed, absently stretching up his hand, and the Metal pulled him to his feet. "I didn't have much time to think before I uploaded you, okay? I knew my mother was coming, and I didn't see any other choice. I thought—I don't know what I thought. I just did it. I'm sorry. I feel like I've been saying that a lot recently."

"That is usually what happens when you mess up," replied the redhead. "Now excuse me—"

Robb caught him by the forearm. "Wait. When my father left the palace, he took the *Tsarina* for a reason. He helped you save Ana, right? Do you know who set the fire? *What* set the fire?"

"I cannot remember."

"*Think*, D09—"

"Di," he absently corrected, shrugging off Robb's hand, "and I cannot remember."

"Try a little harder!"

A muscle in the Metal's jaw fluttered. Oh, good Goddess, this was too human for him. "I said I cannot—"

A floating metal box screeched around a corner, pursued by a Messier.

Robb's jaw went slack. "Is that . . . ?"

"Yes," Di deadpanned.

EOS beeped and slammed into Di's chest, cowering into his arms. Di wrapped his arms around the bot protectively, as if it was his pet.

The Messier came to a stop in front of them. It lowered its blazing blue gaze to the bot. "Thank you. Will you please hand over—"

Di punched his free hand into the Messier's chest, twisted, and pulled back. Its memory core came out with a sigh of wires and optics. He crushed it in his grip, and the Messier's eyes dulled. It slumped to the floor.

"*Goddess.*" Robb gave the Metal an incredulous look. "Remind me not to piss you off."

Di shook his free hand as if the impact had actually hurt. "It was chasing my can opener."

The small bot bleeped in agreement and flew out of Di's arm, swirling around him.

Di cocked his head. "Other Messiers are coming. Ten, perhaps twelve." He narrowed a glare at the bot. "*You* got into trouble. I told you to find the exit code for the moonbay, not trouble."

It bleeped sadly in reply.

Robb hoped he had heard right. "Moonbay codes? So you have a way out?"

"Of course. Riggs parked a skysailer at the docks. Why?"

"Because Jax is here in the palace, and I need to get him out before my mother does something terrible. I didn't have a way to do that until you. You're here for Ana, right?"

Di looked annoyed. "No, I am here to tour the palace."

"Sarcasm, not the time."

"Sorry, the literary device is still new to me. I need to get Ana out of here—tonight. The malware is here. I can hear it—I just saw it."

"You *what?*"

"It was terrifying," he said, and turned his attention down the long hallway. Robb could hear the Messiers coming now, their boots clomping on the marble floor in striking precision. He stepped over the smashed Messier and followed Di down the hallway. The bot swirled around them, as if it was *happy*.

Di glanced over to him. "I will meet you at the docks in three hours and twenty-seven minutes, unless something goes wrong."

"Why three hours and twenty-seven minutes?"

"Because that is when the moonbay resets its docking permissions," he replied as they came to an intersecting hallway. They stopped. Di was to go one way to Ana's room, and he the other.

"How do you know that?" Robb asked.

"The bot told me."

". . . *Right*. Three hours and twenty-seven minutes, and if you're not there?"

"Leave without me."

He didn't like the idea, but he nodded anyway. Di could find his own way out—he'd found his own way *in*, after all.

Robb started for his mother's room—where he hoped Jax was being kept—when he heard his name called. He looked over his shoulder.

The redhead smiled, and it was such a human moment, Robb faltered. "Thank you, Robb."

"For what?"

"Saving me."

Then Ana's Metal turned the corner and was gone.

JAX

These four walls were going to drive him mad.

He tried another combination on the keypad, but it blinked red again. He kicked the door—and the Valerio guard on the other side kicked back. Ana could be dying right now for all he knew. By Erik's knuckle-ringed hand.

And here *he* was, locked up in Lady Valerio's private chambers like a pet! Oh, if his father was alive, he would've had a field day with Jax's predicament now.

This is what happens when you try to defy your stars, he would say.

The doorknob rattled, and he quickly retreated, raising his hands to fight.

But it was the lady herself, followed by three of her private guards. "I hear you've been trying to escape," she chided, taking a seat on the floral fainting couch. "Is my hospitality not good enough for you?"

One of the Valerio guards waved a small remote beside Jax's collar, and the incessant humming quieted.

Jax rubbed his throat above the collar. "I don't like being locked places," he replied, his voice brittle and hoarse. It hurt to talk.

"I doubt many do," she replied, and dismissed the guards. They left him alone in the room with this madwoman.

Jax shifted his weight from one foot to the other, growing anxious because there was only one reason why she'd come back from the gala.

"So, you want me to read your stars?" Jax asked, trying to keep his voice level.

The woman surveyed Jax. "I do not believe in magic, or superstitions, or some 'Great Dark.' I believe in what I can see. But my sons mean a great deal to me, and I aim to give them the best life I can. So, yes. Use whatever unholy power you have to read my future. To read my son's legacy."

Singular or plural? It was hard to tell.

He hesitated, clenching his fists, feeling the way his leather gloves tightened around his knuckles.

"That was our agreement, C'zar Taizu," Lady Valerio reminded him.

"It was half of our agreement," he said. "My half."

The woman looked tired. "Of course. And that's truly what you ask? That my son doesn't come to harm? Do you think me a fool?"

"I think I want you to keep your end of the bargain."

"Fine. I promise I will not let anyone harm Robbert—"

"No, the unbreakable way."

Her lips pursed. "I promise on iron and stars, Solani."

An unbreakable oath. He felt the pull of it, the sway of the stars at the promise, her words knotting together.

He took a deep breath and nodded. "All right."

Kneeling in front of her, he peeled off his gloves and folded them neatly in front of him. His hands were pale in the dim light of the room. They were normal hands, long fingers and short nails. There was nothing special about them, but there didn't need to be. It didn't have to be his hands—a brush of an elbow, a bump of knees, a *kiss*—they all worked the same. But in his hands he could control his gift, feeling his way through the stars.

He asked her to lean forward.

She did, and closed her eyes.

He hadn't *purposely* used his gift in ten years—Robb's small tryst aside—not since he'd left his home on Iliad. Not since his father had forced him to read his stars—for the future of the Solani, his father had said. That same night, he kissed his mother good-bye because he refused to be used as a weapon. He would not flare and burn out.

But as his father said, one could not defy one's stars.

He reached out and pressed his thumbs against the middle of Lady Valerio's forehead. The contact sent a jolt through him. Searing. He concentrated as his father had taught him, focusing on the star-stuff inside this horrid Ironblood—the same star-stuff inside every person—his senses already spiraling up to the pinions of lights above them, past and futures stretching far, far, farther than eternity. He was one of the last Solani who could read them.

The very last, perhaps.

He sensed the glow, the warmth, of Lady Valerio's stars.

And then he pressed the rest of his fingers against the Iron-blood's temples and drank in the sky. Whispers, mutterings, images so sharp they felt visceral—

A coronation, a thousand candles lighting the shrine, panic, a grating and horrid noise, a bloody crown, the muzzle of a pistol—

He gasped, wrenching his hands away from her.

Lady Valerio opened her eyes. She studied him.

"I am going to die," she inferred calmly.

"Yes," he gasped, shaking. He had seen before *how* someone was going to die, but he'd never seen it so close. So thoroughly. The emotions leaked into his head, filling him to the brink. "Soon."

"Very well," she said, but there was a flicker, finally, in her cold eyes. She touched the remote to his collar again, a warm buzz filling his ears, and left the room.

Jax sank to his knees and pressed the palms of his bare hands against his eyes, the sting of tears fresh and scathing. Because of the promise they'd made. Because it was unbreakable.

A promise on iron and stars.

ANA

D09—*her* Di.

Robb said there was only one Metal stationed there that evening—the one her parents trusted. It was D09, and D09 had saved her, so he couldn't have been the one to start the fire. And if he was the only Metal in the tower that night, then what Metals were Rasovant talking about when he said they set fire to the tower? And why had Robb's father called the guards *before* the fire broke out?

Now she had more compelling proof than ever. *Something had happened. Something that someone wanted to keep quiet—*

"Ana . . ."

A chill curled down her spine. She quickly pocketed the note from Machivalle. "Hello?"

But no one answered.

Taking off her heels, she got to her feet, cocking her head to listen for the voice again. It was faint—and sounded like her *name.* Coming from the wall.

No, not the wall—the servants' entrance.

She should go get Viera, but had she actually heard anything? It was so faint—what if it had been in her head?

Her fingers ran along the sides of the hidden door, feeling for the seams. She shoved against it, but it didn't budge. She tried again—harder.

The wall swung open into a dark corridor.

"Anyone in here?" She nervously rubbed her pendant as she reached out her hand to skim the dusty wall, and felt her way through the darkness, so thick her eyes began to float with spots of color.

A soft, hushed breeze tickled her ear.

"Ana . . ."

She spun around—

"Who's there?" she asked. "Where are you?"

The dark responded with the sound of pattering feet—running. Echoing down the long corridor, away from her.

Her hand sank to her hip before she realized she didn't have her pistol. She'd never missed it more.

Another voice whispered, sounding a thousand miles away.

"Hurry up!"

She knew that voice, didn't she? From somewhere. If only she could *remember*.

"Follow us, Ana!" called a third voice.

"Wait," she whispered. She could almost taste the memory on her tongue. A little girl running through secret corridors, bare feet scurrying across the floor. "Wait a second—please!"

She stumbled after the voices, her hands pressed against the walls, rushing across the years of dust and cobwebs.

"What are you waiting for, Ana?" one of the boys said. The eldest. *"Hurry up!"*

Rhys—

He let her taste the sweets from the kitchen. The scent of cinnamon. Warm brown eyes, a melting smile. He used to kiss her bruises when her middle brother, *Wylan*—a cocky smile and a mess of black curls—knocked her down when they pretended to be outlaws. All the horseplaying would scare her youngest brother—*Tobias*. Valerio blue eyes and a small smile and a love of violins and sweet candies and stories.

Rhys. Wylan. Tobias.

She *remembered*.

A sob caught in her throat. They had died. They had not escaped. They had never escaped—they were still here. Still in the ashes and soot and dust of the palace.

And she had forgotten them.

She stumbled to a stop, leaning against the wall with a hand over her mouth, trying to keep herself quiet. Tears burned in her eyes. Her brothers. They'd been there the whole time, waiting just at the edge of her memories.

"Aren't you coming?" Wylan's voice echoed off the walls.

"It's dark in here," the youngest complained.

She closed her eyes. This couldn't be real—*they* couldn't be real. This was a trick. Like the redheaded Metal in the ballroom—a trap.

"Scared the Great Dark'll eat you?"

"Stop scaring him, Wy," Rhys chided. *"Ana, come find us!"*

She would—if only she knew where they were. Had she taken a right? Or two lefts? She couldn't remember how to get back to her door, and she could barely see the hands in front of her. Swallowing her fear, she continued toward the laughter.

Until, like dawn breaking over the edge of the moon, the glowing outline of a door came into view. She rushed toward it, pressing herself against one side to swing it open, and she tumbled through.

Her elbows hit the hard marble and she hissed at the sting, ash rushing up around her in a cloud. She coughed in it, squinting her eyes against the bright gray light. Ash coated her tongue, stale and tasting like cinders.

Shakily, she got to her feet.

It was a room, but not like any she'd ever been in before. It was burned, charred wood crumbled against the floor, resembling a bed and chairs and a wardrobe, all covered in seven years of ash and dust. Black marks slithered up the sides of the marble, a wall of bright bay windows letting the silver light of Eros's other moons into the room.

It was the North Tower.

She stepped lightly over the blackened wood, the bent metal scraps and bits of trash, when movement caught her eye. She looked up, but it was only herself in the remnants of a dressing-table mirror. The glass was fractured, split into dozens of pieces. A girl with a shaved head and long eyelashes, a latticework of scars crossing one side of her face.

When she was younger, she used to look into the mirrors in the *Dossier*'s bathroom and imagine what her parents looked like—if she'd gotten her hair from her mother or her eyes from her father, but she was a mixture of two people she didn't know. Two strangers staring back through the mirror.

But things were coming back in slow, steady trickles—like remembering a dream. Her smile came from her mother, and her ears, and her temperament. Her eyes came from her father, but the quirk of her lips came from a woman with fiber optics in her hair and a coat the color of blood.

Even when she remembered her parents, she missed Siege more.

Something snapped behind her.

Ana lurched forward and grabbed a piece of the mirror and whirled toward the noise. But no one was there. The mirror cut into her hand, and a thin line of blood trickled down her arm.

It would've been really nice to have a pistol right about now.

Where had those voices gone?

As she began toward the door that hopefully let out into the main hallway, she heard footsteps.

Slow, sliding.

She froze.

There was something behind her.

She looked over her shoulder. A Messier stood on the opposite side of the room, the silvery moon making its metal skin shine.

She pulled at the door—but it was melted shut. The knob broke off in her hand.

"Goddess's *spark*," she cursed.

The blue-eyed Messier picked up a piece of broken mirror and lunged.

She dodged its first attack, snagging up a blackened metal tray from the floor, and deflected the next. The sound of the mirror shard against the tray made a loud *ping*, and shattered in the android's grip.

"Stop! I'm not an intruder!" she tried to reason with it. "I'm Princess Ananke—"

"*Burn*," it snarled in her eldest brother's voice. The Metal's eyes deepened to a bloody red.

Then it said in Tobias's sweet tenor, "*You should have burned.*"

Her stomach twisted. She knew that phrase, echoed to her again and again in the *Tsarina*. The malware. But this Metal had a memory core. It wasn't hollow like the ones on the *Tsarina*. It was HIVE'd. So how had the malware taken over?

"*You should have burned,*" it repeated in Wylan's voice, and attacked again. "*With us.*"

Gripping the tray tightly, she slammed it against the side of its face. The android stumbled sideways, its neck cracked open, hissing with broken fuses. It snapped its head back and turned to face her.

She held the metal tray out like a shield.

The Messier punched through it, hand reaching for her neck.

With a scream, she let go of the tray and scurried back toward the door. It threw the tray—she stumbled—and the tray flew across the room, shattering through one of the windows.

"You should have burned," it kept repeating, her brothers' voices. *"You should have burned."*

"I *did!*" she cried. "Can't you see it? I burned with the rest of this damned place!"

She pressed her back against the melted door.

The Messier fisted its hand and threw a punch. She ducked.

It slammed its fist through the melted door, and with a fierce groan it gave, sending both of them out into the hallway. Ash and dust kicked up in a cloud. She scrambled to her feet, gasping and coughing, but she couldn't get a deep enough breath. Her head swam.

The Messier got to its feet. Sparks spewed from broken wires in its neck, igniting the dust around them like lightning in a thundercloud.

Oh, how she *wished* she had her pistol.

The Metal reached out to snag her, but she slipped through its hand and darted away as fast as her dress would let her.

Everything was burned and gray, black scorch marks licking up the sides of the marble, around white outlines of people, she realized, only their skeletons remaining, furniture turned to cinders, tapestries half melted, singed Armorov crests papering the ground.

She had to find someone—anyone. She needed to tell the Grand Duchess or—or Robb!

She tripped on a piece of debris—a charred piece of furniture—but she pushed herself back up and kept running, hoping to find—

A door, sealed shut.

A dead end.

It was a dead end.

She slammed her hands against the sealed door it with a cry of rage.

"*You should have burned, Ana. You should have burned with us,*" her brothers' voices taunted.

This was her nightmare, but real. It was the aftermath, the moment just before waking up, when the fire still scorched her skin, when she could still taste the ash, cough from the smoke. Fear rose in the back of her throat.

And from down the corridor, the Metal with red eyes slowly approached. As if it had all the time in the world.

Knowing she couldn't escape.

Maybe Erik had been right. Di would be alive if she had died in the fire. So would Barger, and Wick, and she wouldn't have ruined anyone's lives—

Don't start thinking that, she urged herself.

The Metal's footsteps were close now. How would it kill her? Punch a hand through her sternum and rip out her heart, like Di ripped out memory cores? Then let it take her heart. It hurt when she didn't need it to, it mourned and made her careless.

What she wouldn't give for a different kind of heart.

Think.

She beat her fists against the sealed door again—and felt it give. Just a bit. Ash flaked out between seams. Seams? It wasn't melted shut—not like the other door. It'd been opened recently. The keypad—dark beside every other door—glowed red.

The power was still on—why would the power still be on

in the abandoned wing of the palace if no one came in here? Unless someone *did* come into the North Tower. *Goddess's spark*—she'd walked right into a trap. Of all the stupid things Siege had told her not to do, one should've been *Don't compulsively follow the voices of your dead brothers.*

Her ears perked at the sound of broken fuses in the Metal's neck. Spitting sparks. Hissing. It was a foot away—maybe two.

She hadn't survived mine raids on Cerces and exploding ships and foul-breathed mercenaries to be taken out by a murderous red-eyed Metal *here*. Who would be left to remember her family? Who would be left to remember Di?

Then the Metal lunged.

She might have been born of Ironbloods, but she was a child of distant starships and buried treasure, and if a Metal thought it could kill her that easily, it was mistaken.

She sidestepped, spinning away as the android brushed past her, slamming its hand into the sealed door.

Before it could pry its hand out, she grabbed a handful of the broken, exposed wires in its neck and pulled.

The Messier jerked, trying to reach for her, but she wrapped the wires around her hand and wrenched them out. Sparks hissed from its neck, burning the tips of her fingers, but she didn't let go until the lights in its eyes dimmed and it toppled to the floor.

"That was for Di," she rasped, and sank down to her knees beside it.

She wasn't sure she could stand at the moment. That had been too close. A Messier with the malware, *here*. After everything that had happened, she knew—the malware had been here the night the tower burned.

But Ana remembered that evening now—there were no Metals. Her mother had tucked her in to sleep while her father read her and Tobias a bedtime story. Before he could finish, he was called away . . . but not by Mercer Valerio.

By Rasovant.

The next thing she knew, Robb's father was shaking her awake, and the fire was everywhere. Her nightmare—the one from the *Caterina*—it had been *real.* And that meant . . .

She touched her cheek, her burn scars.

Di had saved her.

She scrambled to her feet again. She needed to tell Robb that she remembered—when she noticed the red keypad again. And hesitated.

A chill crept down her spine, the kind she got with the thrill of a hunt—a part of her she'd thought had died with Di.

A sealed room in the burned tower that was off-limits and continuously guarded? It was the perfect place to hide something, if she were to hide it. And only secrets needed locks.

She tried a few numbers that came to mind.

The keypad blinked red each time.

"I hate technology," she muttered, and slammed her hand against the sealed door in frustration—

But then she got an idea.

It was too tightly closed to pry open with her bare fingers, but maybe she could with an object. Rolling the prone Metal over, she wrenched a rectangular slat from its face. That would work.

She might not have been tech savvy, but Great Dark take her if she didn't know how to break into a damn room.

Jamming the slat of metal into the seam in the door, she pushed as hard as she could, door groaning, until it opened with a snap.

Cautiously, she stepped inside.

It was a small room, no bigger than the infirmary on the *Dossier*. Spare robotic parts cluttered the countertops beside dog-eared books, scattered diagrams, holo-pads full of schematics, maps of the kingdom—and what theoretically lay outside the asteroid belt. Bookshelves lined the walls, filled with medical texts on anatomy and brain chemistry, and studies of failed AIs.

She slid a glass holo-pad to the side to get a better look at one of the schematics. The image looked like a memory core.

There were photos on the counters of Plague victims, their limbs blackened, others amputated. Before Rasovant created Metals, the androids in the kingdom had not been sophisticated enough to treat the Plague victims, and the doctors who went to help the sick eventually became ill, too.

Against the near wall, a dusty computer console woke up to her entry.

"*Good evening, Gregori,*" it said, a staticky blue holo-screen appearing over the console.

Rasovant? Tensing, she glanced back to the entrance—but there was no one there. She was alone.

The computer meant her.

"*I have five thousand forty-three abnormal readings from our data cores. Would you like to examine them?*"

A *YES*-or-*NO* dialogue box appeared on the screen.

The computer wasn't an AI but one of those older analog consoles Siege had told her about, older than the *Dossier's* consoles.

YES, she pressed.

The screen expanded to fill half the wall, bringing up vitals for thousands of names, maybe more. The computer monitored RAM and processing speed.

At least a quarter of them were marked blue, others dark and flat-lined.

D204. D710. D1489.

Her breath caught in her throat. They were *Metal* vitals. The blue-colored ones must have been HIVE'd—there were so many—and the dark ones smashed. The others, judging from the spikes and dips in vitals, were rogues. There were so few of them left.

She paused the screen once it reached the beginning of the list, a number she knew best of all. D09.

But his vitals weren't dark. Her eyebrows furrowed—why weren't they dark?

Hope fluttered in her chest as she keyed up the prompts.

D09 COORDINATES, she typed.

"*Error. Cannot locate.*"

She pressed her lips together and tried again. *D09 STATUS.*

"*Unknown.*"

She slammed her hands against the keyboard. Took a deep breath.

It's wishful thinking, Ana, she told herself. It didn't matter if this computer knew. She knew. He was dead.

And she wasn't here to remind herself of that.

This must have been Rasovant's lab from before the Rebellion. He said it had burned, but here she was, standing in it. This was where it all started. His research, his breakthroughs, his studies.

Everything that could have saved Di was right here. Schematics of memory cores, blueprints, *answers.* It hadn't been lost after all. But why did Rasovant *hide* it? Why not share this information with the kingdom to understand Metals? To save ones like Di?

Could Di have been saved? She had to know.

Bittersweet, she typed in *MEMORY CORES.*

"Gathering content."

Screens upon screens popped up over each other, each denser in content than the last. Photos. Videos. Case studies. Experiments. Schematics of memory cores. There were notes with case files, different experiments detailing human consciousness and the quantity of memory. Different processing speeds—

And then there were photos of Plague victims, the black patches on their skin—as though their flesh was rotting away. She'd heard stories. She'd seen photos. But nothing as terrible or as extensive as this.

The computer must have been confused. It was bringing up Plague files.

METAL CREATION, she tried.

"Content gathered."

But nothing had changed. Frustrated, she prompted the console again.

"Error. Content gathered."

"How is it . . ." Her words lodged in her throat. She looked at the case files again, the experiments, the studies on the Plague, the contagion rate, the lack of a cure. The growing number of Metals, the experiments on human memory, the megabytes needed, the RAM, the processing speed, the—

D03, Retains little knowledge in transfer, but not memory. Slow. Must up RAM.

D05, Retains most knowledge in transfer, little memory. Perhaps need essential memory supplement?

D08, Retains all knowledge in transfer, but no memory—yet. Memory core functional.

There was a file with this next case number. She clicked it, and a video popped up. A shaky holo-pad recording, pixelated and almost unwatchable. It showed a Metal sitting in a chair, watching someone behind the camera with bright moonlit eyes.

"Now, I want you to think hard," said the gravelly voice of Rasovant—the man behind the camera. *"Identify AI."*

"D09," it said.

Her heart jumped into her throat. D09? *Di?*

She reached for the holo-screen, toward his face, but her hand fell through the screen.

"No, let's try this again. Your real name. You must remember it. Identify AI."

"I am D09," it repeated. Di repeated. *"I am D09."*

"No! Your human *name."*

FILE CORRUPTED, the blank screen read.

Her eyebrows furrowed. His human name? But what did that . . .

"Oh, Goddess," she whispered, retreating from the console as if it had burned her, and she searched the lab for some-thing—anything—to prove her wrong, but all she saw was the Plague and memory cores and death.

Metals had once been people—the Plague victims.

All the Plague victims were burned after they died, so no one would know the difference if their bodies went missing. The disease was so contagious, if you so much as touched an infected person, you would also begin to rot. The kingdom sent out guards to take the infected away, so no one was there when they died. Or when they were put into Metals.

Oh, *Goddess.*

Then . . . D09 . . . he was . . .

She typed in the prompt and hit enter.

IDENTIFY SUBJECT D09.

The files—all of them, the schematics, the experimental files, the lab results—went dark. Words typed out over the screen.

Tsk-tsk, little Ananke.

The screen changed to a mirror—just her reflection in the dimly lit room. But in the doorway to the lab stood the red-eyed Metal, its head bowed to the side, sparks frizzing, a slat of metal missing from its cheek.

I told you, you should have burned like the others.

The screen glitched, and the Metal disappeared, replaced by her brothers, dressed in proper waistcoats and trousers, ashen, with smudges of soot on their cheeks.

But she knew the Metal was there. Its footsteps were heavy, patient, slow. She trembled, unable to look away from the screen—she was afraid to. In the reflection, her brothers prowled closer, shifting, shimmering, growing taller, older, with stares as dark as space. How old they would be, if they had survived. This was a cruel trick. A fabrication.

"You burned the tower," she whispered, and the malware grinned through her eldest brother's mouth. "You're the Metal who burned the tower and killed my family."

The eldest brother, Rhys, bent toward her. His voice was right in her ear. *"We did burn the tower, but it was Father's idea."*

"Your *father*? You . . . you mean Rasovant."

"Father lost his patience with the Emperor. He did not mean to kill him." Wylan shrugged.

Her mouth went dry. "Why?"

"Because Father thought the Great Dark was coming. He needed an army. He wanted to HIVE all Metals, to conscript them, and the Emperor would not let him."

"That's because the Great Dark doesn't exist," Ana replied. "It's just a story."

"But all stories have their beginnings, little Ananke," replied Rhys. *"Like the story of the Rebellion. It was not all lies, was it? There was a fire, and humans died."*

"But my father didn't die in the *fire*," she snarled. "Rasovant killed him, and then you burned the tower to cover up the evidence! There's a difference."

Her eldest brother seemed pleased. *"The only difference is who is telling the story."*

"Then who . . . *what* are you?" Her voice shook with the question.

All three of her brothers grinned at that, and all their eyes flickered—until they were the brightest neon blue.

HIVE blue.

Her eyes widened. "You're the HIVE."

Her not-brothers laughed in unison, but it never reached their dead eyes.

"Why do you want to kill me?" she asked. "What could I possibly do to you?"

"What could your D09 do?" asked the eldest. *"He died on that ship trying to save you, but for naught."*

"Shut up."

"You can join him," said her middle brother. *"We can put you into metal armor. We can make sure your heart never breaks again. We know you hurt."*

"I said shut up." But her voice cracked.

Their grins widened.

"We will help," her older brother echoed. *"Are you not tired of running?"*

"Come home," the youngest said.

Home. It felt like she had wanted that for so long. Her eyes filled with tears, because there was no way to escape the Metal behind her, as it wrapped its cold fingers around her neck—

Someone wrenched them away.

The reflection rippled and she spun around as a Royal Guard tossed the Metal across the lab with inhuman force. It slammed against the bookshelves, toppling them, burying the Metal under the heavy tomes.

It tried to right itself.

"*You shall burn . . . ,*" the red-eyed Metal said.

"She shall *not,*" the guard hissed, wrapping his arm around its neck, then prying his fingers underneath its chin and ripping its head off. Wires sparked and hissed.

She'd seen that move before.

The Metal did not stir again.

She stared, wide-eyed, at the guard. His uniform hat had toppled off, revealing red hair and dark eyes. It was the boy from the ballroom. Rasovant's Metal.

Goddess, she really *was* going to die here.

He looked pained, like he could hear something that was terribly off, but she couldn't hear a thing. "We must leave."

She snapped to her senses, backing away.

"*He is more monstrous than we are,*" said her brothers' voices in unison from the console.

And that was the last she could take.

"I said *shut up!*" she roared, grabbing the metal stool from under the counter and raising it over her head. She memorized what her brothers looked like—the curve of their cheeks, the curl of their hair, the depth of their eyes, committing them to a memory she wished she already had.

And then she slammed the stool into the computer. Again and again. And again. How dare this malware use her brothers.

How *dare* it taunt her with ghosts. She already had enough of them living in her head.

This was for her brothers. For Wick. For Barger.

For Di.

When she went to raise the stool again, the guard stayed her hand. "It is broken," he said.

She reeled away from him, raising her makeshift weapon against him instead. "Don't you come *any* closer."

"I am not here to harm you."

"*Bull*shit," she hissed, her arms shaking from the weight of the stool. "You're Rasovant's Metal. The one from the ship—"

"I am *not* Rasovant's," he interrupted. "I am my own. I am me."

"And who is *me*?"

He met her glare and his eyes sparkled to life—bright, fluorescent. Like moonlight. "You once promised you would always come back for me," he said hesitantly, "but it was I who should have promised to come back for you."

She dropped the stool, and it clattered to the floor.

ROBB

Hiding a tool kit he'd swiped from the Royal Guard station under his suit, he waved at the Valerio guard standing outside his mother's door. "Good evening," he greeted. The guard put a hand up to stop him.

"I'm sorry, sir, but this is your mother's room."

"Oh, is she not in?"

"She is not, sir."

"Not a problem, I can just wait inside. . . ." But the guard put up his hand again, not letting Robb pass. Robb set his lips into a thin line, annoyed.

The guard stood stalwart. "I'm sorry, sir—"

He slammed his fist into the unsuspecting man's face. The guard slumped against the wall, unconscious. Robb shook his hand, hissing through his teeth. Goddess, that *smarted*. When he'd shaken the pain off, he wiggled the guard's lightsword out from his belt—he'd rather try to escape the palace *slightly* armed than not armed at all—and went inside.

To his relief, Jax sat on the fainting couch, staring at the carpet. He didn't even look up when Robb came in. "We're getting that voxcollar off tonight," he said, tossing the lightsword onto the bed.

But the Solani didn't move.

"Jax?"

Finally, the Solani glanced up with bloodshot eyes. Had he been crying? Jax blinked, wiping the tears away with the back of his gloved hand.

"Are . . . are you okay?"

"*Leave,*" Jax mouthed. His voxcollar sparked in warning, making him wince in pain.

"I can't do that. I promised to get you out of here, and tonight's the best chance for you to escape. Don't you *want* to?"

The Solani looked uncomfortable, tugging at his obsidian collar.

"Then you're here for a reason," Robb realized. "But . . . *why?*" When Jax didn't reply, he knelt down in front of the silver-haired boy. "Jax, Di is in the palace—"

Jax gave him a dumbfounded look.

"You know that Metal we found on the *Tsarina?* Well, I tried uploading D09 into it—and it worked. And he's here, trying to rescue Ana, because the malware from the ship is in the palace and she isn't safe. None of us are. So please, you have to *leave.* Or at least let me take this voxcollar off you so you can tell me why you can't."

For a moment it didn't seem like the words registered, until Jax tilted his head to the side, flourishing a hand at his neck.

Robb sighed in relief. "Thank you."

Taking the tool kit out of his coat, he found the omnitool and situated himself beside Jax, as close as he dared without touching him. Even having been in the palace, Jax still smelled of fresh lavender, like he had on the *Dossier*.

That felt like lifetimes ago.

Robb slowly lowered his omnitool against the voxcollar. Sweat prickled the back of his neck. "So, to be honest, I can't remember anyone ever *successfully* picking themselves out of a voxcollar. It just doesn't happen, you know? My grandfather was a genius with circuitry—"

He lightly tapped the circuit board with his omnitool, and the collar gave a jolt. Jax bit his tongue, squeezing his eyes closed against the pain.

"*Goddess's spark*," Robb hissed, sucking on his burned finger-tips. The chip in his wrist throbbed. Could it be overloaded?

Too late to find out, he thought, and lowered the omnitool against the circuitry again—when Jax caught his wrist.

"What? I never said I wouldn't barbecue us both," he began to laugh—but Jax's face widened with horror.

At something behind him.

The bedroom door slammed shut.

Robb whirled around. To his brother, knuckle rings glinting in the soft night-lights around the room. Erik looked like a feral animal in the low light, a creature of shadow with marble-like eyes. His tongue rubbed between his canine and incisor. "You're trying to free him, aren't you?"

"Free who?" Robb asked, playing dumb, knowing his brother hated it.

"You *are*," Erik snarled. There was a horrible glint in his blue eyes. Robb had learned to be wary of that look. To run as fast as he could the other way. "Mother was right about you. You're a piss-poor Valerio. You ruin *everything*."

Robb stood, putting himself between Erik and Jax.

"At least you won't be on the throne—"

Erik shoved him. He stumbled and fell backward over the side table. The omnitool went skittering out of his grip. He tried to reach for it, but his brother grabbed him by the collar and pulled a fist back, knuckle rings ready.

"I *will* be Emperor," Erik seethed, and slammed his fist into Robb's jaw.

Pain sliced across his face, bursting out like an explosion. His vision swam. He'd almost forgotten what this felt like.

Out of the corner of his eye, he saw Jax grabbing the omni-tool and trying to get the collar off by himself.

Don't, he thought. *Don't—you'll kill yourself.*

He tried to struggle out from underneath his brother, but Erik punched him again. His vision filled with white. Then red. The room melted and swirled together.

"But you know what? I'll let the star-kisser tell you I'll be Emperor, once he reads my fate."

"What?" Robb slurred.

"Oh, you didn't know? It's quite a show, I hear."

Robb thought of what a fool he was, actually, not to have realized it sooner. That answer in the infirmary—

Please don't ask, Jax had pleaded.

A curl had slipped from Erik's greased pompadour, his snarl

eating up half of his face. Behind him, creeping up like a shadow, was a silver-haired ghost with the voxcollar in his hands.

"I'll have him read my fate," Erik went on, "and I'll let you watch while I slice his face up. What do you say?"

"I think you won't get the chance," Robb replied, and with a hard kick, he forced his brother backward into the waiting Solani, who fastened the voxcollar around his neck.

"What the—" Erik barely got the words out before fifty thousand volts of electricity sparked through the nodes in the voxcollar, sending him convulsing onto the floor. He gasped, spittle oozing out of his mouth, and clawed at the collar.

Jax stepped over Erik and took the lightsword from the bed. There was a burn from the voxcollar on the side of Jax's neck like a spiderweb, almost black against his pale skin. He twirled the sword in his grip and let the blade come to rest at Robb's throat.

"You're joking," Robb said.

"Look me in the eye, Robb Valerio," the Solani rasped, "and tell me the truth: Did you have four queens?"

His eyebrows furrowed. "What?"

"During the Wicked Luck game on the *Dossier*," Jax clarified. "Did you really have four queens?"

"Goddess no, no one's *that* lucky."

Jax studied him for a moment, then sheathed the blade. "Good, then I would have won."

They locked Erik in the wardrobe in the corner of the room and set a chair under the door handle to make sure he wouldn't be escaping anytime soon. It would give them a few minutes, at least. And it wasn't like Erik could *yell* for help.

"So," Robb said, wiping his bloody lip on the arm of his coat, "you can read the stars?"

The silver-haired boy tugged at his gloves. "If you're looking for a free fortune, I already gave it."

Robb's eyebrows jerked up. "When we kissed?"

Jax nodded. "It's why I don't touch people without gloves on," the Solani went on. "That's why I'm here. Because I saw something in your stars about Ana and— What are you doing?"

Robb bowed, as far as he could go. "I'm sorry. That I hurt you. When we kissed, I should have asked. I'm sorry." He was afraid to stand from his bow, waiting for Jax's response.

The seconds felt like eons.

"Stop making a fool of yourself—and stop bowing to me, stars above," Jax added exasperatedly, and waited for Robb to stand again. "I'm not worth *that* much groveling."

"But you are."

Jax sighed, and held out his hand. "Come on—Di and Ana are waiting."

Robb hesitated. "Well? Don't you want to take a dashing boy's hand?" Oh—oh did he.

And he wanted to win a Wicked Luck game against this dashing boy. And he wanted to know why he had left his home, what his favorite color was, what food he liked best—what *flavor*.

Robb wanted to know him as intimately as a sailor knew the stars.

But there was so much space between them, filled with all the things Robb had never said, and all the secrets Jax kept.

They were victims of an empire built on iron and blood.

But for a moment, the space looked no bigger than the distance between their hands.

He reached out and intertwined their fingers.

"This isn't me forgiving you," the Solani chided.

Robb squeezed his hand tightly, and they left the room together.

DI

In the dim lights of the lab, Di watched Ana's golden-brown eyes flicker across his face. Once, he thought she could recognize him in any body, in any form, in any corner of the universe—

But she did not recognize him at all.

"Promise?" she echoed, voice trembling, and sank away. Horror swept over her face like a thunderstorm. "How do you know about that? What are you?" Her voice was rising, rising, like a tide.

What are you, she had asked. *What.*

A thing. Not *who*.

His chest tightened uncomfortably, but he fisted his hands, nails digging into his palms, to concentrate on that hurt more.

"What do you want from me?"

"Ana," he said thickly, "I do not want anything—"

She grabbed a book from the counter and threw it at him. He dodged, but another slammed him in the forehead.

"*Goddess*," he cursed—from both the pain and her wickedly good aim.

"I don't know how you know me or know about that—that *promise*," she raged, "but I swear to the Goddess, if I find out you're working for *Rasovant*—"

"No—"

"Or the *Valerios*," she added, "I'll gut you spleen to throat, I'll—"

A high-pitched squeal cut her off a moment before EoS shot into the room like a bullet and hid underneath Di's coat.

"Not the time," he told it, his voice cracking, until he remembered that EoS was prone to getting into trouble. The bot tugged at his coat. "What is wrong?"

Messiers, the bot relayed, feeding a brief video through their link. The patrol was not yet to the North Tower, but the HIVE knew they were there. He could hear the signal, screeching and raw, and how—the longer he listened—it began to sound like a song.

"You have to trust me, Ana," he said urgently.

Ana reached for another book to throw.

"Messiers are coming and we *cannot* be caught here. I will leave you alone if you just trust me this once. I will go away—forever." The words hurt, but he would honor them, because his next tore a hole through his center. "I promise you on iron and stars."

An unbreakable vow.

He held out his hand.

She hesitated a moment longer. She could hear the footsteps now.

"If you are found here," he tried to reason with her, "then

Rasovant will know what you know. The HIVE already does."

And the HIVE was the malware. It controlled the Messiers, the newsfeeds, the docks on the moonbay, and it could infiltrate any ship in kingdom space that didn't predate the *Dossier*.

And that was very, very bad news.

Hesitantly, she took his hand, and he pulled her out of the lab and down the scorched hallway. He walked briskly, not sure where he was heading, but his feet seemed to know all the same. Like they knew the scent of sage on his uniform, and how the Eros globe in Rasovant's study squeaked.

It was something so inherent, he was worried what it meant, now that he had seen the lab.

EoS followed them, beeping again.

They left the North Tower, stepping over the prone Metals he had disposed of earlier. Ana gaped down at their ruined chests—and he could see the horror in her eyes, afraid that he would do the same to her.

Messiers came from the hallway to the left, their footfalls like the heartbeat of a great monster.

Like him—a monster.

Ana's grip tightened in his.

EoS beeped again and swirled ahead of them, knocking against a closed door near the East Tower. Di took it as a sign and slipped inside. It was a parlor of sorts, where large portraits of ancient Armorovs hung on the walls and delicate vases stood on podiums. Two fainting couches sat against the windows facing the moon garden, a tea set on the coffee table. The room was immaculate, but it looked like it had not been used in years.

Close, he ordered, and the door clanged shut, the lock switching red.

Ana quickly let go of his hand, jumping at the automated door. "Who did that?"

"I did," he replied, and put a finger to his lips.

EoS hid underneath his uniform jacket again.

The march of Messiers grew louder until they were right outside the door—*right, left, right, left*—as a sharp, grating signal filled the air. He winced against it, recognizing the HIVE.

The Messiers passed by.

For a moment he did not want them to, because then he would have to keep his promise.

Because she sees you as a monster, he thought as the sound of the Messiers faded. Ana backed away from him, her eyes red-rimmed with tears. He did not want to hurt her like this. He would tell Siege to rescue her. Siege could. Perhaps that was the better plan after all, guns blazing.

He did not know why he had thought Ana would recognize him. It was an error on his part. She was human, after all.

And he was exponentially less.

He forced himself to bow, unable to meet her gaze. "I will go."

He turned to leave when her voice stopped him.

"If you don't work for Rasovant, who are you?"

Who.

With his back turned, he said, "You called me Di."

"Di?" she echoed, and before he could respond, she had grabbed a handful of his uniform collar, turning him around to face her. "I watched him die . . . I killed him! You don't even *look* like him. You don't sound like him. You don't . . ."

"I know," he replied, trying to gently uncurl her fingers from his collar—so he could leave. He had promised to. "I must admit, this is one of my worse plans—definitely worse than that mine on Cerces, and the time you ran me over with a skysailer."

Her eyes widened. "How did you . . . No one . . ." She sank to her knees, dragging him with her. "You can't be . . ."

But still, she would not let go.

As if she wanted to believe.

There were over a million possibilities more likely, a million chances more probable. But he was here, and he could finally feel her warm hands, run his thumbs along her calluses.

He was *here*.

And without planning, without calculating, without thinking, he leaned forward—as if it was the most natural thing in the world—and pressed his forehead against hers. Like they always had. Ever since he could remember. The smell of her flooded his senses, moonlilies, rich and wonderful, her forehead warm against his. She looked so different without hair. Stronger, sharper edges and bolder curves.

Her scars were a star chart of latitudes and longitudes crisscrossing, string across string, painting a constellation across her cheek. He ran his thumb across it, tracing the lines, and finally raised his eyes to look into hers, as golden and as brilliant as a sunrise.

He had never known this feeling, and now there was an ache for all the time lost. He drank her in, filling every program, every errant code, every dormant function, with nothing but her. With the imprint of her, the memory, the moment.

She searched his eyes, strangely, wonderingly, trying to find something inside. He did not know what she wanted to find, but he hoped she found him. Her Di.

Hesitantly, she touched his face, her fingertips quivering against his skin as if he was a mirage about to fade, and he leaned into her warmth, closing his eyes, savoring, thinking, *I am here, I am here.*

"He died," she whispered. "I saw him die."

Di smiled sadly. "I will always come back to you."

And with all his iron heart, he believed it.

She heaved a sob and wrapped her arms around his neck. She buried her face into his shoulder, so tightly, as if she were afraid to be pried away.

He set his chin on her head. "I am sorry, I am so sorry," he repeated, feeling her tears dampening his uniform shoulder.

"Why are *you* sorry? I was the one who wanted to sneak onto that ship. I was the one who led you into danger. I *killed* you—"

He pushed her away from him. "No," he said, looking into her eyes so she would understand, "I went because I wanted to."

"You went because you *always* go," she argued, "and I always lead you into trouble."

"Because I will follow you anywhere," he insisted. "To the ends of the galaxy, if I have to. I want to exist where you exist, and that is enough."

Then she leaned forward, and he made a move to try and catch her, worried she was falling—

She pressed her lips against his. They were warm and soft. It was like the kiss from Astoria, a second, a moment, a breath—

One point three seconds—and gone.

"Oh, *Goddess!*" she gasped, pulling away, leaving the tingling, electric sensation against his lips. "I'm so sorry. I didn't mean . . . that was . . . I didn't—"

He wrapped an arm around her waist and pulled her into another kiss, and she melted into him, pressing as close as she could, and still he wanted to be closer. Her fingers threading into his hair, his around her waist, moving, exploring. Calculations had no room here, probability and chances washed away to a deeper longing. His tongue traced the contour of her lips, memorizing her taste, her motion, her method. The kiss lit a million suns in between his zeroes and ones, and made him infinite.

He did not want to let go. He did not want to leave—he *would* not. It was that voice that cried this, deep inside him, growing louder and louder. It was selfish. It was damning. But he did not want to forget the taste of her, her warmth, her curves, her smell. It was selfish and it was human.

And for a moment he allowed himself to be.

Until finally, she slid away, coming up for air. "You, too?"

she whispered, her breath hot against his lips, hopeful, her eyes blazing like suns rising for him.

He pressed his forehead against hers. "On iron and stars," he promised.

ANA

She wanted to drink him in like the dawn, and she wasn't sure if that was good or bad. He was a stranger. He was *stranger*.

The way he looked, red hair and pale skin, sharp jaw and thick eyebrows. So human it almost scared her—it *had* scared her. The body was still Rasovant's creation. It was still a secret the Adviser had tried to hide, but every time she looked into his pitch-black eyes the fear ebbed. Because there was her Di, staring back.

He took her hand tightly, brown to pale skin, where there used to be silver, and she thought how different they both were now.

"Is something wrong?" he asked, his voice strange—tight. Afraid? Did he sound afraid?

"How can you—you know? You can't feel or—I mean you couldn't. Because—you can't—it's not . . . you're . . ."

One side of his lips twitched up. He raised their joined hands and rubbed his thumbs against her knuckles. "I can feel that," he said, flipping her hand over to trace her lifeline, "and that as well . . ." Then he brought her hand to his lips and kissed the tender spot on her wrist, and she shivered. "And that."

A warm, ravenous feeling burned in her stomach.

"But I assure you," he said, turning her hand back over, "I am ninety-nine-point-nine-eight percent me."

"How about that point-oh-two percent?"

"Everyone needs a little mystery." And he smiled. The way he looked at her made her want to stay in this moment until the sun exploded and the cosmos caved in on itself. He was here. He was alive.

Di was alive, and it felt like she could finally breathe again.

But looking at him, a stranger with the heart of her best friend, reminded her of what she had discovered in the dark lab. About Rasovant. About the HIVE. And painfully—achingly—she stood, her hand slipping out of his, which left the ghost of an impression on her skin.

"I can't stay here," she muttered. "I have to go tell Robb about the lab, and the Metals, and—and *you*."

"He already knows about me," Di replied matter-of-factly, rising to his feet too. He dusted off the knees of his trousers. "Well, *this* me. In this body. We had quite a good conversation—"

"It doesn't bother you?" she asked him. "What we learned in that lab? Don't you wonder who you were? Don't you care what the Plague took away—what Rasovant stole?"

He sighed, and said quietly, "Of course I do, Ana."

"You used to be *human*." She tucked a piece of his red hair behind his ear. "You used to be alive. And then Rasovant took your memories, your life—and used you to make a *Metal*.

Goddess," she gasped. "I destroyed the computer. It had everything on it!"

"It needed to be destroyed."

"But I could have shown it to the rest of the kingdom, Di. I had *proof!* Rasovant killed my father because he was afraid the Great Dark would come back. He's taking away Metal sentience—your sentience—because of some *story.* He's a madman."

"Yes," Di agreed, "and a madman with a lot of power is very dangerous. Imagine if other bad people got their hands on a way to create Metals—people worse than Rasovant. Ana, it needed to be destroyed."

"But Rasovant murdered the entire royal family—"

"No. *You* are still alive."

She jabbed a finger back at the door. "Then I want to make that *bastard* sorry he ever let one little girl get away!"

Di pursed his lips. Ana hadn't meant to snap at him—but she didn't know how else to feel. Happy that Di was alive, heartbroken to have remembered her brothers and watched them fade again, angry that she had destroyed the evidence of Rasovant's corruption? The Iron Adviser had killed her father—and Mercer Valerio had found his body. That was why Robb's father called the guards, but before they could arrive . . . the HIVE set the fire.

And so no one knew—everyone believed Lord Rasovant and his lies. The kingdom *let* him HIVE innocent Metals and pretended not to notice.

"I'm sorry," she said, shaking her head. "I'm not angry at you. I just . . ."

"It is okay. I understand," he replied, pulling his bloodred hair back into a ponytail. It was such a strangely human thing to do, as if he'd done it half his life. "But try to understand me, too. The HIVE will do anything to protect its creator. It set the fire in the North Tower—and then on the *Tsarina* it tried to kill us for finding the ship. There is no telling what else it will do if you provoke it."

Her hands curled into fists. "The HIVE is a monster."

He winced at that, and her feet slowed to a stop.

"It is, Di."

"No more monstrous than I," he replied to the floor. "I would do anything for you, too."

"It's nothing like you, Di. You saved me when the fire broke out. We ran with Robb's father onto the closest ship we could find."

He glanced up at her, surprised. "You remember?"

She looked away and gave a slight shrug. There were so many strange memories in her head, trying to fit together like puzzle pieces with the wrong shapes. "But the HIVE—the malware—was on the ship. The only way to get us out was to eject our escape pod manually. He said he would be in the next one, but he lied . . . he just ejected ours."

"Then Siege found us," Di filled in, and Ana scoffed at the mention of her captain. "She told me what had happened."

"She *lied* to me."

"Siege wanted to protect you."

Ana's brows furrowed. "I wish she could've."

Di rubbed the back of his neck, his lips pressed into a thin line as though he heard something she couldn't. "I asked her to keep you hidden, and to wipe my memories—I do not think I will ever get them back. But that led to my glitches."

"And the glitches led us to the Iron Shrine, and Mokuba, who led us to the *Tsarina* again."

"Which led us here."

"Led *you* here," she corrected.

"To you."

He took her hand, twining their fingers together, and kissed her knuckles, his lips so light it melted the anger in her bones and left butterflies instead.

Suddenly, out in the hallway, a door slammed. Ana jumped, startled, as the sound of the distinct march of Messiers returned. This time she could hear the guards opening doors, checking each room.

"We must leave," he said, squeezing her hand tightly. "Let's go home."

Home. She wanted to go home more than anything else.

He pulled her toward the open parlor window. It dropped out into the garden, where moonlilies were beginning to open again like springtime buds on Eros. "I have memorized the guard patrols. We can jump down into the garden and leave the way I entered. Riggs parked a skysailer for us on the docks—"

"Check the next one down," snapped a familiar voice out in the hallway. Rasovant. "The intruder has to be here somewhere."

Ana and Di froze until another door opened. Not theirs yet, but closer. It was only a matter of moments before the Messiers opened theirs. Rasovant was relentless. Even if they fled, he wouldn't stop until he found them again, and he *would* find them. Perhaps not now, but in some other corner of the universe. They would never truly escape.

"Di," she whispered, stopping him from climbing over the windowsill. "I can't."

He turned back to her, confused. "What?"

"I can't go," she repeated, and her voice warbled with the weight of those words. "If I don't stay, then Rasovant will create his army and innocent Metals will die. But if I survive until my coronation, I can dismantle the HIVE. I can destroy Rasovant—"

"And if *you* die?"

She tried to smile. "Apparently, I'm a lot harder to kill than people think."

Di looked away, probably trying to calculate another way for her to leave before Rasovant and his Metals found them—she knew him. She knew he would try again and again and again. And she loved that about him. He was her Di, good and selfless and logical, but it was the .02 percent that she did not know that surprised her.

He turned his dark eyes back to her and said, "Then I will stay with you."

The good-bye she had formed on her lips fell away. "What if someone finds out you're a Metal? You should be afraid of the HIVE—"

"Of course I am afraid," he replied, and it hit her, finally. That he *felt*, and that it didn't matter that he was afraid. "I could not stay with you in Astoria because I was a Metal—but now I have the chance. Let me try." He brought her hand up to his cheek and pressed his face against it. "Tell me to stay by your side."

She wanted to. The way he looked at her, as though she was the moon in his night sky, made her braver than she thought she could ever be. Brave enough to realize that there were no good good-byes.

She was afraid of Messiers finding them—of finding *him*. Would Di be HIVE'd? And if he could now feel, would it hurt? Or would he simply slide away like rain across a starshield? There and then gone?

She didn't want to find out.

So she memorized how the light from the windows slanted across the sharp edges of his face, the way he leaned toward her like a shield, how there were a thousand stars in his eyes, which sometimes made them shine as silver as moonlight—as they did now.

In any other universe, she and Di probably would have met in a room like this, with plush carpet and dour-faced portraits, and sat on the fainting couch by the window. They would've talked for hours.

She would have liked him. Maybe someday, she would've liked to marry him, too.

But in this universe, for a moment she existed where he existed, and that was enough.

"Next room!" snapped the Iron Adviser. The Messiers' march was so loud, it rattled the antique china on display in the curio cabinets. They were coming for their door, overriding the locked keypad.

"I want you to stay," she whispered, taking off the half-melted pendant and tying it around his neck. Because it would protect him. Because it had protected her for so long. "But you can't."

And for a split second his face began to fracture, the metal heart inside his chest breaking, before she shoved him out of the window with all her might, and sent him tumbling into the garden below.

Bleeping, E0S swirled out of the window after him as the Messiers unlocked the parlor door. She turned to their blue-eyed stares with a pleasant smile.

"We are searching for an intruder," the first Messier said.

Of course they were. "Good luck," she said with a smile.

DI

Di hid behind a statue of the Goddess until the patrol passed the entrance to the garden.

His mind was numb, his fingers rubbing the pendant she'd given him—the slightly melted ouroboros—as another group of Messiers passed, moving in perfect precision.

She had pushed him away; she didn't want him to stay.

You knew you could not, he thought, but he wanted to so badly, it ached in places so deep, he could not think.

He did not want to feel anymore. How foolish he was. Humans did not love Metals, and Metals could not love. And she would rather stay and fight than leave with him. The irrational, emotional part of his programming hated it, but the Di he used to be understood. The lives of many outweighed the lives of the few. And Ana was stubborn enough to know it.

Eros's second moon drifted into the corner of the sky, shedding silver light across the garden, exposing the shadows. EOS flew up beside him, hovering over his shoulder.

"Almost out," he told it.

Around him, moonlilies began to open, and he tried not to step on them. Two hundred feet separated him from the side garden where he'd come in last night, and then he could sneak out into the square and—

The footsteps were so quiet, he almost did not hear them.

"I know someone is there," he called to the shadow behind him as EoS dove into the shrubbery to hide.

A Royal Guard stepped out of the shadows of the garden, blond hair shining like a halo of gold in the moonlight. A hand rested on the hilt of her lightsword. "I think you're on the wrong patrol, guardsman."

"My patrol was boring," he replied, turning to face her. She knew he was not one of her guards. Her breast pocket was much too decorated. "Royal Captain Viera, is it?"

"Put your hands up—slowly," the woman commanded.

"I am not a threat."

"We'll see about that." She unlatched her cuffs from her belt clip. "You're under arre—"

EoS darted out of a bush and slammed into her head.

As she stumbled, Di grabbed her lightsword and drew it, sheath in one hand, blade in the other. She reached for her pistol from inside her uniform jacket and aimed.

"Just let me leave," he said, inching back toward the side garden and escape.

Instead, she grabbed for the comm-link on her lapel. "I found th—"

"NO!" he cried. A jolt snapped through his body, and the comm-link sparked. The young woman gasped, dropping the communicator. It exploded before it even reached the ground. He watched in horror. "I—I did not mean to do that."

She pulled the trigger.

The bullet scraped across his cheek. He winced, the sound reverberating in his head, and with him distracted, she grabbed him by his hair and slammed the side of his face against a statue of the Goddess. She pressed the barrel of her gun against the side of his head.

"I warned you—"

Di glared. The dark of his irises flickered, faintly, like a slow-kindling fire, and morphed into a silvery-white as it caught the light. The mark on his cheek where the bullet grazed did not bleed. It looked like part of the earth cracked open, revealing a vein of silver.

Her eyebrows furrowed. "What *are* you?"

"In a hurry," he replied, and E0S rammed into her again, bleeping triumphantly.

Di caught the Royal Captain by the neck and put her in a choke hold. She thrashed, but he was much stronger.

One second, two, three.

He waited, closing his eyes, trying to concentrate on something else—anything else—as the guard captain gasped and clawed in his grip. But all he could think of was the man in the square, the bone protruding from his arm, the calls of *monster*.

He was not a monster.

Her struggling finally died, and she slumped against him. He gently laid her on the grass full of moonlilies, her chest rising and falling in steady breaths.

"I am sorry," he said, and stood.

"Why?" asked a voice behind him.

He glanced over his shoulder.

Flaxen hair, narrow face, wearing the deep purple of a royal handmaiden. It was her again—the girl from Astoria. The one who first called him "monster" in the square. Rasovant's servant.

"Never apologize for being what Father created," she said, and raised her hand toward him.

The air spiked and static filled his head. Loud, grating. It seized his processors, made him want to swallow his own tongue, it was so painful. His body began to lock up like a hundred thousand volts overloading his system.

Faintly, through the buzz in his ears, there were voices. Familiar voices. Robb, he recognized—and Jax. They were close.

He tried to open his mouth to shout for them, but his vocal box crackled.

The girl smiled. "They will not hear you."

Fear crawled up his spine. He was helpless. It hurt to move, like razors slicing over his skin. But he had to do something— so he did the only thing he could think of.

Wincing, he grabbed for E0S and pushed a node of data— instructions, the memory core still in the infirmary, how to fix it—into the little bot, and blasted it away with an electric spark. E0S tumbled into the darkness of the garden and escaped into the nearest bush. This girl could not catch it *and* keep him detained.

The girl bared her teeth. "That made me angry, brother."

The air turned sharp—cutting, like a knife through his core. His vision blitzed between static and color, warnings swarming his sight like storm clouds. He tried to move, but his arms weren't his anymore, and his body was something he couldn't control until, like a switch, the whirring thing inside him shut off.

But not him. He still existed. In the nothing.

The void.

He remembered the void from before.

JAX

The crowd in the square made his head spin.

The warm glow of lanterns and tents and food stands was such a sharp difference from the cold, dark palace that the sight overwhelmed him—and the *sky*. Goddess, the sky was so wide, and all the billions of stars shone down on his skin. He drank the starlight in. It filled him, expanding, and the dull ache that had crept into a corner of his chest subsided.

He'd never longed for such an open expanse before in his whole life.

"So, let me get this straight. You read my mother's stars?" Robb asked as they bobbed through the crowd. "See anything exciting? Torturing poor citizens? Erik becoming Emperor? Sucking human blood?"

Jax wasn't in the joking mood. "I didn't see anything I wanted to," he replied gruffly, and his tongue felt heavier and heavier, the almost-lie tasting like iron. So much blood—a crown covered in it.

He hoped Ana was at the docks. He couldn't wait to see her

again—golden-brown eyes and a smile that curled with trouble. He missed his best friend.

But when they arrived at the docks, no one was there.

"Aren't they supposed to be here?" he asked as a cold knot of dread curled in his stomach.

"Yeah. There's the skysailer Riggs left. . . ." Robb moved toward the *Dossier*'s skysailer. It was a sight for sore eyes. "Maybe they're running late—"

A loud bleep filled the docks. Screaming. Coming from the square. Speeding toward them as fast as the little bot could was EoS.

It dove into Jax's arms.

"Please say this is part of your plan," he said to Robb, who was quickly paling.

"I don't—I mean, I don't think—"

From the square, Messier voices rose up over the chanteys sung by the merrymaking crowd, asking them to kindly move. Jax would bet his left ear they were heading for the docks. Ana, he realized, wasn't coming.

Jax held the bot tightly. He was foolish to think he could change anyone's stars—that the stars were theirs to change. He resigned himself to it until the Ironblood turned back to him, fire in his eyes.

"You need to leave," Robb said, "before the moonbay exit codes expire. I'll stay and distract them—they can't do much to me. I'm a Valerio."

"You're lying," he replied. "I can tell now when you do."

"I'll be *fine*—"

In the square, the Messiers broke through the crowd, making their way toward the moonbay, marching in unison, blue eyes blazing.

"—Please, Jax," Robb pleaded. "You have to go—you'll be fine. If your visions are right, then Ana *is* still in trouble. Go find help. I'll distract them and you can—"

Jax took Robb by the face, fingers spreading into his hair, dark curls wrapping around his fingers, snarling them, so Robb could look at no one else. He memorized the constellation of freckles crossing Robb's nose, peppering his sun-kissed cheeks. The way the human boy looked at him made a strange, burning feeling turn in his stomach. He wanted to kiss off the freckles and place them in the sky as guiding stars.

Closer, closer the Messiers came. Down the ramp, past the first ships

"The Solani have a saying," he said, his voice soft. "*Al gat ha astri ke'eto.* It means something like 'Until the next star shines on you'—until we meet again. So, *Al gat ha astri ke'eto, ma'alor.*"

Robb grinned despite his fear—Goddess's fiery spark, Jax hated that grin, arrogant and insufferable and now he could think of little else. "What does *ma'alor* mean?"

"Stop," one of the Messiers said, drawing its Metroid. "Please step away from the ship."

"I'll save you," Jax said.

And Robb replied, "I know."

Then he shoved Jax into the skysailer, kicked the ropes holding it, and pushed it off from the dock. It rocked away, and the curly-haired boy gave a last nod before he turned back to greet the Messiers.

Jax scrambled to sit up, reaching back toward Robb desperately, but the words he needed sat lodged in his throat.

The guards were one hundred feet away, closing in, and without knowing what else to do, he started the skysailer. Its golden wings fanned out as the engine gave off a sweet, faint hum, and EoS sent out the exit codes to leave the moonbay.

Goddess, give us new stars, he prayed as the skysailer lifted into the starry night, and out into the darkness of space, watching Robb's shadow grow smaller and smaller until it was nothing at all.

Or give us the power to change ours.

ROBB

The Messiers led him out into the moon garden.

He was wondering if there was some prison below the garden he didn't know about when he caught sight of a lone shadow sitting on a bench where roses bloomed. His mother inclined her head as he approached, her face lit by the steady glow of the candles shining out of the Iron Shrine. She dismissed the Messiers.

"Come," said his mother, and patted the bench beside her once they were gone. Hesitantly, he sat, wondering what sort of trap this was. "You let the Solani go. I am honestly surprised it took you so long."

He shifted uncomfortably, noticing the open voxcollar in her hand. Erik must have gotten out of the wardrobe and come running to their mother. Typical.

"Is he gone?" she asked.

"Yes, Mother."

"Then why did you not leave, too?"

"Because I want to see Ana on the throne."

She raised an eyebrow, more amused than angry. "You truly are your father's child."

"I hope so."

Her grip on the voxcollar tightened. She'd yet to look at him, only at the Iron Shrine, as if he wasn't worthy anymore. "You care too little about legacy, about the Valerio name. *Toriean el agh Lothorne*—Glory in the Pursuit, but you never cared for glory. You never went to pursue it, not like your brother. Erik is ravenous for it. He is strong; he will carve our name across the galaxy for the glory of it all."

Robb scoffed, shaking his head. "Erik's a monster, Mother. He doesn't care about *family*, he cares about himself. That isn't a Valerio—"

"And *you* know what being a Valerio means?" she asked, her voice like dry ice.

"*Yes!*" And in that word was all the pent-up rage he had carefully stored. Every moment, every motive, every syllable, bubbling up until he couldn't be quiet anymore. "Our family's motto is Glory in the Pursuit—the pursuit of honor, of family, of love. It isn't pursuit of your *own* glory. It never was. My father taught me that."

"And he died for it, too," said his mother, and she could have said anything else. Absolutely anything, and it would have broken his heart a little less. It would have made the next moment harder.

He stood, and bowed to her. "Then if he is not a true Valerio, neither am I."

He waited for a moment as the wind carried his words

through the rosebushes and willow trees, picking the dying petals of the moonlillies into the air. He waited for her to say otherwise, but she never did, and the hope that maybe, somewhere in that twisted, small speck of dirt she called a heart, she cared for him, went out in a breath.

Blinking back hot tears, he said, "I'll leave after Ana's coronation tomorrow so as not to draw suspicion to the family."

"I will find you if you leave."

"Then I will just escape again, and again, until you grow tired of finding me."

Then, like she had done to him his entire life, he turned his back and left her in the quiet of the moon garden, alone.

DI

Eventually, the void split apart in a blaze of light. It swarmed him, rushing, rushing, until he could feel his hands and feet, and the sharp ache from the bullet that had grazed his face— and he awoke with a gasp.

"So you've come back online," said a deep, dry voice. Lord Rasovant.

Di trailed his eyes up to the man sitting on the stool across from him, one leg over the other, watching. Once, the Adviser would have been a nice-looking man, but sixty years had pulled his skin downward and freckled his face with sunspots.

Blinking, Di tried to clear the fuzzines out of his head. He was bound to a chair in the center of a small, dark room. He had been here before. Moments before, it felt like. Papers were scattered beneath the chair legs, a pile of overturned books in the corner, a headless Metal underneath. The computer on the far wall was dark, crumpled in with the weight of Ana's fury.

How long had it taken for him to reboot? Had he missed the coronation?

Captain? he called hesitantly, but there was no answer. The communications were still blocked.

He tested the handcuffs that bound him to the back of the chair, but they were stronger than normal handcuffs. Titanium, by the sound of them.

"Don't waste your energy," said the Iron Adviser.

"Let me go," Di rasped. "You have no right to keep me here."

The Adviser leaned over onto his knees and picked Ana's pendant off Di's chest, studying it with a thoughtful expression. "Identify AI," he said.

There was a prompt—an instruction to comply. Impulsive, as if it was built in as a reflex. But he bit his tongue, focusing on the pain. *D*—

"A—*person*," he forced out.

"Interesting." Rasovant dropped the pendant and leaned back on his stool. "Identify AI," he repeated.

The command was a fail-safe. A back door built into his code, and he heard the closed door rattling in his head. He felt the compulsion—but he was *not* a serial number. He had not been for some time. He was not a unit. He was not a commodity.

He was more than the sum of his parts.

"My friends," he struggled out, "call—call m-me—*Di*."

The man's face twitched. "I will give you one more chance, Metal. Identify AI—"

"Di," he repeated. Sharper. "Shall I—spell it? *D-I*."

The Adviser struck him across his cheek with the back side of his ringed hand. Di glared up through his red hair, a muscle in his jaw twitching.

"Don't look at me like I am the villain," the Adviser warned.

Di gritted his teeth. "You turned Plague victims into Metals."

"I could not create an AI smart enough without some layer of existing consciousness," replied the Adviser easily, as if it was the most normal response. "The Plague was spreading, and we needed to stop it."

"You made it so we could not *feel*. You took away the part of us that made us *human*—"

"Identify AI," Rasovant tried one last time.

The reaction was so visceral and caught him so off guard that the words ripped out of him, this strange and jumbled mess of syllables he had not expected.

"I am *Dmmm*—"

But he choked on the words as that stranger part of him, the part that remembered the smell of sage and the fit of the uniform and that the globe of Eros squeaked, rebelled—*I am*, it screamed.

Rasovant's jaw worked, as if he was about to say something, when the keypad to the door beeped.

Hope rose in Di's chest, because it could be someone come to find him. Ana or Robb, or *someone*—

The door rose.

"Father, it is almost morning. Is brother awake yet?"

His hope turned to lead. He recognized the voice. It was young, sweet-sounding—flaxen hair and a purple dress. Something was wrong with her—something that made his skin crawl. How had she rendered him unconscious in the garden? What *was* she?

"Brother?" he asked in growing alarm. There was only one other thing that ever called him "brother." "Who are you? What do you want with me?"

The girl smiled, "What we want for every Metal."

A clawing, desperate fear slithered up his throat. No—he could not be HIVE'd. Then he would join that program, the one wanting to kill Ana. He could not kill Ana.

He *would* not.

"But I am not every Metal," he tried to reason, turning back to Rasovant. "You created this body so it could feel and understand emotions, right? What would you get out of HIVE'ing me? What *purpose* was this body for then?"

The Adviser's mouth twisted. "It was an experiment. Because, you see . . . you're right. When I created Metals, I took away your emotions. I didn't realize how important they were. None of my creations retained their memories. This was not a problem but a curiosity. Where did I go wrong? Memories, it turns out, are laced with emotions. A happy memory, a sad one. One cannot exist without the other. Then my son began to die."

Di's eyebrows furrowed. "Your son?"

"He was brilliant. He was good—a talented medic. And the Emperor sent him down to treat a strange disease that would later be known as the Plague. Of course, he contracted it—"

The uniform he now wore, belonging to a son who died during the Plague. A sterile hangar, the smell of sickness, voices crying out, begging, his hands blackened beyond—

The room swam, and Di blinked. That was . . .

"—So I thought of a way to save him—and all the others lost to this incurable Plague—but after I made my son a Metal, he didn't remember me. No Metal remembered who they were, even though their memories were there, captured and frozen, but entirely inaccessible. I spent years researching emotional programming, fine-tuned rational processors, until I built the body you now inhabit. But then that mess with the Rebellion," he said flippantly, as if killing the Emperor and his children were but an asterisk. "And this body"—he gestured to Di—"was lost to me."

"You don't sound all that distraught."

"It is all in the Goddess's plan," he replied, and turned his gaze to Di again. They were dark and listless, as though he were already dead. "But tell me, do you remember anything from your previous life, Metal? Does this body work, at least?"

Di clenched his teeth. Did this body *work*? It was a question with innumerable answers. Did he know what it was like to touch? To smell? To taste? —*Oh*, he could recount every moment. The feel of Ana's warm skin, the scent of her, moonlilies and stardust, and her mouth that tasted like stardust. He knew the fit of Siege's warm coat across his shoulders, the sound of the crew happy to see him alive, and the smile on Ana's lips, and how it made him want to kiss them to make sure they were real.

Yes, it worked.

And with every moment more, every experience, every memory, a piece of him he could not recall lit up, slowly, like a forgotten shrine filling with candles. Memories, from the person he was long ago, drifting in and out of his processors in a waltz. They were his.

They had been *him*.

But Rasovant did not deserve that sort of answer.

The old man shifted in his chair, annoyed at Di's silence. "Identify AI," he commanded one last time.

Di did not even have to fight the prompt—he did not want to anymore. He did not have to. The words tumbled out of his mouth as if they had always been waiting on his tongue, the whisper between his processors of *I am, I am,* the words just out of reach.

"I am Dmitri Rasovant."

Rasovant's face went red. *"Liar.* My son is dead."

"And he would have rather not seen the monster you became," Di agreed.

That made the Adviser angrier. But somehow Di knew it would. Like the smell of sage on the uniform. Like the fit of a pistol. Like the constellation of scars across Ana's cheek.

All these memories—of a life he lived before, and the one now—collided like galaxies.

"I will *save* this kingdom, Metal," the Adviser snapped. "The Goddess gave me an army before I knew I needed one. Don't you see? It is all in Her plan."

"You're a madman. You killed the Emperor"—Nicholii, a man Dmitri had known when they were kids together, in that other life—"and his children and blamed it on Metals to create your *army*."

"I did what I had to!" the Adviser cried. "I—"

"Calm, Father," said the flaxen-haired girl, putting a hand on Lord Rasovant's shoulder. "Sacrifices had to be made for the greater good."

Rasovant nodded, as if the idea actually calmed him. "Yes, like the new Empress—"

"Ana is not a *sacrifice!*" Di snarled, a flash of anger flickering against his chest. His vision filled with static, electricity humming over his wires as it had in the square, turning fury to power, singeing the old man's beard, taking hold of the numerous decorative medals on his breast—none of which he was worthy of anymore—

The girl pulled Rasovant out of the way and slammed Di against the back of his chair with inhuman force.

So close, it seemed as though her face was a fraction too still, her skin too pale, too smooth—like his. She was like him. "Ana," she said, "was *always* a sacrifice."

He jerked against his restraints. She smiled.

The Adviser stood from his stool, his old joints popping. "Submit him, Mellifare. We could use the body."

Panic clawed up Di's throat. "Father!" he cried, the name ripping from his throat, foreign and familiar all at once, as the Adviser left the lab. "Father—wait—please *wait*—"

"*Quiet!*" the girl snapped, and in her voice screeched the HIVE's song—scratching, clawing, loud enough to rattle his insides.

He winced against it, against her, the pain so sharp in his head he could barely think. It was everywhere, screeching. And it was—it was coming from *her.*

He looked up at her, frightened, seeing his end closer than he ever had on the *Tsarina*. Her eyes were red like coals, like fire, like suns about to burst. No beginning and no end.

Nothing at all.

"*You* are the HIVE," he whispered.

She grinned wider. "Oh, my brother, I will let you in on a secret not even Father knows." Then she pressed her lips against his ear, and said in a language of hums and whispers—

"*I have come from the edges. I have come from the end.*"

No, no, no, no—this was not how it was supposed to go. This was not—

The girl forced her hand against his forehead. He tried to twist out of her grip, but the handcuffs held tight. The screeching song of the HIVE grew louder—so loud it rattled his insides like an earthquake. He squeezed his eyes closed.

The HIVE broke the barriers that shielded him and sank its red talons into his code. It felt like his last moment on the *Tsarina*, the malware sinking into his processors like fangs, seeping its venom into the roots of his system, and pouring its data into his circuits.

But there was a last frantic plea in him, and as the HIVE tore against his code, he saw the breaks between it, as he had in the *Tsarina*, and it felt like clear blue sky.

He went without a second thought.

The girl gave a cry as he pushed back, threading between her coding like streams of water in a raging fire. The HIVE here was much stronger than the piece of it on the *Tsarina*, but he did not have to do much.

Into the clear airwaves of the kingdom he sent out one final push through the comms barriers and found the *Dossier* like a ray of sunshine in endless dark. It was home.

Save Ana, please. You must save—

The red coding tore against him, scraping memories, moments, clean.

"Di? Di! What's going on?" Siege cried, frantic. He already missed her voice. He just wanted to go home. *"Di!"*

I am sor—

The girl gripped his hair tightly. "You are *mine*," she snarled, and the red of the HIVE sank deep into his memory core, scrambling him, freezing him—and then it broke him, and she forced herself inside.

He thrashed, pulling at his handcuffs. The breach was a pain he had never felt before. It was not real, like from a blade or paper cut. It was deeper. Like everything inside him that made him unique was being sorted by zeroes and ones.

Tearing him. Shredding him.

It went fast, spearing, separating, picking out left from right, programs from memories from stashed protocols. Deleting them. His self from his functions. He was losing himself, piece by piece, gobbled away. His entire life disassembling.

Dying.

The memories burned, hotter and hotter. Searing away. Ana once said that when you died, your life flashed before your eyes. Was this his life? His existence?

No—he refused. He *would not die.*

"Ana. *Dossier.* Siege. Jax. Robb. *Tsarina.* Nevaeh. Di. Cerces."

He forced his eyes open, staring at the girl whose smile was hungry and whose gaze was a pit of despair. He repeated the words. He knew them. He knew them so well, saying them to try and keep something. Anything.

"Brother, stop fighting. Did I not say I would fix you?"

"Ana. *Dossier.* Siege. Jax. Robb. *Tsarina.* Nevaeh. Di. Cerces," he recited, memorizing them, the curve of their sounds. But they slipped away like sand through his fingers.

Again.

Ana. Dossier. *Siege. Jax. Robb.* Tsarina. *Nevaeh. Di. Cerces.*

Ana. Dossier. *Siege. Jax. Robb. Nevaeh. Di. Cerces.*

Ana. Dossier. *Siege. Jax. Robb. Nevaeh. Di.*

Ana. Dossier. *Siege. Jax. Robb. Di.*

Ana. Dossier. *Siege. Robb. Di.*

Ana. Dossier. *Siege. Di.*

Ana. Dossier. *Siege.*

Ana. Dossier—

Ana.

Ana

A . . .

. . .

V

IRON HEART

ANA

Dawn was fast approaching.

Ana stood out on the balcony, looking over the moon garden. The Iron Shrine, where she would be crowned, looked ominous against the coming light. The moonlilies in the garden closed up, one by one, as pink bled across the sky, eating away the night.

She had seen so many sunrises in the seven years she had just been Ana. Too many for her liking, to be honest. She would watch them with Di from the cockpit, sipping warm tea as she sat on his lap.

"Far above the crown of stars," Ana had once recited. She had been fourteen, and she had finally seen someone die—it had been an accident, but the face of the man haunted her every time she closed her eyes. Di sat up for hours with her when she couldn't sleep, watching the screens in the cockpit shift and change. "Do you believe in the story? That a single girl could drive the Dark away?"

"It is improbable," Di had replied, his fingers patiently

weaving her hair into a braid. "But I do like the sentiment."

"Of a girl shining? She'd be burning."

"No, I like the sentiment of hope."

Hope.

She had waited for a week to feel like the girl of light—the Goddess. But perhaps she was waiting for the wrong thing. She had been waiting for power, for control, but what if the Goddess's only power was hope?

How strong was a power like that?

Sunlight broke over the horizon, warming her face, her smooth cheek and her scars.

Last night, a skysailer had left the docks with a stolen exit code. She hoped it was Di and Jax. Robb had tried to come see her this morning, but the Messiers at the door wouldn't let him in. Not even when she asked.

So she was rather glad for the Royal Captain's stalwart guard this morning. It meant the Messiers had to get through at least *one* body before they killed her, although she hoped Viera could hold her own if she tried. The captain kept her collar up higher than normal today, hiding the bruises Ana saw anyway underneath.

Ana reached for the pendant at her throat—then she remembered it wasn't there. She'd given it to Di last night, though she could still feel the ghostly weight of it against her chest.

Far out in the square, she heard her name being chanted—

Ananke. Ananke. Ananke.

—with a conviction that could hold up the stars.

But she was not the Goddess, and she did not know how she

could be. She clung to a small part of her that was still Ana, who'd kissed an iron boy, and who cared for him deeply, and if that was love—if wanting him to be safe, and happy for the rest of his life . . . if *that* was love . . .

It felt a lot like hope.

"Your Grace, are you ready?"

Ana turned around, smoothing out her dress to make sure no one could see the dagger hidden underneath. It was Viera's, borrowed without question. Siege had taught her never to go into a fight empty-handed, and she'd be damned if she would start now. If the kingdom expected her to shine, it'd be from the blade at her hip.

"Yes," she told her Royal Captain. "I think I am."

HIVE

Nine hundred and ninety-nine candles burned low in the Iron Shrine.

He sat in the rafters of the shrine, a hood pulled low over his brow, chewing on his thumbnail as he waited.

Ironbloods fanned themselves, waiting impatiently for the princess's entrance. They sweated in their satins and starched collars like pigs in a hot pen, speaking with wet and smacking words. He crinkled his nose at their smell. Meat trying to mimic flowers. What fleshy things. One tipped candle and they would all burn.

The shrine was dimly lit. News drones circled in the rafters and around the Goddess's outstretched arms. One of them turned a prying lens to him—that would not do. He caught its information stream and slithered inside. The camera glitched, and slowly buzzed away.

The Grand Duchess was old enough to only want humans present during the ceremony, so the HIVE lined its Messiers outside. They would not be of much assistance, however.

In fact, he was sure they would not even move.

Ananke Armorov knelt in front of Rasovant, the thousandth candle lit in her hands. She was the last surviving member of a lost bloodline, presumed dead, pieces and parts of what the kingdom wanted her to be, stuck together.

It would be a relief to pry her apart.

Can I yet? he asked, the dirt under his nail tasting like ash.

"*Patience, brother.*"

For how long?

"*Until she takes her vows,*" the voice in his head cooed. Gentle, sweet, like a song.

Why?

"*Because that is what we want. Listen harder, brother.*"

He shifted, impatient. If he listened harder, he could have come to the conclusion himself, but he was still adjusting. When he rebooted last night, she told him it would take time. He only needed to listen. Listening became easier the longer he did it.

"Blood of the Moon and Sun," Lord Rasovant droned on, "and blood of the Iron Kingdom, the first daughter in a thousand years, it gives me great honor to pass this holy privilege to you . . ."

Lying in wait, he was bored. His fingers twitched, eyes roaming the shrine. On the ceiling, the painted murals told the story of the kingdom of shadow and the daughter of light.

Far above the crown of stars . . .

He had heard that before. Sitting two in a cramped cockpit. Braiding dark hair. Warm eyes. The sound of—

"Listen!" she hissed.

A knife of pain sliced through his head. He winced. *I was. I am. I—*

The command was a strike of red in his processors; it was a shift of prompts. When at one moment his thoughts ran one way, she twisted them like readjusting a cog, and suddenly he understood her wholly. And there was no more pain.

Yes. I will listen, he replied.

"Good," she cooed.

Lord Rasovant droned on.

He surveyed the room. In the front row, Lady Valerio stood beside her sons. They matched the princess in white tuxedos, although the youngest Valerio's crimson bow tie was crooked from pulling at it uncomfortably.

In the rafters, he blinked, watching. He must have stared too long, because the young Valerio glanced up—and saw him.

The human's eyes went wide. Shock morphed into recognition. Robb Valerio's lips formed a name. One syllable, two letters.

The name did not belong to him. It was a mask. Dust knocked off his core.

He pulled his hood over his face to hide his hair, so no other Ironblood could spot him. He was clad in black, from his hood to his soft boots—better for mimicking shadows than the human D09 once strived to be.

Lord Rasovant finally finished the rites, reached forth for the crown. The tines could cut flesh with enough pressure. What an entertaining thought. The crown rusted red against the Adviser's fingertips, staining his human flesh.

Above them, like the ticking of a great clock, the planets moved into position. The Goddess stared up at them, as if she had waited a thousand years to see them again.

His father placed the crown upon the girl's head. "May the stars keep you steady and the iron keep you safe, Empress Ananke."

The girl held out her candle and set it at the base of the Goddess's feet, a thousand candles for a thousand years. For less than a second, the thousand candles flickered as if the shrine itself had sighed.

Now, the voice whispered.

The word filled him with purpose.

It made him yearn to *impress*.

As the crowd rose, erupting in applause, he leaped over the edge of the rafters and landed on top of a Royal Guard stationed by a statue. The human broke in multiple places, fingers twitching on the hilt of his lightsword.

He grabbed the sword, standing, as a guard a few feet away turned to shout for help. He shoved his sword through the guard's throat. No one heard her gurgles over the applause. The guard's blood hissed off the blade.

In his other hand, electricity sizzled against his fingertips. A gift, she had told him. Currents he could control, in exchange for his thoughts. He was a weapon. Weapons did not need to think.

Empress Ananke noticed him first as he prowled down the aisle. She took a step back before she stopped herself. Rose to stand tall.

Something in the corner of his processors spiked, but he shoved back the errant code. A girl kissing his Metal mouth. Honeysuckle vines. Soft lips. A smile.

Oh, what a pretty lie.

From under his hood, his eyes glowed a burning, brilliant red.

"Guards!" she called, but he wanted her to shut up.

He slashed at her.

She jumped out of his way, surprisingly quick for a human in a dress. The crown toppled off her head and clattered to the ground. He picked it up. Toyed with the idea of using it to scrape her face clean.

"It's an assassin!" someone yelled.

"Why aren't the Messiers doing anything?" cried another.

"Is the HIVE broken?"

The crowd erupted into chaos. They shrieked. The sounds rattled the rafters, shook the flames in the candles. Frightened Ironbloods clambered over each other, kicking away the dead guards, pushing open the doors, letting the sweet dawn light inside. Abandoning the Empress they seemed to love so much. He reveled in the chaos. The sound spurred him on, the voice in his head crooning sweet promises. He needed to kill her. It did not matter why.

"Save the Empress!" Rasovant cried as he ran with the other Ironbloods, as if he was worried for his own life.

But it was a ruse—scripted to make him seem innocent.

With Rasovant gone, he turned his gaze back to the Empress. Overturned candles set fire to the tapestries.

The Empress backed up against the altar, weaponless and alone.

This was no fun at all.

"You won't kill me. Whoever you are—"

He grinned beneath his hood. "You should have burned, Empress." He advanced, crown tight in his grip, tines pointed toward her.

"I . . . I *know* that voice," she said in horror.

The crowd emptied out of the shrine like sand out of an hourglass. The HIVE warned him more Royal Guards were arriving—there were only fifty-seven in the palace, not including the Royal Captain. They spewed into the garden like rats from a hole, but their progress was slow against the tide of Ironbloods rushing to leave.

He lunged at her, raising the crown high over his head. A bullet ricocheted off one of its sharp tines and embedded itself into the floor. He glanced over his shoulder to the source.

"Robb Valerio," he greeted the Ironblood, his lips twisting into a grin. "So you have finally joined the fray."

"I won't miss next time," said the Ironblood, and pulled the hammer down on his pistol again.

Ignoring the Ironblood, he turned back to the Empress—

Another bullet clipped his fingers. Made him drop the crown. It landed on the steps with a heavy thud and rolled under the stone pews. Pain blossomed in his fingertips, a hiss escaped his lips. Involuntary. He looked at his metal-tipped fingers, the skin scraped away.

"Be patient," he told the Valerio with a growl. "You are next."

"No, he won't be!" cried the Empress. When he turned back to her, she slammed the thousandth candle across his face.

He stumbled back, wiping the burning wax from his face, and his hood fell back to reveal his identity. "You little *bitch.*"

"Di," she whispered. The betrayal in her eyes burned him to his core.

His grip on the lightsword faltered.

Kill her! What are you waiting for? Kill her! Kill her! the HIVE screamed. Louder and louder. Forcing code. Bright red bursts of pain. Splitting his processors, fingers curling around his hard drive, covering up something that was beginning to break through, this whisper he faintly remembered. *Kill her!*

Her face brightened. Hopeful.

Like a sunrise—

A body slammed against him. Forced him to the ground. Robb Valerio pinned him down, but he threw the Ironblood off like a blanket, tossing him into the pews. The boy got to his feet again, drawing his pistol. At this short range, he would likely not miss.

"Run, Ana!" the Ironblood cried. *"RUN NOW!"*

"But—"

"You can't save him if you're dead!"

The Empress, pursing her lips, picked up her dress—and ran.

She slipped between the Royal Guards flooding inside, coming to the distress call. A guard took her by the arm—old, gray hair, a mechanical leg, someone he *knew*—

Kill her! the voice in his head cried. *Kill her now!*

He went after her, but the Ironblood shot him again, this time in the shoulder. He hissed, but the red code in his head blocked out the pain. Until he was better.

"You're just another mindless Metal," the Ironblood said.

"And you are just *meat*," he retorted, then lunged forward and knocked the pistol out of Robb Valerio's grip. He grabbed Robb by the throat and sent him swinging into a line of oncoming guards.

He picked up Robb's pistol and pointed it at the retreating Empress as she raced out of the shrine. He aimed for her head—not his first choice, but he did not have time to kill her with the crown. Pity. That would have been so fitting.

His hand shook. He tried to steady it. But there was a noise in his head.

A scream, leaking between the tendrils of his new programming.

Begging, pulsing, swelling.

No, you are mine, the HIVE commanded.

The Grand Duchess rounded a statue from where she had been hiding, grabbed a candle, and threw it at him. It bounced off his shoulder, rolling under a pew. "Monster! You will not kill my Ananke!"

He swung his aim toward the Grand Duchess and pulled the trigger.

It was not his aim that had made his hand shake after all.

The old woman slumped back, painting a red streak across the base of the Goddess's statue as she slid to the ground. He tossed the empty Metroid to the ground.

After the Empress! the voice cried, the red code grinding, grinding. He winced, wanting it to stop.

The Ironblood was getting to his feet.

· He pushed Robb back down into the pews. "Get up again and I will kill you," he warned the boy, not sure why he did not kill him now, and pursued the Empress out of the shrine, plucking a lightsword off a dead guard as he left, the sound of the HIVE so loud and sweet, it tasted like blood on his lips.

ROBB

Robb struggled to his feet. The Royal Guards, led by the captain herself, drew their weapons on Di—they would stop him. The Metal couldn't possibly get through half a dozen of the kingdom's finest *and* Viera. The hum of their Metroids filled the shrine like a haunting hymn. They'd kill Di. Robb couldn't watch, turning his face away.

"You will *move!*" Di flung out his hand to the guards.

Robb felt the hair on his neck stand on end. A wave of electricity pulsed from the end of Di's fingertips, rippling outward like a wave toward the guards. The comms on their lapels sparked—and the voltage sent the guards, including Viera, to their knees in gut-wrenching screams.

Di stepped over the guards writhing on the ground and was gone.

Robb cursed, grabbing a Metroid from one of the guards' holsters, hurtling over the stone pews after him, when a shadow stepped into his way. He hadn't notice her before—hadn't all the guests left screaming? The girl was small, fragile, although her eyes glowed as red as death. The same color as Di's. She cocked the pistol she was holding.

"You got up—what a pity," she *tsk*ed, and aimed for him.

Surprised, Robb froze. He didn't have a moment to think—even a second. Someone screamed his name, and the air around him shifted. A blur stepped in front of him, shielding him. Dark peppery hair spun high into a tight bun, a white dress, tall and cold and—

The girl fired.

A firework of red exploded into the air, and warm droplets splattered on his cheek. He quickly wiped them away—blood.

The world came into focus with a jolt, and his mother stood in front of him, arms outstretched. Blood stained her beautiful white dress—she had made her sons match her, in insufferable white tuxedos. White only ever looked good on her, and now it was stained in red. Robb couldn't breathe, frozen in a moment when his mother still existed. And then her arms fell to her sides, and she toppled to the ground like a doll and did not stir again.

He looked down again to the blood he'd wiped off his cheek. Her blood. "No," he whispered, sinking down to his knees beside her. "No, no, no . . ."

The flaxen-haired girl aimed again. "Seems I missed."

Robb turned his gaze up to the monster with the familiar face. Round cheeks and pursed lips, golden-peach skin and high eyebrows. She was unmistakably Ana's handmaiden. He had seen her a hundred places before. Mellifare. He stared at her until he had memorized her face—until he could pick her out of a crowd of thousands.

"I like that look, Lord Valerio. Hate really suits you," said the girl, and she squeezed the trigger—

A flashbang ignited the shrine in a blinding white light.

He winced, covering his eyes with his arm as the explosion swept through the room, extinguishing all one thousand candles in a single puff, until the only light came from the doorway—a bright, burning dawn.

No—it wasn't the dawn, it was a woman's hair blazing as brilliant as the sun. Captain Siege stepped into the shrine, her Metroid fixed on the golden-haired girl.

Talle hurried over to Robb and pulled him to his feet. "Robb! *Where's Ana?*"

Dazed, blinking, he took one last look at his mother's corpse on the ground and told her, "She ran—she ran with Riggs."

"Perfect," Talle began, but he caught her shoulder.

"Di went after them. He's HIVE'd—Di's HIVE'd. So is that girl," he added, turning his gaze back to Mellifare, who was pressing her palms into her hands, unable to reset her optics. "She's a Metal, too. Like Di."

"*Shit,*" Siege cursed.

Mellifare blinked, resetting her vision, turning to them— when a Royal Guard slammed into her, throwing her to the ground. Then the guard grabbed a lightsword from one of her dead comrades, turning it on the girl.

Robb's eyes widened. Viera.

"I'll keep her busy," said the Royal Captain. One of her ears was bleeding, her coat singed and smoking from the charge that had downed her guards. She could barely stand. "Just get Her Grace to safety."

Viera Carnelian's eyes flashed to Robb, and there was that aristocratic stubbornness he always saw—the kind of stubbornness that had them dueling in their underwear on the Academy rooftop and playing thirteen rounds of Wicked Luck.

There was no way of stopping her.

"Iron keep you, Vee," he said, and turned to leave the shrine. "This way!"

Siege and Talle followed.

Outside the shrine, the bulbs of the moonlilies were red with postdawn light, almost red enough to disguise a young man with golden hair in them. A Carnelian pendant smashed in the flowers. Footprints dirtied his evening coat. Robb knew him— one of Erik's lackeys. Vermion.

Robb tore his eyes away from the body, hurrying to catch up with the captain. People lay abandoned in the garden, moaning, some trampled, others simply afraid to move.

Overhead, three large ships dove in close to the palace, so fast they plucked the moonlilies from the ground and spun them into the air, leaving the stench of burning tapestries and airship exhaust. The ships flew pirate colors, painted silver and black.

Siege's fleet?

Smaller Messier fighter ships screamed across the skies in pursuit, painting dawn in exhaust-white clouds. The crackle of explosions lit the skies like bloodred fireworks, rumbling across the palace.

Robb made his legs go faster, because Viera was a good swordswoman, but she couldn't hold out for long. He refused to look back. He couldn't watch her die, too.

So he trained his eyes on the palace doors, Talle and Siege just behind him, and ran.

ANA

"This way!" Riggs cried.

In the corridors, the Messiers stood guard like metal statues, blue eyes blazing as they watched. They didn't move, they didn't turn their heads. They simply stood—not wanting to kill her but not saving her, either. They were supposed to look impassive. The HIVE had planned this all along.

The booming sound of ships in the skies overhead quaked the walls of the palace in long, terrible growls. The lanterns bobbed frantically overhead, rushing faster as if they, too, knew something was wrong.

Her heart hammered in her throat.

Di . . . Di was . . .

"Why did you come for me?" she asked Riggs, whose mechanical leg made sharp thunks against the ground with every step. "You're going to get yourself killed! Like Di . . ." Her voice cracked at his name, at the memory of those red-ruby eyes glinting from under that black hood. He hadn't escaped after all.

If she hadn't sent him away—maybe if she'd kept him close, maybe if she'd . . .

"Erik was right," she croaked. "I destroy everything—"

Riggs grabbed her by the shoulders and shook her one good time. "Never say that. Never even *think* it. Wick wouldn't let you, so I won't either. We *protect* our family. We're nothing without it."

Tears brimmed in her eyes. But what about all the family who had died because of her? All the family who haunted her shadow, breathing across the back of her neck?

The old man pressed a kiss on her forehead. "You're ours, Ana. And we'll always come for—"

He choked, his reply cut short. Blood dribbled from his mouth. Ana gave a cry as Lord Rasovant pulled the dagger out of Riggs's back, letting him drop to the ground. Rasovant stepped over him, wiping the blade clean on his pristine white ceremonial cloak.

"I am dearly sorry, Empress Ananke," he said, turning the dagger on her, "that it's come to this."

Riggs went still on the ground, eyes open, as if he was staring into some great distance. Dead—he was dead.

Because everyone around her died.

"At first, I thought I wouldn't have to kill you after all," said Rasovant, and she gritted her teeth against the fire-hot hatred inside her. "I loved your father. Your parents were like a second family to me. I had to kill the Emperor, and the fire . . . it just seemed like the best story. It had to be done to stop the Great Dark," he said as Riggs's blood dripped from the blade. "It was only by chance you survived—Erik would have been a grand pawn. He still will be, when you meet your tragic end!"

He jabbed the dagger at her, but he was slow, and she was full of rage and heartache, and it made her blood pump fast as she dodged the attack and wrapped her fingers around the hilt of the dagger.

"There's nothing to fight! There's no *war*," she snarled.

"I have the will to save this kingdom from the Great Dark," Rasovant declared, "and you will not stand in my way!"

She twisted the dagger out of his grip and slammed her foot into his gut. He fell back onto the floor, and she pressed her knee against his sternum, the dagger at his throat.

He looked up at her with wide, unblinking eyes, as if he'd never thought *she* had that sort of anger. "Mercy . . . ," he gasped.

"Mercy?" She pressed the dagger deeper. "You killed my family for *nothing*. You killed Di for *nothing*!"

"Mercy," he repeated. "Goddess, have mercy . . . The Great Dark is coming—"

"Then we'll defeat it with iron, not *blood*!"

Her hand holding the dagger shook.

If she let him go, he would keep hurting people. He would keep taking Metals away until the only ones left were ones run through with the HIVE. He would keep preaching his fear of the Great Dark, a sort of fear that ensured that the only thing that burned bright was fire, consuming everything it touched.

But in the corner of her eye she could still see Riggs, and she couldn't bring herself to shove that extra inch into this horrid man's neck. Because if she did, then she was no better than Rasovant.

Then she would be like him, too.

And Di had saved her from those sorts of monsters.

Slowly, she eased the dagger away from his throat.

"You will tell the kingdom what you did," she said, getting to her feet, trying to make her voice as strong as she could. "You will tell the kingdom what Metals are—who they are. You will tell them what happened the night of the Rebellion. That *you* killed the Emperor, and that *your* HIVE set the fire."

Lord Rasovant staggered to stand, rubbing the thin cut from the dagger at his throat. He gave her a sharp, dark look.

"And then you will end the HIVE, and you will *never* be seen in this kingdom again," she finished. "Do you understand?"

For a moment, the Adviser didn't say anything at all. Until his lips twisted into a scowl and he said, "She was right. You should have burned!"

Then he reached into his robes for the outline of a Metroid at his side and she was turning her dagger on him.

Captain Siege told her to count her bullets. A dagger wasn't a bullet, but no bullet aimed as true.

Goddess bright, she prayed the moment before her dagger sank into Lord Rasovant's stomach, *give me a heart of iron.*

JAX

An explosion ripped through the left sail, sending the *Dossier* spiraling out of the moon's orbit. Letting Siege and Talle off in the garden was the easy part. Getting *out* of Luna's orbit—now there was the magic trick.

He pulled up on the helm, ignoring the half dozen warning signs. Yes, he *knew* the left sail was punctured. Yes, he *knew* he was losing power to the bottom level of the ship. Oh yes, and he definitely knew he was being fired on by three Messier fighters. It didn't take a surgeon to figure out he was being followed.

Accelerating the right thruster, he leveled the ship with a lurch. Lenda hung on for dear life at the communications console, looking like she was about to vomit all over the incoming messages ordering them to surrender.

"Hey! Lose it to the *side* of the console!" Jax snapped at her. "And pay attention to the messages! I need to know when the captain has Ana."

"I'm trying," Lenda moaned. "Can you please make it stop spinning?"

"Yeah sure, love, if you want us to die." A warning signal blipped up—two incoming missiles. Another hit to their sails and they wouldn't be going anywhere anytime soon, but the *Dossier*'s thrusters weren't powerful enough to dodge the attack.

Think, think, he urged himself, trying not to listen to the voice in his head that said, *I told you so. You can't change your stars.*

But to be honest, when he looked out of the starshield at the millions upon millions of lights, swirling in their nebulae of purples and blues and greens, he couldn't think of a better view. His father would never have approved, but his father had never approved of anything Jax did.

So when his father commanded him, a child of eight, to read his stars, Jax wanted to do one thing right. Just once. Besides, one never disobeyed an order from a C'zar.

What Jax had not known at the time was that while the stars were infallible, his father was not. In his father's stars he found out the true fate of the Solani who could read them. Why they never lived long, and why they never fathered children.

Because nothing—not even a glimpse into the future—came without a price.

"I'll die," he told his father, his hands still shaking after the reading, chilling him to the bone like nothing ever had before. "I'll die if I keep doing this. I'll *die* if I keep—"

"What did you see?" his father had interrupted. "Did you see who the next Emperor will be? Did you see the Holy Conjunction?"

In their tiny bungalow in the city of Zenteli on Iliad, Jax had stared at his father with a growing horror. "You knew. That every time I used my power I'd shorten my life. You knew and you want me to *keep doing it*?"

"You do not have a choice," his father had replied. "You are a powerful asset to the Solani legacy—"

"I'm not a *weapon!*" he had cried.

That night, Jax left.

He didn't know what would have happened if he had stayed. Would he have died before now? Would it have been slow, in his sleep under the stars, with the taste of his mother's cider still on his tongue?

How *boring* that sounded.

Lenda's voice rose, frantic, from the comms chair. "Jax! I—I think there's a missile—"

He reached out to the lever commanding the sails and grabbed ahold of it tightly. If he drew the sails back into the ship, they'd only have their inertia to coast with, and they weren't yet out of the moon's gravity.

So, obviously, what went up must go down.

He was counting on it.

"Hold on!" he cried, pulling the lever.

The sails sucked into the sides of the *Dossier* with a sharp noise, and the *Dossier* slowed out of speed with a sharp jerk. The Messier fighters went screaming past them, missiles exploding in a sharp blast. The blowback knocked the *Dossier* backward, and with an excited cry, Jax let gravity wrap its fingers around the old girl and pull her—like a meteor—toward the ground.

HIVE

His father slid, like a melting piece of iron, to the Empress's feet. And did not stir again.

As he watched, a tremor went through him, the voice in the back of his head screaming, so loud even the song could not block it out. It made him advance quicker, it made the song sweeter. It no longer felt like a minor chord in a major key, but an accompaniment, a sorrow that ached in a place he had long since forgotten. His father—his father was dead, both the voice and the song wailed.

He gave a cry, clutching his lightsword, and charged the Empress.

A moment before he swung, she looked up and ducked, scrambling out of the way. He slashed again with reckless abandon, carving a glowing mark down the wall. She stumbled on her dress, fleeing.

But there was nowhere she could run where he would not follow.

The HIVE's song roared in his thoughts, prickling the back

of his neck like splinters. The Empress had killed him. She'd killed Father. He gripped the hilt of his sword tightly.

Kill her! the song cried, and he agreed.

He stepped over the corpse of his father, the dagger embedded in the man's stomach. The old man's yellowing eyes found his face. He reached up a bloodied hand, mouth forming words, but no sound came out.

There is not time for this, the red song screamed. *Go after her!*

But he did not want to leave Father. He did not—

The song spiked, puncturing any sorrow, any separate thoughts. He placed a hand on his father's neck and squeezed. The man gave a gurgle, gasping, before his hand fell limp against the bloody floor.

After her, the song sang, and he obeyed. The Empress could not hide.

A group of guards rounded the corner to stop him, but he felt his way into the communicators inside their lapels and overheated them. They exploded, leaving gaping holes carved into the guards' chests. They dropped with barely a scream.

Their Messier counterparts watched. Good statues.

He stepped over the bloody bodies, his lightsword humming hungrily in his grip. He could follow her to the ends of the cosmos without tiring.

He would follow her until she was dead.

It did not take long for her to reach the end of the hall. She did not know the palace well enough, and humans made the most foolish mistakes. She stopped in front of the closed doors to the North Tower. There were new chains locking it shut.

She turned around. Her face imperfect. Illogical.

He advanced slowly.

There was no need to rush. Moments like these were to be savored.

"Snap out of it," she said, pressing her back against the door. He could hear her heart thrumming, the pump of a fleshy organ in a brittle cage. "I know you're still in there. I know you are—"

"You ruined me. Do you remember? I did not want to go onto the *Tsarina*, but you did not care."

"You said you would go anywhere with me." Her voice was barely more than a whisper.

"But then, last night. You could have come away with me. You could have *saved* me. You could have been my *home*." The hurt on her face deepened with every word, how it made the scars seem sharper. "But you did not love me enough to try."

"I love you more than iron and stars, Di," she whispered.

Di. Yes, she would die. He would be her death.

But he was not *her* Di.

Ana shook with a sob. Tears. She often woke up with those. Streaming down her cheeks.

You are mine, the HIVE sang.

"You're my best friend," she said.

He faltered. Blinked. "Friend?" He pressed his free hand against his forehead. "I—I think—Ana . . ."

"Di?" Her voice sounded hopeful.

He lowered his lightsword. It hummed, hummed, ready and waiting. She took a hesitant step forward.

"Di? Are you—is it *you*?" she asked, and when he looked back to her, he knew his eyes were moonlight. It was so easy to change their color. Her face broke into a smile, and she took another step forward. Then another. He helped close the distance. The HIVE, sweet and soft, sang like the whisper he had once heard a lifetime ago. "Di—Di it's you, I'm so sorry I—"

"Ana!" someone shouted behind them.

He glanced over his shoulder to their uninvited guests.

The captain's hair glowed the color it did when she was angry. Orange. And it seemed as though she was accompanied by what was left of her lackeys. The pirate captain aimed her Metroid at him. "Get away from her!"

"Captain?" he asked, turning to her. "Thank you for coming. I am . . . fine. I am myself again. The HIVE told me things. So many things . . . I could barely think."

"He's fooling you, Ana," the Ironblood beside Siege warned. Blood painted his face, but it was not his. What had happened to Mellifare? "He's not in there. He can't be."

"He has to be," the Empress argued. "He *has* to be somewhere in there."

The captain's face hardened to stone as she tensed to pull the trigger. "I'm sorry—"

He quickly grabbed the Empress to use her as a shield, back toward them so she could only see his face when he killed her, and pressed his lightsword against her stomach.

The captain did not shoot. He smirked.

Humans were so predictable, he thought, until he became distinctly aware of a sharp prick against his ribs. He glanced down. She had a dagger hidden in her dress, it seemed, that she now pressed against his side.

"I promised," she whispered, "I promised you on iron and stars."

Iron and . . .

It was a promise, was it not?

You are mine, the red inside him screamed.

His hand shook, but at this range he could not miss. And neither would she.

"I promised . . . ," she sobbed, the tip of her dagger quivering. She could kill him. The dagger was angled in a way that would not miss his vital components. "Remember what I promised, Di?"

If Metals had hearts, his would have broken, for he had promised, too.

But it was a good thing he did not have one.

He pressed his lips against her ear, relishing her smell. Of a moment long ago, honeysuckle vines and dusky sunlight falling across her cheeks.

"I should have let you burn," he whispered, and slid the blade into her.

ANA

The pain was so bright it fractured the universe.

Someone screamed. Loud and yet so far away, like light from a distant star.

The dagger in her hand clattered to the ground.

Di watched, eyes warming to red again, as he pulled the sword out. The stench of iron filled the air. She pressed a hand against her pain, and it came away slick. Her stomach was wet and warm with crimson—the color of his hair.

Her blood? But she couldn't die. Not yet.

She'd never thought she was afraid of death. She thought it was something she'd be ready for when the time came. But now its cold fingers squeezed around her heart.

And she couldn't tell it no.

As she tried to breathe, a starburst of pain rushed up through her torso. Her head spun as though she was dancing. Dancing— an orchestra. Whirling around the ballroom. Crimson hair and an honest smile. All she ever wanted was to dance with him again, but there was no music.

Everything was so quiet.

Blood coated the back of her tongue. It tasted like iron. She turned her eyes back to him. But she did not recognize the monster staring back.

He let her go, and without anything to keep her steady, she fell.

ROBB

Robb grabbed a flashbang from Talle and lobbed it at the son of a bitch. It exploded, so bright it blinded everyone, giving him time to draw his lightsword and rush the Metal. He slashed. Di deflected with his own sword, still sizzling with Ana's blood. Robb attacked again. Sparks sprayed off their blades as he pushed Di into a corner.

Robb was the best fencer at the Academy. Like hell would some *Metal* beat him.

He tossed his lightsword up, catching the hilt in reverse, and rammed it into the Metal's shoulder like a stake. The sword slid through, although he wanted so angrily to hit his memory core, and sank into the wall behind.

Di hissed in pain as the sword pinned him like a moth to a corkboard.

Try to get out of that fast, Robb thought.

Siege swooped Ana up in her arms and they ran, following the lanterns, finding themselves in the great hall, murals of the Goddess on the ceiling. They ran as fast as they could, so close to the entrance of the palace Robb could see the gilded front doors.

And that was when the Messiers leaned forward from their statuesque perches and pursued them.

Robb dodged the grip of one, but another pulled at his tailcoat. Talle took out her pistols and sent bullets into their chests, dropping them one by one, but they swarmed out of doorways like silver-skinned ants replacing those that fell.

And behind them, pushing through the flooding Messiers, was the unmistakable glow from Di's red eyes, cutting down every body in his way with a sword in each hand. His injured shoulder spit sparks as he went.

The sword hadn't held him long enough.

"Di's coming!" Robb warned, as at the same time Messiers filed into a line at the entrance of the palace, blocking their escape.

"Talle, up ahead!" Siege thundered.

Talle dug into her coat for another flashbang and pulled the pin out with her teeth, pitching it at the Messiers. It exploded in rays of white. Robb dodged between two blinded automatons, the sound of Di's lightswords slicing through them a moment later.

They hurried out into the square, now a graveyard of sweet-smelling food stalls and half-destroyed tents. Di followed, too vicious to be slowed down.

Robb realized they weren't going to make it out of the palace alive.

He turned to Siege frantically. "Where's Jax? What do we do—"

A roar—so loud it sounded like a starship—came from above. The smell of thruster exhaust exploded through the square.

From the dawn-filled sky fell a ship he never thought he'd be happy to see again. The *Dossier.*

Jax.

The ship landed in the center of the square, flattening tents and stalls. The cargo bay door lowered, and in its yawning mouth stood Lenda with a heavy machine gun slung under her arm. She shot cover fire over their heads, raining sparks of white-hot bullets onto the Messiers in pursuit.

"WE'RE ON, JAX! *FLY!*" Siege howled after she'd climbed into the cargo bay, followed by Talle.

She spun back, extending her hand back to Robb. "Grab it!"

Twenty feet away, Di was closing in. His eyes flickered like rubies. A pulse throbbed from his Metal body and made his hair levitate, infused with static. Every comm-link and holo-pad in a twenty-foot radius exploded, leaving gaping holes in the Iron-bloods still trying to escape.

The chip in Robb's wrist sparked. He hissed, shaking away the pain. He took Talle's hand and was pulled up into the cargo bay.

Siege cradled Ana in her arms. Blood was everywhere, soaking her opal dress crimson. The fiber optics in Siege's hair shimmered with panic. "Ana, darling. Please—please, darling. Talle! Get a med kit! We have to stop the bleeding. Stay with me. *Ana,*" she choked, cradling her. "You're safe, you're safe. . . ."

But being safe didn't matter now.

Thrusters hummed as the ship shifted, rising.

Robb glanced out between the closing cargo bay doors one last time and met Di's ruby eyes. He was still coming, quickly, without remorse. Fifteen feet—ten.

The *Dossier* rose higher into the air.

Then Di stopped. He reached his hand up as if to grab the ship. Robb felt a shift—brief, like a magnetic pull—

And Di snapped his fingers.

The chip in his wrist lurched. Robb clutched it with a cry, dropping to his knees. Pain, swirling, throbbing, raced up his swordfighting arm as the chip grew brighter. And brighter. Blazing like the sun through his skin. He screamed. Pain curled up around his shoulder, seized hold of his heart, and squeezed. It squeezed so hard he barely felt it when the chip burned away the nerves in his wrist. When it tore apart the blood vessels in his hand. When it spread like molten lava, up and up and up his arm until the pressure was too much and the light was too bright—

The tracking chip burst.

JAX

The stars passed by slower and slower the farther they sailed from Eros, the stretches between them growing larger the longer they sped. Their destination was Xourix, a space station hidden in the asteroid belt, out beyond Cerces. Out of kingdom space. It was safe only for the right price, and Jax didn't want to know what price Siege would pay.

Jax had never flown so recklessly in his entire life. Messiers had pursued, relentlessly hot on their solar trails, until Siege's friends finally helped him shake them off around Iliad's rings. It was a detour they couldn't afford, and now the quickly-patched sails groaned at full mast, catching the solar winds out into no-man's-land.

He hadn't slept in two days, his hands barely leaving the helm. He couldn't risk autopilot. Too much computer interference might tip off the Messiers, and he didn't want to risk that. The entire kingdom was on high alert, and so little sleep was making him bleary-eyed and numb.

He tapped his fingers on his armrest, eyeing the comm-link. He was tempted to radio the infirmary. He wanted to know if . . .

A knot swelled in his throat.

He didn't know Robb's fate anymore, and worry kept him company as he watched the screens for any ships that might try to ping them.

And Ana . . . he would rather not think of Ana. Thinking of her only made his chest ache, and he didn't think he could hurt any more in his lifetime.

"Jax?" Talle greeted him, knocking on the cockpit door-frame. "I can keep the cockpit for a while."

Jax twirled his chair around. "Nah, I'm fine. It's quiet up here—"

"He woke up," she interrupted.

He jumped to his feet. "I hate quiet. Tell me if you see anything pop up on that screen," he said, motioning to the half dozen holo-screens. "*Any* of the screens."

He was out of the cockpit and down the main corridor before Talle had the chance to nod, past the galley and crew's quarters, to the infirmary downstairs. A curtain separated two beds, and he threw it back, not even pausing to catch his breath.

Captain Siege sat in a chair by Robb's bedside. They were talking in quiet tones until Jax appeared. "Sorry," Jax excused himself breathlessly. "I'll wait outside—"

"Nah, he's been asking about you. Couldn't get him to shut up," said the captain, standing. "Think about it, okay?" Robb nodded and she left, clapping a hand on Jax's shoulder.

When she was gone, Jax finally got up the courage to look at Robb.

He lay on a gurney, his face sallow with a thin sheen of sweat. He couldn't look more dead even if he tried, but he was awake, and his blue eyes were piercing like a clear Erosian sky.

Jax had realized, in the moments he thought Robb would bleed out in the cargo bay, that he wanted to fly into those eyes. He wanted to get lost in them. Just once. If they just opened one more time.

But now, standing in front of the Ironblood, he realized how silly that sounded. Because he didn't care *that* much for an insufferable Ironblood who was quite possibly from the worst family in the universe.

Really he didn't.

"I wasn't asking about you," the Ironblood said hoarsely.

"I know," Jax replied, fidgeting with his gloves. He came to sit down on the side of Robb's gurney. He didn't know what to say, now that Robb was awake. In the last two days, he had thought up entire conversations, ones that could last for hours, but now face-to-face with him . . . he couldn't think up a single one.

"The captain was giving me her condolences. For my mother." Robb's voice broke at the mention of her, and Jax reached to put a comforting hand over his—

But it wasn't there.

Jax quickly drew his hand back. "I'm sorry, I didn't—"

"It doesn't hurt," Robb said, rolling his shoulder. His arm

faded to a nub halfway to where his elbow should have been, bandaged and spotty with blood. "Not *yet*, anyway. Talle did a good job."

"She and Lenda did the best they could, but . . ."

"I'm alive, and I think that's good enough."

Jax felt his lips twitch up into a grin. "I doubt that'll ever be good enough for you, Robb Valerio."

In reply, the Ironblood gave a sad smile. "I gave that up last night after you left. I'm not a Valerio anymore. My entire life I thought my name made me who I was—I grew up knowing that as truth. That I was just a bad Valerio. But now that I'm not a Valerio at all, I don't feel any different. I'm still me." But then he bit his bottom lip and added hesitantly, "The captain gave me her last name, if I wanted it."

Jax said the proposed name to see how it felt on his tongue. "Robbert Siege—"

"It's not Siege. It's an Ironblood name."

"No shit."

"Yes shit."

"Well, *are* you gonna take it?"

"I'm not sure if I deserve it. I was selfish for a really long time. I only cared about myself. I don't think I've earned it," he replied bitterly. He glanced over to the other bed, sectioned off with a curtain. The soft beep of Ana's heart monitor kept them company. "I don't know how we're alive. She *must* be the Goddess to have survived that."

Jax hesitated. "Di was a medic. He knew what he was doing. The blade missed her vital organs. She didn't survive because she was the Goddess. She survived because Di loved her."

"And then we left him," Robb muttered.

He turned his eyes down to Robb's missing forearm. "He's not Di anymore. Even if we did somehow get him back, he killed people. The Grand Duchess. Countless guards . . . almost Ana. How would you feel if you came back to your senses after that?"

"I don't know." The curly-headed boy sighed, frustated, through his nose. "He didn't kill me back in the shrine—he could've, but he didn't. There was another Metal—a girl, Ana's handmaiden—*she* killed my mother. *She* looked evil. Di . . . Di didn't. He's still in there somewhere."

Jax studied Robb silently. Was this really that boy from Nevaeh—the one who fell out of Jax's skysailer, and fought him in a duel, and bled on his favorite coat?

"Chivalry looks good on you, *ma'alor*," he said, brushing a dark curl out of Robb's face. "And I hate that I like it."

"Your flattery will only get you so far," Robb joked, trying to grin, but it turned sour and bitter. "I like you, but I have no right to say that. For what my mother did—for what *I* did. But . . . if there was a way for you to forgive me, no matter how long it takes, would you let me? Will you let me try to be worthy of you?"

The question took Jax by surprise.

He sat back, quite unable to find a response.

I've seen your stars, he wanted to say, *and this is impossible.*

All his life he'd thought that all fates flowed in a continuous, never-ending river, but now the current was disrupted, the path unsettled. They had changed the stars, and he was falling in love with a boy who should have died.

Robb shifted, uncomfortable. "Or—or if you don't feel the same way—"

"I'm sorry," Jax began, but when he looked into Robb's eyes, there were tears there. Alarmed, he quickly added, "No, no! That's not what I meant! I don't mean—"

"I knew you wouldn't. I'm sorry, I'm so sorry." Tears curved down Robb's cheeks, and, almost exasperated, Jax wiped them away.

"I can't *lie*, you insufferable Ironblood," he chided. "I'm apologizing because I can't forgive you right now, but that doesn't mean I don't want to kiss you, *ma'alor*. And it doesn't mean I don't like you. I do. I like you, but do you really want *me?* Someone who can't touch other people? That's my reality. I'll never kiss you without seeing your fate. I'll never touch you without seeing how you'll die. Am I someone you could be happy with?"

Robb's brow furrowed. "Screw fate. I'll tear down the stars for you."

For *him?* Even though Jax had to wear gloves, and could never brush his lips against Robb's jawline without seeing the stars, never kiss Robb's ears, or trace the lines of his body, or feel the heat that pulsed just beneath his skin, hot and red and wanting. Jax felt his throat tighten as tears pooled at the edges of his eyes. He didn't cry. He never cried.

Robb took Jax's hand, and kissed his gloved knuckles. "And lucky for you," Robb added, "I'm not planning to ever die, so you don't have to worry about my stars."

He laughed. "You make being mad at you hard, *ma'alor.*"

"I plan on making it impossible," replied Robb, and raised an eyebrow. "What does *ma'alor* mean?"

Jax chewed on his bottom lip. "It means . . ." But he couldn't bear that sort of embarrassment, so he simply leaned into the Ironblood and kissed him. Savoring the moment, the unknowingness of it all.

Until new images came flooding across his senses like a wave of darkness across the stars.

HIVE

The Royal Guard patrolling the door jumped when he approached. "Sorry, sir, this is a private Iron Council meeting—"

"I am expected." He grabbed the woman by her chin and flicked her head to the left. There was a crack, and she slumped to the floor.

Inside the meeting, the poor Ironbloods were bickering about who would next wear the crown. They sat around a glass table, either too young to remember the face he wore, or too old to care. All the great heads of family were there—well, the ones who were left.

There were no video feeds of the massacre. There were no reports. The HIVE had successfully altered or wiped all accounts from the feeds. The survivors would not be believed. The HIVE would see to that. More importantly, no one knew his face—at least, not outside of history books.

The only thing left of that day was the blood he could not seem to get out from underneath his nails, and a creaking in his shoulder.

He straightened his black suit as he came into the Iron Council meeting, his hair pulled back loosely with a silver tie.

The Iron Crown gleamed in the middle of the table.

Some of the Ironbloods tucked their rust-stained fingers into their laps; others clenched their fists. He smirked. They'd all tried to wear the crown. Pity none of them could.

"Who are you?" asked Lord Carnelian, the arrowhead markings under his eyes faded with age.

"I wish to test the crown," he told the council. "Perhaps the Goddess has chosen me."

"That still doesn't tell us who you are," replied a young woman with strawberry blond hair and light eyes—the Wysteria girl. The one who danced with Ana. Her fingertips were the only ones not rusted. She had not tried to wear the crown. "I've never seen you before."

"What house do you hail from?" asked another young Ironblood. Blue eyes, curly black hair. The eldest Valerio—*Erik.*

He took the pendant from around his neck, and tossed it onto the table. The half-melted Valerio crest rolled to a stop. There were only four known in the kingdom.

Erik Valerio prickled. "I don't recognize you. Who are your parents? You don't even *look* like a Valerio."

He turned his eyes blue like an Erosian sky and lifted his gaze. "Are you sure?"

Erik Valerio stiffened. "It doesn't matter. They've decided on *me*. The Grand Duchess—"

"Does not speak for the Goddess," he interrupted. "And bless her stars, she is no longer with us."

There was a murmur through the council as they shifted in their seats, weighing his words.

He flourished his hands toward the crown. "May I?"

Erik Valerio opened his mouth to object when two other Ironbloods slid the crown, sitting on a pillow of crushed velvet, to the end of the table. They watched him with unease—with the exception of the Wysteria girl, who looked as though she had finally placed his face. No matter. The HIVE's sweet song was loud and strong, drowning out the roaring, horrible sound of the shadow he used to be.

And he reached for the iron crown.

ANA

At first, she thought she was dreaming.

The *Dossier*'s infirmary was quiet and bright, the place she always felt safest, but she couldn't quite remember how she'd gotten here.

Slowly, she pulled her legs over the side of the bed and felt the cold tiles under her feet.

Where was everyone?

She tried to stand, but pain throbbed in her stomach, and she remembered—the palace, the HIVE, Di. She had her dagger pressed against his ribs, and she knew where to aim, where to slice, but she . . .

She couldn't.

And he ran her through. He—

The steady blip of her heart monitor began to quicken and skip, until she tore the patches off her neck and the beeping went silent.

A whirring overhead caught her ears, and she glanced up to find EoS in the corner.

"What're you doing here?" she asked, her voice tight and scratchy, as if she hadn't used it in a while. The bot turned and floated over to her, sinking onto her lap, and she noticed something small in its retractable arms. "What do you have there?"

It bleeped, its lens closing, as she pulled a small cube out of its grip. It was barely bigger than a copper. A memory core. It pulsed gently, flaring and dimming with a gray-white light. Her eyebrows furrowed as she held it, the scrapes and dents across its surface like old battle wounds.

"Is this Di's?" she whispered.

EoS bleeped again. *Yes.*

She closed her fingers around it as the bot grabbed her by her nightshirt and pulled. She got to her feet and followed the bot up the stairs. There was a voice coming down the hallway. It was familiar, and loud—much too loud.

She climbed the stairs and turned down the hallway toward the cockpit, like she had done her entire life, but it felt so strange now. The hallway was too small, the ship too cramped. She gripped the memory core tightly, pressing it against her stomach. The wound throbbed, but it was a pain she could endure, because she knew that voice.

She followed it like a siren's song.

Her fingertips brushed the rusted walls, the sounds of Wick's fiddle and Riggs's voice playing phantom songs in her head. Barger's boisterous laugh, the hum of Di's Metal parts as she pressed her forehead against his.

The ship was full of ghosts.

Ahead in the cockpit, the crew stood watching the starshield.

They didn't hear her come to the doorway and lean against it, her very bones aching. She was just so tired.

In the video, the steward, in a too-tight morning coat, addressed the crowd from a podium in front of the palace. *"It is with a heavy heart that we announce the death of our Empress."*

Her death? Was she dead?

She gripped the doorway, looking around at the crew, or whoever was left. Robb was in a chair, his shoulder bandaged up with gauze, tapering to nothing at all. He looked sunken, terrified. Jax stood behind him like the backbone Robb needed. Lenda shifted against the wall, arms crossed, as Talle massaged Siege's shoulders. The captain sat in the pilot chair, hair dark for the first time Ana could remember, and she could finally see the gray between her black curls.

The cockpit felt empty and heavy with all the people they'd lost. Wick, Barger, Riggs . . . *Di.* Her Di. But now every time she thought about him, her wound flared, crippling.

The steward's face flickered on the screen as the *Dossier* caught another solar draft. She could feel the shift under her feet, the spirals of stars rushing past. On a small screen in the corner of the starshield, a dot moved toward the asteroid belt. Toward Xourix.

Her captain was desperate enough to go to Xourix.

"Four days ago, a Metal attacked the heart of our kingdom. The lives of countless Ironbloods were lost, including the Grand Duchess Armorov, Cynthia Valerio, Quintin Machivalle, Vermion Carnelian, and Gregori Rasovant."

Her fists clenched at the feeling of driving the dagger into him.

She had killed someone.

Count your bullets, Siege had said, but the guilt of killing someone didn't suffocate her like she thought it would. She could have spared Rasovant, but as he'd reached into his robes she'd made her choice, and she had prayed for a heart of iron. In that moment, she had thought that the Moon Goddess hadn't answered.

But maybe she had.

Her hands were not shaking, and blood washed off like every other stain. She'd tried being the daughter the kingdom wanted. The girl who studied the law and followed the rules. But now she knew—there were no rules. There was no peace.

Only blood, and iron, and flames.

"But in this hour of great need we need a great leader. We need someone chosen by the Goddess to combat these terrible crimes. We need someone with merit, someone with knowledge of the demons we fight. Someone who can unite our kingdom in this time of darkness."

"It's going to be Erik, I know it's going to be Erik," Robb murmured from his chair, his hand over his mouth.

Jax squeezed his left shoulder tightly. "He'll be a terrible ruler. Someone will kill him off."

"That's not any better," Siege replied.

"And the Goddess gifted us a ruler in our greatest moment of need. We look to him for guidance."

But the man who came into view was not Erik Valerio.

She knew that gait—too smooth and too unnatural—and

the color of his bloodred hair. He was dressed in all black, a crimson ascot knotted at his throat. His face was just as she remembered, seared into her nightmares. The sharpness of his cheekbones, the slant of his lips, the constellation of freckles across his nose.

She clutched the memory core against her stomach, feeling the core pulse again, and again, in a steadying rhythm. A heartbeat.

The redheaded young man knelt on one knee, and as the steward placed the crown upon Di's head, Ana felt a strange shift in the universe, as if the stars had turned upside down and the sun was no longer theirs.

"Rise, Emperor of the Iron Kingdom," said the steward, and the man rose to his feet again, turning his gaze to the crowd. His eyes shone blue—pupils as dark as space. Lightless, unending nothing.

A kingdom cast in shadows.

"Will you lead our great kingdom in our time of need? Will you sacrifice all you have for the greatness of our Goddess? Will you give your life for Her?" the steward asked, reciting the same oath Lord Rasovant had said to her a lifetime ago.

Captain Siege slammed her hand on the disconnect button and cursed under her breath. She turned back to the crew when she finally noticed Ana in the doorway. She gave a start, jumping to her feet. "Darling! You're awake!"

The rest of her family turned, too.

"Ana!" they chorused, and she had never been happier to see familiar faces.

In two quick strides, Siege crossed the cockpit and drew Ana into a hug, and she sank into it with relief. The captain smelled like gunpowder, her coat scratchy, her hug bone-crushingly tight—and it was home. Her home. "I was so worried, so worried," the captain sobbed, holding Ana tightly.

Tears brimmed in Ana's eyes. "I'm so glad to see you. I'm sorry—for fighting with you after Di died. I'm sorry."

"Oh, darling, I was never mad," replied her captain. "And *I'm* sorry—for keeping your past from you."

"It's okay. I forgive you."

Siege pulled away, blinking the tears out of her eyes. "You do?"

"You love me unconditionally. You didn't treat me like a princess but like . . . like you would a daughter."

"You *are* my daughter," Siege said, and the words made Ana's heart sing. "I'll never let anything happen to you again. We're heading to Xourix, where you'll be safe. No one will look for you there."

That sounded nice. She could disappear into the kingdom and never be seen again. She *was* dead, after all. Was that what Di had thought when he'd stabbed her? She could let herself fade into history and live the rest of her days being a girl with no destiny, no stars, no *fate*.

But Di's memory core pulsed in her grip, beating softly, reminding her of who she was, and what had been taken, and of a Great Dark that now sat on the kingdom's throne, having waited a thousand years to return.

She swallowed her trepidation and looked at the crew. "I

don't want to run away, to go to Xourix and just disappear. The HIVE has control now, and I'm not going to sit by and watch it destroy the kingdom."

"But the kingdom doesn't care about us," Lenda argued, "so why should we care about it?"

"And it's dangerous, darling," the captain added, frowning.

But then Jax said, "Yet don't we always go looking for danger?"

"And we have a Metal to save," Robb added.

Talle shook her head. "Who is now a brainwashed murdering robot who wants to *kill* us."

"But he didn't," Ana argued, painfully aware of the wound in her stomach. If he had wanted to kill her, he could have. He knew how. She didn't tell them what Di had whispered before he plunged the blade into her, wishing to have let her burn. That was not Di. So, she kept it to herself, a secret between her and her new scars. "And that means the HIVE didn't take everything. The HIVE *won't* take everything. The Iron Kingdom isn't mine—it's ours. We're the outcasts, the rebels, the refugees—"

"And the royalty," said Jax.

"And the royalty," she agreed. "We're part of the Iron Kingdom. We're the parts no one remembers, so they'll never see us coming. Who's with me?"

Jax and Robb raised their hands without hesitation, and then Lenda, and Talle. The captain pursed her lips, blinking the stray tears out of her eyes, and then she nodded because Ana knew she just wanted to keep her safe—but now it was Ana's turn to save people.

"To the ends of the universe, darling," Siege finally replied.

Ana's heart swelled. She held tightly to Di's memory core, a lifeline glowing with hope in the dark. Once, she had not known who she could be without Di, and once she couldn't have fathomed the thought. But now she knew she carried Di with her, and Barger, and Wick, and Riggs—and Siege, and Talle, and Lenda and Robb and Jax, and Machivalle and Wynn, and Viera, and her late parents and lost brothers, tucked within the steady thrum of her heart. They were the sum of her parts that made her whole.

She was Ananke Armorov. She was the heir to the Iron Kingdom. She was a girl born in fire and raised in the stars, and she would burn against the darkness—and drive it away.

ACKNOWLEDGMENTS

I can't find the right words.

Perhaps it's because *Heart of Iron* means a great deal to me. But see? Even those words don't really convey how I feel. They don't have the weight I'm looking for, the moments in a quiet room while Di braids Ana's hair, the seven years in search of Jax's stars, the different coats Robb tried on before he found a perfect blue vintage number that fit like a *dream*. I daresay all these characters have become a part of me, as things often do when you carry them long enough.

Everyone says that writing is a solitary thing, but it's because of *Heart of Iron* that I met so many wonderful people, and they are all carried in these pages.

I want to thank my agent, Holly Root, for being my greatest champion, and for believing in me even when I didn't believe in myself.

And I also want to thank my wonderful editor at Balzer + Bray, Kelsey Murphy, who gave Ana a home. She took my words and shaped them into a story that I am so dearly proud of, and without her this book would not be half of what it turned out to be.

The road to publication was long, and rife with terrors, but the Fellowship was a bright spot in an otherwise murky Mordor. Thank you, Hannah Fergesen, Bess Cozby, Lauren Spieller, and Chelsea Fought, for all of our text threads and cathartic conversations over bottles of wine.

Without Eric Smith, Ana would've been lost on the dark side of Palavar forever, and without Sara Taylor Woods and our writing dates, I would've never turned anything in on time.

To all the friends who believed in me over the years— Savannah Apperson, Rae Chang, Nita Tyndall, Jarad Greene, Paul Krueger, Nicole Brinkley, Julie Daly, Alona Fryman, Shae McDaniel, Meredith Rich, Victoria Schwab, Katherine Locke, Christianna Marks, and Cera Osmialowski, who dared me to write a bad-ass heroine.

And without my weirdo, wonderful family, I would have never been able to chase the dream tucked into the corner of my heart. Thank you for letting me chase it.

Thank you to everyone at Balzer + Bray—Alessandra Balzer, Donna Bray, Jordan Brown, Kristin Rens, Tiara Kittrell. To the stellar sales team, Andrea Pappenheimer, Kerry Moynagh, Kathy Faber, Heather Doss, and everyone else I haven't named. To my cover designer and the artist who thought up such a star-studded cover, Sarah Kaufman and John Dismukes. To the rad souls in marketing, Nellie Kurtzman, Bess Braswell, Tyler Breitfeller, Ebony LaDelle, Audrey Diestelkamp, Sabrina Abballe; and to Caroline Sun in publicity; and to the powerhouses in production, Allison Brown, Meghan Pettit, and Nicole Moulaison. Y'all rock.

Last but not least, thank *you*, reader, for taking this journey with me. May you be as brave as Ana, as noble as Di, as ambitious as Robb, and as confident as Jax.

You are my Iron Kingdom.

May the stars keep you steady and the iron keep you safe.